Jack Finney (1911-1995) was born in Milwaukee, Wisconsin with the given name of John Finney. He was three when his father died and he was renamed Walter Braden Finney, in honour of his father, but the nickname Jack remained with him throughout his life. He was educated at Knox College and his writing career began when he won a short story competition sponsored by *Ellery Queen's Mystery Magazine* in 1946. As well as publishing novels and short stories, he contributed articles to a number of popular periodicals, including *Saturday Evening Post* and *Good Housekeeping*. A number of his novels were turned into films, most famously *The Body Snatchers*, which was filmed as *Invasion of the Body Snatchers* twice and then as *Body Snatchers*. He died not long after writing *From Time to Time*, the long-awaited sequel to *Time and Again*.

'One of the most original, readable, and engaging novels to have come along in a long time'
The Washington Post Book World

'Mind-boggling, imagination-stretching, exciting, romantic entertainment' *San Francisco Examiner*

'For a few precious hours his fascinating novel will push back the sands of time and give you your heart's desire: to live in another age, a better world, the good old days when things were more to your taste'
Houston Post

ALSO BY JACK FINNEY

Five Against the House (1954)
The Body Snatchers (1955)
The Third Level (1957)
The House of Numbers (1957)
Assault on a Queen (1959)
I Love Galesburg in the Springtime (1963)
Good Neighbour Sam (1963)
The Woodrow Wilson Dime (1968)
Marion's Wall (1973)
The Night People (1977)
Forgotten News: The Crime of the Century
  and Other Lost Stories (1983)
About Time (1986)
From Time to Time (1995)

Fantasy Masterworks

TIME AND AGAIN

JACK FINNEY

Copyright © Jack Finney 1970
All rights reserved

The right of Jack Finney to be identified as the author
of this work has been asserted by him in accordance with the
Copyright, Designs and Patents Act 1988.

This edition published in Great Britain in 2001 by
Gollancz
An imprint of the Orion Publishing Group
Orion House, 5 Upper St Martin's Lane, London WC2H 9EA

A CIP catalogue record for this book
is available from the British Library

ISBN 0 57507 360 8

Printed in Great Britain by
The Guernsey Press Co. Ltd, Guernsey, C.I.

For Marg, who liked it

1

IN SHIRT-SLEEVES, the way I generally worked, I sat sketching a bar of soap taped to an upper corner of my drawing board. The gold-foil wrapper was carefully peeled back so that you could still read most of the brand name printed on it; I'd spoiled the wrappers of half a dozen bars before getting that effect. This was a new idea, the product to be shown ready for what the accompanying copy called "fragrant, lathery, lovelier *you*" use, and I had the job of sketching it into half a dozen layouts, the bar of soap at a slightly different angle in each.

It was just exactly as boring as it sounds, and I stopped to look out the window beside me, down twelve stories at Fifty-fourth Street and the little heads moving along the sidewalk. It was a sunny, sharply clear day in mid-November, and I'd have liked to be out in it, the whole afternoon ahead and nothing to do; nothing I had to do, that is.

Over at the paste-up table Vince Mandel, our lettering man, thin and dark and probably feeling as caged-up today as I was, stood working with the airbrush, a cotton surgical mask over his mouth. He was spraying a flesh-colored film onto a *Life* magazine photo of a girl in a bathing suit. The effect, when he finished, would be to remove the suit, leaving the girl apparently naked except for the ribbon she wore slanted from shoulder to waist on which was lettered MISS BUSINESS MACHINES. This kind of stunt was Vince's favorite at-work occupation ever since he'd thought of it, and the retouched picture would be added to a collection of others like it on the art-department bulletin board, at which Maureen, our nineteen-year-old paste-up girl and messenger, refused ever to look or even glance, though often urged.

Frank Dapp, our art director, a round little package of energy, came trotting toward his partitioned-off office in the northeast corner of the artists' bullpen. As he passed the big metal supply cabinet just inside the room he hammered violently on its open door, yodeling at full bellow. It was an habitual release of unused energy like a locomotive jetting steam, a starting eruption of sound. But neither Vince nor I nor Karl Jonas at the board ahead of mine glanced up. Neither did anyone in the typists' pool outside, I knew, although strangers waiting in the art-department reception room just down the hall had been known to leap to their feet at the sound.

It was an ordinary day, a Friday, twenty minutes till lunchtime, five hours till quitting time and the weekend, ten months till vacation, thirty-seven years till retirement. Then the phone rang.

"Man here to see you, Si." It was Vera, at the switchboard. "He has no appointment."

"That's okay. He's my connection; I need a fix."

"What you need can't be fixed." She clicked off. I got up, wondering who it was; an artist in an advertising agency doesn't usually have too many visitors. The main reception room was on the floor below, and I took the long route through Accounting and Media, but no new girls had been hired.

Frank Dapp called the main reception room Off Broadway. It was decorated with a genuine Oriental rug, several display cases of antique silver from the collection of the wife of one of the three partners, and with a society matron whose hair was also antique silver and who relayed visitors' requests to Vera. As I walked toward it my visitor stood looking at one of the framed ads hung on the walls. Something I don't like admitting and which I've learned to disguise is a shyness about meeting people, and now I felt the familiar slight apprehension and momentary confusion as he turned at the sound of my approaching footsteps. He was bald and short, the top of his head reaching only to my eye level, and I'm an inch short of six feet. He looked about thirty-five, I thought, walking toward him, and he was remarkably thick-chested; he'd out-weigh me without being fat. He wore an olive-green gabardine suit that didn't go with his pink redhead's complexion. *I hope he's not a sales-man*, I thought; then he smiled as I stepped into the lobby, a real smile, and I liked him instantly and relaxed. *No*, I told myself, *he's not selling anything*, and I couldn't have been more wrong about that.

"Mr. Morley?" I nodded, smiling back at him. "Mr. Simon Morley?" he said, as though there might be several of us Morleys here at the agency and he wanted to be certain.

"Yes."

He still wasn't satisfied. "Just for fun, do you remember your army serial number?" He took my elbow and began walking me out into the elevator corridor away from the receptionist.

I rattled it off; it didn't even occur to me to wonder why I was doing this for a stranger, no questions asked.

"Right!" he said approvingly, and I felt pleased. We were out in the corridor now, no one else around.

"Are you from the army? If so, I don't want any today."

He smiled, but didn't answer the question, I noticed. He said, "I'm Ruben Prien," and hesitated momentarily as though I might recognize the name, then continued. "I should have phoned and made an appointment, but I'm in a hurry so I took a chance on dropping in."

"That's all right, I wasn't doing anything but working. What can I do for you?"

He grimaced humorously at the difficulty of what he had to say. "I've got to have about an hour of your time. Right now, if you can manage it." He looked embarrassed. "I'm sorry, but . . . if you could just take me on faith for a little while, I'd appreciate it."

I was hooked; he had my interest. "All right. It's ten to twelve; would you like to have lunch? I can leave a little early."

"Fine, but let's not talk indoors. We could pick up some sandwiches and eat in the park. Okay? It's not too cool."

Nodding, I said, "I'll get my coat and meet you here. You interest me strangely." I stood hesitating, looking closely at this pleasant, tough-looking, bald little man, then said it. "As I think you know. Matter of fact, you've been through this whole routine before, haven't you? Complete with embarrassed look."

He grinned and made a little finger-snapping motion. "And I thought I really had it down. Well, it's back to the mirror, and more practice. Get your coat; we're losing time."

We walked north on Fifth Avenue past the incredible buildings of glass and steel, glass and enameled metal, glass and marble, and the older ones of more stone than glass. It's a stunning street and unbelievable; I never get used to it, and I wonder if anyone really does. Is there any other place where an entire cloud bank can be completely reflected in the windows of one wall of only one building, and with room to spare? Today I especially enjoyed being out on Fifth, the temperature in the high 50's, a nice late-fall coolness in the air. It was nearly noon, and beautiful girls came dancing out of every office building we passed, and I thought of how regrettable it was that I'd never know or even speak to most of them. The little bald man beside me said, "I'll tell you what I've come to say to you; then I'll listen to questions. Maybe I'll even answer some. But everything I can really tell you I will have said before we reach Fifty-sixth Street. I've done this thirty-odd times now, and never figured out a good way to say it or even sound very sane while trying, so here goes.

"There's a project. A U.S. government project I guess you'd have to call it. Secret, naturally; as what isn't in government these days? In my opinion, and that of a handful of others, it's more important than all the nuclear, space-exploration, satellite, and rocket programs put together, though a hell of a lot smaller. I tell you right off that I can't even hint what the project is about. And believe me, you'd never guess. I can and do say that nothing human beings have ever before attempted in the entire nutty history of the race even approaches this in absolute fascination. When I first understood what this project is about I didn't sleep for two nights, and I don't mean that in the usual way; I mean I literally did not sleep. And before I could sleep on the third night I had to have a shot in the arm, and I'm supposed to be the plodding unimaginative type. Do I have your attention?"

"Yes; if I understand you, you've finally discovered something more interesting than sex."

"You may find out that you're not exaggerating. I think riding to the moon would be almost dull in comparison to what you may just possibly have a chance to do. It is the greatest possible adventure. I would give anything I own or will ever have just to be in your shoes; I'd give years of my life just for a *chance* at this. And that's it, friend Morley. I can go on talking, and will, but that's really all I have to say. Except this: through no virtue or merit of your own, just plain dumb luck, you are invited to join the project. To commit yourself to it. Absolutely blind. That's some pig in a poke, all right, but oh, my God, what a pig. There's a pretty good delicatessen on Fifty-seventh Street; what kind of sandwiches you want?"

"Roast pork, what else?"

We bought our sandwiches and a couple of apples, then walked on toward Central Park a couple of blocks ahead. Prien was waiting for some sort of reply, and we walked in silence for half a block; then I shrugged irritably, wanting to be polite but not knowing how else to answer. "What am I supposed to say?"

"Whatever you want."

"All right; why me?"

"Well, I'm glad you asked, as the politicians say. There is a particular kind of man we need. He has to have a certain set of qualities. A rather special list of qualities, actually, and a long list. Furthermore, he has to have them in a pretty exact kind of balance. We didn't know that at first. We thought most any intelligent eager young fellow would do. Me, for example. Now we know, or think we do, that he has to be physically right, psychologically right, temperamentally right. He has to have a certain special way of looking at things. He's got to have the ability, and it seems to be fairly rare, to see things as they are and at the same time as they might have been. If that makes any sense to you. It probably does, because it may be that what we mean is the eye of an artist. Those are just some of what he must have or be; there are others I won't tell you about now. Trouble is that on one count or another that seems to eliminate most of the population. The only practical way we've found to turn up likely candidates is to plow through the tests the army gave its inductees; you remember them."

"Vaguely."

"I don't know how many sets of those tests have been analyzed; that's not my department. Probably millions. They use computers for the early check-throughs, eliminating all those that are comfortably wide of the mark. Which is most of them. After that, real live people take over; we don't want to miss even one candidate. Because we're finding damn few. We've checked I don't know how many millions of service records, including the women's branches. For some reason women seem to produce more candidates than men; we wish we had more we could check. Anyway, one Simon L. Morley with the fine euphonious serial number looks like a candidate. How come you only made PFC?"

"A lack of talent for idiocies such as close-order drill."

"I believe the technical term is two left feet. Out of fewer than a hundred possibilities we've found so far, about fifty have already heard what you're hearing now, and turned us down. About fifty more have volunteered, and over forty of them flunked some further tests. Anyway, after one hell of a lot of work, we have five men and two women who just might be qualified. Most or all of them will fail in the actual attempt; we don't have even one we feel very sure of. We'd like to get about twenty-five candidates, if we possibly can. We'd like a hundred, but we don't believe there are that many around; at least we don't know how to find them. But you may be one."

"Gee whiz."

At Fifty-ninth Street as we stood waiting for the light, I glanced at Rube's profile and said, "Rube Prien; yeah. You played football. When was it? About ten years ago."

He turned to grin up at me. "You remembered! You're a good boy; I wish I'd bought you some thick gooey dessert, the kind I can't eat anymore. Only it was fifteen years ago; I'm not really the young handsome youth I know I must seem."

"Where'd you play again? I can't remember."

The light clicked green, and we stepped down off the curb. "West Point."

"I knew it! You're in the army!"

"Yep."

I was shaking my head. "Well, I'm sorry, but it'll take more than you. It'll take five husky fighting MPs to drag me back in, kicking and screaming all the way. Whatever you're selling and however fascinating, I don't want any. The lure of sleepless nights in the army just isn't enough, Prien; I've already had all I want."

On the other side of the street we stepped up onto the sidewalk, crossed it, then turned onto the curve of a dirt-and-gravel path of Central Park and walked along it looking for an empty bench. "What's wrong with the army?" Rube said with fake injured innocence.

"You said this would take an hour; I'd need a week just for the chapter headings."

"All right, *don't* join the army. Join the navy; we'll make you anything you like from bosun's mate to lieutenant senior grade. Or join the Department of the Interior; you can be a forester with your very own Smokey-the-Bear hat." Prien was enjoying himself. "Sign up with the post office if you want; we'll make you an assistant inspector and give you a badge and the power to arrest for postal fraud. I mean it; pick almost any branch of the government you like except State or the diplomatic corps. And pick any title you fancy at no more than around a twelve-thousand-a-year salary, and so long as it isn't an elective office. Because, Si—all right to call you Si?" he said with sudden impatience.

"Sure."

"And call me Rube, if you care to. Si, it doesn't matter what payroll you're technically on. When I say this is secret, I mean it; our budget is scattered through the books of every sort of department and bureau, our people listed on every roster but our own. We don't officially exist, and yes, I'm still a member of the U.S. Army. The time counts toward my retirement, and besides I like the army, eccentric as I know that sounds. But my uniforms are in storage, I salute nobody these days, and the man I take a lot of my orders from is an historian on leave from Columbia University. Be a little chilly on the benches in the shade; let's find a place in the sun."

We picked a place a dozen yards off the path beside a big outcropping of black rock. We sat down on the sunny side, leaning back against the warm rock, and began opening our sandwiches. To the south, east, and west the New York buildings rose high, hanging over the park's edges like a gang ready to rush in and cover the greenery with concrete.

"You must have been in grade school when you read about Flying Rube Prien, deer-footed quarterback."

"I guess so; I'm twenty-eight." I bit into my sandwich. It was very good, the meat sliced thin and packed thick, the fat trimmed.

Rube said, "Twenty-eight on March eleventh."

"So you know that, do you? Well, goody goody gumshoes."

"It's in your army record, of course. But we know some things that aren't; we know you were divorced two years ago, and why."

"Would you mind telling me? I never did figure out why."

"You wouldn't understand. We also know that in about the last five months you've gone out with nine women but only four of them more than once. That in the last six weeks or so it seems to have narrowed down more and more to one. Just the same, we don't think you're ready to get married again. You may think you are, but we think you're still afraid to. You have two men friends you occasionally have lunch or dinner with; your parents are dead; you have no brothers or sist—"

My face had been flushing; I felt it, and took care to keep my voice quiet. I said, "Rube, I think I like you personally. But I feel I have to say: Who gave you or anyone else the right to poke into my private affairs?"

"Don't get mad, Si. It isn't worth it; we haven't snooped that much. And nothing embarrassing, nothing illegal. We're not like one or two government agencies I could name; we don't think we're divinely appointed. There's no wiretapping or illegal searches; we think the Constitution applies even to us. But before I leave I'll want your permission to search your apartment before you go back tonight."

I felt my lips compressing, and I shook my head.

Rube smiled and reached out to touch my arm. "I'm teasing you a little. But I hope you don't mean that. I'm offering you a crack at the damnedest experience a human being has ever had."

"And you can't tell me *anything* about it? I'm surprised you got seven people. Or even one."

Rube stared down at the grass; thinking about what he could say; then he looked up at me again. "We'd want to know more," he said slowly. "We'd want to test you in several other ways. But we think we already know an awful lot about the way you are, the way you think. We own two original Simon Morley paintings, for example, from the Art Directors' Show last spring, plus a watercolor and some sketches, all bought and paid for. We know something about the kind of man you are, and I've learned some more today. So I think I can tell you this: I can just about guarantee you, I believe I *can* guarantee you, that if you'll take this on faith and commit yourself for two years, assuming you get through some further testing, you will thank me. You'll say I was right. You'll tell me that the very thought that you might have missed out on this gives you the chills. How many human beings have ever lived, Si?

Five or six billions, maybe? Well, if you should test out, you'll become one of maybe a dozen out of all those billions, maybe the *only* one, who just might have the greatest adventure any human being has ever had."

It impressed me. I sat eating an apple, staring ahead, thinking. Suddenly I turned to him. "You haven't said a damn thing more than you did in the first place!"

"You noticed, did you? Some don't. Si, that's all I *can* say!"

"Well, you're too modest; you've got your sales pitch worked out beautifully. Will you accept a down payment on the Brooklyn Bridge? My God, Rube, what am I supposed to tell you? 'Sure, I'll join; where do I sign?' "

He nodded. "I know. It's tough. There's just no other way it can be done, that's all." He sat looking at me. Then he said softly, "But it's easier for you than most. You're unmarried, no kids. And you're bored silly with your work; we know that. As why shouldn't you be? It doesn't amount to anything, it's not worth doing. You're bored and dissatisfied with yourself, and time is passing; in two years you'll be thirty. And you still don't know what to do with your life." Rube sat back against the warm rock, staring off at the path and the people strolling along it through the sunny fall noon-hour, giving me a chance to think. What he'd just said was true.

When I turned to look at him again, Rube was waiting. He said, "So this is what you have to do: take a chance. Take a deep breath, close your eyes, grab your nose, and jump in. Or would you rather keep on selling soap, chewing gum, and brassieres, or whatever the hell it is you peddle down the street? You're a young man, for crysake!" Rube sliced his hands together, dusting off crumbs, and shoved several balls of waxed paper into his lunch sack. Then he stood up quickly and easily, the ex-footballer. "You know what I'm talking about, Si; the only possible way you can do this is to just go ahead and do it."

I stood up too, and we walked to a wire trash-basket chained to a tree, and dropped our wastepaper into it. Turning back toward the path with Rube, I knew that if I took my wrist between thumb and forefinger my pulse rate would be up; I was scared. With an irritation that surprised me, I said, "I'd be taking a hell of a lot on the say-so of an absolute stranger! What if I joined this big mystery and didn't think it was all that fascinating?"

"Impossible."

"But if I did!"

"Once we're satisfied you're a candidate and tell you what we're doing we have to know that you'll go through with it. We need your promise in advance; we can't help that."

"Would I have to go away?"

"In time. With some story for your friends. We couldn't have anyone wondering where or why Si Morley disappeared."

"Is this dangerous?"

"We don't think so. But I can't truthfully say we really know."

Walking toward the corner of the park at Fifth Avenue and Fifty-ninth Street, I thought about the life I'd made for myself since I'd arrived in New York City two years ago looking for a job as an artist, a stranger from Buffalo with a portfolio of samples under my arm. Every now and then I had dinner with Lennie Hindesmith, an artist I'd worked with in my first New York job. We'd generally see a movie after dinner or go bowling or something like that. I played tennis fairly often, public courts in the summer, the armory in the winter, with Matt Flax, a young accountant in my present agency; he'd also brought me into a weekly Monday-night bridge game, and we were probably on the way to becoming good friends. Pearl Moschetti was an assistant account executive on a perfume account at the first place I worked; ever since, I'd seen her now and then, once in a while for an entire weekend, though I hadn't seen her for quite a while now. I thought about Grace Ann Wunderlich, formerly of Seattle, whom I'd picked up almost accidentally in the Longchamps bar at Forty-ninth and Madison when I saw her start crying out of overwhelming loneliness brought on from sitting at a table by herself having a drink she didn't want or like when everyone else in the place seemed to have friends. Every time I'd seen her after that we drank too much, apparently following the pattern of the first time, usually at a place in the Village, a bar. Sometimes I stopped in there alone because I knew the bartenders now and some of the regulars, and it reminded me of a wonderful bar I'd been to a few times on a vacation, in Sausalito, California, called the No-Name Bar. Mostly I thought about Katherine Mancuso, a girl I'd been seeing more and more often, and the girl I'd begun to suspect I'd eventually be asking to marry me.

At first a lot of my life in New York had been lonely; I'd have left it willingly then. But now, while I still spent two or three and sometimes more nights a week by myself—reading, seeing a movie I wanted to see that Katie didn't, watching television at home, or just wandering around the city once in a while—I didn't mind. I had friends now, I had Katherine, and I liked a little time to myself.

I thought about my work. They liked it at the agency, they liked me, and I made a decent enough salary. The work wasn't precisely what I'd had in mind when I went to art school in Buffalo, but I didn't know either just what I did have in mind then, if anything.

So all in all there wasn't anything really wrong with my life. Except that, like most everyone else's I knew about, it had a big gaping hole in it, an enormous emptiness, and I didn't know how to fill it or even know what belonged there. I said to Rube, "Quit my job. Give up my friends. Disappear. How do I know you're not a white slaver?"

"Look in the mirror."

We turned out of the park and stopped at the corner. I said, "Well, Rube, this is Friday: Can you let me think about it? Over the weekend, anyway? I don't think I'm interested, but I'll let you know. I don't know what else I can tell you right now."

"What about that permission? I'd like to make my phone call now. From the nearest booth, in fact, at the Plaza"—he nodded at the old hotel just across Fifty-ninth Street—"and send a man over to search your apartment this afternoon."

Once more I felt a flush rise up in my face. "Everything in it?"

He nodded. "If there are letters, he'll read them. If anything's hidden, he'll find it."

"All *right*, goddammit! Go ahead! He sure as hell won't find anything interesting!"

"I know." Rube was laughing at me. "Because he won't even look. There's no man I'm going to phone. Nobody's going to search your crummy apartment. Or ever was."

"Then what the hell is this all about!"

"Don't you know?" He stood looking at me for a moment; then he grinned. "You don't know it and you won't believe it; but it means you've already decided."

2

SATURDAY MORNING Katie and I drove up into Connecticut for the day. The clear sunny weather still held, as long a fall as I could remember. It was weather that couldn't last, we didn't want to waste it, and we drove up in Katie's MG. It was the old-style model with running boards and exposed radiator-front, and although New York is really no place to own a car, Kate had this because it just exactly fitted into a narrow areaway beside her shop if she illegally drove up over the curb. When it was parked you had to climb in and out over the back end, but it saved garage rent, making it possible for Kate to have it.

Katie had a tiny antique shop on Third Avenue in the Forties. Her foster parents—she'd been adopted when she was two—had died two years ago within six months of each other; they were elderly, older than her own parents would have been. She'd moved to New York then, from Westchester, worked as a stenographer, didn't like it, and opened the shop a year later with the few thousand dollars she'd inherited. It was failing. She'd added greeting cards and a little rental library which hadn't helped, and we both knew she'd have to give up the shop when the lease expired in the spring.

I was sorry, both for Kate and because I liked the place. I liked poking around it, discovering something I hadn't seen before: a box of old political-campaign buttons under a counter, maybe, or something new she'd just bought such as an admiral's hat I could try on. And whenever there's been time or when I've had to wait for Kate as I did this morning, I'd usually sit down with one of the stereoscopes—the viewers—she had, and one of several big boxes loaded with old stereoscopic views, mostly

18

of New York City. Because I've always felt a wonder at old photographs not easy to explain. Maybe I don't need to explain; maybe you'll recognize what I mean. I mean the sense of wonder, staring at the strange clothes and vanished backgrounds, at knowing that what you're seeing was once real. That light really did reflect into a lens from these lost faces and objects. That these people were *really there* once, smiling into a camera. You could have walked into the scene then, touched those people, and spoken to them. You could actually have gone into that strange outmoded old building and seen what now you never can—what was just inside the door.

The wonder is even stronger with old stereoscopic views—the almost, but not quite, identical pair of photographs mounted side by side on stiff cardboard, that, looked at through the viewer, give a miraculous effect of depth. It's never been a mystery to me why the whole country was once crazy about them. Because the good ones, the really clear sharp photographs, are so *real:* Insert a view, slide it into focus, and the old scene leaps out at you, astonishingly three-dimensional. And then, for me, the awe becomes intense. Because now you really *see the arrested moment*, so actual it seems that if you watch intently, the life caught here must continue. That the raised horse's hoof so startlingly distinct in the foreground *must* move down to the solidness of pavement below it again; those carriage wheels revolve, the girl walk closer, the man move on out of the scene. The feeling that the tantalizing reality of the vanished moment might somehow be seized—that if you watch long enough you might detect that first nearly imperceptible movement—is the answer to the question Kate has asked me more than once: "How can you sit there so long—you hardly move!—staring endlessly at the very same picture?" So I liked the shop; it had things like stereoscopic views to stare at. And I liked it because I'd met Katie through it; it's the only time in my life I ever worked up the nerve to do what I did.

I'd needed a certain kind of antique table lamp to sketch into an ad I was working on, and I came to Katie's shop and stopped to look into the window just as she was taking something out of it. I looked at her; she's a nice-looking girl with that kind of thick dark-brown coppery hair that just misses being red, and the lightly freckled skin and the brown eyes that so often go with it. But it was her face that hooked me; I mean the look of it, the expression. It's the face, you know at first sight, of an extremely nice person, that's all. I liked her instantly, the person as much as the nice-looking girl. And I'm sure that's why, when she glanced up at me, I had the nerve—before I could remember that I *didn't* have the nerve—to touch my lips with my bunched fingers and toss her a kiss through the glass, at the same time crossing my eyes. She smiled, and before I could lose this new untypical courage I walked right on into the shop, trusting that I'd think of something to say, which I did. I said I was looking for another Napoleon hat, that they'd taken my old one away. She smiled again, which shows how kind she was, and we talked. And while she couldn't come out for a cup of coffee with me then, I was back next day, and we went out to dinner.

Katie came down now—her apartment is over the shop—in a short brown-canvas car coat, a yellow scarf over her hair, which was a great combination, and she gave me the car keys, asking if I'd mind driving; she knew I liked to drive the MG.

We had a good time, a nice day, and in the late afternoon I was driving along a little country road I'd found—a dirt road, farmland on each side, occasional stone fences, and a lot of trees, some still with fall foliage. I was going no more than twenty, just lazing along, one hand on the wheel, not thinking of anything much. Off and on during the day I'd thought of Rube Prien, wishing I could talk to Katie about it; I couldn't quite remember whether or not I'd promised I wouldn't mention even the conversation with Prien, so I didn't say anything.

It was still fairly warm, lots of late-afternoon sun, and Katie untied her scarf, pulled it off, then tossed her head to shake out that thick handsome hair, very coppery now in the slanted sunlight, then fluffing it up at the back with one hand—a great combination of feminine gestures—and I glanced at her and smiled. She smiled back, sitting there smoothing her scarf flat on her lap; she was wearing a green tweed skirt. Then she looked at me and slid closer, which was pleasant and flattering. She was holding the scarf by the front two corners now, stretching it out tight between her hands. She lifted it to just above windshield level and the air took it, fluttering it tautly back from the corners she held. She moved it directly over my head, and then very quickly—a scurry of motion—she drew the two corners down past my face to below my chin and let go the scarf. The wind instantly plastered it tight to my face like a pale-yellow skin, and I was absolutely blind. I couldn't even breathe very well, or thought I couldn't, and I let out a strangled yelp and was in a panic for a second or so, unable to think.

Just try it some time: driving along a road with a damn scarf plastered over your eyes. You don't know *what* to do; whether to hang onto the wheel trying to steer from memory, braking as fast as you can without skidding off the road; or whether to let go and try to snatch off the scarf before piling up.

I tried both. One hand still on the wheel, and trying to remember exactly what there'd been along the sides of the road here, I grabbed at the scarf with my other hand but got a handful of hair along with it, and the scarf wouldn't budge. I was braking too hard and felt the rear end swing into a slide and knew that if the ditches were at all deep along here, the car couldn't help but go into one. I was trying to scoop the scarf off my face but my fingers only scrabbled over glossy nylon. Then we were stopped, the motor killed, car slewed halfway around in the road, the rear end off it, and when I finally plucked and dragged that scarf from my face, Kate was leaning back against her door, an arm raised limply to point a finger at me, almost helpless with laughter.

The instant I could see, I checked the road ahead and behind as fast as I could swivel my head, and of course nothing was in sight in either direction or Katie wouldn't have done it; and the ditches beside us were so shallow they were almost nonexistent and entirely dry. I said, "Marvelous. Absolutely great. Let's do it again! On the parkway coming home tonight."

"Oh, God, you were funny," she said, hardly able to get out the words. "You looked so *funny!*" I grinned at her, very pleased with this nutty girl, and at that moment and for all that weekend Rube Prien's mystery project had no chance at all with me.

I'm not going to say everything there is to say about Kate and me. I've read such accounts, completely explicit and detailed, nothing omitted; and when they've been good I've liked them. Sometimes I've even learned something about people from them, almost like an actual experience, and that's very good indeed. But my nature is different, that's all. I don't like to and I could not reveal everything about myself. I like to read them, but I wouldn't like to write one. I'm not holding back anything all that unique, in any case. So if now and then you think you can read between the lines, you may be right; or may not. Anyway, everything I might possibly find to say about Kate and me isn't what I'm trying to get down.

During that weekend I didn't believe I was even thinking very much about Rube and his proposal. Yet at two-thirty Monday afternoon I finished the last of my "lovelier *you*" soap sketches, walked into Frank Dapp's office, laid them on his desk, started to turn and leave, and instead my mouth opened, and I stood listening to myself give notice. I'd saved some money, I told Frank; now, before it was too late, I was going to take some time and see if I could make it as a serious artist. It was a lie, and yet something I'd often thought of. "You want to paint?" Frank said, leaning back in his chair.

"No. Painting's pretty much all abstract and nonrepresentational these days."

"You anti-abstract or something?"

"No. Actually I'm kind of a Mondrian fan, though I think he painted himself into a corner. But my talent, if any, is all representational; so I'm going to draw."

Frank nodded, looking wistful. It's what he wanted to do, but he had two kids in high school who'd be expecting to go to college. He said if I was in a hurry I could leave as soon as I got rid of my current work, that he wanted to buy me a good-luck drink before I left, and I thanked him, feeling lousy about the lie, and took the elevator to the building lobby and the public phone booths. There I dialed the number Rube had given me.

It took a long time to get him on the line. I had to speak to two people, first a woman, then a man, and then wait for what must have been two full minutes; the operator came on for more money. Finally Rube spoke, and I said, "I phoned to say that if I do this I'll have to tell Katherine what's going on."

There was a longish pause. Then he said, "Well, you won't have much of anything to tell until we're sure you're a candidate. If it turns out you aren't, we'll thank you for your trouble, and in that case I don't think you'll have to tell her anything about it. Can we agree on that?"

"Yeah."

"If you reach the point of joining the project, knowing what we're doing"—he hesitated—"well, damn it, if you have to tell her, I guess you have to. We have two guys who are married, and their wives know. We swear them to secrecy, and hope, that's all."

"Okay. What would happen if she blabbed, Rube? Or if I did? Just out of curiosity."

"A man in a skintight black suit and a mask will come down your chimney and shoot you with a soundless blow dart, paralyzing you. Then we seal you in a big block of clear plastic till the year 2001. *Nothing* would happen, for crysake! You think the CIA murders you or something? All we can do is pick people we think we can trust. And we've seen Katherine, you know; inquired about her, very discreetly and all that. Of the two of you, I trust her the most. I take it you're joining us?"

I felt an impulse to hesitate, but didn't bother. "Yeah."

"Okay, the first day you can make it come around about nine in the morning; here's the address."

And so, three days later, on Thursday morning a little after nine, too tense to sit in a cab, I was walking through the rain, the good weather finally over apparently, looking for the address Rube had given me. I was feeling more and more puzzled; this was the upper West Side, an area of small factories, machine shops, wholesalers, binderies. Cars were solidly parked on both sides of every street, their off wheels up over the curbs. The walks were littered with wet paper, crushed orange-drink cartons, broken glass, and there were no other pedestrians. Checking addresses, I walked west, coming nearer and nearer the river. I passed BUZZ BANNISTER, neon-sign manufacturer, in a dirty white-stucco building, the windows piled with cardboard cartons. Next door was FIORE BROS., WHOLESALE NOVELTIES, a padlock on the door and a smashed wine bottle in the doorway. Across the street, silent and deserted in the rain, hundreds of rusting car bodies compacted into cubes were stacked behind a steel-mesh fence.

I was beginning to wonder if I'd been hoaxed, and Rube Prien were . . . what? An actor, possibly, hired to trick me in some elaborate practical joke? It didn't seem likely, yet the number he'd given me, if it existed at all, had to be in the block just ahead but I could see that the entire block was occupied by just one great building, six stories high, of soot-darkened brick, surmounted by a weathered wooden water tower, and in a wide band of faded white paint just below the roof line I read BEEKEY BROTHERS, MOVING & STORAGE, 555-8811, and I could tell by looking at it that that sign had been there for years.

The walls were windowless except at the corner just ahead and across the street from me. There, at street level, two plate-glass windows were lettered BEEKEY BROTHERS in chipped gold-leaf. In the tiny office behind the windows a girl sat at a desk back of a counter operating a billing machine. High up on the wall facing me, a rectangular panel painted on the bricks read LOCAL AND LONG DISTANCE; STORAGE OUR SPECIALTY; AGENTS FOR ASSOCIATED VAN LINES. On the street several stories below this, a green van lettered BEEKEY BROTHERS, MOVING AND STORAGE stood before a metal-slat truck door in the side of the building. Two men in white coveralls stood tossing stacks of protective blankets into the back of the van.

There was nothing to do except walk on toward the building, but I knew the number on its office door wouldn't be the one Rube had given me, and it wasn't. I kept walking. For a full block I walked through the rain beside the weathered brick wall. Between it and the sidewalk in a narrow strip of hard-packed dirt grew a scraggly, uncared-for, foot-high hedge. Cellophane fragments were trapped in its stiff little branches, dirty words were spray-painted on the walls, and I wondered if I'd have the nerve to ask Frank for my job back.

Set in the building wall at the end of the block was an ordinary wood door with a weathered brass knob and key circle. The gray paint was cracked and peeled to the bare wood in places, and the door looked locked. But stenciled on the wet bricks above it in white paint so faded you could barely make it out was the number Rube had given me. I rapped on the door panel, and there was a silence except for the sky-high roar of the Thursday-morning city and the sound of the rain on the hoods and tops of the parked cars behind me. I had no belief that my knock would be answered, or that there was anyone on the other side to hear it.

But there was. The knob rattled, turned, the door opened, and a black-haired young man in white coveralls looked out; in red stitching over a breast pocket it said *Don*, and he had a copy of *Sports Illustrated* in one hand. He said, "Hi; come on in. Boy, what a lousy day," and I walked in past him. As he closed the door I read, BEEKEY BROTHERS, MOVERS, in red block-letters across his back.

We were in a windowless fluorescent-lighted office no more than ten feet square, furnished with a desk, swivel chair, and a couple of yellow-oak straight chairs with most of the varnish worn off. On the wall hung a Beekey Brothers calendar and a lot of framed photographs of smiling crews posed alongside Beekey vans. "Yeah?" said the man in coveralls, sitting down behind his desk. "What can we do for you? Moving? Storage?"

I said I'd come to see Rube Prien, half expecting him to look blank, but he asked my name, then dialed a phone, gesturing with his chin toward a couple of hooks on the wall. "Hang up your hat and coat," he said to me, then into the phone, "Mr. Morley to see Mr. Prien." He listened, said, "Right," and hung up. "Be down in a minute; make yourself at home." He lay back in his swivel chair and began reading his magazine.

I sat there trying to wonder what was going to happen now, but there was nothing for my mind to work on, and I found myself examining the framed photographs: one of them, inscribed *"The Gang,"* 1921, in white ink, showed a Beekey van, an old Mack truck with metal-spoke wheels and solid rubber tires; half the crew wore big mustaches.

There was a click from a door set flush in the wall at my right. I looked up as it swung open, noticing that there was no knob on this side. Rube stood holding the door open behind him with a foot. He was wearing clean wash pants and a short-sleeved white shirt open at the neck; his forearms were fuzzy with red hair and were as large as my biceps and more muscular. "Well, I see you found us." He put out his hand. "Welcome, Si. Glad to see you."

"Thanks. Yeah, I found it. In spite of the disguise."

"Oh, we're not really disguised." He beckoned me in, then let the door swing closed behind us; it made a quiet heavy *thunk*, and I realized it was painted metal. We were standing in a little concrete-floored hallway badly lighted by a bare bulb in a wire cage in the ceiling. A pair of green-enameled elevator doors faced us, and Rube reached past me to poke the button. "Actually the building is the way it's been for years. On the outside. Up to ten months ago this was a genuine moving-and-storage business, a family corporation. We bought it, and we still do some moving and a little storage in a walled-off section of the building; enough to maintain the pose." The elevator doors slid open, we stepped

25

in, and Rube pressed 6. The only other visible button said 1; the other buttons were taped over with dirty adhesive.

"The older employees were pensioned off, the others gradually replaced by our people; I was 'hired' and actually worked as a moving man for a month. Damn near killed me." Rube smiled; that nice genuine smile you couldn't help responding to. "Now our estimates tend to be a little high; not much, just a little. And the business generally goes to a competitor. We look busy as ever, though. In fact, we are. We've even added two new vans. One hell of a lot of stuff has been moved out of here in our own closed vans; the entire interior of the building, in fact. And I guess we've brought even more stuff in." The green doors slid open, and we stepped out onto a floor of offices.

You could smell the newness, and it looked like a floor in any modern office building: polished vinyl-tiled corridors under a string of skylights; beige-painted walls with stenciled black arrows indicating groups of office numbers; looped fire hoses behind glass; occasional drinking fountains; numbered flush doors each with a black-and-white plastic nameplate fastened to the wall beside it. Far ahead, as we turned toward her, a girl in a white blouse and dark skirt, her face indistinguishable, walked toward us carrying a stack of papers in one arm; she turned into an office before reaching us. As we passed them I glanced at the plastic nameplates for some sort of clue, but they were only meaningless names: W. W. O'NEIL; V. ZAHLIAN; MISS K. VEACH. . . .

Rube gestured at a door just ahead; the plastic wall sign beside it said PERSONNEL. "We have to get this over first; withholding forms, Blue Cross, insurance, the works. Even we don't escape this stuff." He opened the door, gesturing me in first, and we stepped into a little anteroom half filled by a desk at which a girl sat typing. "Rose, this is Simon Morley, a new hand. Si, Rose Macabee." We said how-do-you-do, and Rube said, "How long will you need, Rose? Half hour?" She said about twenty-five minutes, and Rube said he'd be back for me then, and left.

"In here, please, Mr. Morley." The girl opened the door and led the way into an ordinary office, windowless and bare-looking, lighted by a large skylight. "Will you sit down, please?" I walked to the flat-topped desk and sat down in a swivel desk-chair. "The forms should be in here." She opened a drawer of the desk and brought out a little sheaf of six or eight printed forms of different colors and sizes clipped together. She pulled off the clip and spread them under my desk lamp, turning on the lamp with the other hand. "They're all here. Just fill in the blanks, Mr. Morley; do this long one first. Here's a pen." She handed me a ball-point pen. "It shouldn't take long. Call me if you have any questions." She nodded at a small table beside my chair; the top was an intricate pattern of inlaid wood about a foot square, just large enough for the white phone it held. She smiled and walked out, closing the door.

Pen in hand, I sat looking around the room for a moment or so. A green filing cabinet stood on the wall opposite me; a mirror hung on the wall behind me; on the wall to my right beside the door was a small framed picture, a watercolor of a covered bridge, not bad work but pretty standard. That was all there was to see, and I looked down at the papers spread out under the desk lamp; they were withholding-tax forms, hospitalization, and the like. I pulled the long one to me—it was headed "Personnel Fact Sheet"—and began filling it out. In the first blanks I wrote my name; place of birth, *Gary, Indiana*; date of birth, *March 11, 1942*; wondering if anyone ever looked at these things. The phone on the little table at my elbow rang, and I swung around in my chair, picked it up, and an actual physical sensation of coldness moved up my spine because the phone was green. It had been white, I was certain of that, but now it was green. I said, "Hello?"

"Mr. Prien is back for you, Mr. Morley. Are you nearly finished?"

"Finished? I just started."

There was a moment's pause. "Just started? Mr. Morley, you've been at it"—there was a pause as though she might be consulting a watch—"over twenty minutes."

I didn't know what to say to her. "You've made a mistake, Miss Macabee; I've barely begun."

I could detect the repressed annoyance in her voice. "Well, please finish up as quickly as you can, Mr. Morley. Mr. Prien has made an appointment with the director." She clicked off, and I slowly hung up the phone; could I possibly have drifted off into a daydream twenty minutes long? I turned back to the form I'd been filling out, then actually jumped to my feet in panic, my chair skidding back and banging the wall. There in the blanks under my name, birthplace, and date of birth were written my father's name, *Earl Gavin Morley*; his birthplace

27

and date of birth, *Muncie, Indiana*, 1908; my mother's maiden name, *Strong*; my hobbies, *sketching and photography*; and my entire history of employment beginning with *Neff & Carter* in Buffalo. All the other forms were filled out, too: every one of them, just like this, in my own unmistakable handwriting. It was impossible for me to have done this without knowing it, but there it was. It wasn't possible that twenty minutes had passed, but they must have. And the white phone—I glanced at it again—was still green. The hair on the back of my neck was prickling, trying to stand erect, and the fear in my stomach was like a clenching fist.

Then it stopped. I had *not* filled out these forms, and I knew it. I'd been in this room no more than three or four minutes at most, and I knew that, too. My eyes were narrowed, I stood staring out across the desk top thinking, then I saw the watercolor on the wall. The covered bridge was gone; now it was a pine-covered snow-capped mountain, and I laughed aloud, the fear instantly shrinking to nothing. The door opened, and Rube Prien walked in. "All finished? What's the matter?"

"Rube, what in the hell do you think you're doing?" I stood grinning at him as he walked toward the desk. "Why am I supposed to think I've been here twenty minutes?"

"But you have."

"And that the picture on the wall"—I nodded at it—"changed from a bridge to a mountain?"

"The picture?" Rube was standing before my desk, and he turned to look back at the watercolor, puzzled. "It's always been a mountain."

"And was the phone always green, Rube?"

He glanced at it. "Yeah, I guess so; far as I can remember."

I was slowly shaking my head, still smiling. "It's no use, Rube; I've been here five minutes at the most." I gestured at the papers on the desk top. "And I never filled those out, no matter how much it looks like my writing."

Through a moment or so Rube stood looking across the desk at me, his eyes concerned. Then he said, "Suppose I swear to you, Si, that you did? And that you've been here"—he looked at his watch—"just under twenty-five minutes?"

"You'd be lying."

"And suppose Rose swears it, too?"

I just shook my head. Suddenly I squatted down beside the little telephone table and looked underneath it. There hung the white phone, held in place and the receiver prevented from falling by a wide U-shaped copper band fastened between two sides of the underpart of the table; near it was fastened a small metal box from which a pair of thin wires ran down the inside of the table leg. I pressed the table top near the edge, and a panel within the intricate design revolved, the white phone rolling up into sight, the green phone sliding down onto the copper holding strip. When I looked up at him Rube was smiling, and he beckoned over his shoulder at the office doorway behind him.

A man in shirt-sleeves walked in. He was young, dark-haired, with a thin trimmed mustache, and he was looking at me in a pleased way. As he walked toward us Rube said, "Dr. Oscar Rossoff, Simon Morley." We each said how-do-you-do, and he reached across the desk top while my hand rose to shake his, but instead of taking my hand he took my wrist between thumb and fingers.

After a moment he said, "Pulse almost normal, and slowing rapidly. Good." He let go my wrist, stood smiling at me happily, and said, "How did you know? What tipped you off?" In the doorway Rose stood watching us, smiling.

"Nothing tipped me off except that it's impossible. I just knew I hadn't filled out those forms. That I hadn't been here twenty minutes." I had to smile again as I nodded toward the picture. "And that a few minutes ago that crazy mountain was a bridge."

"Inner-directed," Rossoff was murmuring before I finished. "This is fine," he said to Rube, "a very good reaction." He turned to me again. "To you it may seem unremarkable but I assure you many people act differently. One man jumped up and ran out through the door; we had to grab him in the hall and explain."

"Well, fine; glad I passed." I tried not to look it, but I felt pleased as a kid who'd just won the spelldown. "But what's the idea? And how'd you work it?"

Rube said, "We already knew the facts. It took an expert forger four hours to do those forms in a chemical ink. All but the first three blanks of the long form; those we left for you. There's a small infrared tube in the desk lamp; it makes the ink visible a few seconds after it's turned on. Rose watches through the mirror behind you; there's a corridor from her desk. As soon as you fill in the first three blanks, she phones you from an extension there and turns on the infrared tube. Time you're off the phone, and look back at the papers—hey, presto!—all the blanks are filled."

"And the picture?"

Rube shrugged. "A hole in the wall behind the glass and frame. While the candidate's writing, I just pull out the bridge and shove in the mountain."

"Well, it beats the Katzenjammer Kids, but what's the point?"

Rossoff said, "To see how you react when the impossible is happening: Some people can't take it. They rely on things being what they ought to be, and behaving as they always have. When suddenly they aren't, and don't, their senses actually surrender, can't cope. Right at that desk, they fail. Don, downstairs, was one; we had to give him a pill even after he knew what had happened. But you're guided from within, not from the outside. You know what you know. Come on into my office now, and have some coffee. A drink, if you want it; you've earned it."

Rossoff's office was down the corridor Rube and I had come along, around a corner, then in through a door labeled INFIRMARY. As Rossoff pushed it open for Rube and me, I was reminded of a hospital, and I realized that the door was wider than most. We walked on through a large room, unlighted except for a skylight. It contained a desk, a row of wicker chairs along a wall, a fluoroscope, an eye chart, and what I took to be a portable X-ray machine. Rube said, "No more tricks from now on, Si, I promise. That was the one and only."

"I didn't mind." Off to one side as we crossed the big room were the doorways of other, lighted rooms; from one I heard voices in casual conversation; in another I saw a man in a white hospital gown, his foot in a cast, sitting on an examining table reading a *Reader's Digest*.

We walked into a small reception room; a nurse in white uniform stood at a filing cabinet leafing through folders in the open top drawer. She was holding a pen in her teeth by the barrel, and she smiled as well as she could; Rube pretended he was going to swat her in the rear as we passed through, and she pretended to believe him, swinging out of the way. She was a big, good-looking, good-natured woman in her late thirties, with a lot of gray in her hair.

In his office Rossoff said, "Sugar? Cream?" walking toward a low magazine table and a glass jug of coffee on a hot plate. "I hope not, because we haven't got any."

"I believe I'll take mine black," Rube said, sitting down in an upholstered chair. "How about you, Si?"

"Black sounds good to me." I sat down in a green-leather chair, looking around me. It was a large rectangular room, windowless but filled with daylight from two immense skylights. I liked the room and felt comfortable in it. It was carpeted in gray and the walls were papered in a cheerful red-and-green pattern. At one end the doctor's desk was a mess, heaped with stacked books and papers. The other end was floor-to-ceiling bookshelves, and Rossoff, handing me a cup of coffee, saw me looking at them.

"Go take a look, if you like," he said, and I got up and walked over, tasting my coffee, which wasn't too good.

I'd expected the books to be medical texts, and a lot were. But six or eight feet of shelving was history: college textbooks, reference books, biographies, all kinds of books on every period, country and historical personage you could think of. And there must have been two hundred novels, many very old judging from the bindings, none of their titles familiar to me. On the way back to my chair, sipping the coffee, I took a quick look at the framed diplomas, New York State license, and photographs that nearly covered a wall above the back of a green-leather davenport. Rossoff, I saw, was an M.D. and a psychologist, from Johns Hopkins. He also had a cheerful-looking wife, two grade-school-age daughters, and a Basset hound. "All mine, the dog especially," he said, when he saw me glance at the pictures.

We had our coffee, talking idly, filling in a five-minute pause. Mostly we talked about the San Francisco Giants, and a plan of Rossoff's to force them back to New York by kidnapping Willie Mays. Then Rube set his cup on a little table beside him and stood up. He said, "Thanks, Oscar; the coffee was atrocious. Si, I'll be back when the doc's finished with you, and we'll go see the director."

He left, Rossoff asked if I wanted more coffee, and I said no. "Okay; now then," he said, "I have some tests I expect I'll be asking you to take presently. Mostly of a kind I'm sure you're familiar with. I may ask you to look at some Rorschach blots and tell me what nasty things they

31

make you think of. That sort of thing. If you do all right, then we may want to find out how good a liar you are. I may ask you to pose, with no advance warning, as something you're not; a lawyer, for example. And withstand the questionings of three or four people apparently suspicious of the pose. Or you may deny you're an artist, or that you've ever been to New York, sitting in conversation with several strangers, all from the project, who will try to trap you. But all that later. There's something else has to be done first. Incidentally, has it occurred to you that we may all be nuts, and that you've wandered into an immense booby-hatch?"

"That's why I joined up."

"Good; obviously you're the type we need." I liked Rossoff; if he was trying to put me at ease he was succeeding. He said, "Have you ever been hypnotized for any reason?"

"No, never."

"Do you have any feelings against it? I hope not," he added quickly. "This is most important; we have to be certain, first of all, that you *can* be hypnotized. Some people can't, as you undoubtedly know; the only way to find out is to try."

I hesitated, then shrugged. "Well, I suppose if it's someone competent . . ."

"I'm competent. And I'll do it. If you're willing."

"Okay. I've come this far; it wouldn't make sense to let that stop me."

Rossoff stood up, walked to his desk, and picked up a yellow wooden pencil. He sat down again, hitching his chair closer to mine till we sat only a yard apart, facing each other. Holding the pencil vertically before me, by the point, he said, "We'll use an object. This or most anything else will do; it doesn't have to be shiny. Just stare at it, if you will, please, not particularly intently; and if you want to blink or glance away do so. The only important thing here is that if you tense up and resist, I won't be able to do it. I need your okay in more than words; you have to agree mentally. Within yourself. And completely. All the way. Don't fight it at all. Don't resist. Are you perfectly comfortable? Just nod, if you are." I nodded. "Fine. If you sense any resistance in your mind, let it thaw. Just sit and watch it melt, then let it drain away. Relax your muscles, incidentally; I want you really quite comfortable. Relax even your jaw; let your mouth hang open a little, and let your eyes unfocus. I think you're feeling it a little now; you're intelligent and perceptive, and I believe you're accepting this very well. Really very well, and it's rather pleasant, isn't it? And nothing to be concerned about. Occasionally I practice auto-hypnosis, which can be done very easily, and which you will learn, too. Just four or five minutes of self-hypnosis, which actually means nothing more than opening your mind to suggestion, your own suggestion, can be wonderfully refreshing. I can cure a tension headache with it; I never use aspirin. I think you're feeling how relaxing this can be. Isn't it a nice way to rest? Better than a drink, better than a cocktail." He lowered the pencil, saying, "I'll tell you how wonderfully relaxed you are, in fact. Look at your right arm lying there on the arm of your chair. It's so completely relaxed, more than ever before in your life, even when you've been asleep, that you can't lift it. The muscles are too relaxed, they refuse to move. When I count to three you'll see for yourself. Try to lift your arm when I say 'three.' You won't be able to. One. Two. Three."

My arm wouldn't move. I stared at it, leaning closer, my eyes fixed on my coat sleeve, my brain willing it to move. But it lay absolutely motionless; it would no more move at my silent command than the doctor's desk.

"All right, don't be in any way concerned; you've willingly put yourself under my hypnotic suggestion, and done it very well, too. I'm going to talk to you for just a few minutes, now. Your arm, incidentally, is entirely free to move now."

I lifted my arm, flexing it, clenching and unclenching the fingers as though it had been asleep. Then I leaned back into the soft leather of the chair, more comfortable and content than I remembered ever having been before.

Rossoff said, "In a sense the mind is compartmented. Various parts of the brain perform various functions; eliminate a certain part of the brain, by accident, for example, and you lose the ability to talk. You have to learn how all over again, training another part of the mind. We can think of memory in that way, too, if it's convenient. Memories can be shut off. Closed down as though they had never existed. When it happens extensively we call it amnesia. Right now we're going to close off only a small part of your memory. When I tap this pencil against the arm of my chair, you will forget the name of the man who brought you

33

here. For the time being it will be gone from your mind, as impossible to recall as though you never knew it." He tapped the pencil against the leather arm of his chair; it made only the smallest sound but I heard it. "You remember the man, don't you, who first talked to you and induced you to come here? And who just had coffee with us? You can picture his face?"

"Yes."

"How was he dressed, by the way?"

"Wash pants, white shirt with short sleeves, brown moccasin loafers."

"Could you draw a sketch of his face?"

"Sure."

"Okay, what is his name?"

Nothing came to mind. I thought. I ran over names in my mind: Smith, Jones; names of people I knew or had known; names I had read or heard. None of them meant anything; I simply didn't know his name.

"You understand why you can't think of it? That you're under hypnotic suggestion?"

"Yes, I know."

"Well, see if you can break through it. Do your damnedest. You know his name. You've used it and heard it several times today. Come on, now; what is his name?"

I closed my eyes, straining. I searched my mind, tried to force out that name, but there was no way to find it. It was as though he were asking the name of a stranger in the street.

"When I tap this pencil on the arm of the chair again, you will remember it." He tapped the pencil against the leather and said, "What is his name?"

"Ruben Prien."

"All right. When I clap my hands together you will come out of hypnosis completely. There will be no lingering remainder, no vestige of it. All hypnotic suggestibility will be gone." He clapped his hands together, not loudly but with a sharp hollow pop. "Feel all right?"

"Yeah, fine."

"Let me just test to be sure. When I tap this pencil against the arm of my chair, you will forget my name. You will be completely unable to recall it." He tapped the chair arm with the pencil again. "Now, what is my name?"

34

"Alfred E. Neuman."

"No, come on now, no kidding around!"

"Rossoff. Dr. Oscar Rossoff."

"Okay, fine. Just testing; you're clear. Well, you did good, a first-rate subject. I have a hunch you'll do. Next time I may have you bark like a seal and eat a live fish."

I looked at Rorschach blots then, and told Rossoff what thoughts they started. I looked at pictures, interpreted them, and drew a few myself. I did a short true-or-false test. I filled in words missing from sentences. I talked about myself and answered questions. Wearing a blindfold, I picked up objects and described their sizes and shapes, and sometimes their uses. Finally Rossoff said, "Enough. More than enough. I've generally run tests for several days, sometimes a week, but . . . we're not really so damned sure of what we're doing that I can pretend to pinpoint the requirements for performing what is probably an impossibility. I have the strongest kind of hunch about you, and no test is going to make me change my mind. They all confirm it, anyway. As well as I'll ever be able to figure it out, you're a candidate." He looked over at the closed door of the office, listening. We could hear the murmur of a man's voice, then a woman's laugh, and Rossoff yelled, "Rube, get your hands off Alice, and come on in here!"

The door opened, and a very tall, thin elderly man walked in, and Rossoff got quickly to his feet. "It's not Rube," the man said, "and my hands weren't on Alice, I'm sorry to say."

"It was the other way around," the nurse said, reaching into the office for the doorknob; she closed the door, smiling.

Rossoff introduced us. This was Dr. E. E. Danziger, Director of the project, and we shook hands. His hand, big and hairy and with prominent veins, wrapped right around mine, it was so large, and his eyes stared at me, excited, fascinated, wanting to know all about me in one look. The words spilling out, he said, "How does he test?" and while Rossoff told him, it was my turn to study him.

He was a man you'd know again if you saw him just once. He was sixty-five or -six, I thought, his forehead and cheeks heavily lined; the cheek lines were a series of three curved brackets beginning at the corners of his mouth and extending up to the cheekbones, widening and deepening when he smiled. He was bald and tanned, the top of his head freckled, his side hair still black, or possibly dyed. He must have been six feet five inches tall, maybe more; and he was thin and lanky, wide-shouldered but stooped. He wore a jaunty polka-dotted, blue bow tie; an old-style double-breasted tan suit, the coat hanging open; and a brown button-up sweater under the coat. He was well into his sixties but he looked strong, he looked masculine and virile; I had a hunch that he might not at all mind getting his hands on Alice, and that maybe she wouldn't mind either.

To Rossoff, speaking slowly, he said, "You say yes?" And when Rossoff nodded, he said, "Then I do, too. I've gone over all we have on him, and he *sounds* right." He turned and stood looking at me soberly and searchingly for some seconds; during this Rube stepped into the office and very quietly closed the door. I was beginning to feel a little embarrassed by Dr. Danziger's stare when he suddenly grinned. "All right!" he said. "And now you'd like to know what you've got yourself into. Well, first Rube will show you, then I'll try to tell you." He gripped his coat lapels in his big freckled fists, his arms hanging loosely, and stood staring at me again, smiling a little, nodding slowly; in approval, I felt, and was more pleased than I'd have thought.

"I'm in charge of this establishment," Danziger continued then. "I began it, in fact. But just now I envy you. I'm sixty-eight years old, and two years ago when I understood that this project was going to become real, I began taking care of my health for the first time in my life. I quit smoking. I never thought I could and never much wanted to, but I quit"—he snapped his fingers—"like that. I miss it." His hand returned to his lapel. "But I'm not going to start again. I drink moderately; medicinally, actually. And I once drank a lot on occasion. Frequent occasion. Because I liked it. But no more now, and I follow a diet besides. Why all this nonsense?" He raised a hand, forefinger pointing up. "Because I want to live and be with this project just as long as I possibly can. I've had an interesting life, I haven't been cheated; I've been in two wars, lived in five countries, had two wives, a great many friends of both sexes, and once for four years I was rich. No children, though; you can't have everything." Again Dr. Danziger stared at me, eyes friendly and envious, hands hung on his lapels. "But if this project should succeed, it will be the most remarkable thing mortal man has ever done, and I'll give up anything, I'd follow a diet of raw turnips and horse manure, just to get an extra year or even an extra month of life for it. No matter how carefully a man lives, though, at sixty-eight his remaining years are numbered, while you—you're what: twenty-eight?" I nodded. "Well, you've got forty years on me then, and if I could steal them from you I'd do it, cheerfully and without compunction. I even envy you this day. Have you ever given someone a book you enjoyed enormously, with a feeling of envy because they were about to read it for the first time, an experience you could never have again?"

"Yes, sir; *Huckleberry Finn.*"

"Right. Well, that's how I feel about the day you're going to have now. Take him away, Rube. There's lots to show him, and we're in a hurry now." He raised a wrist to look at his watch. "Bring him to the cafeteria at noon."

3

_____

OUT IN THE CORRIDORS as I walked along with Rube, people passed us, moving to and from offices. They were men and women, mostly young, and whenever one walked by, speaking or nodding to Rube, he or she would glance at me curiously. Rube was watching me, I saw, smiling a little, and when I looked at him he said, "What do you think you're going to see?"

I tried to find an answer but had to shake my head. "I haven't a glimmering, Rube."

"Well, I'm sorry to be so damn mysterious. But it's the director who explains this, not me. And you have to see it before he can explain it." We turned a corner and then another, into a corridor considerably narrower than the others. We turned once more, and now we were walking along a narrow aisle that stretched ahead for a considerable distance.

One wall of the aisle was blank. The other was a series of tinted windows through which we could see into what Rube told me were instruction rooms. The first three were empty and were fitted out as ordinary classrooms. There were six or eight one-armed wooden chairs in each, the arms widening into writing surfaces; there were blackboards, bookshelves, teachers' desks and chairs. At the fourth window two men were sitting in the same kind of room, one at the desk, the other in a wooden chair facing him, and we stopped to watch. "We can see in, they can't see out," Rube said. "Everyone knows it; it's just a matter of not disturbing people at work."

The man in the student's chair was talking, steadily but with frequent pauses, sometimes rubbing his face in thought. He was about forty, thin and dark, and wore a navy-blue sweater and a white shirt open at the collar. The instructor at the desk was younger and wore a brown tweed sport coat. Beside the window on a stainless-steel wall plate was a pair of buttons. Rube pushed one and now we could hear the speaking man's voice from a loudspeaker behind a grill over the window.

It was a foreign language, and after a dozen seconds or so I thought I recognized it and was about to say so, then I stopped. I'd thought it was French, a language I can recognize, but now I wasn't sure. I stood listening carefully; some of the words were French, I was almost certain, but pronounced not quite correctly. He kept on, fluently enough, the instructor occasionally correcting pronunciation, which the other would repeat a few times before continuing. "Is it French?"

From the way Rube smiled I knew he'd been waiting for the question. "Yep. But medieval French; no one has talked like that in four hundred years." He pressed the other button, and the loudspeaker went silent, the man's lips continuing to move, and we walked on. At the next window Rube jabbed the speaker button, I heard a stifled grunt and the clash of wood on wood, then I stopped beside him and stood looking into the room.

It was completely bare, the walls padded and faced with heavy canvas; in it two men were fighting with bayonet-tipped rifles. One wore the shallow helmet, high-necked khaki blouse, and roll-puttees of a First World War American uniform. The other wore the black boots, gray uniform, and deep flared helmet of the Germans. The bayonets were an odd false-looking silver, and I saw that they were painted rubber. The men's faces were shiny with sweat, their uniforms stained at armpits and back, and as we watched they parried and riposted, heaved and shoved, grunting as the rifles clashed. Suddenly the German stepped back fast, feinted, sidestepped a counterthrust, and drove his rifle straight into the other's stomach, the rubber bayonet bending double against the khaki. "You're dead, pig of an American!" he yelled, and the other shouted, "Hell I am, that's just a little stomach wound!" They both started laughing, jabbing away at each other, and Rube stood glaring in at them, muttering, "Wrong, wrong, the bastards! An absolutely wrong attitude!" I glanced at him: He looked mean and dangerous, his lips set, eyes narrowed. For a moment longer he stared in silence, then punched the cutoff button hard with his thumb and swung away from the window.

A dozen men sat in the next room. Most of them wore white carpenter's overalls; a few were in blue jeans and work shirts. Beside the desk a man in khaki wash pants and shirt stood pointing with a ruler at a cardboard model which completely covered the desk top. It was a model of a room, one wall missing like a stage set, and the man was pointing to the miniature ceiling. Rube pushed the button beside the window. ". . . painted beams. But only at the highest ceiling points, where it's dark." The ruler moved to a wall. "Down here begin real oak beams, and real plaster. Mixed with straw; don't forget that, damn it." Rube poked the cutoff button, and once more we walked on.

The next room was empty of people, but an immense aerial photograph of a town covered three walls from floor to ceiling, and we stopped and looked at it. It had been labeled with a black marking pen: WINFIELD, VERMONT. RESTORATION IN PROGRESS, VIEW 9 OF ELEVEN, SERIES 14. I looked at Rube and he knew I was looking, but he offered no explanation, simply continuing to stare at the big photo, and I silently refused to offer a question.

The next two rooms were empty. In the following room the chairs had been shoved back to the walls, and a good-looking girl was dancing the Charleston to music from a portable windup phonograph on the desk. A middle-aged woman stood watching her, beating time with a forefinger. The swaying hem of the girl's tan dress came to just above her flying knees, and the waist of her dress wasn't much higher. Her hair was cut in what I knew was once called a shingle bob, and she was chewing gum. The older woman was dressed in pretty much the same way, though her skirt was longer.

Rube pushed the speaker button, and we heard the fast rhythmical shuffle of the girl's feet, and the thin, ghostly sound of a long-ago orchestra. The music stopped suddenly with an old-fashioned fillip, and the girl stood breathing audibly, smiling at the older woman, who nodded approvingly and said, "Good! That was the ant's ankles," and on that neat exit line Rube pushed the speaker button, trying not to smile, and we walked on, neither of us saying a word.

There were three more rooms, all empty of people, but in the next-to-last a dozen dressmaker's dummies stood ranged beside the instructor's desk. On the seat of one of the chairs lay a pile of white cardboard boxes that looked as though they might contain clothes.

Again we were walking briskly along skylighted corridors past numbered doors and black-and-white nameplates: D. W. MCELROY; A. N. BURKE AND HELEN FRIEDMAN, ACCOUNTING; N. O. DEMPSTER; FILE ROOM B. Rube was spoken to by, and he replied to, nearly everyone we passed; the men were more often than not dressed informally, wearing sweaters, sport coats, sport shirts, although some wore suits and ties. The women and girls, some very nice-looking, dressed the way they usually do in offices. Two men in overalls edged past us, pushing a heavy wooden handcart, trundling a motor or piece of machinery of some sort, partly covered by a tarpaulin. Then Rube stopped at a door no different from any of the others except that it was labeled with only a number, no nameplate. He opened it, gesturing me in first.

A man behind a small desk was on his feet before my foot crossed the threshold; it was a bare little anteroom, the desk and chair and nothing else in it. Rube said, "Morning, Fred," and the man said, "Morning, sir." He wore a green nylon zipper jacket, his shirt was open at the neck, and he had no insignia or weapon I could see, but I knew he was a guard: He had the shoulders, chest, neck, and wrists of a powerful man, and the only thing he was doing in here was reading a copy of *Esquire*.

Set flush in the wall behind the desk was a steel door. It was knobless, and along one edge were three brass keyholes spaced a few inches apart. Rube brought out a key ring, selected a key, then walked around the desk, inserted the key in the topmost lock, and turned it. From his watch pocket he took a single key, pushed it into the middle keyhole, and turned. The guard stood waiting beside him, and now the guard inserted a key in the bottom keyhole, turned it and pulled the door open with the key. Rube removed his two keys and gestured me in through the open door before him. He followed, and the door swung solidly shut behind us. I heard the multiple click of the locks engaging, and we were standing in a space hardly larger than a big closet, dimly lighted by an overhead bulb in a wire cage. Then I saw that we were at the top of a circular metal staircase.

Rube leading the way, we walked down for maybe ten feet, almost in darkness at first but descending into light; from the last stair we stepped onto a metal-grill floor. Except for the metal floor we were in a space very much like the one we had just come from. Along two walls ran a narrow unpainted wood shelf; on this lay a dozen pairs of shapeless boots made of inch-thick gray felt. They were awkward-looking things made to come up over the ankles, with buckles like galoshes. Rube said, "They pull over your shoes; find a pair that fits well enough so they won't drop off." He nodded at a metal door before us. "Once we go in, it has to be quiet, quiet, quiet all the way. No loud or sharp sounds, though we can talk softly; the sound seems to go up."

I nodded; my pulse, I knew, wouldn't be normal now. What in the *hell* were we going to see? We fastened the buckles of our boots—they were clumsy and too warm—then Rube pushed open the door, a heavy swinging door without knob or lock, and we stepped out, the door swinging shut behind us without a squeak.

We were standing on a catwalk, a narrower extension of the metal-grill floor on the other side of the door just behind us. Only a waist-high railing of steel rods that seemed too thin to me prevented our falling over the edge. My hand was gripping the top rail far more tightly than necessary, but I couldn't relax it and I didn't feel like walking on, because the catwalk under our feet was part of a vast spider web of metal-grill walks hanging in the air over an enormous block-square, five-story-deep well of space, the walks connecting and interconnecting, converging and angling off into the distance.

This great lacy web of narrow metal walkways hung from the roof—which was the underside of the office space we'd just left—by finger-thin metal rods. As we stood there, Rube giving me time to accept the necessity of walking out onto the web, I couldn't yet see anything below us except the tops of thick walls which rose up from the floor of the gutted warehouse five stories below to within a foot of the underside of the walkways we stood on. These walls, I could see, divided the great block-square space below us into large irregular-shaped areas. I looked up and saw a mass of air ducts and subduedly humming machinery suspended from the roof; then I glanced back at Rube. He was smiling at the look of my face. He said, "I know, it's a shock. Just take your time, get used to it. When you're ready, walk on out, anywhere you like."

I made myself walk then, maybe ten feet straight ahead, barely able to resist hanging onto the railings, and still unable to look down. For a few feet the walk led straight out from the door we'd come in through. Then it angled to the right, and I was aware that we passed over the top of a wall that rose from the floor far below almost to the underside of our walk. As we crossed over this wall, I felt a steady updraft of warmth and heard the hum of exhaust fans overhead. Just below the level of the catwalks rows of metal piping hung over the wall tops in places; clamped to them were hundreds of hooded theatrical lights. They seemed to be of every color and shade and of every size; all of them were aimed in groups to converge on specific areas below. I stopped, turned to the side, gripped the railing with both hands, and forced myself to look down.

Five stories below and on the far side of the area over which we were standing, I saw a small frame house. From this angle I could see onto the roofed front porch. A man in shirt-sleeves sat on the edge of the porch, his feet on the steps. He was smoking a pipe, staring absently out at the brick-paved street before the house.

On each side of this house stood portions of two other houses. The side walls facing the middle house were complete, including curtains and window shades. So were half of each gable roof and the entire front walls, including porches with worn stair treads. A wicker baby-carriage stood on the porch of one of them. But except for the complete house in the middle these others were only the two walls and part of a roof; from here I could see the pine scaffolding that supported them from behind. In front of all three structures were lawns and shade trees. Beyond these were a brick sidewalk and a brick street, iron hitching posts at the curbs. Across the street stood the fronts of half a dozen more houses. On the porch of one lay a battered bicycle. A fringed hammock hung on the porch of another. But these apparent houses were only false fronts no more than a foot thick; they were built along the area wall behind them, concealing the wall.

Leaning on the rail beside me, Rube said, "From where the man on the porch is sitting and from any window of his house or any place on his lawn, he seems to be in a complete street of small houses. You can't see it from here, but at the end of the short stretch of actual brick street he is facing now, there is painted and modeled on the area wall, in meticulous dioramic perspective, more of the same street and neighborhood far into the distance."

While he was talking a boy on a bike appeared on the street below us;

I didn't see where he'd come from. He wore a white sailor cap, its turned-up brim nearly covered with what looked like colored advertising- and campaign-buttons; short brown pants that buckled just below the knees; long black stockings; and dirty canvas shoes that came up over the ankles. Hanging from his shoulder by a wide strap was a torn canvas sack filled with folded newspapers. The boy pedaled from one side of the street to the other, steering with one hand, expertly throwing a folded paper up onto each porch. As he approached the complete house, the man on the porch stood up, the boy tossed the paper, the man caught it, and sat down again, unfolding it. The boy threw a paper onto the porch of the false two-walled house next door, which stood on a corner. Then he pedaled around the corner, and—out of sight of the man on the porch now—got off his bike and walked it to a door in the area wall against which the little cross street abruptly ended. He opened the door and wheeled his bike on through it.

I couldn't see what lay on the other side of the door, but a man immediately came through it, closing it behind him. Then he walked toward the corner putting on a hard-topped, flat-brimmed straw hat with a black band. His white shirt collar was open, his tie pulled down, and he was carrying his suit coat. From five stories above the man's head Rube and I watched him stop just short of the corner, shove his hat to the back of his head, sling his suit coat over one shoulder, and bring a wadded-up handkerchief from his back pocket. Dabbing at his forehead with the handkerchief, he began to walk tiredly, and turned the corner to move slowly along the brick sidewalk past the man on the porch, who sat reading his paper.

"Listen," said Rube, cupping a hand beside his ear, and I did the same. From far below but clearly enough, we heard the man on the sidewalk say, "Evening, Mr. McNaughton. Hot enough for you?" The man on the porch looked up from his paper. "Oh, hello, Mr. Drexsler. Yeah, it's another scorcher; paper says more of the same tomorrow." Still trudging by, a hot tired man on his way home from work, the man on the sidewalk shook his head ruefully. "Well, it has to end some-time," he said, and the man on the porch nodded, smiling, and said, "Maybe by Christmas."

The man on the sidewalk turned, cut across the street at an angle, climbed the steps of one of the false fronts across the street, and opened a screen door. "Edna!" he called. "I'm home." The screen door slammed behind him, and we watched him climb down a short ladder, duck under the scaffolding behind, and open a door in the wall. He walked through it, and it swung silently closed behind him.

In the false front next to this a screen door opened, and a woman walked out onto the porch and picked up the folded newspaper. She unfolded it and stood glancing over the front page; she was wearing an unusually long blue-checked housedress, its hem no more than a foot from the ground. At the sound of her opening screen door, the man on the porch across the street had glanced up momentarily, then gone back to his paper. Now, his arms spreading wide, he opened his paper, then folded it back to an inside page. The woman across the street walked back into the false front, carrying her paper. Propped in a curtained window beside her front door was a foot-square blue card printed in block letters, and I leaned forward a little, straining to read it. "It says ICE," Rube said. "On each edge is printed 25, 50, 75, or 100. You set the card in your window so that the number of pounds of ice you want the iceman to deliver when he comes along your street is at the top of the card."

I turned to look at Rube's face, but he was watching the scene below, forearms on the guardrail, his hands clasped loosely together. I said, "I don't see a camera but I assume you're either making or rehearsing some kind of movie down there." I couldn't help sounding a little bit irritated.

"No," said Rube. "The man on the porch is actually living in that house. It's complete inside, and a middle-aged woman comes in to cook and clean for him. Groceries are delivered every day in a light horse-drawn wagon labeled HENRY DORTMUND, FANCY GROCERIES. Twice a day a mailman in a gray uniform delivers mail, mostly ads. The man is waiting to hear whether he's been hired for any of several jobs he's applied for in the town. Presently he'll hear that he's been accepted for one of these jobs. At that point his habits will change. He'll begin going out into the town, to work." Rube glanced at me, then resumed his contemplation of the scene below. "Meanwhile he putters around the house. Waters his lawn. Reads. Passes the time of day with neighbors. Smokes Lucky Strike cigarettes. From green packages. Sometimes he listens to the radio, although in this weather there's lots of static.

Friends visit him occasionally. Right now he's reading a freshly printed copy, done an hour ago, of the town newspaper for September 3, 1926. He's tired; it's been over a hundred down there in the afternoons for the last three days, and in the high eighties even at night. A real Indian-summer heat wave with no air conditioning. And if he looked up here right now all he'd see is a hot blue sky."

Keeping my voice patient, I said, "You mean they're following some sort of script."

"No, there's no script. He does as he pleases, and the people he sees act and speak according to the circumstances."

"Are you telling me that he actually believes he's in a town in—"

"No, no; not that either. He knows where he is, all right. He knows he's in a New York storage warehouse, in a kind of stage setting. He's been careful never to walk around the corner and look, but he knows that the street ends there, out of his sight. He knows that the long stretch of street he sees at the other end is actually a painted perspective. And while no one has told him so, I'm sure he understands that the houses across the street are probably only false fronts." Rube stood upright, turning from the railing to face me. "Si, all I can tell you right now is that he's doing his damnedest to feel that he's really and truly sitting there on the porch on a late-summer afternoon reading what Calvin Coolidge had to say this morning, if anything."

"Is there actually a town and a street like this?"

"Oh, yes; a street with houses, trees, and lawns precisely like that, right down to the last blade of grass and the wicker baby-carriage on the porch. You've seen an aerial shot of it; it's called Winfield, Vermont." Rube grinned at me. "Don't get mad," he said gently. "You have to see it before you can understand it."

We walked on, high up on the spider web under the humming machinery and just above the hundreds and hundreds of lights. We crossed directly over the house with the man on the porch, and it was strange to think that if he should look up here from his paper he wouldn't see us but only an apparent sky. He didn't look, though; just continued reading his paper until the eave of his porch roof cut him from view. Angling to the left onto another length of catwalk, we passed over a wall and the area was gone from sight.

It was instantly cooler, with a hint of dampness and a feel of rain, and we stopped to stare down. Far below lay a section of prairie and through it ran a tiny stream. On the other side of the area from where we stood grew a scattering of thin white-trunked birch trees. These were stragglers at the edge of a much thicker woods which stretched up and over the crest of a rise. Most of the woods, I realized now, was painted on a wall but it looked very real. Almost directly under our feet stood three tepees made of hide and daubed with faded circles, jagged lines, and sticklike figures of men and animals. A thin smoke drifted from the open top of each tepee. Before one of them a puppy lay tethered to a peg; he was worrying something held between his paws. As we stared, some of the lights aimed into the area went off one by one—we could just hear the clicks—and the triangular shadows of the tents slowly deepened on the grass of the prairie, and now we could see an occasional spark in the trickles of rising smoke.

"I love this one," Rube murmured. "Montana, about sixty miles from where Billings now stands. There are eight people—men and women and one child—in those tepees; all of them full-blooded Crow Indians. Come on."

In our felt boots, moving almost soundlessly on the narrow metal grill, we walked on across space, again crossing over a wall. We stopped high above a triangular-shaped area and stood directly over its shortest side facing ahead toward its farthest point. A white stone building rose from the floor almost to our feet. Again, it wasn't what it seemed from its front and one side; there were only two walls, supported at their backs by iron-pipe scaffolding. Extending outward from the base of these walls lay a rough stone pavement. Between the cracks of the pavement four men in overalls were planting narrow strips of sod and little clumps of weeds which they took from baskets. The rough slab paving ended in a short grassy slope which led down to what seemed to be an actual river. Water flowed there, brown and sluggish, moving along one side of the triangular area toward its point, off ahead.

Something about this pseudo building of white stone, which ended only a yard or two under our feet, was becoming familiar, and I walked on along the catwalk to where I could get a better view of its front. The side wall along which I walked was flying-buttressed, and then I saw that the front rose into twin square towers. From the sides of the towers projected carved stone figures; one was nearly close enough to reach

47

down and touch. The figures were winged gargoyles and the buttressed wall and twin towers were those of a cathedral; this was Notre Dame of Paris; now I recognized it from movies and photographs.

Watching my face, Rube saw that I understood what we were seeing, and now he pointed across the river. I saw winding dirt roads trailing off into the distances of the other side; a few score of low wooden or stone structures; most of the area was farmland or woods. "Medieval Paris in the spring of 1451." Rube smiled. "It will be, that is, if we ever get the damn thing finished." His arm lifted, his forefinger pointing again, and now, across the river and far ahead, I saw a man in tan cotton pants and blue work shirt streaked with paint—a giant standing before houses and trees that reached no higher than his knees. A palette lay on his left forearm, and he was carefully painting in an extension of the forest, drawn in charcoal on the area wall on the other side of the brown, slow-flowing Seine. "Hell of a lot more work to be done here," said Rube. "Every stone of the cathedral to be aged with acid washes and stain; after all, in 1451 it was already several centuries old. In a sense this is our most ambitious project, but I doubt if even Danziger really thinks it can work. Ready? Let's move on."

Without stopping we walked over an empty area roughly rectangular in shape, one end a little wider than the other. Far below two men on hands and knees were marking off the area with strips of cloth tape and with colored chalk. "I don't quite remember what's going in here," Rube said, "but I think it will be a field hospital of the AEF near Vimy Ridge, France, 1918."

We looked down at a section of a snow-covered North Dakota farm in the dead of winter of 1924. The air over it was sharply cold; within half a minute we were shivering. We stood over a Denver street corner of 1901; it included a cobbled street with streetcar tracks, and a little grocery store with a tattered awning, into which two overalled men were wheeling supplies. Leaning on the rail beside me Rube murmured, "Reconstructed from seventy-odd photographs and snapshots, including one magnificently clear stereoscope view. Together with Lord knows how many present-day, on-the-site measurements. We're not finished yet; they're stocking the store now, everything absolutely authentic to the time. When it's done, it'll be the way it was, you can be certain of that." He glanced at his watch. "There are a few others, but it's time to meet Danziger now." We turned to walk back, Rube just behind me. "And our New York site doesn't need to be duplicated; we'll catch that after lunch. You hungry? Confused? Tired and irritable?"

I said, "Yeah, and my feet hurt."

4

_____

WE ATE in a small cafeteria on the sixth floor, a windowless fluorescent-lighted room tiled in pale blue and yellow and not very much larger than a big living room. Danziger was already waiting, seated alone at a table. As we picked up trays he waved to us; on the table before him stood a piece of apple pie and a bowl of soup covered with a saucer to keep it warm. Rube and I slid our trays along the chromed rails. I took a glass of iced tea, and a ham-and-cheese sandwich from a stack of them already made up and wrapped; Rube had Swiss steak and mixed vegetables, served up by a nice-looking girl. There was no cashier at the end of the rails, no charge, and Rube picked up his tray, said he'd see me later, and walked over to join a man and a woman just starting to eat. I carried my tray to Dr. Danziger's table, looking the place over as I walked. There were only seven or eight people besides us, with room for about a dozen more, and as I stood unloading my tray after speaking to Danziger, he guessed what I was thinking and smiled.

He said, "Yes, it's a small project. Maybe the smallest of any importance in the history of modern government, a pleasing thought. We have only about fifty people who are fully involved; eventually you'll meet most of them. We can and do occasionally draw on the services and resources of various government branches. But we do it in a way that doesn't suggest what we're up to or arouse questions." He lifted the saucer from his bowl of soup. "No chocolate pie today, damn it."

He picked up his spoon and sat watching me unwrap the sandwich I didn't really want. I was too tense to feel like eating; I'd have liked a drink. He said, "We maintain secrecy not by stamping things 'Classi-

50

fied' and wearing lapel badges but through inconspicuousness. The President, of course, knows what we're doing, though I'm not sure he thinks we do. Or that he even remembers us. Unavoidably we're known to at least two Cabinet members, several members of the Senate, the House, the Pentagon. I could wish that somehow even that weren't necessary but of course they're the people who get us our funds. Actually I can't complain; I make my reports, they're accepted, and they haven't really bothered us."

I made some sort of reply. The couple eating with Rube across the room were the girl I'd seen practicing the Charleston and a young guy about the same age. Danziger saw me looking at them, and said, "Two more of the lucky ones: Ursula Dahnke and Franklin Miller. She was a high-school mathematics teacher in Eagle River, Wisconsin; he managed a Safeway store in Bakersfield, California. She's for the North Dakota farm, he's for Vimy Ridge; you probably saw him bayonet practicing this morning. I'll introduce you next time, but right now: How much do you know about Albert Einstein?"

"Well, he wore a button sweater, had bushy hair, and was terrible at arithmetic."

"Very good. There are only a few other things to say after that. Did you know that years ago Einstein theorized that light has weight? Now, that's about as silly a motion as a man could have formed. Not another human being in the world thought that or ever had; it contradicts every feeling we have about light." Danziger sat watching me for a moment; I was interested, and tried to look it. "But there was a way to test that theory. During eclipses of the sun, astronomers began observing that light passing it bent in toward it. Pulled by the sun's gravity, you see. Inescapably, that meant that light has weight: Albert Einstein was right, and he was off and running."

Danziger stopped for several spoonfuls of soup. My sandwich, I'd found, was pretty good: plenty of butter, and the cheese actually had some taste; I was hungry now. Danziger put down his spoon, touched his mouth with his napkin, and said, "Time passed. That astonishing mind continued to work. And Einstein announced that E equals MC squared. And, God forgive us, two Japanese cities disappeared in the blink of an eye and proved he was right again.

"I could go on; the list of Einstein's discoveries is a considerable one.

51

But I'll skip to this: Presently he said that our ideas about time are largely mistaken. And I don't doubt for an instant that he was right once more. Because one of his final contributions not too long before he died was to prove that all his theories are unified. They're not separate but interconnected, each depending upon and confirming the others; they largely explain how the universe works, and it doesn't work as we'd thought."

He began peeling the red cellophane strip from the little package of crackers that came with his soup, looking at me, waiting. I said, "I've read a little on what he said about time, but I can't say I really know what he meant."

"He meant that we're mistaken in our conception of what the past, present and future really are. We think the past is gone, the future hasn't yet happened, and that only the present exists. Because the present is all we can see."

"Well, if you pinned me down, I'd have to admit that that's how it seems to me."

He smiled. "Of course. To me, too. It's only natural. As Einstein himself pointed out. He said we're like people in a boat without oars drifting along a winding river. Around us we see only the present. We can't see the past, back in the bends and curves behind us. But it's there."

"Did he mean that literally, though? Or did he mean—"

"He always meant exactly what he said. When he said light has weight, he meant that the sunlight lying on a field of wheat actually weighs several *tons*. And now we know—it's been measured—that it really does. He meant that the tremendous energy theoretically binding atoms together could really be released in one unimaginable burst. As it really can, a fact that has changed the course of the human race. He also meant precisely what he said about time: that the past, back there around the curves and bends, *really exists*. It is actually there." For maybe a dozen seconds Danziger was silent, his fingers playing with the little red cellophane strip. Then he looked up and said simply, "I am a theoretical physicist on leave here from Harvard University. And my own tiny extension of Einstein's giant theory is . . . that a man ought somehow to be able to step out of that boat onto the shore. And walk back to one of the bends behind us."

52

I was struggling to keep a thought from showing in my eyes: that this might be an intelligently, plausibly, wildly deluded old man who'd persuaded a lot of people in New York and Washington to join him in constructing a warehouse full of fantasies. Could it possibly be that I was the only one who'd guessed? Maybe not; this morning Rossoff had made a joke—an uneasy one?—about my joining a booby hatch. I nodded thoughtfully. "Walk back how?"

Danziger had a little soup left, and now he finished it, tipping his bowl to get the last of it, and I finished my sandwich. Then he raised his head, his eyes looked directly into mine, and I looked back into his and knew that Danziger wasn't crazy. He was eccentric, very possibly mistaken, but he was sane, and I was suddenly glad I was here. He said, "What day is this?"

"Thursday."

"What date?"

"The . . . twenty-sixth, isn't it?"

"You tell me."

"The twenty-sixth."

"What month?"

"November."

"And year?"

I told him; I was smiling a little now.

"How do you know?"

Waiting for a reply to form itself in my mind, I sat staring across the table at Danziger's intent, bald-headed face; then I shrugged. "I don't know what you want me to say."

"Then I'll answer for you. You know the year, the day and the month, for literally millions of reasons: because the blanket you woke up under this morning may have been at least partly synthetic; because there is probably a box in your apartment with a switch; turn that switch, and the faces of living human beings will appear on a glass screen in the face of that box and speak nonsense to you. Because red and green lights signaled when you might cross a street on your way here this morning; and because the soles of the shoes you walked in are a synthetic that will outlast leather.

"Because the fire engine that passed you sounded a hooter, not a siren; because the teen-aged children you saw were dressed as they were;

53

and because the Negro you walked by eyed you warily, as you did him, each of you trying to conceal it. Because the front page of the *Times* looked precisely as it did this morning and as it never will again or ever has before. And because millions and millions and millions of still other such facts will confront you all day long.

"Most of them are possible only in this century, many only in the latter half of it. Some are possible only this decade, some only this year, others only this month, and a few only on this particular day. Si, you are surrounded by literally countless facts that bind you to this century . . . year . . . month . . . day . . . and moment, like ten billion invisible threads."

He picked up his fork to cut into his pie, but instead he raised it to touch his forehead with the handle. "And in here there are millions more of those invisible threads. Your knowledge, for example, of who is President at this moment of history. That Frank Sinatra could now be a grandfather. That buffalo no longer roam the prairie, and that Kaiser Wilhelm isn't generally considered too much of a threat any more. That our coins are now made of copper, not silver. That Ernest Hemingway is dead, everything is turning to plastic, and that things don't go one bit better with Coke. The list is endless, all of it a part of your own consciousness and of the common consciousness. And it binds you as it binds us all to the day and to the very moment when precisely that list and only that list is possible. You never escape it, and I'll show you why." Danziger crushed his paper napkin and set it on the edge of his plate. "Finished? Want anything more?"

"No, that was fine. Thank you."

"Pretty frugal lunch but good for you. So they say. Let's go up on the roof. I'll take my pie along."

Outside, at the end of a short corridor, we climbed an enclosed flight of concrete fire stairs to a door that opened onto the roof. The morning rain had stopped, the sky was nearly clear again except for horizon clouds, and several girls and men were sitting out there in canvas chairs, their faces lifted to the sun. At the sound of our feet on the gravel as we stepped out onto the roof, they turned and spoke, and Danziger smiled and flicked his hand in a wave. The rooftop was immense; a city-block square of tar and gravel, ordinary enough except for scores of new skylights set into it, and a forest of stacks and vents. Ducking under

54

rusting guy wires attached to the taller stacks, walking around an occasional puddle, we crossed to a glob of noon shade around the base of the
wooden water tower. Danziger cut into his pie, and I stood looking
around.

Far to the south and east, I could see the outsize bulk of the Pan Am
Building overshadowing and dwarfing the entire area around Grand
Central Station. Beyond it I saw the dull-gray tip of the Chrysler Building, and to the right of that and farther south the Empire State Building. After that, there was only a nearly solid wall of mist already stained
yellow with industrial smoke. To the west, only a block or so away, lay
the Hudson River looking like the opaque gray sewer that it is. On its
other shore rose the cliffs of New Jersey. To the east I saw a between-
buildings sliver of Central Park.

Danziger gestured at the invisible horizons with his fork and said,
"There lies what? New York? And the world beyond it? Yes, you can say
that, of course; the New York and world of the moment. But you can
equally well say that there lies November twenty-sixth. Out there lies
the day you walked through this morning; it is filled with the inescapable facts that *make* it today. It will be almost identical tomorrow, very
likely, but not quite. In some households things will have worn out,
used today for the last time. An old dish will have finally broken, a hair
or two come out gray at the roots, the first flick of a new illness begun.
Some people alive today will be dead. Some scattered buildings will be a
little closer to completion. Or destruction. And what will lie out there
then, equally inescapably, will be a little different New York and world
and therefore a little different day." Danziger began walking forward
toward an edge of the roof, cutting off a bite of pie as he walked. "Pretty
good pie. You should have had some. I made certain we got a damn
good cook."

It was nice up here: As we walked, the sun, deflected up from the
rooftop, felt good on the face. We stopped at the edge of the roof and
leaned on the waist-high extension of the building wall, and again
Danziger gestured at the city. "The degree of change each day is usually
too slight to perceive much difference. Yet those tiny daily changes have
brought us from a time when what you'd have seen down there instead
of traffic lights and hooting fire engines, was farmland, treetops, and
streams; cows at pasture, men in tricornered hats; and British sailing

ships anchored in a clear-running, tree-shaded East River. It was out there once, Si. Can you see it?"

I tried. I stared out at the uncountable thousands of windows in the sooty sides of hundreds of buildings, and down at the streets nearly solid with car tops. I tried to turn it back into a rural scene, imagining a man down there with buckles on his shoes and wearing a pigtailed white wig, walking along a dusty country road called the broad way. It was impossible.

"Can't do it, can you? Of course not. You can see yesterday; most of it is still left. And there's plenty of 1965, '62, '58. There's even a good deal left of nineteen hundred. And in spite of all the indistinguishable glass boxes and of monstrosities like the Pan Am Building and other crimes against nature and the people"—he waggled a hand before his face as though erasing them from sight—"there are fragments of still earlier days. Single buildings. Sometimes several together. And once you get away from midtown, there are entire city blocks that have been where they still stand for fifty, seventy, even eighty and ninety years. There are scattered places a century or more old, and a very few which actually knew the presence of Washington." Rube was up here now, I saw, wearing a felt hat and a light topcoat, deferentially waiting a few token paces out of earshot. "Those places are fragments still remaining, Si"— Danziger's fork swept the horizon once more—"of days which once lay out there as real as the day lying out there now: still-surviving fragments of a clear April morning of 1871, a gray winter afternoon of 1840, a rainy dawn of 1793." He glanced at Rube from the corner of his eye, then looked back to me. "One of those survivals, in my opinion, is close to being a kind of miracle. Have you ever seen the Dakota?"

"The what?"

He nodded. "If you'd ever seen it, you'd remember that name. Rube!" Rube stepped smartly forward, the alert lieutenant responding to the colonel's call. "Show Si the Dakota, will you, please?"

Outside the big warehouse, Rube and I walked east to Central Park; I'd picked up my hat and coat in the little ground-level office. In the park we turned onto West Drive, which is the street just inside the western boundary of the park. We walked along under the trees; a few still had their leaves, clean and greener now after the morning's rain, and Rube said, looking around us, "This park itself is something of a miracle of survival, too. Right here in the heart of what must be the world's most changeable city are, not just acres, but several square *miles* that have been preserved practically unchanged for decades. Lay a Central Park map of the early eighteen eighties beside a map of today, and there on both maps are all the old names and places: the reservoir, the lake, North Meadow, the Green, the pool, Harlem Mere, the obelisk. We've photocopied some of the old maps to precisely the size of a modern one, then superimposed one over the other between glass sheets, and shot a good strong light through them. Allowing for small mapmakers' errors, they've coincided, the sizes and shapes of the things in the park unchanged through the years. Si, the very curve of this road, and nearly all the roads and even the footpaths, are unaltered."

I didn't doubt it; off to our left, the low boundary wall of the park was not quick-poured concrete but old carefully mortised cut-stone, and the very look of the park, of its bridges and even its trees, is old. "Details are changed, of course," Rube was saying. "The kinds of benches, trash baskets, and painted signs, the way the paths and roads are surfaced. But the old photographs all show that except for automobiles on the road-ways there is no difference you can see from, say, six or seven stories up." Rube must have timed what he was saying, or maybe it was past experience at this, because now as we passed under a final tree beside the walk, rounding the curve that led off the West Drive and onto the Seventy-second Street exit from the park, he lifted an arm to point ahead. As we walked out from under the branches of the tree he said, "From an upper apartment of *that* building, for example," and then I saw it and stopped dead in my tracks.

There across the street just outside the park stood a tall block-wide structure utterly unlike any I'd ever before seen in all New York. One look and you knew it was what Danziger had said: a magnificent survival of another time. I later came back—it was after a snowfall, as you can see—and took photographs of the building, a whole roll of them, the super even taking me up to the roof. The one at the top of the next page I took from where Rube and I stood; the building you see there is pale yellow brick handsomely trimmed in chocolate-colored stone, and as one of my later shots shows, each of its eight stories is just twice as high as the stories of the modern apartment house beside it.

It's a wonderful sight, and the roof almost instantly pulled my eyes

up; it was like a miniature town up there—of gables, turrets, pyramids, towers, peaks. From roof edge to highest peak it must have been forty feet tall; acres of slanted surfaces shingled in slate, trimmed with age-greened copper, and peppered with uncountable windows, dormer and

flush; square, round, and rectangular; big and small; wide, and as narrow as archers' slits. As the shot that I took on the roof shows—at the bottom of the opposite page—it rose into flagpoles and ornamental stone spires; it flattened out into promenades rimmed with lacy wrought-iron fences; and everywhere it sprouted huge fireplace chimneys. All I could do was turn to Rube, shaking my head and grinning with pleasure.

He was grinning, too, as proud as though he'd built the place. "That's the way they did things in the eighties, sonny! Some of those apartments have seventeen rooms, and I mean *big* ones; you can actually lose your way in an apartment like that. At least one of them includes a morning room, reception room, several kitchens, I don't know how many bathrooms, and a private ballroom. The walls are fifteen inches thick; the place is a fortress. Take your time, and look it over; it's worth it."

It was. I stood staring up at it, finding more things to be delighted with: handsome balconies of carved stone under some of the big old windows, a wrought-iron balcony running clear around the seventh story, rounded columns of bay windows rising up the building's side into rooftop cupolas. Rube said, "Plenty of light in those apartments: The building's a hollow square around a courtyard with a couple of spectacular big bronze fountains."

"Well, it's great, absolutely great." I was laughing, shaking my head helplessly, it was such a fine old place. "What is it, how come it's still there?"

"It's the Dakota. Built in the early eighties when this was practically out of town. People said it was so far from anything it might as well be in the Dakotas, so that's what it was called. That's the story, anyway. I know you won't be astonished to learn that a group of progress-minded citizens was all hot to tear it down a few years ago, and replace it with one more nice new modern monster of far more apartments in the same space, low ceilings, thin walls, no ballrooms or butler's pantries, but plenty of profit, you can damn well believe, for the owners. For once the tenants had money and could fight back; a good many rich celebrities live there. They got together, bought it, and now the Dakota seems safe. Unless it's condemned to make room for a crosstown freeway right through Central Park."

"Can we get in and look around?"

"We don't have time today."

I looked up at the building again. "Must get a great view of the park from this side."

"You sure do." Rube seemed uninterested suddenly, glancing at his watch, and we turned to walk back along West Drive. Presently we walked out of the park; ahead to the west I could see the immense warehouse again, and read the faded lettering just under its roofline: BEEKEY BROTHERS, MOVING & STORAGE, 555-8811.

If I'd expected Danziger's office, as I think I did, to be luxurious and impressive, I was wrong. Just outside it the black-and-white plastic nameplate beside the door merely said E. E. DANZIGER, no title. Rube knocked, Danziger yelled to come in, Rube opened the door, gestured me in, and turned away, murmuring that he'd see me later. Seated behind his desk, Danziger was on the phone, and he gestured me to a chair beside the desk. I sat down—I'd left my hat and coat downstairs again—and looked around as well as I could without seeming too curious.

It was just an office, smaller than Rossoff's and a lot more bare. It looked unfinished really, the office of a man who had to have one but wasn't interested in it, and who spent most of his time outside it. The outer wall was simply the old brick of the warehouse covered by a long pleated drape which didn't extend quite far enough to cover it completely. There was a standard-brand carpet; a small hanging bookshelf on one wall; on another wall a photograph of a woman with her hair in a style of the thirties; on a third wall, a huge aerial photograph of Winfield, Vermont, this view different from the one I'd seen earlier. Danziger's desk was straight from the stock of an office-supplies store, and so were the two leather-padded metal chairs for visitors. On the floor in a corner stood a cardboard Duz carton filled to overflowing with a stack of mimeographed papers. On a table against the far wall something bulky lay covered by a rubberized sheet.

Danziger finished his phone conversation; it had been something or other about authorizing someone to sign vouchers. He opened his top desk drawer, took out a cigar, peeled off the cellophane, then cut the cigar exactly in half with a pair of big desk scissors, and offered one of the halves to me. I shook my head, and he put it back in the drawer, then put the other half in his mouth, unlighted. "You liked the Dakota," he said; it wasn't a question, but a statement of fact. I nodded, smiling, and Danziger smiled too. He said, "There are other essentially unchanged buildings in New York, some of them equally fine and a lot older, yet the Dakota is unique; you know why?" I shook my head. "Suppose you were to stand at a window of one of the upper apartments you just saw, and look down into the park; say at dawn when very often no cars are to be seen. All around you is a building unchanged from the day it was built, including the room you stand in and very possibly even the glass pane you look through. And this is what's unique in New York: *Everything you see outside the window is also unchanged.*"

He was leaning over the desk top staring at me, motionless except for the half cigar which rolled slowly from one side of his mouth to the other. "Listen!" he said fiercely. "The real-estate firm that first managed the Dakota is still in business and we've microfilmed their early records. We know exactly when all the apartments facing the park have stood empty, and for how long." He sat back. "Picture one of those upper apartments standing empty for two months in the summer of 1894. As it did. Picture our arranging—as we are—to sublet that very apartment for those identical months during the coming summer. And now understand me. If Albert Einstein is right once again—as he is—then hard as it may be to comprehend, the summer of 1894 *still exists.* That silent empty apartment exists back in that summer precisely as it exists in the summer that is coming. Unaltered and unchanged, identical in each, and existing in each. I believe it may be possible this summer, just barely possible, you understand, for a man to walk out of that unchanged apartment and into that other summer." He sat back in his chair, his eyes on mine, the cigar bobbing slightly as he chewed it.

After a long moment I said, "Just like that?"

"Oh, no!" He shot forward again, leaning across the desk toward me. "*Not* just like that by a long shot," he said, and suddenly smiled at me. "The uncountable millions of invisible threads that exist in here, Si"— he touched his forehead—"would bind him to *this* summer, no matter how unaltered the apartment around him." He sat back in his chair, looking at me, still smiling a little. Then he said very softly and matter-of-factly, "But I would say this project began, Si, on the day it occurred to me that just possibly there is a way to dissolve those threads."

I understood; I knew the purpose of the project. I'd understood it for some time, of course, but now it had been put into words. For several seconds I sat nodding slowly, Danziger waiting for me to say something. Finally I did. "Why? Why do you want to?"

He slouched back in his chair, one long arm hooked over its back, and shrugged a shoulder. "Why did the Wrights want to build an airplane? To create jobs for stewardesses? Or give us a way to bomb Vietnam? No, I think all they really had in mind was to see if they could. I think it's why the Russki scientists shot the first satellite into orbit, no matter what supposed purposes they advanced. For no other real reason than to see if they could, like kids blasting a firecracker under a tin can to see if it'll really go up. And I think it was reason enough. For their scientists and ours. Impressive purposes were invented later to justify the horrible expense of these toys, but the first tries were just for the hell of it, boy, and that's our reason, too."

It was okay with me. I said, "Fine, but why Winfield, Vermont, in 1926? Or Paris of 1451? Or the Dakota apartments in 1894?"

"The places aren't important to us." He took the half cigar from his mouth, looked at it distastefully, and put it back. "And neither are the times. They're nothing but targets of opportunity. We're not especially interested in the Crow Indians. Of 1850 or any other time. But as it happens, there are some thousands of federally owned acres of Montana land still virtually untouched, unchanged from the 1850's. For four or five days at most the Department of Agriculture will undertake to close the road through it—no cars or Greyhound buses—and to keep the jets out. They can also provide a herd of approximately a thousand buffalo. If we could have the area for a month we wouldn't need the simulation down on the Big Floor. As it is, our man will get used to it here, and—we hope—be ready to make the most of the few days we'll have in the real location.

"As for Winfield—" he nodded toward the wall photograph. "It's just a very small town in an area of played-out farmland, virtually abandoned when we got it. For forty years the town was slowly dying, gradually losing population. For the last thirty of those years hardly anyone wasted money modernizing and trying to fight the inevitable. It's an old story in parts of New England; the ghost towns aren't all in the West. This one was more isolated than most, so we bought it through another agency simply as a target of opportunity. Supposedly to build a dam on its site."

Danziger grinned. "We've closed off the road into it, and now we're restoring it; God, it's fun! The reverse, for a change, of running a freeway through the heart of a fine old town or replacing a lovely old place with a windowless monstrosity; it would drive the destroyer mentalities insane with frustration, but our people are having a wonderful time." He sat smiling like a sailor talking about his all-time-best shore leave.

"They're ripping out all the neon, they'll tear out every dial phone, unscrew every frosted light bulb. We've carted out most of the electrical appliances already: power lawn mowers and the like. We're removing every scrap of plastic, restoring the buildings, and tearing down the few new ones. We're even *removing* the paving from certain streets, turning them back into lovely dirt roads. When we're finished, the bakery will be ready with string and white paper to wrap fresh-baked bread in. There'll be little water sprays in Gelardi's store to keep the fresh vegetables cool. The fire engine will be horse-drawn, all automobiles the right kind, and the newspaper will begin turning out daily duplicates of those it published in 1926. We're working from an extensive study and collation of photographs and town records, and when we're finished I think forgotten little Winfield will once more be the way it was in 1926; now what do you think of that?"

I was smiling with him. "Sounds impressive. And expensive."

"Not at all." Danziger shook his head firmly. "It will cost, all told, only a little over three million dollars, less than the cost of two hours of war, and a better buy. All this for the benefit of one man; you saw him this morning out on the Big Floor."

"The man on the porch of the little frame house."

"Yes; it's a duplicate of one in Winfield. In it, as well as he can, John is doing his level best to work himself into the mood of living in Winfield, Vermont, in the year 1926. Then, when he's ready and when we are, for about ten days—the longest period that is practical—some two hundred actors and extras will begin walking the restored streets of Winfield, driving the old cars, sitting out on the porches if it's warm enough. They'll be told it has to do with an experimental movie technique; hidden cameras catching their impromptu but authentic actions, which must be maintained at all times when outdoors. Among the two hundred—all those having actual dealings with John—will be some twenty-odd people from the project. We hope John will be mentally ready to make the most of those brief ten days." Chewing his cigar stump, the old man sat staring across his office at the huge photograph on the wall.

Then he looked at me again. "And that's the purpose of all our constructions down on the Big Floor. They're preparatory: temporary substitutes for the real sites because they're either not available yet or not available for a long enough time. There aren't many thousand-year-old buildings anywhere, for example, but one of them is Notre Dame cathedral in Paris. The actual site will be given to us for less than five hours, between midnight and dawn of one night only. Electricity and gas to be turned off on the Île de Cité and along the Right and Left banks within eye range of the cathedral. And we'll be allowed to stage-set the immediate area. It's the best we could arrange—through the State Department—with the French government. They think it's being done for a movie. We even prepared a full shooting script to show them; realistically bad, which I expect convinced them. No one in the project has a great deal of hope for this particular attempt; there will be only a matter of hours in which to make it, not nearly enough, I'm afraid. And it's reaching a long way back; could anyone really achieve a sense of what it was like? I must doubt it, but still I have hope. We do the best we can, that's all, with the sites we discover."

Danziger stood, and beckoning me to follow, he walked to the covered table. "And now, except for countless details, you know what this project is. I've saved the best for last: your assignment."

He pulled the dust cover from the table and exposed a model, three-dimensional and beautifully made. From a body of white-capped green water a wooded island rose to a peak. Facing the island across a strait, a slanted cliff rose from a boulder-strewn beach. Above the rock face of the cliff grew timber, and among the trees stood a white house with a railed veranda.

"We're building this down on the Big Floor." Danziger touched the peak of the wooded island. "This is Angel Island in San Francisco Bay; it is state and federally owned. Except for a long-abandoned immigration station and an abandoned Nike site, both hidden by trees, the island looks now as it looked at the turn of the century when this house"—he touched its tiny roof—"was new. It was the first house built here, and it took the best view, nearest the water. The actual house still exists, and except from its rear windows you can't see the newer houses

66

around it. And Angel Island blocks off the Bay bridges. So the site is as it was except for modern shipping and power boats passing through the strait. For two full days and three nights we can have the strait as it was, including two cargo sailing-ships and some smaller ones." Danziger smiled at me and put a big heavy hand on my shoulder. "San Francisco has always been a charming place to visit. But they say the city that was lost in the earthquake and fire of 1906 was particularly lovely, nothing like it on earth anymore. And that, Si—San Francisco in 1901—is your assignment."

No one likes anticlimax: There was a kind of innocent drama about this moment that I liked, and I hated to spoil it. But I had to, and I shook my head, frowning. "No. If I have a choice, Dr. Danziger, then not San Francisco. I want to be the man who tries in New York."

"New York?" He moved one shoulder in a puzzled shrug. "Well, I wouldn't myself, but if you like, you may. I thought I was offering you something exceptional, but—"

I had to interrupt, embarrassed. "I'm sorry, Dr. Danziger, but I don't mean the New York of 1894."

He wasn't smiling now; he stood staring intently into my eyes, wondering if he hadn't made a big mistake about me. "Oh?" he said softly. "When?"

"In January—I don't remember the date, but I'll find out—of the year 1882."

Before I'd even finished he was shaking his head no. "Why?"

I felt foolish saying it. "To . . . watch a man mail a letter."

"Just watch? That's all?" he said curiously, and I nodded. He turned abruptly, walked to the side of his desk, picked up the phone, dialed two digits, and stood waiting. "Fran? Check our records on the Dakota; they're on film. For parkside vacancies in January 1882."

We waited. I put in the time studying the model on the table, walking around it, stooping to squint across it. Then Danziger picked up a pen, scribbled rapidly on a scratch pad, said, "Thank you, Fran," and hung up. He ripped the sheet from the pad, turned to me, and his voice was disappointed. "I'm sorry to say there are two vacancies in January of 1882. One on the second floor, which is no good. But the other is on the seventh floor and runs for the entire month, from the first of the year on into February. Frankly, I'd hoped there would be none, and that your purpose would therefore be impossible, ending the matter. Si, there can be no private purposes in this project. This is a deadly serious venture, and that's not what it's for. So maybe you'd better tell me what you have in mind."

"I want to. But I don't want to just tell you, sir, I want to *show* you. In the morning. Because if you actually see what I'm talking about, I think you may agree."

"I don't think so." He was shaking his head again, but once more now his eyes were friendly. "By all means show me, though; in the morning if you like. Go on home now, Si; it's been quite a day."

5

ABOUT THREE MONTHS or so after I met Katherine Mancuso I brought
her home one night; I don't remember now where we'd gone. We'd
been out in the MG, and I bumped it up over the curb, parked it in its
slot between her store and the next building, and we crawled out over
the back end. Up in her apartment over the store, Kate put water on for
tea. All this was about as usual, yet I think we both knew even while
taking our coats off that in some mysterious way tonight—mysterious
because the evening until now hadn't seemed any different from a lot of
others—we'd crossed some sort of invisible line, and that our relationship was no longer tentative but was headed somewhere. Because Katie
began telling me all about herself.

She carried in our tea, a full cup on its saucer in each hand—I knew
she'd added sugar to mine in the kitchen—handed me mine, sat down
beside me on the chesterfield, and began talking as though we'd both
understood she was going to, as I guess we did. Most of what she told
me that night is of no importance to this, but after a while she said,
"You know I'm an orphan?"

I nodded; she'd told me that much long since. When Kate was two,
her parents took a weekend trip, and as usual left her with Ira and Belle
Carmody next door; this was in Westchester. They were much older
than the Mancusos but good friends, childless, crazy about Kate. Her
parents were killed driving home.

In the days that followed, the Carmodys kept Kate with them. And
when it turned out there were no relatives to take her except a cousin of

her mother's in another state who had never seen her, the Carmodys legally adopted Kate, the cousin glad to agree. They raised her, and of course to Katie they were her parents; she didn't remember her own.

I nodded; yes, I knew she was an orphan. And Kate got up, went to her bedroom, and came back with an accordion folder, the kind made out of shiny red cardboard that ties with an attached red cord. She opened it on her lap, found the right compartment, reached in, and—we're all actors by instinct, hams from birth—she didn't withdraw her hand but sat talking, letting my curiosity build. She said, "Ira's father was Andrew Carmody, a fairly well-known financier and political figure of nineteenth-century New York, though not one of the really famous ones. Later on he seemed to lose his moneymaking ability, and whatever fortune he had along with it. His chief claim to fame was that he was some sort of adviser to President Grover Cleveland during Cleveland's second term in the nineties, which is when Ira was born."

I nodded and, just for something to say, said, "What'd he advise him about?"

Kate smiled. "I don't know. Nothing much, I imagine; as an historical figure he was pretty minor. Ira used to say that in a very complete history of Cleveland's second administration his father would probably rate one small footnote. But he was important to Ira, because when Ira was small, I don't know how old, his father killed himself. And for the rest of Ira's life I don't think his father was ever very far from his mind."

Kate brought her hand out from the folder; she was holding a square little black-and-white snapshot. "Andrew Carmody was broke, the last of his money finally gone, and in 1898 he and his wife moved to Montana, a little town called Gillis. Years later in the thirties, long after Ira was grown and had left Gillis, he drove back there, halfway across the country, just to make sure he was right and that his father's grave was really the way he remembered it as a child.

"It was—exactly." Kate handed me the little photograph. "That's the picture Ira took that summer: That's his father's gravestone. I suppose it's still there; someday I'd like to go see."

I couldn't make out what I was looking at, staring at the glossy little snapshot on my palm. Then I recognized the shape: It was the kind of gravestone cartoonists draw, the old-fashioned straight-sided slab with the top rounded into a perfect half-circle. This one seemed to stand no more than a foot and a half or so above ground—it was much shorter than most—and was no longer perfectly upright, but canted to the left. It was sharp and clear; he'd taken this when the light was just right. There stood the stone at the head of a sparsely grassed grave, several gone-to-seed dandelions plainly visible. It was an old grave, the mound shallow, almost level again with the surrounding earth. Then I realized with a small sense of shock that the markings on the stone weren't letters; there was no inscription on the headstone, only a design, and I brought the little snap closer, tilting it toward the lighted lamp at the end of the chesterfield.

The design was a nine-pointed star inside a circle. It was formed of what must have been ninety or a hundred or so dots. The engraver had simply tapped it out, one dot after another, the points of the star touching the circle, the design covering almost the entire surface of the tombstone right down to the ground. The photograph was good, each dot a tiny shadow-blackened pit in the flaking stone surface, the weathered round-topped shape of the tombstone sharply outlined against the much darker background of hard-packed earth and sparse grass behind it, other neighboring headstones slightly out of focus in the near distance.

I have an idea that I sat staring at the little photograph for as much as a full minute, which is a long time. It had the fascination of absolute reality; somewhere far across the country outside a small Montana town this strange stone still stood, very likely, stained and roughened by years of heat, cold, and the alternate wetness and dryness of many seasons. I looked up at Kate finally. "This is what his wife put up at his grave?"

Kate nodded. "It disturbed Ira all of his life." Her hand was rummaging in the folder again; then she brought out a paper, a long rectangle of robin's-egg blue. It was an envelope, and Kate said, "His father shot himself. One summer afternoon. Sitting at his desk in a little frame house. And this is what he left on his desk."

I took the envelope. It bore a canceled three-cent green stamp bearing a profile of Washington in a design I'd never seen before, and the postmark circle read: "New York, N.Y., Main Post Office, Jan. 23, 1882, 6:00 PM." Under this it was hand-addressed in black ink to "Andrew W. Carmody, Esq., 589 Fifth Avenue, City." The lower right corner of the envelope was slightly charred as though it had been lighted and almost

71

immediately put out. I turned it over—the back was blank—and Kate said, "Look inside."

There was a white sheet inside, folded in half and charred at one side as though it had been in the envelope when the envelope was lighted. In black ink above the fold, in the same neat script as the address, was written: *If a discussion of Court House Carrara should prove of interest to you, please appear in City Hall Park at half past twelve on Thursday next.* In blue ink below the fold, in a large half-illegible scrawl, blot-stained in four places, it said: *That the sending of this should cause the Destruction by Fire of the entire World* (a word seemed to be missing here at the end of the top line where the paper was burned) *seems well-nigh incredible. Yet it is so, and the Fault and the Guilt* (another word missing in the burned area) *mine, and can never be denied or escaped. So, with this wretched souvenir of that Event before me, I now end the life which should have ended then.*

I felt a corner of my mouth move up into a faint smile; this seemed unreal. As I looked down at the charred little sheet, it was hard to understand that once people could actually write a florid overblown note like this, then pick up a gun and kill themselves. But it *was* real; however written, this thing in my hand—I glanced down at it again, and stopped smiling—was a desperate message from the last moments of a man's existence. I slid it back into its envelope and looked up at Kate. "End of the world?" I said, but she shook her head.

"No one ever knew what it meant. Except, I suppose, Ira's mother. She came running—I've pictured this so often, Si, though I hate to, I don't like it—and with the sound of the shot still in her ears, the room filled with the smell of gunpowder, she stood beside her husband's body sprawled across the desk top, read this, then set it afire. Suddenly she slapped out the flame instead, and kept it. She didn't call a doctor. He'd shot himself through the heart, she said at the inquest after the funeral; any fool could see he was dead. Instead, and immediately, she washed and dressed the body for burial. It wasn't unusual at that time and place not to have a body embalmed; but she didn't let an undertaker or anyone else set foot in the place till the body was ready for its coffin.

"It was a town scandal, as Ira was reminded more than once as a boy. But she faced it down. She looked them in the eye at the inquest, said she had no idea what the note meant and that what she'd done was

nobody's business but hers. Ten days later she had the stone you saw erected at the grave, and no one ever heard one word of explanation about that either.

"It shadowed Ira's life. As long as he lived he wanted to know—why, why, why? And so have I."

I did, too. We talked a lot that night. I told Kate a good deal about myself; mostly about my marriage and divorce and what I understood and did not understand about it. It wasn't something I'd ever much felt like discussing with anyone before. But even blabbing away about myself to an interested and willing listener, part of my mind was still thinking about Andrew Carmody, and wondering why, why, why.

It may be that the strongest instinct of the human race, stronger even than sex or hunger, is curiosity: the absolute need to know. It can and often does motivate a lifetime, it kills more than cats, and the prospect of satisfying it can be the most exciting of emotions. And so on Friday morning in Dr. Danziger's office I sat hardly able to wait till he was ready to give me an answer. He'd listened. He'd looked at the little snapshot and the blue envelope I'd borrowed from Kate. And now he sat regarding me from behind his desk; today he wore a dark-blue double-breasted suit, a white shirt, and a maroon bow tie; I wore the same gray suit I'd worn yesterday. After a moment or so he picked up the blue envelope again, and read aloud, " 'That the sending of this should cause the Destruction by Fire of the entire World . . . seems well-nigh incredible. Yet it is so. . . .' "

He grinned suddenly. "And you'd like to watch the 'sending of this,' would you? Well, who could blame you? So would I. But what *good* would it do you, Si? What would you learn? If anything, only a meaningless fragment more of a mystery that would continue to tantalize you and which you could not pursue. Because surely you've understood"—he leaned across the desk toward me—"that there cannot be the least intervention of any kind in events of the past. To alter the past would be to alter the future which derives from it. The consequences of that are unimaginable, and it is an utterly unacceptable risk."

"Of course! And I understand. But just to watch that letter *mailed*, Dr. Danziger! I wouldn't learn much, I know. Nothing, probably. But . . . well, I can't explain."

"You don't have to. Because I understand. Nevertheless—"

73

"If this should succeed, I'll be watching *something*. Why not that?"

"In theory I suppose there's no reason why not; I was afraid you might put it that way. All right, Si. After you left yesterday I phoned the board members. We have a bimonthly meeting scheduled for later this week, and I asked them to move it up to today. I didn't know last night what you had in mind but I thought it might be something they'd have to decide; I don't have an entirely free hand, you know. I'll present this to them. And they'll say no, too."

A little later Danziger introduced me, in the board room. It was a fairly large conference room typical of the kind in many an ad agency: a portable blackboard up front; a good many enlarged photographs and sketches pinned to the cork-board walls, most of them of settings or the plans for settings down on the Big Floor; a long conference table surrounded by men in shirt-sleeves, sweaters, or suit coats. Danziger led me around the table, introducing me. Some I'd met already—Rube was there, wearing a suit today; he just grinned and winked at me—and there was an engineer Rube had introduced me to in the hallways. Now I met a history professor from Columbia, an intelligent-looking, surprisingly young man; a bald, chubby meteorologist from Cal Tech; a professor of biology from Chicago University who looked like a professor; a professor of history from Princeton who looked like a nightclub comedian; a tense bright-eyed army colonel named Esterhazy, in a civilian suit; a mean-looking U.S. senator; and several others. It was a fairly distinguished gathering, I suppose, but I realized from the way each of them looked at me as we'd speak and shake hands that I was the guest of honor for the moment. Each of them in turn would stand, smiling and speaking, and I'd smile and respond, but as we shook hands he'd be searching my face. It made me realize that I and a half-dozen others were what this and every other meeting was about: We *were* the project, and I felt suddenly important, walking to the cafeteria, where I sat over a cup of coffee waiting for Danziger.

He walked in about twenty minutes later, looking pleased and a little surprised. Sitting at my table then, he told me that the board had agreed to my request. It was Rube, the Princeton professor, and Esterhazy who'd carried the ball for me, he said. They argued that there was no harm and there might even possibly be some advantages in what I wanted to do, and presently it was so decided. Danziger smiled and said, "So now you

74

present me with a temptation. My mother was sixteen years old in 1882. She was born February sixth, and on her birthday her father, mother and sister took her to Wallack's theater, and that was the occasion on which she met my father; it was a family anecdote all their lives. He arrived at the theater, an exuberant young man-about-town, saw Apple Mary, a character of the day who sold apples outside the theaters, and on impulse handed her a five-dollar gold piece, saying it was good luck for her and good luck for him. She replied that his evening would be blessed; he walked on into the lobby and his eye was caught by a green velvet dress, and by the girl who wore it. He knew the people she and her family were talking to, went over, was introduced, and they were married several years later. You can guess the temptation you've presented me with now." I nodded, smiling, and Danziger sat back in his chair. "There are many times when I have no least faith in this project; none. The whole thing seems absurd, hopeless. But if it *should* succeed, Si, if you should actually reach the New York of that time, and standing inconspicuously in a corner of the lobby were able to witness that meeting . . . well, if we're to have one personal purpose, we can have a second. I'd value very very much, Si, your sketch, a portrait of them as they were then." He stood up abruptly. "And now we're in a hurry." They could be ready for me on Monday, he said, by working over the weekend, and I sat nodding, listening, aware that in the very moment of elation I'd felt at the news Danziger had brought me the excitement had perversely subsided, and that all belief in this odd old man's project was draining away as though some sort of plug had been pulled. It was a feeling I was to have again and again and even get used to in the time that began on Monday morning.

6

I SHAVED for the last time on Sunday. On Monday morning, ten dummies covered by sheets stood in a row across the front of the classroom Danziger had told me to report to. I walked along the row looking them over, wanting to lift one of the sheets and peek. But before I could work up the nerve, a skinny young man of about twenty-six, I thought, came hurrying in, and introduced himself. This was Martin Lastvogel, my instructor, and we shook hands and agreed it would be sensible to use first names. I sat down in a one-armed classroom chair and watched him standing behind the desk hunting through a worn-out briefcase; the straps were curled from years of use, and below the lock was the remnant of a round paper sticker that had once read *Columbia U.*

My God, he's homely, I thought. He didn't have quite enough chin to balance his nose, which was big, sharp and too long; his hair was also too long by about three weeks and hadn't been combed for four. But when he glanced up and smiled, his eyes were friendly, eager with intelligence, and I found out later that he had a marvelous-looking wife who thought he was a wonder, and that Martin was forty-one years old.

"Okay," he said; he'd found what he was looking for, a packet of file-card notes which he riffled affectionately with a thumb, then set neatly on a corner of the desk top. "I'm not really a teacher, so just speak up whenever I'm not clear or make no sense. I'm a researcher, one of the lucky people who can earn a living doing what they like to do, in my case historical research. Ask me how streets were lighted, if at all, in fourteenth-century Paris, or what an eighteenth-century peruke was made of, or how they wrapped lard in a New England butchershop in 1926. And I'll poke around in the debris of the past, and try to find out for you. Over the weekend I've been digging into the eighties, and I'll be doing a great deal more. It's a terribly neglected period, though I don't know why because a great deal of interest seems to have been going on then.

"But I'm not here just to stuff you with facts about the period. You get along in the twentieth century without knowing everything about it." Martin walked out from behind the desk to stand beside the nearest figure; he took hold of the sheet. "And I don't think you have to know all about the eighties either. But you *do* have to *feel* them." He pulled the sheet from the figure.

There hung an old dress. It was a drab drooping tube of some heavy dark material, and I got to my feet and walked up to take a look. It hung motionless on the dummy, its hem touching the floor, the long full sleeves limp and straight at the sides. The neck was high, and an intricate pattern of tiny dull black beads lay across the chest and encircled the cuffs. Martin said, "We borrowed this from the Smithsonian. For your benefit. Flew it up here. It was made and worn in the early eighties. People walk through the Smithsonian, look at things like this, and think this is how women dressed." He began shaking his head. "But it's not. Get it through your head that it's not. Look at the color! If you can still call it a color. The old dyes don't hold up, Si!" he said as though I'd been arguing that they did. "For decades that thing has been fading, altering; into no color at all, finally. And look at the cloth. Shriveled. Shrunken in places. While in other places it sags; I think all the life has gone out of the threads. Even the bead trim has turned black!" Martin reached out and tapped my shoulder. "This is what you've got to understand, and more than that you've got to *feel* it: The women of the eighties weren't ghosts. They were *living women*, and they would never have worn that rag!" He jerked a thumb at the ancient dress. "The woman who once owned that—what did she *really* wear when she first put it on? *Here's* what she wore! To a party!"

Martin snapped the covering from the next figure, and there stood—I won't call it a dress but a *gown* of bright wine-red velvet, the nap fresh and unworn, the material magnificently draped in thick multiple folds, front and back. The bead trim caught the light, glittering a clear deep red, shimmering as though the garment were moving. It was spectacular;

under the overhead lights the gown glowed like a jewel. "We chose this original"—Martin touched the sad, drab dress from the museum—"because they have a diary at the Smithsonian, donated with the dress, that records when and how it was made, including the dressmaker's pattern and an unfaded swatch of the material. We've had a replica made"—he reached out, his fingers unable to resist the rich new red velvet—"that is far more the dress a living woman once wore than what's left of the actual original." He stood peering at me anxiously, then gestured to the brand-new gown. "Can you see an actual breathing woman, Si, a *girl*, wearing this and looking absolutely great?"

And I said, "Hell, yes: I can see her dancing!"

In the next couple of hours we looked at a brown-at-the-edges cloth wreck that, unimaginably, had once actually been a child's party dress. Then we studied a duplicate in some kind of fresh flouncy pink cloth, that looked the way it did the day the girl first put it on. And I saw—as they had survived and as they had been when new—a boy's suit with brass buttons and knee pants; a postman's uniform; and a man's suit including a cutaway coat with silk-faced lapels, raveling and dusty in the original, fresh and shiny in the replica.

During that week—I couldn't keep my hands off my beginning new beard—we looked at a collection of men's and women's hats of all kinds, originals and duplicates; and of purses, muffs, gloves. And one morning I stood turning a woman's shoe in my hands, studying the brittle gray-black leather crisscrossed with cracks. The toe and a band around the top were oddly discolored, the mother-of-pearl buttons chipped; it was no longer a shoe but a curiosity. Then Martin handed me its counterpart in new leather, and it was supple in my hands, the buttons of newly cut mother-of-pearl, the toes and a wide strip around the top brilliantly scarlet. Martin was imaginative; the shoe wasn't quite new. It had the fragrance of new leather but the sole was a little scratched, the heel had lost its sharp edges, and the faint beginning of a crease lay across the shiny instep. Martin smiled and said, "The trouble with everything that comes down from the distant past is that it's old. A relic. It may tell us something of what the past was like, yet it generally contradicts any feeling that it could possibly have been used by someone really alive." He nodded at the shoe in my hands. "But that's a shoe a living person could own. We had to create it, though." I nodded; it wasn't hard to see a young girl sitting on the edge of her bed pulling this on, buttoning it, then admiring it as she revolved her foot on her ankle to make the new leather catch the light.

During several days Martin and I sat leafing through books whose pages had gone brown and whose covers were sometimes speckled with mildew. As you turned the pages, corners flaked off; only a ghost could ever have read these. Then, from a box, Martin brought out the same books, identical except that now their covers were bright new reds, blues, and greens, their titles fresh-stamped in shining gold leaf, their pages pure white, the fresh black print still smelling of ink. Obviously these had never been read—not yet. And in my mind the eighties had begun to stir a little with life.

Rube was in the cafeteria lineup one noon, and he joined Martin and me for lunch. Then, during the rest of that afternoon, he took me into every office, into the carpentry and metal work shop, a small library, the conference room, the tailor's and shoemaker's shop, the control room for the Big Floor, a tiny projection room, and into every other place in the building where people were working; and he introduced me to them all.

I met Peter Marple, a young designer for the project, formerly a set designer in the New York theater, and a good one; I'd seen several plays of his, it turned out. I met Larry McDermott, the project photographer, who'd occasionally done work for an ad agency I'd once been with. I met technicians, stenographers, engineers, an accountant. I met an associate professor of history from the University of California, and people whose work wasn't mentioned; Rube referred to one of them as "our chief briber," at which the man just grinned.

Except for the two already out on the floor—John McNaughton in the Vermont house, and George Wing, a Crow Indian and former chief petty officer who was living in the tepee I'd seen—I also met my fellow candidates. One was the man I'd seen studying medieval French; we had a mutual friend whose first name neither of us could recall. Another was Miss Eileen Jorgensen, a thin, anxious-looking young mathematics teacher from Lincoln, Nebraska, who began studying turn-of-the-century San Francisco in the classroom next to mine. And I met the good-looking Charleston girl and the man I'd watched practicing with a rubber bayonet.

79

In a corridor walking toward the elevator, Rube said, "We made a mistake with that pair. They started having coffee together in the cafeteria, then lunch together, then meeting outside. Now, of course, all they're interested in is each other. They'll be getting married soon, and I suppose that's great. But we're not running a lonely-hearts club, and no one gives either of them much chance of succeeding anymore. So we've locked the barn door, and now the rule is: Pass the time of day with the other candidates when you see them around, but no fraternizing; okay?"

"Sure, as long as I'm too late for the Charleston girl." We rode down in the elevator—it was ten after five—and walked across town together, stopping in at the Algonquin for a drink.

I spent an hour, one morning, in Doc Rossoff's office, while he taught me the technique of self-hypnosis. It was surprisingly easy; at least the technique was. He had me sit down in his big green-leather easy chair and get comfortable. He said, "Close your eyes if you like, though it's not necessary." I closed them. "Now, just silently tell yourself that you are becoming more and more comfortable, more and more relaxed in body and mind both. And let it become true. Then tell yourself that you are slowly, gradually, moving into trance. A light trance, fully awake and aware. Don't let the word 'trance' bother you; it's simply a convenient term for a state of somewhat advanced receptiveness to suggestion; nothing mysterious about it. Presently, when you feel you've achieved it, tell yourself in so many words that you are under self-hypnosis. Then test it: Tell yourself that you are temporarily unable to lift your arm. Try it, and if you really can't lift your arm you're in trance. Make any self-hypnotic suggestion you wish, then. If you had a headache, for example, you'd tell yourself you were going to count to five, and that your headache would have faded away before you finished. Or you can blank out thoughts, emotions, memories, and make them return later by posthypnotic suggestion. Okay? It's really a remarkable tool."

I nodded, and he left me, to try it out. I did what he'd said, and felt myself grow wonderfully relaxed and comfortable. Presently I told myself I was gradually moving into light trance, and it seemed to me I could feel it happening. Sitting there, motionless, almost drowsy, I told myself that I could not lift my arm, that it was powerless to move. Then, my eyes on my coat sleeve, I tried to lift my arm, and almost hit myself in the eye as it popped right up.

I tried again, taking more time, feeling every muscle relax; and the only part of me that didn't know I was in hypnosis was my arm; up it came every time like an eager but stupid dog who doesn't quite understand the trick. Doc came back presently, listened, and told me to practice at home, preferably when I was actually tired and sleepy.

One morning Martin Lastvogel had a screen pulled down across the blackboard at the front of the classroom, a slide projector on a stand at the back. We sat side by side, Martin with a remote-control gadget in his hand. He clicked it, the air fan of the projector started up, and a round-cornered square of white light, fuzzed at the edges, filled most of the screen. Another click, and the square turned into a sharp-focused black-and-white drawing, an old-fashioned woodcut. It was a street scene, a busy one—of the eighties, I supposed; there were carriages, wagons, pedestrians. It was well done—the artist a good draftsman—but in a style that hasn't been used for half a century. "Done directly from a photograph, very likely," Martin said quietly; unconsciously he'd dropped his voice as people do in the dark. "A lot of illustrative woodcuts were copied from photos, before photoengraving. If so, you're looking at what could be an absolutely accurate representation of an actual moment. That's what it *did* convey to someone of the time. With the help of that woodcut in his weekly picture magazine, a man of the eighties could visualize the scene."

This was my own field, and I said, "But it's not how we convey reality. Reminds me of Japanese art, the perspective flat, and even Westerners' eyes slanted. To us his drawing is unreal, but to his own audience—"

"Right. Supply your own lecture; and do me out of a job. I've got a family to support, you know. Okay; we gave a copy of that cut, and a batch of others, to Sidney Urquhart. You know him?"

"I've seen his work: street scenes, city scenes. Watercolors, mostly. He's pretty good."

"He knows how to tell you what a city is like; you think he succeeded here?" Martin clicked his control, and a Sidney Urquhart that I wanted to own filled the screen. It was the scene we'd just looked at, detail for detail. And it was also a drawing. But this was in color, the pen-and-ink outlines filled in with brushed-on india inks in strong shades. It was the same scene but impressionistic; the thing *moved*. What I'd so often tried to do staring at Katie's stereoscope views, he'd got down on paper; the carriage horses were really trotting, the dray horses beside them sweaty and straining with effort. Carriage wheels were revolving, the spokes catching the light, and a mustached man dodging through the traffic was *darting*, his feet nimble and busy; you *saw* it. As Urquhart's sketch flashed onto the screen there was an instant when I was standing on the curb watching the scene and it was almost real.

Martin's control clicked, the screen went white and empty, another click and the big square was a sepia photograph: Two women in long dresses and big hats were walking, their backs to the camera, down a wide sidewalk shaded by immense trees; one of them carried an open umbrella against the sun. To their left lay a grassy parkway in which great trees grew, shadowing the street; to their right, long sloping lawns. Beyond the parkway lay the shade-dappled street, empty except for an open buggy, its horse tethered to a hitching post. It was a good moment; the photographer had caught a nice scene. Sitting in the semidarkness studying it, I could believe—I knew—that it had once really happened. But it was frozen in time, infinitely remote, and the two women up there were never going to take the next step.

A double click, and Sidney Urquhart's glimpse of the same moment filled the screen in color. It was only a sketch now, an impression, but the women's next step was imminent. They were really walking, their bodies flowing into the next step, feet just lifting from the last one, and you knew that up out of sight the leaves of those trees were stirring and that the women, if somehow you could strain enough to hear, were quietly talking.

We spent all that morning looking at, first, a drawing or photograph of the early eighties, then a "translation," which was Martin's term, and a good one, by Urquhart, Karl Morse, Murray Sidorfsky, or someone else. Not all of them succeeded, and some only partly. But some of them worked, and I'd suddenly experience the thrill of glimpsing the actuality of a moment of the past.

Long before we were finished I knew I could do the same thing. I didn't need Urquhart now or anyone else; I, too, could look at an old cut or photograph and do the work of getting myself into and fully perceiving it until I found and touched the long-ago realness that had produced it. I could do it as well now as the makers of most of the new drawings

I'd seen up there on the screen—better, I thought. Whether I could show it as well, whether I was artist enough, I wasn't sure; I doubted it. But I knew I could do it in my mind.

Walking to the cafeteria for lunch, I said so to Martin, and he nodded. "It's how we hoped you'd feel; Rossoff predicted it. But you won't have much time for actually sketching, and the point of this morning was to give you a head start; we've got a lot of stuff for you to study and translate for yourself." I spent three days then, alone with the projector looking at scene after scene of the eighties, staring, working at finding the actuality that lay under the surface of each, gaining experience and speed as the time passed.

At four o'clock one afternoon, in the tailor's workroom, I was measured from head to foot. Then I stood in my socks, holding a pail of sand in each hand, while a bootmaker traced the outlines of my feet.

During most of one week Martin lectured from file-card notes. What was the population of the United States in 1880? he asked me for a starter. I cut our present population in half and said a hundred million, but Martin told me to cut it in half again; there were only fifty million Americans then, most of them living east of the Mississippi. In the West, buffalo still roamed the open prairie, the new transcontinental railway was a national marvel and excitement in a way that even space travel isn't today, and Indians were still scalping Whitey. It was a very different country and world; there were animals alive that are now extinct, and social systems, too; Europe was full of kings, queens, emperors, czars and czarinas then, and they weren't figureheads, they *ruled*.

Martin talked about how the world traveled and moved its goods. There were steamships, and the railroad was decades old. But just the same, cargo vessels still moved largely by sail and most of the world traveled as it always had, on foot or by horse. Most people in America lived and died in the state or even the town they'd been born in; more people traveled across the ocean than across the country. Yet different as the world of the eighties was, Martin said, it was closer to ours than it seemed; walking through that horse-and-buggy United States, Lee De Forest was a nine-year-old boy already thinking about the problems involved in the invention of radio, sound movies, and television. At the end of one day, waiting at the elevator with me, Martin said, "It's a hell of a different world, Si, but it isn't alien to this, and I think you could be at home in it."

Kate thought my collar-length hair and my new brown beard—I'd begun trimming it—made me particularly handsome, and I agreed. She'd begun helping me with my homework at night now. I'd taken her to lunch one day, at a Madison Avenue restaurant, inviting Rube and Dr. Danziger, and they'd liked her. Katie is attractive, physically and personally; she's intelligent, tactful, and can be witty if she's in the mood; she has charm. And after that, they let her visit the project; Dr. Danziger himself showed her the Big Floor, then his secretary showed her through most of the rest of the project. I wasn't along; I was too busy with Martin Lastvogel.

So now, in a sense, Kate was fully in on the project, and on more nights than not, usually at her place though sometimes at mine, she drilled me on facts from Martin's lectures, using his notes. And she worked with me on getting the feel of the eighties from the photographs and woodcuts I brought home. One Saturday morning I took her to the project and showed her the reconstructed dresses, hats, gloves, and shoes of the period, and she was fascinated, wishing she could try an outfit on. She was a big help, and I think she speeded up the learning process for me. Martin thought so anyway. And she was a tremendous help with the self-hypnosis technique; Kate got it right away just from my description of how you were supposed to do it. That made me realize it was really possible, and from Kate's description I got an idea of the actual feel of slipping into "trance." So that one night at her place, sitting in her antique rocker, a very comfortable chair actually, I made it: My arm genuinely would not, could not, move, and I sat staring at it, fascinated. I told myself then that it was now free to move, tried it, and it did. Now I told myself that I would forget my own street address and stay in trance until Kate spoke. Then I sat there trying to recall my address, and it simply wasn't there to remember; it was both fascinating and a little frightening. I looked over at Kate who was reading through some of Martin's notes, and she happened to look up at the same time. She smiled and said, "Any luck?" and I knew my own address just as always, and could feel that I was out of trance.

"Yeah, finally," I said. Then we spent an hour studying samples of money; coins of the sixties, seventies, and early eighties, including gold pieces; big old bank notes issued by local banks pretty much in their own designs and actually signed by the bank presidents; and the ones I liked best of all, gold certificates redeemable not in silver but in gold and printed on the backs in an orange-colored ink suggesting gold.

Once in a while Kate and I did other things: took a drive on a weekend, took a walk, even saw some friends. And one night—Kate and I had been seeing almost too much of each other, I felt, and I think she did, too—I phoned Matt Flax, but got no answer. Kate was going to iron, wash her hair, that sort of thing, and get to bed early. But I felt restless, and I phoned Lennie, and then Vince Mandel, who lived in town, but got no answers. So I stayed home and read, deliberately getting my mind off the project in a one-night vacation from it. In my living room I sat reading a one-volume complete Sherlock Holmes which I generally picked up whenever I had nothing else to read. At Dr. Danziger's request I'd quit reading newspapers, magazines, and modern novels; I'd also unplugged the television and my radio, no hardship.

Every day at the project I sat listening to Martin, a clipboard in my lap, and I spent part of one afternoon tasting food. That was after lunch, which I'd skipped at Martin's request, and the cafeteria was empty except for the fat middle-aged cook, Dr. Rossoff, and me. First the cook brought in a plate of mutton, potatoes and beets, all boiled, and set it down in front of me. Rossoff sat across from me, and the cook stood beside the table, both watching me, and grinning a little. I ate a little of each of the things on the plate, tasting, staring off into space like a wine connoisseur. I'd never had mutton before, and didn't know what to expect; it seemed all right. But the potatoes and beets tasted— not quite the way they should have: I chewed away, trying to figure out the difference, and pretty soon Rossoff said, "Well?" I swallowed, and said, "They're better, they taste better. They have more flavor than I'm used to."

They both grinned some more, and Rossoff said, "Vegetables were grown in the eighties without chemical fertilizers, insecticides, or special treatments before planting. Also, no preservatives or additives." The cook said, "And they were boiled in chlorine-free water."

I had some fudge made with sugar refined in a way I didn't follow; it tasted about like any other. I had a small piece of longhorn steak, tougher and distinctly different in taste from any other I'd ever had. I had some marvelous ice cream made with unpasteurized cream. And I had a straight shot of whiskey, especially distilled for me; rough, raw, and powerful.

And then one night I had supper at home, washed the dishes, and threw out everything in the refrigerator that wasn't canned or bottled. Then I sat down at a card table in my living room, and wrote a note or postcard to everyone I knew who might wonder about me.

The work wasn't going very well here in New York, I said in each of them; and this was January 4th, a new year, so I'd bought an old station wagon on impulse, packed, and was leaving in the morning before I could change my mind. I was just going to tour around, I didn't really know where—I might head for one of the Western states—drawing, sketching, and taking reference photographs as I went. I'd write when I could, I said, and would be in touch when I got back. I didn't like doing it this way but I knew I wasn't up to convincingly answering questions if I tried doing it in person or by phone.

I mailed my cards and notes on Lexington Avenue, a block from my apartment. I dropped them into the box, then stood looking around for a moment at New York in the second half of the twentieth century. But there wasn't much to see besides the walls of the buildings around me, a long stretch of asphalt on which only a single cab was moving and a fragment of gray-black sky directly overhead too hazed for any stars to be visible. The day's car-exhaust seemed to have settled down here and was making my eyes smart; it had turned cold; and half a block down the cross street, on the corner of which I was standing, a group of young Negroes was walking toward Lex, so I didn't hang around to encounter them and explain how fond I'd always been of Martin Luther King. I walked on, up Lexington and then across town toward the warehouse; I felt tired, a little sleepy, yet so excited I was conscious of the beat of my heart.

At ten minutes after one in the morning, an hour and a half later, we left the warehouse; Rube had his car, a squat little red MG sedan, parked in the street at the side door. He drove, Doc Rossoff sat on the outside, and I was more or less hidden between them wearing Doc's raincoat over the costume I'd put on at the warehouse, though I tried not to think of it as a costume. No need to hide my long hair and beard, of course.

I like New York late at night, most places closed and dark, the streets as nearly empty of movement and as quiet as they ever get. We could hear the sound of our own tires on the asphalt, and at Amsterdam Avenue, waiting for a light, I heard someone cough half a block or more away. We didn't talk to amount to anything; we crossed Broadway, stopped for another light at Columbus, and Rube said, "Funny-looking dog," nodding toward a woman walking a clipped poodle in a jeweled dog-coat. A block or so further on Oscar Rossoff pointed at a darkened restaurant and said, "Good seafood there." I don't recall saying anything, but I yawned a lot from nervousness. Rossoff understood the reason, glancing at me occasionally to smile.

Rube parked a dozen yards from the Dakota's main entrance; he held out his hand to me, and I took it. All he said was "Good luck, Si; I wish it were me." Rossoff had his door open, and he stepped out, and I slid across the seat to follow him.

The uniformed doorman was expecting us; he simply nodded and we walked on past him, under the great main arch, then on across the courtyard; the two huge green-bronze fountains were empty. We climbed the wide old staircase in the northeast corner of the Dakota, meeting no one, stepping out onto the seventh floor; my apartment was a few doors off, and I brought out my key. "My coat, Si," Oscar said, and I took off the raincoat and handed it to him. "Want to come in?" I said, but he shook his head; he was staring at my clothes, then he lifted his eyes to stare at my hair and mustache as though he'd never seen them; he seemed suddenly awed. "No," he said, "I don't think anything of the present belongs in there now, Si." He held out his hand. "Good luck. You know what to do when you're ready."

We shook hands, then I walked to my door, slid my key into the lock, and turned the big ornamented brass knob; the door swung soundlessly back on its hinges as though it were weightless, but I could sense its solidity. I turned to say a final goodbye, but Doc Rossoff was down the hall, just turning onto the stairway again; he turned to glance back at me, then he was gone.

I walked in, closing the door behind me, my eyes widening, accustoming themselves to the faint light from the tall rectangles of the windows. I knew the layout and appearance of the apartment; I'd been here with Dr. Danziger and Rube the day it was completed. Now I walked over to one of the windows, stopped, and stood looking down onto the pale curves and jumbled shadows that were the paths and greenery of Central Park under the moon. Directly below my window if I'd cared to lean forward and look straight down, I knew I could have seen the street, Central Park West, and its traffic lights and occasional cars. Far across the park, if I'd lifted my eyes to look, I could have seen a few still-lighted windows in the block-after-block row of great apartment houses bordering Central Park's eastern side. By turning my head to the right, I could have seen the rooftop neon of the hotels at the southern end of the park, and the lights of the great midtown office buildings beyond.

But I looked at none of these. Instead I stared down into the shadows of Central Park, and almost directly ahead the moon shone on the surface of the lake just as it must have, I thought, on another such night when the building I stood in was new. On the curved roads of the park widely spaced streetlamps burned, each with a nimbus of late-at-night mist, and it seemed to me that from here they couldn't look very different, if at all, from the way they had looked long ago.

There was a heavy green window shade, I knew, and in the darkness I pulled it down, then drew the velvet drapes. I did this with each of the other windows, then brought a matchbox from my pocket. I struck a match on the sole of my boot, it spluttered, then caught and burned steadily, the wax running thinly down its stem. Cupping the flame with my other hand, I lifted it to an L-shaped ornamented brass tube projecting from the wall. Fastened to the short arm of the tube was a bracket on which a flowered glass shade was fitted; a key-shaped brass handle projected from the underside of the tube. I turned it, heard the soft hiss of gas, then touched my lighted match to the open end of the tube. A wedge of blue-edged flame popped into existence under the glass shade, and a wavering circle of flowered gray carpet appeared at my feet, then steadied.

I looked at the room and its furnishings for only a moment or so. It was approaching two in the morning, two o'clock in the morning of January 5, 1882, I said to myself, suddenly realizing that the experiment had actually begun. But I was tired, empty of all energy now, and my hand still on the fixture, I turned the light out, then walked down the hall to my bedroom.

7

I CAN COOK fairly well in a top-of-the-stove, smoke-up-the-kitchen style, the way a man who lives alone usually learns. But I'd been doing it for nearly a week now, and my memories of good food were growing dim. Tonight I was having pork chops and a sliced-up potato fried in lard, hoping that for a change they'd both be finished at the same time, but my hopes weren't high. I'm fed up with my own cooking, I thought, as I bungled around the big old kitchen, then I smiled; "fed up" was hardly the phrase.

The boy from Fishborn's Market had delivered the chops that morning at the service door of the apartment. I'd stood at the door in my black, unpressed, cuffless wool pants; wide suspenders; heavy black buttoned shoes; green-and-white-striped shirt with no collar, though both front and back studs were in the neckband; and I wore a double-breasted black vest with braided edges, a heavy gold watch chain stretched across it. I'd stood there handing the boy my pencil-written order for next day's meat and groceries, then I gave him a nickel tip. The nickel had a shield design on one side and a big 5 on the other; the boy was glad to get it, and thanked me nicely. Putting the meat in the icebox, I pictured him out on the street again, climbing up to the seat of his light delivery wagon with the canvas sides that could be rolled up in summer. When it snowed, as it would any day now, I knew he'd switch to the big delivery sled.

The meat, which I laid on top of the ice, was wrapped in coarse butcher's paper tied with string—no gummed-paper tape or cellophane allowed. Someone had forgotten that the first day, but someone else apparently saw to it that they remembered from then on. They remembered about the butter and lard, too; these came wrapped in the same kind of paper, and packed into shallow scoop-shaped trays made of paper-thin wood.

My potatoes were frying away on the big, black coal-burning stove, and I stood watching them, turning them occasionally. I liked it here in the kitchen; it was an enormous room with plenty of space for a big round wooden table and four tall wooden chairs in the center of the room. The stove was big as an office desk, ornamented with nickel-plated castings. A huge wooden cupboard covered an entire wall, floor to ceiling; back of the glass-paned doors stood all the china, glassware, and pots and pans on oilcloth-covered shelves.

It was a fine room, warm and comfortable from the fire, the windows steamed opaque. I turned from stove to cupboard, took half a loaf of bread from the big red bread-box, and cut off three thick slices. I knew I'd eat all of them; this bread was the only thing I ate that still tasted good. Probably all that's keeping me alive, I said to myself silently; I wasn't talking aloud to myself, not yet. It was homemade bread baked by an Irishwoman who sold it door to door, she said.

The chops were nearly done, as far as I could tell by staring at them, and now I ground some coffee in a little hand grinder made of wood and fancily carved. I filled the tin coffeepot and set it on the stove.

I'd gotten into the habit of eating most of my meals in the kitchen; it was easier than carrying food and dishes all over the place. And tonight as usual, when supper was ready, I sat eating and reading the evening paper which was left at the door each night. This was January 10, so I was reading a crisp fresh copy of the *New-York Evening Sun* of January 10, 1882. Sitting there reading, eating—the chops were all right though a little dry, but the half-raw potatoes would have been turned down by a starving vulture—I took out my watch and pressed the little stud in its side which released the gold cover that protected its face. It showed just past seven, four minutes faster than the kitchen clock, which hadn't yet struck. I didn't know which was right, and it didn't matter; the evening ahead wasn't too exciting. It was seven o'clock, and would be seven thirty when I finished the dishes. Then I'd play a few games of patience till around nine, go to bed and read this week's copy of *Frank Leslie's Illustrated Newspaper*, which the mailman had delivered in the second afternoon delivery.

A few days later, though, I had company. Once again I was washing dishes after supper, which I didn't really mind once I got started. I'm a daydreaming type, something that's often got me into trouble, starting with kindergarten when I was sent home with a note saying I was "lackadaisical." No one in my family knew what that meant so nothing was done about it, and I've stayed fairly lackadaisical ever since. When I'm doing a routine job that keeps my hands busy, like washing dishes, I slide into a daydream.

Now, as usual during dishwashing time, I let myself slide into one; pretty much the same one every night. What I'd do was picture to myself what was probably going on here and there around town. Down in Central Park, my mind said to itself, if I were to walk into the living room and look out the window, there might be a cabriolet clip-clopping along under the lamps and the bare-branched trees. I didn't actually look out the windows too often, and when I did it was down toward the center of the park late at night or in the very early morning. Because of course this was the twentieth, not the nineteenth century, and the fewer reminders of that the better. So standing at the sink I imagined the man in the cabriolet down in the park at this moment, its top folded back. He was holding the reins in one hand, whip in the other, wrapped to the waist in a light blanket, wearing a black cutaway and a high-crowned derby. And earmuffs? No, it wasn't that cold, but he'd be wearing fur gloves.

Then, in my mind, I watched a man and his wife in a landau heading in the opposite direction, the plate glass glittering each time they passed under a light; they were going somewhere for dinner, I supposed. Helped by Martin Lastvogel's woodcuts, I pictured a liveried servant driving, high on the outside front seat between lighted carriage lamps. The man inside, visible through the oval back window, wore a black coat and a silk hat. His wife wore a round fur cap, and the collar of her coat was fur. Landau and cabriolet passed through a yellow circle of light, and the occupants nodded, the men tipping their hats.

Adelina Patti was singing tonight at the Opera House, according to the *Evening Sun*; right now, I supposed, overalled mustached men were testing the footlights, and in my mind I watched them turn each one on, light the gas, watch for a moment, then turn it off.

At the firehouse half a mile south a man in hip boots was currying the big horses in the stalls at the back of the station, averting his face from the swishing tails, keeping his feet from under the hoofs that occasionally stomped hollowly on the heavy worn planking, leg muscles quivering.

The dishes washed and draining, I lighted a candle in a porcelain holder, turned out the gas jets over the sink and table, and walked down the long hall to the living room, my hand cupped around the flame. There I lighted a single wall jet, and a lamp on a table beside my favorite chair. I glanced cautiously at the windows—it was dark out, there was nothing to be seen—and I sat down in my chair. It was upholstered in plum-colored cloth, with a million tassels hanging from the arms and around the lower edges.

When the doorbell rang, I actually jumped. It hadn't occurred to me that anyone would ring it; the boy from the market always knocked. I hadn't known there even was a doorbell, and I almost ran to answer it, afraid something was wrong.

Rube Prien and a black-haired brown-eyed woman stood in the hall smiling at me. He was wearing an ankle-length overcoat with a brown fur collar, and in one hand held a high-crowned derby and something else I couldn't quite make out in the shadows of the hall. The woman with him had on an ankle-length navy-blue coat with a cape attached, and a white scarf tied under her chin. "Hello, Si," Rube said. "We were just passing by and thought we'd stop in for a moment. I'm glad to find you at home."

"Come in, come in!" I was as elated as a kid. "I'm glad you did!"

Rube introduced me to the girl—her first name was May—and I took their things. Rube was carrying a couple of pairs of skates, just blades attached to wood platforms fitted with leather straps. They were going skating in the park, he said; the flag was up and bonfires were lighted. He asked me to come along, but I said no, I didn't skate. I got them some coffee, and when I carried it in, May was sitting at the organ, looking through the sheet music.

The organ was the size and shape of an upright piano, and only a little more ornate than the Taj Mahal. It was of light yellow wood—oak, I think—and was jigsawed, lathed, and carved beyond belief: Apparently an entire family of demented woodcarvers had gone berserk and would have carved it to a mound of chips if they hadn't been forcibly dragged away. May took her coffee; she wore a plain ankle-length wool dress, brown to match her eyes; it had a white collar fastened in front with a little silver brooch; her black hair was parted in the middle and tied up in back in a bun. Rube was sitting in a wooden rocker, and he looked great: His suit had four buttons and high tiny lapels, and he wore a stand-up wing collar and a four-in-hand black tie with a gold stickpin; his shoes were high, black, and buttoned, like mine.

May set her cup down, opened a sheet of music, and played something called "Hide Thou Me," and then "Funiculi, Funicula!" She played pretty well, and Rube and I sat there, smiling faintly, nodding our heads to the music, pretending we liked it. We talked for a few minutes then: about the weather, about a fire yesterday in Ninth Street, about progress of the digging of the Hudson Tunnel. I offered a drink, but Rube said no, it was time to go skating if they were to go at all, and they left. But it was an hour or so—I was so excited by that little visit—before I could make sense out of the book I was trying to read.

Next day that visit caused trouble. After breakfast and the *Times*, I was suddenly fed up with nothing to do but playacting for myself. The whole pretense turned into foolishness, and standing in the living room, a book in my hand that I thought I was about to read, I tossed it to a chair instead. Then I just stood in what had become not clothes but a tiresome costume, fiercely aware of the real New York City all around me. It was full of movies, plays, nightclubs, radio, television, and, above all, people I knew and wanted to be with; and all I had to do to have them was walk out. Planes flew over the city around me; I heard them. And automobiles choked it, and just out of my sight the city rose to the sky in glass, steel, and stone, and the New York of the eighties was dead.

But almost as it began the rebellion was fading and I knew it wasn't going to be hard, in a moment or so, to resume the pretense. I suppose most everyone has had the experience of a vacation in a fairly remote place away from newspapers and television. Under those conditions the reality of the world you've left recedes, and the real world becomes wherever you are and whatever you're doing.

That had been happening here. The idea of turning on a television set was remote. The remembered feeling of how it is to sit at the wheel of a car was a little fuzzed. And the last national and international news I'd heard was long since stale. All the memories of the world I'd left had just perceptibly lost a degree of vigor. And since most of what we do, think, and feel is habit, it wasn't very hard now to blink, look around, then pick up my book and resume reading where I'd stopped last night, back in the mood once again.

Yet as the days passed I didn't even make an attempt, because I knew it would fail. Time flowed by as it does for a convalescent; slowly, effortlessly, without real boredom or restlessness, the hours and days disappearing almost unnoticed like melting ice. The world outside was far gone now, my routine the only reality. Everything about it was consistent with January 15, 16, 17, 18, 19 . . . 1882. And I could almost, *almost*, believe that it was. But outside . . . From up here Central Park seemed unchanged except for the buildings around it; the view opposite I took from the middle window the first time I was in the apartment. And often now, late at night and at dawn, I stared down at the park trying to achieve the feeling of a nineteenth-century world beyond it. But once when I'd thought I might be succeeding or beginning to, a maroon Mustang with aluminum wheels and a raised rear-end moved across the scene. And I had never, in any case, dared lift my eyes from the old roadways and paths, knowing that the twentieth century, as my picture shows, stood stark and visible all around them. I knew I'd fail if I made the attempt, so I waited.

One afternoon I was reading in the living room, and around four o'clock—the kitchen clock, I thought I remembered, had struck the hour not long before—I looked up from my book; something in the room had changed. I glanced around, but everything seemed the same. Then I looked up, and the ceiling was brighter; the light from outside had altered. Something else had changed, too. The walls of this building were thick; from the outside I never heard any but the loudest sounds, and they were muted. But now I couldn't hear even these; no horns, air brakes, tire squeals. The silence was absolute. Then, far away, a child shouted for joy.

Carrying my book, I walked to a window, and whatever it is that leaps in your chest with excitement sprang up now; there were six inches of new snow, unmarked and sparkling, on every horizontal surface outside, ten billion more fat flakes rushing past my window. Nothing moved on

the street below me, and there wasn't a parked car in sight, every one of them moved from the curbs before the snow trapped them. Under my window Central Park West was level with untouched snow, the traffic lights uselessly clicking from green to red, red to green, and across the street Central Park was a delight. There things moved: Little kids in red, blue, brown, green, were running, toddling, and falling down in the snow; they were rolling in it, scooping it up, throwing, and eating it. A few had sleds, and one struggling cluster was rolling a ball of snow already taller than they were.

I'm a nut for lightning- and snow-storms, and I stood at the window for what must have been half an hour, watching the big flakes whirl past the glass, watching Central Park turn into an etching as the black branches loaded up with white, watching the humps and depressions that marked paths and streets level off and disappear.

After a while I made coffee, dragged a chair to the window, and sat next to it, sitting sideways, legs over the chair arm. Then—it was early for supper, but I felt hungry—I made a sandwich and brought it, with an apple, back to my chair. The light had dwindled, and the white of the vast expanse of snow outside had picked up a blue tint. I sat eating, watching the day disappear. The traffic lights on the street under my windows had stopped, I noticed presently; either shut off to save current or interrupted by the storm. They looked different now, their tops and hoods mounded high with snow; they could have been streetlamps. In the cooling air the falling flakes became smaller, and a little wind began and carried the fine snow horizontally like a curtain of mist. Now I couldn't see beyond the center of the park; far on the other side the apartments along its eastern edge had vanished in the curtain; so had the buildings to the south and, of course, far to the north. The last of the children left; it was colder—I could feel it through the window-pane—and it was nearly dark. Then the streetlights came on. Nothing moved outside now but the snow in the wind, and the silence was complete. Staring down into Central Park, I wondered suddenly if it had also snowed in January 1882.

I didn't know but it was likely, of course. And if it had, at this time, then now *in every way* the scene I sat staring down at was exactly and without difference what I'd have seen from here then. I stood up and stepped to the window, glancing at my own dim reflection in the glass, and in these clothes, in this room, in this building, I knew I could have stood here then precisely as I stood here now.

I turned away, walked to the chandelier, struck a match, then reached up to light the lamps, one by one. There was coffee, still warm, in the china pot I'd set on the carpet beside my chair, and I poured out another half cup but I never drank it. I sat down again beside the window, the room warm and comfortable, silent except for the tiny hiss of the gas jets and the occasional hard flick of a snowflake against the pane. I lay back in my chair, legs stretched out, holding the cup in my lap, staring up at the blue-edged flames shaped like tiny medieval ax-blades behind the etched patterns of the glass shades.

I was no longer thinking; you couldn't call it thought. I sat at rest, almost blank-minded, except that a picture involuntarily formed itself in my mind momentarily: of the people who had to be out in the streets, farther south, downtown in the busier parts of the city. I saw them bent against the blowing snow, men touching the rims of their derbies, women's hands snug in their muffs, and in the streets beside them the horses' feet were sliding, staggering for a footing. For an instant I had a glimpse in my mind of a lifted hoof wet with slush, the fetlocks balled with gray snow. And now I could—not imagine; that wasn't the word—I could *feel* the city around me, all the others, I mean: the people in their houses tonight like me, in the soft yellow light of a million gas flames.

I hated to move; it was so white and silent outside, the flakes scudding past my lighted window; it was so comfortable in here, the room's shadows occasionally shifting as the wedgelike flames momentarily flickered. I kept meaning to sip my coffee but never did. Finally I set down the cup, made myself stand, and walked to the last window to the left and pulled the blind. Who, watching from somewhere, would see that this one window was now darkened I didn't know and hardly cared.

And when the bell over my door jounced on its coiled spring I was nearly asleep in my chair. It was Oscar Rossoff, I saw without surprise when I opened the door, stomping off the snow clinging to his unpolished, heavily greased boots. He wore a shiny black beard trimmed to a point. "Hello, Si." He stood snapping off beads of moisture from a high-crowned derby in his hand. "I was passing by, and stopped to catch my breath, if it's convenient. A fine night, but hard walking."

"Come on in, Oscar! I'm glad to see you."

He stepped in, and stood smiling, unbuttoning his ankle-length fur-collared overcoat. Then he handed it to me and rubbed his hands together quickly, glad to be warm; he wore a black cutaway coat with silk lapels, black-and-white-checked pants, and a wing collar with a black ascot tie. We walked across the room to facing chairs, and Oscar unbuttoned his coat as he sat down. Across his vest hung a heavy gold chain strung with gold and ivory ornaments.

"Oscar, I'll make a fire. Would you like a drink first? Or coffee, if you'd rather. Have you had supper?" I was pleased to have company, and almost chattering.

"No, I can't stay, Si; I only stopped for a moment. So don't trouble with anything on my account. Except a drink; I would like a whiskey! Neat." He rubbed his hands together again, glancing at the windows. "Quite a night!"

I brought whiskey in miniature cut-glass tumblers, we raised them in salute, then tasted the liquor. "Fine," Oscar said, and sat back in his chair, and began absently playing with a coin-shaped gold ornament on his watch chain. "This is fine, sitting here with a glass of whiskey, the storm dying outside."

I nodded. "Yes. I'm glad you came, Oscar; I was falling asleep."

"A man could do that easily enough on a night like this." He sipped at his whiskey, then sat back again, idly fingering the disc on his chain; I sat watching it glow dully in the gaslight. "Nothing could be more relaxing, it's so quiet outside, so warm and peaceful in here." I nodded, and started to make some reply, but Oscar shook his head slowly, smiling, lying comfortably back in his chair. "Don't trouble to make small talk, Si; I don't need entertaining. It's so pleasant in here it should be enjoyed without thought, the mind at rest, content and serene. And the whiskey helps, doesn't it? You can feel your nerves and muscles relaxing. I think the wind has died down, it's so absolutely silent now. Still snowing, though; big soft flakes again. You're very contented right now, Si, I can see it. So relaxed and at ease. At peace. And I believe I am helping. Because although you're listening to me it's not so much to the words as the sound; the tone, the murmur, the suggestion. It's draining away all tension; I can see that you feel it happening. You're so at peace that even the glass in your hand is becoming a little heavy to hold; notice? You're more content and serene, more than you've ever been before in your life, just sitting here in peace listening to the sound of my voice. That glass *is* too heavy; set it down on the floor beside you. That's better, isn't it? If you tried to pick it up again it would be too heavy now. And you don't want to anyway, you don't care to. And you couldn't. Try, though, Si; just try to pick it up for a moment. Try harder; lift it for just an inch or so, then let it drop back. You can't. Well, no matter. It doesn't matter at all. You're very tired, and in a moment I'm going to let you sleep. I only want to tell you something first, then I'll go.

"You'll sleep for only a little while, Si. But it will be a marvelously restful sleep. Deep and dreamless. Restful as you've ever known. And when you wake, everything you know of the twentieth century will be gone from your mind. As you sleep, that entire body of knowledge will shrink in your mind; it will dwindle to a motionless pinpoint deep in your brain, and lost to you.

"It's beginning to happen now. There are no such things as automobiles, Si; there are no planes, computers, television, no world in which they are possible. 'Nuclear' and 'electronics' appear in no dictionary anywhere on the face of the earth.

"You have never heard the name Richard Nixon . . . or Eisenhower . . . Adenauer . . . Stalin . . . Franco . . . General Patton . . . Göring . . . Roosevelt . . . Woodrow Wilson . . . Admiral Dewey. . . . Everything you know of the past eight decades is washing out of your mind; everything. All of it. Large and small. From the important to the smallest of trivia.

"But you know what the world is like; you know that very well. You know all about it. Why shouldn't you know what the world is like tonight, January 21, 1882? Because that *is* the date; that is the time we're in, of course. That's why I'm dressed as I am, and you as you are. That's why this room is as it is. Don't sleep quite yet, Si. Hold your eyes open just a bit. For just a few seconds longer.

"Now, hear what I say. I am going to give you a final, irrevocable instruction; you *will* hear it, you *will* obey it. You will sleep for twenty minutes. You will awake rested. You will go out for a walk. Just a little walk, a breath of air before you go to bed. You will be as careful as you possibly can be . . . that no one sees you. You will be absolutely certain to speak to no one. You will allow no act of yours, however

99

small, to influence anyone in any way, however trivial.

"Then you will come back here, go to bed, and sleep all night. You will awaken in the morning as usual, free of all hypnotic suggestion. So that as you open your eyes, all your knowledge of the twentieth century will light up in your mind again. But *you will remember your walk. You will remember your walk. You will remember your walk.* Now . . . let go. And sleep."

I was embarrassed; the moment I woke up in my chair I glanced quickly over at Oscar's chair and saw that he was gone, his glass on a table, and I wondered what he must have thought at my falling asleep while he sat here, a guest. But I knew he wouldn't mind; we were old friends and he'd be amused.

I felt rested now, though; alive and energetic, a little too restless to feel like going to bed, and I decided to take a walk. It was still snowing, but big soft flakes. There was no wind, I'd been indoors too long, and I wanted to get out, into that snow, breathing chill fresh air; and I walked to the closet and put on my overcoat, chest protector, boots, and my round fur cap of black lamb's wool.

I walked down the building stairs, somehow glad to encounter no one; I didn't feel like chatting, and if I'd heard someone on the stairs I think I'd have stood waiting till he'd gone. Downstairs I walked out of the building, glancing quickly around, but saw not a soul—tonight I didn't want to see anyone—and I turned toward Central Park just across the street ahead. It was a fine night, a wonderful night. The air was sharp in my lungs, and snowflakes occasionally caught in my lashes, momentarily blurring the streetlamps just ahead, already misty in the swirls of snow around them.

Just ahead the street was almost level with the curbs, unmarked by steps or tracks of any kind. I crossed it and walked into the park. There was no path to be seen or detected; I simply avoided bushes and trees, and it was hard going, the snow seven or eight inches deep now. It occurred to me that I'd better not go too far from the lights of the street or I could easily become lost, and I turned to look back. The streetlamps were plainly visible, and I could still see my own footprints in their light, but they were covering over very quickly and I knew that in only minutes they'd be gone again and that I'd never be able to follow them back if I went on much farther.

I plodded on just a little way more though, feet lifting high, boots clogged with damp snow, enjoying the exercise of it, exhilarated by the feel of this snowy luminous night, and my aloneness in it. Behind me and to the north I heard a distant rhythmical jingle, perceptibly louder each time it sounded, and I turned to look back toward the street once again. For a moment or two I stood listening to the *jink-jink-jingle* sound, and then just beyond the silhouetted branches, down the center of the lighted street, there it came, the only kind of vehicle that could move on a night like this: a light, airy, one-seated sleigh drawn by a single slim horse trotting easily and silently through the snow. The sleigh had no top; they sat out in the falling snow, bundled snugly together under a robe, a man and a woman passing *jink-jink-jingle* through the snow-swirled cones of light under each lamp. They wore fur caps like mine, and the man held a whip and the reins in one hand. The woman was smiling, her face tilted to receive the snow, and the only sounds were the bells, the muffled hoof-clops, and the hiss of the sleigh runners. Then their backs were to me, the sleigh drawing away, diminishing, the steady rhythm of the sleigh bells receding. They were nearly gone when I heard the woman laugh momentarily, her voice muffled by the falling snow, the sound distant and happy.

It was enough of a walk, I had no desire to push on into the park, and I turned back. The slim parallel lines of the sleigh runners were still there, down the middle of Central Park West, but they were fading quickly, and my own earlier footsteps were already completely gone. I climbed the stairs of the Dakota, took off my cap and coat, then turned off the living-room jets, ready for bed. I walked to the windows for one last look outside. Then I wanted to feel the snow once more, and I opened the french windows, and stepped out onto the balcony. Down on the street I'd crossed, the marks of the sleigh runners and of my steps were gone, the snow level and unmarked once more. I stared into the black-and-white park for several moments, then turned to look north. All I could see, barely visible through the curtain of snow, was the Museum of Natural History several blocks ahead, one row of its windows lighted, then I turned back into the living room. In bed I fell asleep almost instantly.

8

Rube said, "Tell us again. *Think*, goddammit!" the frustration and anger growing in his voice. "Was there anything *else* about the sleigh, anything at all? Didn't they say *anything*, for crysake?"

"Easy, Rube, easy," Dr. Danziger murmured. He, Rube, and Oscar Rossoff, who wore his own clothes now, were sitting in my Dakota living room, each with a cup of coffee in his hand or beside him. Oscar was smoking a cigarette; I'd never seen him smoke before, and after he'd smoked a couple, Danziger asked him for one, and now he was smoking, too.

I sat in shirt-sleeves, wearing carpet slippers, sipping coffee, and forcing every detail of my walk last night to life again, examining the pictures in my mind for anything new. Then once again I shook my head. "It was just . . . a sleigh. I'm sorry. And they didn't say a thing. She laughed after they'd passed, but if he said anything to cause it I didn't hear it."

"Well, what about the streetlamps?" Oscar said irritably. "Were they gas or electric? That's not hard to tell."

Irritability is contagious, and I said, "Oscar, I no more paid any attention to streetlights than *you* do when you go out at night."

"And you saw no one else?" Rube said, squinting at me. "Nothing else? Heard no sound? What about that: Did you *hear* anything else, anything at all?"

I hated to do it again—I felt guilty about it as though it were my fault—but after several seconds of trying to remember anything more of what I'd already told them in every possible detail, I had to shake my head once more. "It was absolutely silent, Rube; snow everywhere, nothing else moving."

His mouth quirked in annoyance, lips pressing tight together to hold in the anger. Then he made himself smile at me to show he understood. But he had to find some physical release, and he stood, hands shoving into the back pockets of his army pants, and began walking the room. "Damn it, damn it, *damn* it! It could have been 1882, it *could* have! Or it could have been today! Someone got out granddad's old sleigh, and the traffic lights were out because of the storm." Rube swung around to Rossoff, flinging his hands helplessly, laughing without amusement. "It's ridiculous! He might have made it! Maybe he *did!* And there's no way to tell—Jesus!" He walked to his chair, dropped into it, and reached for his coffee on the carpet beside him.

His voice slow, rumbling a little, lowering the level of irritability in the room, Danziger said patiently, "You came back up here, Si, after your walk? Meeting no one?"

"Right." I nodded again.

"Then you came into the living room here, walked to the windows, and looked down at the park."

"Right." I nodded, staring at his face, hoping he could draw something from me I didn't know was there.

"And you saw—nothing, really."

"No." I sat back in my chair, suddenly depressed. "I'm sorry, Dr. Danziger, terribly sorry. But to me last night, it *was* 1882. At least in my mind. So there was nothing unusual about that fact, and I paid no special attention—"

"I understand." He nodded several times, smiling at me; then he turned to the others, shrugging a shoulder. "Well, that's that. We'll simply have to wait for another opportunity and try again, that's all."

They nodded, then we all just sat there. Dr. Danziger looked at the lighted cigarette in his hand, made a disgusted grimace, and ground it out in an ashtray, and I knew he'd just quit smoking again. After a little, maybe a couple of minutes, Rossoff said, "Si, walk over to the windows, will you? And step out onto the balcony the way you did last night." I walked over to the french doors, opened them, and stepped out, turning to Rossoff inquiringly; I was tired of this but felt obligated to go on as long as anyone wanted me to. Rossoff said, "Close your eyes." I closed them. "Okay; it's last night. You're standing out there looking down at the park. Keep your eyes closed, and see it again in your mind. As soon as you see it, describe it, Si; exactly."

After a moment, eyes shut, I said, "Perfectly white snow still untouched, unmarked; it's beautiful . . . the trees look carbon-black against the whiteness. The street is level with snow, completely unmarked: I can see that my footprints are gone, and the snow is still falling. In the light around the bases of the streetlamps the snow sparkles, and nothing is moving, nothing; there isn't a sound. I stand here, looking down at the park for a few seconds longer, then decide to go to bed. I'm turning away now, to step back inside. I see that several windows are lighted—the cleaning women, I suppose—in the Museum of Natural History; then I pull the curtains shut, and . . . that's all, I'm sorry." I turned to look at the three of them, stepping back inside the room. "I went to bed then, and slept all—"

I didn't finish. Dr. Danziger was slowly standing, unfolding to his full six-five, his face coming to life. He walked quickly toward me, his hand reaching out ahead of him to grip my shoulder so hard it was painful. He swung me around, back to the balcony again, pushing me out onto it ahead of him. He stepped out, too, and said, "Look!" His big veined old hand moved past my eyes, seized my whole jaw, and swung my head to the north. "There's where you looked last night! Look again! *Where is the Museum?*"

I couldn't see it, of course: Between my eyes and the Museum stood four solid blocks of apartment houses rising far above the roof of the Dakota. The Museum hadn't been visible—not from this balcony— since the early eighteen eighties, and as the realization roared through my brain, it did in Rube's, it did in Oscar's, and Rube whispered, "He made it."

Then, his face an instant pink from the effort, he yelled. "He *made* it! Oh, my God, he *did!*" Rube and Oscar were grabbing at my hand then, shaking it, congratulating me and each other, and I stood grinning, nodding, trying to get hold of the knowledge that last night for a few moments I had stepped out of this apartment into the winter of 1882. Dr. Danziger's eyes were half closed, and I saw him sway for just an instant; I believe he came close to actually fainting. Then he and all of us were gabbling at each other, grinning, making lousy jokes, and while I

104

was a part of it, responding, grinning back, elated, excited, in my mind at the same time I was back on the balcony in the dead of a silent white night staring across five city blocks of empty space which had long since and for decades been solidly filled.

In the warehouse twenty minutes later I sat in a room I remembered vaguely from a tour of the building I'd taken with Rube. I sat in a swivel chair, the little tube of a chest microphone suspended by a tape around my neck. On a wall panel beside me, recording tape revolved, and a girl sat at an almost silent electric typewriter, a tiny headset over her ears, my recorded voice replaying into her ears only a matter of seconds behind my actual voice. Danziger, Rube, Rossoff, the Princeton history prof, Colonel Esterhazy, and a dozen others I'd met were standing around the room, leaning against the walls, listening, waiting.

I said, "Frederick Boague—Frederick N. Boague—Buffalo, New York. I last saw him in an art class three and a half years ago." I sat thinking for a second, then said, "There was a movie called *The Graduate*. Anne Bancroft was in it. And a guy named Dustin Hoffman. Directed by Mike Nichols." I paused, listening to the muffled clatter of the electric typewriter. "There are Hershey bars, chocolate. Brown paper wrappers with silver lettering." A pause. "Clifford Dabney, New York City, about twenty-five, is an advertising copywriter. Elmore Bob is dean of girls, Montclair College. Rupert Ganzman is a state assemblyman. Living in Wyoming is a full-blooded Sioux Indian named Gerald Montizambert. There was a fire in an apartment building on East Fifty-first Street just off Lexington last October. Penn Station has been torn down."

A young guy I'd seen in the halls came quietly into the room, almost tiptoeing. He carefully tore off the top typed half of the paper in the electric typewriter and walked out; the girl continued typing on the bottom half of the sheet. I continued talking onto the tape: names of people I knew or knew of, both obscure and prominent; facts large and small; any and every scrap of knowledge that came into my mind of the world as I remembered it before last night. "Queen Elizabeth is queen of England, but the *Queen Mary*—the ship, I mean—was sold to a town in southern California. . . . There's a barber named Emmanuel in the shop on Forty-second just west of the Commodore. . . ." A man opened the door and stepped into the room, grinning; he was around forty and bald; I'd met him in the cafeteria. "So far, okay!" he said.

"Everything we've been able to check." There was a murmur, everyone excited; the man left, and I continued. "There's a comic strip called *Peanuts,* and not long ago Lucy told Snoopy . . ."

At eleven o'clock Danziger cut me off; it was enough, he said. And by noon we knew. Every random fact I'd recalled of the world as I remembered it before last night was still a fact today. The few steps I'd taken, across the snow into the world of 1882 and back, hadn't altered that world—or in consequence altered ours. There was no one I'd known or known of yesterday, for example, who didn't exist this morning. No one else was in any way changed. No truth of any kind, large or trivial, was found to differ from my memory of it. Things were as I'd left them, there had been no detectable change, and that meant the experiment could cautiously continue.

But before it did I saw Katie. I walked across town after lunch, she closed her shop, and we sat upstairs for forty minutes while I told her three times what had happened. "What was it like? How did it *feel?*" she kept asking in a variety of ways. I'd try to tell her, hunting for the words that would do the job, and Katie would sit leaning toward me, eyes narrowed, lips parted, straining to extract the full meaning of what I was trying to convey from my mind to hers. At times her head would shake unconsciously in wonder and awe, but of course she was disappointed: I couldn't really transfer my experience, and when I had to get up to go finally, I knew she still wondered, "What was it like? How did it feel?"

At the warehouse again, I changed clothes in Doc Rossoff's office, and he had *his* questions while I dressed. They were mostly along the line of, Could I emotionally feel as well as intellectually believe in the reality of what had happened? And, always obliging, I thought about it as I got into my clothes. In my mind I saw the sleigh drawing away through the swirl of soft snowflakes, the jingle of the harness bells diminishing. And again I heard the clear musical sound of the woman's laugh in that marvelous winter night, and a thrill of pleasure touched my spine. I nodded at Doc and said yes.

He drove me to the Dakota then; we were in a hurry now. It had taken me a long time of living in the Dakota apartment to reach the point of last night's success; now I had only this night, tomorrow morning, and part of the afternoon to reach the same point again—if I were to see Katie's long blue envelope mailed in "New York, N.Y.; Main Post Office, Jan 23, 1882, 6:00 PM." And this time, to advance the experiment, I was to try it alone with no help from Doc Rossoff.

By four I was climbing the building staircase. The package from Fishborn's lay on the hallway floor before my door, I picked it up, and when I unlocked the door and stepped into my living room, it was astonishingly like coming home. At six, standing at the kitchen stove, a long fork in my hand, waiting for my potato to boil and reading the *Evening Sun* for January 22, 1882, it was as though I'd never left this familiar routine. Just before I'd come up I'd seen that last night's snow had been removed from the street below my windows, that the traffic lights were working and the cars flowing past again. But these things no longer mattered. Because now I knew—I *knew*—that January of 1882 existed out there, too. And I knew—*knew*—that when the time came I was going to be able to walk out into it once again.

I poked into my potato; it was still hard in the center, and with my paper folded lengthwise I stood at the stove reading on. The trial of Guiteau, Garfield's assassin, had continued today, Guiteau conducting his own defense as usual; the inquiry into the Star Route scandals dragged along, an entire family living on an isolated Wyoming farm had been found scalped. My front doorbell jangled.

Newspaper at my side, I walked down the long, wide old hall in my carpet slippers, opened the front door, and Katie was standing in the hallway. In an ankle-length winter coat, a scarf tied on her head, she stood smiling nervously, waiting for me to say something. After a moment during which I just stood staring, she slid quickly past me and into the living room. I turned, automatically closing the front door behind me, saying, "Katie? What the hell?" But she was crossing the room, shrugging out of her coat. She tossed it to a chair and turned to face me in a bottle-green silk dress trimmed in white lace, buttoned at neck and wrists, and its hem, still swaying from the motion of her turn, brushed the insteps of her buttoned shoes. In one swift sweeping motion she peeled off her dark scarf as though afraid I'd make her keep it on if she didn't hurry. Her hair was parted in the middle, drawn straight back off her forehead, and gathered in a bun at the nape of the neck.

I had to smile with pleasure, she looked so good; that thick dark coppery hair, her pale slightly freckled skin, those big brown defiant eyes, with the shimmering bottle-green of her dress; she knew what she was doing when she picked that color. As soon as I smiled she said quickly, "I'm going with you, Si. To see the letter mailed. It's mine, and I'm going to see it, too!"

I like women, I never run them down as somehow inferior to men, and I have a contempt for men who do. And I think, for one thing, that women are just as principled as men—but they sure as hell aren't the same kind of principles. I knew I could trust Kate in virtually anything, relying on her absolutely, her sense of right and wrong as lively as mine. Yet now we argued interminably: Kate at the stove, where she'd taken over dinner preparations, I at the kitchen table, waiting; then, sharing my two chops, we continued the battle at dinner. I began to feel like a hick upholding my own stuffy notions of morality. Because it simply did not matter to Kate that this was a government project, of the utmost seriousness, brought into being at tremendous expense and effort, and involving important people from all over the country. With no trouble at all Kate saw through the transparency to the truth—the feminine truth—underneath the serious pretense. She knew this was really a great, big expensive fascinating toy; we were all of us playing with it, and like a determined tomboy on a playground shouldering her way into a circle of boys, she was damn well going to play, too.

I switched to practical arguments but that was a blunder. Because she was instantly able to point out—shaking her fork at me, her food getting cold—that she was prepared, too; that she'd learned as much about the 1880's as I had. As a matter of fact, she pointed out, she was better prepared now than I'd been at this time last night, because now she knew as I did that it was really possible.

Under my verbal argument lay the knowledge that she was right. I knew in my bones that I'd succeed tomorrow; it wasn't just optimism but a matter of certain knowledge. And I knew, if I can convey this, that the sheer strength of my certainty could carry Kate along with me. I knew absolutely that we could succeed, both of us, and in the living room after dinner, the dishes washed, the argument dwindled out.

I never agreed in so many words. But she was pacing back and forth arguing, that long skirt swinging and making an audible swishing sound as she'd turn. I sat watching her, having a little trouble now not to smile because she looked so fine—her hair had a new special shine as she'd pass under the gaslights of the overhead chandelier. She looked so great, I just got up, finally, walked over, took her in my arms, and kissed her. She responded, we kissed again, then she stepped back. She'd won; the arguing was over. We'd said it all and she knew I wasn't going to throw her out bodily. She said, "No more, Si. Only one thing matters, and that's success tomorrow. We can't let anything at all interfere with that."

During the days and weeks I'd spent here alone, I'd daydreamed about having Kate here with me, and now she *was* here. But what she'd just said was so clearly true that there could be no question about accepting it, and we spent a quiet, domestic evening of the eighties: reading *Harper's Weekly, Leslie's*, then trading; and finally, over a cup of tea, we played some dominoes.

We went to bed around ten thirty. While I turned out the overhead chandelier, Kate walked to the closet beside the front door. From the pocket of her heavy winter coat she brought out a rolled-up white bundle, her nightgown, and I smiled, shaking my head, at her certainty that I'd let her stay. My hand on the key of the little green-shaded student lamp on the game table where our dominoes still lay, I waited for Kate to light the hall light. I heard the faint pop of the gas, then the wavering light steadied on the wall of the hallway, and I turned out the student lamp.

Kate stood waiting in the doorway of her room; the L-shaped bracket of the open-flame hall light was just over her head and to the right of her doorway, and again I noticed the special glow that gaslight gave the red of her hair. She said, "Good night, Si; see you in the morning."

"Right. Good night, Kate."

"It's going to work, isn't it, Si?"

I nodded. "I think so. You shouldn't be here but I'm glad you are. And I think it'll work."

We spent most of the next day—once breakfast, the dishes, and the morning paper were out of the way—reading aloud. I got a coal fire going in the living-room fireplace first. Then I found, where I'd left it on the floor near the windows, the book I'd been reading when I'd glanced down at the park and seen the snowstorm—only day before yesterday, I was mildly shocked to realize. This was a book from the living-room shelves: a bright, fresh new copy of *Tried for Her Life*, by Mrs. Emma D. E. N. Southworth, published a year or so ago, in 1880. It was a two-bit paperback but there were no semi-naked women on the cover, just black type on plain red paper.

I gave Kate a synopsis of what I'd read so far, then—sitting comfortably slouched in a chair, my feet in carpet slippers up on a hassock—I found my place and picked up the story aloud. It was a good day to be in here, snug and comfortable, the fire occasionally snapping; outside it looked cold, the sky gray and completely overcast. " 'When Sybil recovered from her death-like swoon,' " I read, " 'she felt herself being borne slowly on through what seemed a narrow tortuous underground passage; but the utter darkness, relieved only by a little gleaming red taper that moved like a star before her, prevented her from seeing more. A presentiment of impending destruction possessed her, and overwhelming horror filled her soul and held her faculties.' " I looked up to smile at Kate, who was on the settee, her feet tucked under her. I was smiling in acknowledgment of this overblown prose; I was certain that reasonably sophisticated people of the eighties *did* smile a little at this sort of thing, too. But I didn't smile much, and Kate took her cue from me. I'd read a lot of these books now, and whatever slight amusement there might be in their style, it was worn thin long since, and—skipping a lot—I was able to read for the stories, which weren't any better or worse than many a modern mystery I'd read.

We took turns reading, stopping for coffee, and stopping for lunch, finishing the book by midafternoon. It ended the way nearly all these books did by giving you some idea of what happened to the characters after the story ended. It's not really a bad idea; I've read many a book and wished I had some notion of whatever happened after the final page to the people I'd come to know, especially those I liked. In fact, the better the book and more real the characters, the more I've wanted to know.

Well, Mrs. Southworth let you know. Kate was reading when we reached the final page. " 'There is little more to tell,' " she read. " 'Raphael Riordan and his stepmother, Mrs. Blondelle, came over to view the corpse, and see to its removal. Gentiliska, now a very handsome matron, gazed at the dead body with a strangely mingled expression of pity, dislike, sorrow, and relief.' "

"Hold it," I said, and when Kate looked up at me I widened my eyes, frowned a little, then lifted one corner of my mouth. "That look like pity to you?"

"Sort of."

I deepened the frown, kept one eye wide with pity, then narrowed the other a little. "I've just added dislike. Now watch: here comes sorrow." I opened my mouth plaintively. "And now, in the center ring, juggling all four at once: relief!" I threw my chin high, opening my mouth all the way, trying to hang onto all the other expressions. Without moving my mouth I said, "How do I look?"

"Strangling."

"I was afraid of that. But I'll bet Gentiliska managed without strain. She could probably have piled on horror, chagrin, and ecstasy, without straining a facial muscle."

"You kind of like Gentiliska, don't you?"

"My all-time literary favorite. Pray continue."

" 'Raphael, now a grave and handsome man, met Mrs. Berners with a sad composure. He worshipped her as constantly and purely as ever. He had known no second faith. The widow Blondelle sold out her interest in the Dubarry White Sulphur Springs, and with her step-son Raphael Riordan, returned to England. Mr. and Mrs. Berners have but one child—Gem! But she is the darling of their hearts and eyes; and she is betrothed to Cromartie Douglas, whom they love as a son.' "

Kate closed the book, and we both sat smiling a little. But then she said seriously, "I'm glad Gem and Cromartie got engaged. Even though it was long after the story ended. I thought they would be eventually, but it's nice to know."

"Right. As for Gentiliska and her mingled emotions, the more about her the better. And I'll tell you something else I like: I think I like the kind of people who like a story like this." Katie nodded, and we sat silent. The draft in the fireplace made a subdued miniature roar, then a coal fell. I said, "Kate, they're out there now." I nodded toward the windows across the room; all we could see was the silvery winter sky. I meant what I said; all day I'd felt the living presence of the New York winter of 1882 gathering itself around us—with more strength and reality now than in all of the days and weeks just past. Because now one truth could never change: I knew that that time existed. "They're waiting for us, Kate," I said, and—strong moods and powerful certainties reach from one mind to another—Kate nodded, believing and knowing, too, caught up in my absolute certainty. I said, "Kate, I think it's time," and for an instant she looked frightened; then she nodded, and closed her eyes.

I close mine, reached over and took Kate's hand, then sat, warm and comfortable, letting each muscle relax, letting all least tensions drain away. And presently—as Kate, too, was doing—I silently spoke to myself. *In a few moments, and for a few moments, your mind will give up thinking; and you will almost sleep. This is January 23. And that will be the date, of course, when presently you open your eyes again: January 23, 1882. You and Kate have an errand to do; you will walk into the park with her, and there will be nothing at all of any other time in your mind. All you will be thinking is that you're going to the post office. Be there by five-thirty, no later. And see who mails the blue envelope. Do not interfere with events. Observe them, move through them, but do not cause or prevent any. One difference: This is new but it is going to work, it is going to work. At some point, walking through the park very likely, at some point when you know absolutely that this is a winter afternoon of the year 1882 . . . you will remember the present. You will remember the present and for the first time be truly an observer.*

I jumped a little, and my eyes popped open; I'd actually dozed, it seemed to me. Kate sat watching me, her hand in mine. She said, "I was asleep, too. We have to go to the post office, Si. Do you feel like it?"

"Yes." I nodded, and stood up, yawning. "Do me good to get outdoors and wake up; come on."

At the hall closet, yawning, I got into my overcoat with the attached cape, my overshoes, my round black fur cap. Kate put on her coat and tied on her scarf. I no more gave thought to what year or century this was than anyone else getting ready to go out today. And downstairs, walking out of the Seventy-second Street building entrance, our shoulders hunching and our chins ducking into our collars as we stepped into the cold, I didn't look behind me to the west, and crossing the street bordering the park, I glanced neither north or south. Why should I have? It never occurred to me; the air was sharp and cold, and I kept my head down.

In the park we angled across it to the east and south, toward the entrance at Fifty-ninth and Fifth. It was cold, we saw no one, and here in the park the city seemed nearly silent. We heard only the steady scuff of our feet on the path, and I felt snug in my greatcoat, a little less sleepy, and began enjoying the exercise. Except for the paths, the snow was nearly unmarked, though there were occasional trails of footprints. For a few dozen yards our path paralleled the winding roadway, and on its packed snow I heard, absently, a faint axle squeak and the slow muffled clop of hoofs, but didn't trouble turning to look, and neither did Kate. We simply walked across the park, used to the cold now, enjoying it and the walk, hardly thinking at all.

We came out of the immense rectangle of Central Park at its southeast corner, at Fifth Avenue and Fifty-ninth Street, and I unbuttoned my coat to reach into my pants pocket for our fares. Katie moaned, and I looked at her quickly. She had a hand pressed to her forehead, her eyes were squeezed shut, and I saw her face turn paper-white. I turned to grab her but instead I staggered half a step sideways to keep my balance, and had to stop, feet wide apart and braced, slowly bending almost double, my elbows jamming into the pit of my stomach, both hands sliding up over my face, fighting against fainting as memory lighted up every cell of my brain.

Neither of us had anticipated physical shock. I got an arm around Kate's shoulders and she was trembling. Trying to support us both, I stood leaning against a tree trunk at the curb, feeling the sweat pop out on my forehead and upper lip, and knew I must be deathly pale. My eyes were fixed on my own shoe tips, and I stood drawing deep breaths of the sharp chill air; then I felt the sweat drying on my face and knew I would be all right. I looked at Kate; her eyes were open now, her tongue moistening her lips. "I'm okay now; thanks," she said, and straightened up. "But, oh, my God, Si!" she whispered, and I could only nod.

We didn't turn immediately; we couldn't quite bring ourselves to do that. But we heard the squeal of iron tires crunching cold dry snow, heard the loose wood-and-iron rattle of the body, and the crack of leather reins on solid flesh. Then, very slowly, we turned our heads to look again at the tiny, arch-roofed wooden bus with high wooden-spoke wheels, drawn by a team of gaunt horses, their breaths puffing whitely into the winter air at each step. It was closer now, filling our vision; and staring at it I knew now from where and when I had come. It took a moment of actual struggle for my mind to take hold of what it knew to be the truth: that we were here, standing on a corner of upper Fifth Avenue on a gray January afternoon of 1882; and I shivered and for a moment felt shot through with fear. Then elation and curiosity roared through me.

9

I LOOKED AT KATE and she was grinning; then I turned to look south, down the long familiar length of Fifth Avenue, and once more the faintness touched me.

Everyone has seen in actuality or on film the splendid glittering length of Fifth Avenue, the wide wide street solidly lined with incredible towers of metal, glass, and soaring stone: the sparkling Corning Glass Building, its acres of glass walls rising forever; the enormous aluminum-sided Tishman Building; the great stone masses of Rockefeller Center; weather-worn St. Patrick's Cathedral, its twin spires submerged down among the huge buildings which dwarf it. And the sparkling stores: Saks, Tiffany's, Jensen's; and the big, old soiled-white library at the corner of Forty-second Street, its stone lions flanking the wide steps of its main entrance. They must be the most famous seventeen blocks of the world, and beyond them even farther down the length of that astonishing street, the unbelievable height of the Empire State Building at Thirty-fourth Street, if the air should happen to be miraculously clear enough to see it. That was the picture—asphalt and stone and sky-touching towers of metal and glass—that was in my mind instinctively as I turned to look down the length of that street.

Gone. All gone! This street was *tiny!* Narrow! Cobbled! A tree-lined residential street! Mouths open, we stood staring at rows of brownstone houses, at others of brick and stone, at trees, and even patches of fenced snow-covered lawn before the houses. And all down the length of that quiet street, the highest structures I could see were the thin spires of churches, nothing above them but gray winter sky. Coming toward us, rattling on the cobbles of the bare patches of this strange little Fifth Avenue, was another horse-drawn bus, the only moving vehicle, at the moment, in several blocks.

Katé was gripping my arm, whispering. "The Plaza Hotel is gone!" She pointed, and I turned to stare across Fifty-ninth Street to where the Plaza ought to be; instead there was only empty space as though the hotel had been wiped from the scene. We had to stop thinking this way: It hadn't disappeared; it wasn't yet built. But the plaza itself, the little square directly beside Fifth Avenue across the street from the park—it was there, with a fountain at its center, turned off now for the winter. I nudged Kate: "Look. The hack line!" There they stood waiting, the familiar line of half a dozen horse-drawn hacks along the Fifty-ninth Street curb beside the park, where they've been ever since.

We heard the sound, and swung around: The little wooden bus was stopped at the curb beside us, its lantern smudged, and as we walked toward it I caught the sharp stink of oil. The door was at the back, just over a jutting wooden step, and as I opened it for Kate I glanced ahead at the driver, but he was only a motionless, blanket-wrapped figure high on an outside seat at the front, under a heavy umbrella. I followed Kate in, heard reins slap the horses' rumps, the bus jerked forward and we pulled out from the curb. Opposite is a sketch I made from memory of the moment we began rattling down Fifth Avenue on the winter afternoon of January 23, 1882.

Inside, two benches ran the short length of the bus under the windows, and Kate sat down beside the rear door while I walked to the tin box up front labeled FARE 5¢. I found two nickels, dropped them in, and noticed the hole in the roof through which the driver could look to see that I did.

And then we sat—there were no other passengers—heads swiveling, trying to see both sides of this alien little street at once. Half meaning it, I said, "This isn't Fifth Avenue, it *can't* be," and Kate pointed. Sliding past the window opposite us was a tiny curbside streetlamp, four horizontal strips of painted glass forming a shallow boxlike frame around it, and the painted legend on the panel facing us said 5TH AVENUE.

Kate was pulling my coat sleeve, and when I turned she gestured with her chin at the view behind us. "The Seventies, on the East Side," she

said, and I nodded. It was true: The block we were jogging through now looked precisely like some of the tree-lined streets of the East Seventies in modern New York; a row of tall, dignified three- and four-story houses that said *money*, and I knew that different though it seemed this *was* Fifth Avenue. Between Fifty-eighth and Fifty-seventh streets, in fact, on the east side of Fifth, the houses were all of white marble and looked spectacular; and the entire block on the west side of Fifth was filled with a brick-and-gray-stone château.

A gong sounded, not loud, just the touch of a clapper, and I turned and saw the source: a dark-green-enameled light wagon just turning off Fifty-fifth Street ahead into Fifth Avenue, then heading south. Almost immediately it swung to the right into a driveway crossing the sidewalk and a strip of snow-covered lawn, and we could see the driver in profile now. He had a heavy mustache and wore a dark-blue cap with a straight absolutely flat peak, and on the side of the wagon I saw the brass gong I'd heard. ST. LUKE'S HOSPITAL, said the gold-leaf lettering along the green side-panel, and the wagon stopped in the curving driveway. The building—we could see it now—was utterly strange, big and with a long wing stretching down Fifty-fifth: the hospital. Trundling toward him, we watched the driver tying his leather reins to the dashboard, then saw him climb down—first a foot on top of the wheel, the other foot next onto the brass hubcap, then a hop to the ground. Now a second man, mustached and wearing an ankle-length white coat, came out to meet him at the back of the wagon. The bus windows were open an inch, and we could hear the sudden chain-rattle as the tail gate was lowered; then we watched the two of them slide a wood-and-canvas stretcher out the back. As we passed the hospital, a bearded man lay on the stretcher, motionless, staring straight up at the sky, a dark blanket tucked neatly under his chin. Turning to look back, we saw them carry him quickly up the stone steps and inside, and as we rattled over the cobbles past the big stone building he'd disappeared into, I sat glancing up at its tall, lean, round-topped windows. It was a strange sight to me, a hospital here on Fifth Avenue, and I thought of the man on the stretcher about to be attended by long-skirted nurses and bearded doctors. Quietly, so the driver couldn't hear, I said so to Kate, then she leaned close to murmur, "Doctors and nurses who've never heard the words *penicillin*, *antibiotics*, or *sulfa*." I couldn't remember if Martin Lastvogel had ever mentioned this, and I wondered if, in this hospital, they even had anesthetics.

In a window of a house on the southwest corner of Fifth and Fifty-third Street, I saw a sign reading ALLEN DODSWORTH'S SCHOOL FOR DANCING, then two old friends slid past our windows. First, on the southwest corner of Fifty-second Street: one of the Vanderbilt mansions. I could barely remember, as a child on a visit to New York, standing with my father for half an hour watching as the old building was slowly smashed down to make room for the Crowell-Collier Building. It was old, stained, dirty, worn out; now here it stood in its youth, a shining château of clean white limestone. Across the street from it was the Catholic Orphan Asylum, and then in the block beyond I caught a glimpse of a really old friend. We sat grinning as we approached it, and Kate whispered, "I'm so glad, so *relieved*, to see it."

I nodded. "Just looking at it," I said, "I'm almost converted to Catholicism." Because there it was, an old friend, St. Pat's good gray cathedral, looking immense, higher by far than anything else near it, but unaltered—no, it was changed, somehow: What was different? I pressed my face to the glass to look out and up, and the twin spires were—not gone, of course; they weren't yet built. We were passing directly before it now, the gray cathedral completely filling the windowpane, our own reflections swaying ghosts before it. The sight of it was so utterly familiar that it suddenly seemed as though the Fifth Avenue I knew *had* to exist, and I turned my head to look back up the street toward Central Park. But once more I felt the shock of it: I was staring up miles of bare-branched shade trees and houses, church spires rising to the sky high above them. I swung around to look forward—we were passing something utterly alien called the Buckingham Hotel, just across Fiftieth Street from St. Pat's—and saw still more miles of elegant residences stretching unbrokenly, apparently, to the Battery.

I realized that we'd stopped and that the door was opening. A man climbed in, dropped his fare in the tin box, and sat down across the aisle with a casual uninterested glance at us. Then he crossed his knees and turned sideways to stare out the window as the reins slapped and we started up again. And I sat watching him from the corner of my eye, tense, excited, almost frightened at my first really close look at a living human being of the year 1882.

In some ways the sight of that ordinary man whom I never saw again is the most intensely felt experience of my life. There he sat, staring absently out the window, in an odd high-crowned black derby hat, a worn black short-length overcoat, his green-and-white-striped shirt collarless and fastened at the neck with a brass stud; a man of about sixty, clean-shaven.

I know it sounds absurd, but the *color* of the man's face, just across the tiny aisle, was fascinating: This was no motionless brown-and-white face in an ancient photograph. As I watched, the pink tongue touched the chapped lips, the eyes blinked, and just beyond him the background of brick and stone houses slid past. I can see it yet, that face against the slow-moving background, and hear the unending hard rattle of the iron-tired wheels on packed snow and bare cobbles. It was the kind of face I'd studied in the old sepia photographs, but this hair, under the curling hat brim, was black streaked with gray; his eyes were a sharp blue; his ears, nose, and freshly shaved chin were red from the winter chill; his lined forehead pale white. There was nothing remarkable about him; he looked tired, looked sad, looked bored. But he was alive and seemed healthy enough, still full-strengthed and vigorous, perhaps with years yet to live—and I turned to Kate, my mouth nearly touching her ear, to murmur, "When he was a boy, Andrew Jackson was President. He can remember a United States that was—Jesus!—still mostly unexplored wilderness." There he sat, a living breathing man with those memories in his head, and I sat staring at the slight risings and fallings of his chest in wonder.

The Rev. and Mrs. C. H. Gardner's Boarding and Day School for Young Ladies and Gentlemen moved past our windows near the corner of Forty-ninth; at 603 Fifth, said the polished brass plate on its brownstone front. Then just past Forty-eighth, Kate whispered, "There it is: five-eighty-nine!" I didn't understand, and she hissed, "Carmody's house!" and I swung around in my seat to look. It was wonderful: a big, beautifully proportioned brownstone mansion with a marvelously ornate bronze fence around it and the tiny patches of lawn. We stared as it slid past our window, and I was baffled; I felt almost certain I'd seen it before. It seemed astonishingly familiar, then I remembered; it looked like the big brownstone James Flood mansion surviving on Nob Hill in twentieth-century San Francisco, even to the bronze fence, and I wondered if the same architect hadn't done them both. We were nearly past it, staring back at it, wondering if Andrew Carmody—alive now, years before he was to shoot himself in Gillis, Montana—was somewhere inside it.

The cross streets slipped by—Forty-ninth, Forty-eighth, Forty-seventh, Forty-sixth—all strange unfamiliar identical streets of uninterrupted row after row of high-stooped brownstones precisely like blocks still existing on the West Side. As we'd moved down toward the thick of the city, the street became more and more alive. There they were now, moving along the walks, crossing the street—the people. And I looked out at them, at first with awe, then with delight; at the bearded, cane-swinging men in tall shiny silk hats, fur caps like mine, high-crowned derbies like the man's across the aisle, and—younger men—in very shallow low-crowned derbies. Almost all of them wore ankle-length great coats or topcoats, half the men seemed to wear pince-nez glasses, and when the older men, the silk-hatted men, passed an acquaintance, each touched his hat brim in salute with the head of his cane. The women were wearing head scarfs or hats ribbon-tied under the chin; wearing short, tight-waisted cutaway winter coats, or capes or brooch-pinned shawls; some carried muffs and some wore gloves; all wore button shoes darting out from and disappearing under long skirts.

There—well, there they *were*, the people of the stiff old woodcuts, only . . . these moved. The swaying coats and dresses there on the walks and crossing the street before and behind us were of new-dyed cloth—maroon, bottle-green, blue, strong brown, unfaded blacks—and I saw the shimmer of light and shadow in the appearing and disappearing long folds. And the leather and rubber they walked in pressed into and marked the slush of the street crossings; and their breaths puffed out into the winter air, momentarily visible. And through the trembling, rattling glass panes of the bus we heard their living voices, and heard a girl laugh aloud. Looking out at their winter-flushed faces, I felt like shouting for joy.

Within two blocks half a dozen people had climbed into the bus; one of the pince-nezed top-hatted men, several others, and then, somewhere along in the Forties we pulled to the curb, and a woman got on, walking past us to the fare box, her long skirt brushing our legs. She wore a flower-trimmed felt hat, a plain black coat, a long pale-green scarf around her neck, and the hem of her dress, just below her coat, was deep purple. She was a woman in her thirties, and my first impression as she walked down the narrow aisle past us was that she was beautiful. But then her coin rattled into the fare box, she turned back, and—Kate and I sat directly beside the door at the rear—she sat down up ahead. This is a drawing I've made from memory. Now I saw her face clearly and

glanced quickly away so that I wouldn't offend her, because her face was scarred with dozens of pitted cavities, and I remembered that smallpox was almost commonplace still. No one else paid her the least attention.

We passed the Windsor Hotel, the Sherwood, and then something called Ye Olde Willow Cottage, according to an old-English sign running the width of the building just over the doorway: a wooden colonial-looking building with shutters, a wide veranda, and a short flight of wooden steps, like a country store. In front of it a big tree grew out of the pavement, pedestrians walking around it, and if Ye Olde Willow Cottage didn't date from colonial times, it sure looked it. Right next door, on this astonishing Fifth Avenue, stood Henry Tyson's Fifth Avenue Market, apparently a butchershop because I caught a glimpse of skinned carcasses hanging in rows.

Street traffic had grown heavier. We were passing carriages now; and a light delivery wagon, enameled deep purple and lettered *Moquin* in gold script, cut around us. As I watched it, Kate touched my arm, and I turned. She was frowning, shaking her head. "Si, I've had enough. I'm seeing too much. I'd like to . . . just retreat somewhere and close my eyes."

"I know: I know what you mean." I stood up, stooping to look ahead. I knew we must be approaching Forty-second Street and I was unconsciously looking for the landmark that would confirm it, the main library on the west corner just across Forty-second. Again a moment of utter disbelief, because of course it wasn't there. Where it should have been stood what looked like the base of an enormous pyramid: tall blank walls slanting inward, running clear down to Forty-first Street on Fifth, and west on Forty-second out of sight. Martin had briefed me with pictures, and I knew what this was: the Croton Reservoir. But it was one more bewildering sight in a city completely familiar to me and now terribly different. The bus was edging toward the curb, I beckoned to Kate, and we got off directly in front of a two-wheeled hansom cab parked just short of the corner. I opened the cab door and helped Kate in. Settling down beside her, I glanced at her, and her head was back, her eyes closed. The driver sat in the rear on a high seat where he could look over the top, and now I heard a sound overhead, and looked up to see a panel slide back and reveal a small open square in the roof. Framed in it a moment later, I saw one eye, half of the other, a nose red with cold, and the beginnings of a large and drooping mustache. "The main post office," I said; then I got out my watch, pressed the stud, and the lid sprang back to reveal the face. It was nearly five. "Can you do it in half an hour?"

"I don't know," he said disgustedly, and clucked at his horse, snapping the reins. We pulled out into the street. "The way traffic is nowadays, it gets worse every day, you never know anymore. We'll try it; straight down Fifth to the square shouldn't be too bad yet, this time of day. Then over to Broadway, and miss the damned El; pardon me, ma'am." My head was back, too, my eyes closed; I'd seen enough for the moment, almost more than I could take. But as the roof panel slid shut I was smiling; however different, New York wasn't really changed.

10

THE SLOW absolutely regular *clip-clop*, *clip-clop* of our horse's hoofs on the hard-packed snow—a little louder and more ringing when we crossed bare cobbles—was soothing, and so was the rhythmical sway and slight jounce of the hansom body on its springs. I began to recover from too much all at once, and opened my eyes now and then. But the glimpses I had were more of the same: This was a narrow, pleasant, tree-lined, expensive residential street, mostly. Occasionally we passed hotels with strange names: St. Marc . . . Shelburn. And the Union League Club looking just like a Union League Club.

Then I heard the distant frantic sound of a bell, growing louder with every clang, and as we crossed Thirty-third Street it was suddenly a brain-numbing fury of sound to the west. Kate scrambling upright beside me, I turned to look, and here it came straight for us, a team of immense white horses, manes flying, hoofs pounding, drawing a red-and-brass fire engine, the driver slashing his whip at the horses, a flat stream of white smoke lining out behind it like the wake of a ship. The bell was wild now, the pound of hoofs on the cobbles so fast and in such unison that the sound was a throb. It was frightening to see that smoke-belching fury roaring straight at us, and our driver lashed out at his horse, and we jolted on across the street and out of its way. Behind us, we saw it dash on across Fifth, red-and-gilt spokes flashing, drivers reining up to hold the path clear. Four or five blocks farther on we heard the sound again, this time to the south, and I remembered that this was a city of wooden beams, floors and walls, and of open-flame lighting and heat.

All the while we clip-clopped on, block after block downtown into the busy part of the city, the street traffic grew heavier. Then suddenly Kate and I were bumped hard against each other. The cab had stopped abruptly, slewing sideways in the slush of the pavement. Then it jerked, starting forward again, and I sat up, hearing our driver cursing, and I lowered my window to stick my head out, and the noise was hard to believe.

We were at the intersection where Broadway crosses Fifth, and vehicles were pouring from Broadway to join our traffic stream, which was just possible, or to fight their way across it, which was almost impossible. Nearly every vehicle had four wheels and every wheel was wrapped in iron that smashed and rang against the cobbles, every horse had four iron-shod hoofs that did the same, and there was no control whatsoever. Wheels clattered, wood groaned, chains rattled, leather creaked, whips cracked against horseflesh, men shouted and cursed, and no street I've ever seen of the twentieth century made even half that brain-numbing sound.

Bulling their way across Fifth or Broadway were varnished delivery wagons, each with a single slim horse; enormous-wheeled, flat-bedded wagons loaded sky-high with barrels, crates, sacks, some pulled by as many as three tandem teams of immense steam-breathing dray horses; carriages of black, maroon, green, brown, some shabby, some elegant and glinting with glass and polish. They trotted, lumbered, or rattled over the stones, or they slowed or stopped short in little knots and clusters; Kate was leaning out her window and we saw a carriage horse at the intersection rear high on his hind legs, whinnying, and I saw a truck driver come out of Broadway, standing before his seat to force his way across Fifth, slashing out with his whip at his own horses and at any others who got in his way. Other drivers simply sat in numb patience, hunched and motionless against the cold, completely out in the open on their high wooden benches, wrapped to the waist in drab torn-edged blankets, wearing fur or knit caps pulled down low, and enormous coats of stained cloth or balding fur. Then we were across, resuming our steady *clip-clop* down Fifth, and I yelled at the driver, "There ought to be traffic lights!" and he opened his slide.

"What's that?"

"They ought to have signal lights to control the traffic," I said, but of course he just looked at me, then slid the panel closed. At Washington

Square we turned left—there was no arch at the entrance, and to me, again, it looked as though it had been *removed*—over to Broadway, and I sat with Kate's hand in mine, my body, senses, and capacity for surprise used up. Kate laid her head back on the hard tufted-leather upholstery, and I did, too, watching the telegraph wires, which had appeared as soon as we turned into Broadway, angle endlessly across the top of my window. I didn't sit up or look out again till Chambers Street. Then, a block ahead on Kate's side, I looked out and saw City Hall, and it was so good to see something familiar that I dragged out my watch; it was five twenty, there was time to walk, and I rapped on the roof.

We walked south, on past City Hall and the little park before it. I said, "This is the original City Hall you can't fight, you know," and Kate smiled. Then we crossed the street to the big main post office which filled the triangle of land just across from City Hall Park where Park Row ends at Broadway. By the time we got around to the front entrance of the post office, Kate and I were grinning at each other; it was such a ridiculous building, all windows and ornamental stone columns rising five stories to a roof of shingled towers; cast-iron railings; an ornamental cupola; and, fluttering from a flagpole, a long pointed pennant on which was lettered POST OFFICE.

Inside, it was tiled floor and brass spittoons, dark wood, pebbled glass, and gaslights. We found an enormous panel of ornate brass letter-drops labeled CITY, BROOKLYN, STATEN ISLAND, ANNEXED DISTRICT, together with separate drops for each state and territory, and CANADA, NEWFOUNDLAND, MEXICO, SOUTH AMERICA, EUROPE, ASIA, AFRICA, and OCEANIA. Beyond this great panel was an entire wall of thousands of private numbered boxes. It was just past five thirty, and Kate at one side and I at the other, we took positions beside the big panel and began our wait.

I suppose some fifty-odd people came in and dropped letters into those slots in the next fifteen minutes, nearly all of them men; and the look of astonishment and disgust on Kate's face was something to see. Because just about every last man, without breaking stride, aimed a shot of thick brown tobacco juice at one of the several dozen cuspidors scattered around the big floor. Some were expert, hitting the mark squarely and audibly, then walking on toward or past us looking pleased and self-satisfied. Others missed by a foot or more, and now, our eyes used to the gloom of the feeble lighting, we saw that the floor was soiled everywhere you looked; and I saw Kate reach down the side of one leg, gather up her skirts, and stand holding them a good two inches from the floor.

We waited, minute after minute, people streaming in and out, the squeak and clatter of the hinged brass flaps of the many letter drops almost never entirely stopping. I was sure Kate was picturing, as I was, the blue envelope, singed at one end, covered on the back with a man's last words. Were we about to see it again? Maybe not; it was possible that it had been posted at an outside mailbox, and at the thought I was instantly certain it had been, that we were never going to see "the sending of" the letter that would "cause the Destruction by Fire of the entire World. . . ."

And then here he came, at ten minutes of six by the big lobby clock, shoving through the heavy doors. Here he came, walking fast and full of purpose, a black-bearded round-bellied John Bull of a man, and the excitement flared so that for an instant I literally could not see. Filling my vision now, here he came heading across the great tiled floor directly for us, and his hairy right hand held the long slim robin's-egg-blue envelope. His stubby, flat-topped plug hat hung jauntily on the back of his head; and his unbuttoned overcoat, swept behind him by the speed of his walk, exposed the long curve of his belly shoved belligerently forward. His chin was lifted, thrusting his stiff beard almost horizontally outward as though he were defying the world, and a corner of his mouth gripped a cigar butt, lifting his lip so that he appeared to be snarling.

He was an imposing and memorable man, and he didn't see me, didn't see anyone; his brown fierce little eyes looked straight ahead, lost in his own concerns and purpose and the importance of the act he was about to perform. And then we saw what we had come across the years to see.

He thrust the long blue envelope toward the brass slot marked CITY and there was an instant when I had a glimpse of its face. I saw the strange green stamp, slightly tilted to the right; saw it in memory, canceled, and saw it in actuality, queerly unmarked; saw the slanted script, old and browning in memory, fresh-written and sharply black in actuality, but reading identically: *Andrew W. Carmody, Esq., 589 Fifth Avenue. . . .* The end of the envelope, unsinged and unopened now, pushed the brass flap inward, the hand holding it turned at the wrist, a diamond ring gleaming. Then the blue envelope was gone, the brass flap still swinging, its mysterious journey toward the future begun.

The man had turned on his heel, was walking swiftly toward the outer doors, and—that was all we'd come to see but we simply weren't *able* to let him walk out and away, into the night and lost forever—Kate and I stepped forward to follow.

We pushed through the doors, and it was dark out now. Our man turned north, back the way we'd come, walking along the Broadway side of the post office. We followed, watching him pass through the yellowy circles at the base of each streetlamp, the light sliding along the silk curves of his hat. Beyond the curb Broadway lay in almost complete darkness, its traffic still noisy but much less heavy. And now the traffic was dim shapes and moving shadows visible only in bits and pieces. You'd see a fan shape of muddy spokes revolving through the swaying light of a lantern slung from a van's axle, but the wagon itself and its driver and team would be lost in the blackness; or see the shine of a silvery door handle and the waxed curve of a jouncing carriage body under its own flickering side lamp, and nothing more of it. Across the dark street, the windows and doorways of business houses were almost dark, their shapes silhouetted only by turned-down night-lights. Pedestrians—the last of the office workers, I supposed—hurried past us, their faces yellowing and coming momentarily clear as they approached and passed through the cones of dim street-lighting, pale and almost lost in the in-between blackness. Across the street a man, a dark blur against the dimly lighted doorways and windows, carried a pole, and with this, as he walked, he reached up into each dark streetlamp, touching it into light.

I'd felt Kate's arm tighten under mine, drawing my arm closer to her side, and I understood why. This strange dim street, still clattering steel against cobble in a blackness relieved by squares, rectangles and cones of vague light whose very color was strange, had me uneasy, too. And yet—oh, God, just to *be* here!—something in me responded to it and the mystery of the hurrying, dimly seen people around us, and I knew Rube Prien had been right: This was the greatest possible adventure.

My arm squeezed down on Kate's, halting her beside me. Just beyond a streetlamp ahead, our man had abruptly turned to the curb and stepped out into the street. Now he stood within the slightly trembling circle of light on the cobbles, hat gleaming on the back of his head, belly jutting, looking past us to the south, his head moving from side to side trying to see through the oncoming traffic in the unmistakable attitude of a man impatiently searching for a bus. Vague in the dark of the street beside us, a heavy wagon trundled past. Kate and I watched its lantern jolting and swaying under the rear axle, watched its heavy black bulk clatter toward the puddle of yellow light ahead and the man standing inside it. The driver stood up, sharply silhouetted for us against the streetlight ahead. He was shouting, cursing, and we saw his arm move fast and heard the crack of his whip. The man standing in the street facing him lifted his head, jutting his beard, and we stood watching him stare up at the driver high above him without a change of expression and without budging or intention to budge. We stared at the driver's back, saw his whip arm lift high in threat. Then we saw the move of his left shoulder as he twitched his left rein. And under the lamp the horse and then the wagon curved around the man on the street. The upraised whip passed directly over the shining hat; but neither whip nor the man under it moved. Then, disappearing into the darkness ahead, the driver shouted an obscenity over his shoulder, and our man tossed back his head and—I thought his hat would tumble down his back, but it did not—he laughed.

We'd had to resume our walk, slowing our pace, but we were very nearly abreast of him as he peered once more to the south, then swung impatiently away toward the curb. "A *bus?*" he said, as though suddenly astonished. "Why should I ever wait for a bus again!" He stepped up onto the walk, Kate and I looking out into the street pretending to ignore him; he was only a step ahead of us now. He turned to walk rapidly north, and we stopped, giving him time to draw ahead.

He didn't go far. We stood waiting, watching, and he walked quickly along a row of four or five hansom cabs lined up to the street corner ahead, and stopped at the first in line. "Home!" he said, his voice ringing out happy and exuberant as he reached for the door handle. "All the way home, and in style!"

"And where might that be?" The faint silhouette of the driver leaned over the side of his exposed seat, his voice sardonic.

"Nineteen Gramercy Park," the man said, climbing in; then the cab door slammed, I heard the driver cluck at his horse, heard the reins crack, and stood watching the cab pull out and into the thin stream of wavering lamps and lanterns. I turned to Kate, but she was staring at the walk.

At the base of a curbside wooden telegraph pole lay a half oval of snow out of the pedestrian path, protected by the pole and still untouched. The patch of snow lay just within the circle of pale light from a streetlamp, and at the edge of the patch, sharply and clearly impressed in the snow, was a replica in miniature of the tombstone whose photograph Kate had shown me over the grave of Andrew Carmody outside Gillis, Montana.

Almost matter-of-factly Kate murmured, "It's impossible." She looked up at me. "It's *impossible!*" she said again, her voice suddenly angry, and I knew what she felt; this was so far from any sensible explanation that it made you mad, and I nodded.

"I know," I said. "But there it is." And there it still was; we bent forward to stare at it. All we could do was stand looking at that shape in the snow; straight-edged at bottom and sides, the top perfectly rounded in a cartoonist's tombstone shape, and, in its interior, the design formed of dozens of tiny dots, a nine-pointed star contained in a circle.

The cab was long gone when I looked up, lost in the traffic and dark. I stood staring, eyes narrowed, but I wasn't looking after it. A second or so before, above the iron rattle of the thinning Broadway street traffic, I'd heard a sound, a familiar sound at the very edge of my attention, and now I realized what it had been. I said, "Kate, would you like a drink? In front of a great big fire?"

"Yes. Oh, my God, *yes,*" she said, and I took her arm, and we walked half a dozen yards ahead to the corner. Across the street one of the illuminated signs framing the streetlamp read BROADWAY, the other PARK PLACE. And a short block west on Park Place I saw the source of that familiar clackety-racketing sound. Its three tall slim windows were lighted redly, the familiar gabled shape of its roof black against the night sky: There, perched over the street, was an El station like an old old friend.

We crossed Broadway—it wasn't hard now, the traffic sparse—and on the other side I turned to look back. This was a dark city, but just beyond the rear of the post office on the far side of City Hall Park I saw a five-story building that still stands in twentieth-century New York. But now the upper floors were brilliant with the light of hundreds of gas jets. Carved in the stone of the side of the building, clearly readable in the light streaming out the upper windows, was THE NEW YORK TIMES. They were up there now—I could walk back, climb a wooden staircase, and actually see them—derbied reporters scribbling in longhand; dozens and dozens of typesetters in sleeve protectors standing in long rows plucking type letter by letter from wooden cases, their hands blurred by motion as they set every word, sentence, paragraph, column and page of what would presently be, ink still wet, tomorrow morning's *New York Times*. They were there now as I stared across the darkness at those brilliantly lighted windows, preparing a paper I might already and long since have seen brown and crumbling at the edges, lying forgotten in an old file. I shivered, turning away, and we walked on a short block to the El station.

As I climbed the steps, even the ironwork of the railings seemed wonderfully familiar. I'd visited New York often as a boy, ridden the El many times. And now here again, inside the little station, were the bare worn floorboards, the wooden tongue-and-groove walls, the little scooped-out wooden shelf projecting from under the change-booth window, grained and polished from ten thousand hands. There was a cuspidor on this floor and the station was lighted by a single tin-shaded kerosene ceiling lamp. But even the dimness was familiar; as late as the 1950's I'd been in stations just like this.

I shoved two nickels in through the little half-moon hole at the bottom of the wide-meshed grill between me and the mustached man in the booth. He took them without looking up from his paper, and shoved out two printed tickets. Then we walked out to the platform, and for just an instant it was once again a tiny shock to see the dozen or so passengers: the women in skirts that nearly brushed the platform, wearing bonnets and shawls, some carrying muffs; and the whiskered men in their derbies, silk hats, and fur hats, smoking cigars, carrying canes. Then a whistle toot-toot-tooted, a high happy sound, we turned to look down the tracks, and I was astounded. Martin had told me, shown me pictures, but I'd forgotten; a short, squat, toy locomotive was chuff-chuffing toward us, red sparks flaring into the night from its miniature stack. Its brakes grabbed, the *chuff-chuff* slowing, white steam jetting from its sides, and the train—engineer leaning out its side window—slid into the station and on past us.

There were three cars, enameled light green and trimmed with gilt arabesques. Inside, seats ran the length of the car; they were upholstered in brown, and at intervals along the backs *New York Elevated Rail Road* was elaborately woven into the cloth; there was a kerosene ceiling lamp at each end of the car. We'd hardly sat down before a conductor in a low-crowned, flat-brimmed uniform cap came through, walking fast, collecting tickets.

The car was nearly filled, but once more I was used to the way people looked, and glancing at Kate's face, I could see that she was, too. It didn't pop into my mind that the brown-bearded man directly across the aisle from us might be going to a wedding; the shiny silk topper he wore was the hat he wore every day, of course, like many another man in this very car. Next to him, staring absently into space, sat a woman wearing a navy-blue scarf tied under her chin, brown knit shawl, a long dark-green dress, and—I caught a glimpse—between the end of her skirt and the tops of her black button shoes she wore heavy white knit stockings with broad horizontal red stripes. But I could see more than the clothes now; I could see the girl who wore them. And see that in spite of the clothes she was young and pretty. I even thought I could tell—I don't know how, but I thought so—that she had a nice figure.

Kate was nudging me. "No ads." She nodded toward the spaces over the windows.

I looked, and said, "I wonder how long before some genius thinks of them?"

We'd taken a right-angled curve to the left almost immediately after starting up, then a curve to the right a block or so farther on. I didn't know where we were, or what street we were over now. But we were heading in the right direction, steadily and rapidly north, stopping for only seconds at each station. We were no longer curious about the people around us, but just sat staring out the windows. We were facing west, and looking past the shiny topper of the man opposite, I peered through the shiny window out at the strange nighttime New York sliding past us.

There were lights, thousands of them, but of no brightness: these

133

were thousands of tiny flecks affecting the darkness not at all; they were gaslights, most of them, white at this distance and almost steady; but there was candlelight, too, and, I supposed, kerosene. No colors, no neon, nothing to read, just a vast blackness pricked with lights, and all of them, I realized, below us. This was a Manhattan in which we looked out over the rooftops, its tallest structures the dozens of church spires silhouetted against—yes, the Hudson River, just becoming visible under a rising moon. A few minutes later—we couldn't see the moon, but it was higher now—the river brightened, its dark surface glinting, and suddenly I saw the darker bulk of sailing ships anchored offshore, and the silhouettes of their bare masts. I shivered then, staring out that window at the strangeness of the city flowing past. This was Manhattan and there lay the Hudson, but I was a very long way from anything I knew.

We got off at the last stop, Sixth Avenue and Fifty-ninth Street, only a block from where we'd come out of Central Park this afternoon. We crossed the street and again entered the park, walking through it silently, postponing anything we had to say till we reached the sanctuary of the Dakota; we could see it far ahead, towering alone against the moonlit sky.

Then Kate and I sat in my living room, our second drinks in our hands: good stiff drinks, whiskey and water. The fire was going again, and we'd said, and then said once more, all there was to say about the blue envelope and the man who'd mailed it, and the tiny image of the Gillis tombstone marked in the snow. Now, after a little silence, I said, "What's the one single thing of all you saw that made the strongest impression? The streets, the people? The buildings? The way the city looked from the El?"

Kate took a sip of her drink, thinking, then said, "No; their faces." I looked at her questioningly. "They aren't like the faces we're used to," she said, shaking her head as though I were disputing her. "The faces we saw today were different."

I thought possibly she was right, but I said, "An illusion. They dress so differently. The women have hardly any makeup. The men have beards, chin whiskers, side-whiskers—"

"It's not that, Si, and we're used to beards. Their faces are actually *different*; think about it."

I sipped at my drink, then said, "You may be right. I think you are. But different how?"

We couldn't say, either of us. But staring at the fire, sipping my drink and remembering the faces we'd seen—on the bus, the sidewalks of Fifth Avenue, on the El, in the gaslighted marble-and-dark-wood lobby of that strange vanished post office—I knew Kate was right. Then I realized something: "Vanished," I'd just said to myself, and I looked over at Kate. Testing her impression, I said, "Katie, where are we? What's outside the windows right now? Are we in 1882 still?"

For a moment she considered it, then shook her head.

"Why not?"

"Because . . ." She shrugged. "Because we came back, that's all. We were finished, so we came back to the apartment, and we came back in our minds, too." Suddenly doubtful, she said, "Haven't we?"

We got up and, glasses in hand, walked over to the windows and looked down into the blackness of Central Park, hesitating. Then we leaned forward and, foreheads touching the windowpane, looked straight down into the street. And saw the long string of traffic lights, red as far as we could see in both directions. They all flicked green, the cars starting up, and a cab horn shrieked in rage at a car speeding out of the Park to beat the light at Seventy-second. I turned to Kate, shrugging, lifting my drink to finish it. "Yep," I said. "We're back."

11

WE'D INEVITABLY BEGUN calling it my "debriefing," and I sat as I'd done before, a microphone hung on my chest, reciting names and random facts onto tape. As I spoke, I watched the people who sat or stood leaning against the walls; every one of them was staring at me. My voice droned on, the muffled clatter of the electric typewriter accompanying it, and they watched me, knowing I was different from all of them now. Staring back at them, so did I.

Rube was there in faded, very clean sharply pressed army pants, and shirt without insignia. He lay tilted back in a molded-plastic chair, hands clasped behind his head, looking at me. He grinned when our eyes met once, quirking a mouth corner and shaking his head in mock awe and wonder, his eyes filled with friendly aching envy. Dr. Danziger just stood there, his great hands hung on the lapels of his double-breasted brown suit; his eyes, blazing with fierce joy, never left me. Colonel Esterhazy, neat and cool in a gray suit, stood against a wall, a hand clasping a wrist, regarding me thoughtfully. The Columbia and Princeton history men were there, too; so was the U.S. senator, several others I'd met, and even three or four neatly dressed strangers.

After I'd finished we waited in the cafeteria for forty minutes or so. I sat with Rube, Danziger, and Colonel Esterhazy, and had three, maybe even four, cups of coffee. Every chair at the other tables was occupied, and people were sitting on the radiator cover against the far wall. I had to respond to a good many jokes from people pausing at our table, most of them being questions about whether I'd bought any Manhattan real estate at bargain prices. Oscar sat down with us for a minute. He said,

"What one thing hit you the hardest?" and I tried to tell him about the man, the living *actuality* of the man, who had sat opposite us on the bus, and who might have remembered Andrew Jackson as President. Oscar sat nodding, smiling a little; he knew what I meant. As soon as he'd left, Rube leaned toward me and said, " 'Us'? Who else was there, Si?" and I told him there were one or two other passengers on my side of the bus.

The tall bald man of the day before came hurrying in, the room going silent as he stopped at our table. Grinning, he said that everything they'd been able to investigate so far had checked out okay. He felt certain now that the rest would, too, and the room broke into an excited gabble.

At one fifteen the board assembled, I sat at an end of the long conference-room table, and for the fourth time today I began describing what had happened. Every chair at the table was filled, and along one side there was a second row of folding chairs, all occupied. As far as I could tell, looking around the table as I talked, everyone I'd met here before was here again today plus at least a dozen others I didn't know. One of them, Danziger told me later, was a personal representative of the President.

Again I spoke in the singular, saying nothing about Kate. I'd have to tell Danziger what she'd done but I wanted to do that when we were alone. I described every move I'd made, every sight I'd seen and sound I'd heard, the room silent. Something like two dozen men sat around that table or on the folding chairs and no one coughed or glanced away from me. It may be that some of them lighted cigarettes during the twenty minutes I spoke, or sat back in their chairs, shifted position, crossed their legs; I expect they did. But my impression was of motionless silence, complete except for my voice, and of a focused concentration on me so absolute I felt I was talking with a kind of invisible searchlight bathing me in the glare of their attention.

I finished, then sat answering questions for half an hour more. Mostly, whatever the specifics, it was the same unanswerable question: What was it *like?* What was it *really like?* And now they *were* restless. They stirred, frowned, whispered, lighted cigarettes. Because no matter how I tried or how complete the detail, I couldn't give them the essence of what had happened to me; the mystery remained.

One set of questions, the senator's, had a tone different from the others. For reasons I don't understand he was antagonistic. It was as though he suspected or thought it was a possibility at least that I might be hoaxing them. I suppose it wasn't an unreasonable suspicion under the circumstances, though no one else showed it. But the senator, for example, didn't remember his grandfather's ever mentioning the kind of bus I'd described. He sat looking at me shrewdly then, as though he'd caught me. All I could do, of course, was shrug politely and reply that nevertheless that's what I'd seen. I suspect he was simply following the politician's sleazy instinct to protect himself in case something later went wrong. Presently Esterhazy cut in on him smoothly with some minor question, and then forgot to give him the floor back. He simply thanked me, and asked if I'd mind keeping myself available here in the building till the meeting ended. When I said yes, of course, he thanked me again, and I understood that I was dismissed, and left. There was actually a little applause as I walked out, and my face flushed.

I sat forever in Rube's office then, turning the pages of old copies of *Life*, discovering again, as in a doctor's waiting room, that it's very hard to tell, looking through back issues of *Life*, whether or not you've seen them before. I looked through a *Playboy*, a copy of the *U.S. Infantry Journal*, and I walked out once and down the corridor to the cafeteria for a Coke I didn't want. Rube's girl came in twice, wanting to know, of course, what it had been like, *really* like, and once again I did my damnedest to find the words that would convey it. It was after four o'clock when she came in the third time. She'd just gotten the call: Could I come back to the conference room, please?

I've never really walked into a jury room after they've been locked up for hours, but I think this must have been like it in appearance and atmosphere. The room was air-conditioned so it wasn't full of smoke, but the ashtrays overflowed and the air smelled of cigarettes. And ties were pulled down now, coats were off, note pads were doodle-filled, crumpled paper balls lay on the table, and I noticed a pencil snapped in half; faces were set, some actually sullen. Esterhazy stood up as I came in, smiling affably, looking unruffled. *His* suit coat was still on, his tie and shirt neat as ever. He gestured me to the chair I'd had before, waited till I'd sat down, then he sat down too, resting his forearms on the tabletop, his hands loosely clasped, very relaxed.

He said, "I'm sorry to have kept you waiting like this; you must be quite tired, physically and mentally." He sounded as though he meant it, and I murmured a polite response. I realized that I'd expected it would be Danziger who'd speak, and I glanced down the table at him. One big hand lay on the tabletop at the edge; his chair was pushed back from the table as though—the thought popped into my mind—he were disassociating himself from the meeting. Did he look angry? No, I decided; actually his face was expressionless. There was no way to know what he was feeling or thinking; he might only be tired. Esterhazy was talking. "We have had to hear, *wanted* to hear, every shade of opinion in reaching a decision as important as the one"—he looked slowly around the table—"that we are now agreed upon."

Then he smiled and sat looking at me for a moment or so, and I had the sudden feeling that he was interested in me as a person as well as just someone who'd done what I had. "Your first 'visit,' if that's the term, couldn't have been more cautiously made. No one so much as glimpsed or heard you, and no least trace of your brief presence was left behind. There was no interference whatever in even the smallest events of the past, and you had no effect upon it. But your second visit—deliberately, by design—was more bold. Again you made no interference with events, except"—he unclasped his hands to raise his forefinger, a West Point lecturer requiring attention—"that your very presence was an event. A tiny one, but this time people saw you, and spoke to you, momentarily at least. What trains of thought might possibly have resulted? Influencing events that followed in what ways, large or small? It was a danger and a profound one, but"—soundlessly striking the table with his fist, he emphasized each slow word—"*it is a risk already over and past*. We accepted the risk, the full report is now in, and once again there is no least evidence that your presence affected subsequent events in even the slightest way."

He sat silent for a moment, then again smiled, suddenly and very pleasantly, adding, "And I'm not a bit surprised. This confirms, most of us feel—and as all of us, I'm certain, will come to feel—a theory we've been calling 'twig-in-the-river.' Would you like to hear it?" I nodded. "Well, time is often compared to a river, a stream, as you know. What happens at any one point in the stream depends at least partly on what happened upstream earlier. But a tremendous number of events occur every day and every moment; billions of events, some of them enormous. So if time is a river, it's infinitely bigger than even a Mississippi at full raging flood. While you"—he smiled at me—"are the very tiniest of twigs dropped into that torrent. It's possible, or would seem so, that even the smallest of twigs might have an effect; might lodge, for example, and eventually cause a barrier that could affect the entire course of even that great stream. The possibility, the *danger*, of important change seems to exist. But does it really? What are the chances? There is virtually a one-hundred-percent probability that a twig tossed into that enormous and incredibly powerful current, into the inconceivable momentum of that vast Mississippi of events, will not and *cannot* affect it *one goddam bit!*"

For just an instant his face had pinkened; then it was white and almost pale again, and he sat back in his chair, an arm lying relaxed on the tabletop, and said quietly, "That is the theory, and that is the fact."

The room was silent then, of course, for as long as six or seven seconds; if there'd been a clock we'd have heard it tick. Then without moving his hand lying on the table edge and without sitting forward, Danziger said gently, "That is the theory. And I agree with it. As I should, since it's largely mine. But is it a fact?" He nodded slightly. "I think so, I suspect so." He turned his head slowly, looking all around the table. "But what if we're wrong?"

I was surprised. Esterhazy murmured, "Yes," and nodded gravely in agreement. "It's an enormous possibility. A real one and a terrible one. And yet"—he moved one shoulder in a slow reluctant shrug—"unless we are simply to abandon the project, abandon it actually *because* it has succeeded—"

"No, of course not," Dr. Danziger said just a little brusquely. "And no one argues for that, least of all me. I say—"

"I know," Esterhazy said, voice regretful, and he nodded in agreement again. "Go slow," he said, finishing Danziger's sentence. "Proceed, but with infinite caution. Over a period of weeks, months, even *years*, if that's necessary to be absolutely sure. Well, I might very well think so, too . . . if that were an option open to us. But as the senator knows, as I and a good many of us know, and as perhaps you, Dr. Danziger, haven't ever had the opportunity to know—it is simply not the way government works." He gestured to indicate the entire building around us. "This has cost *money*, that's the trouble. So that now, simply because it *has* succeeded, it must justify its cost with practical results. Mr. Morley is to go back; we're all agreed on that. It's unthinkable that he should not. But . . . he is to continue at a pace faster and bolder than we might all wish. Pure research, left to itself, would proceed with infinite patience. But this is money. Federally appropriated. Secretly spent. Without even the consent of Congress. Now it damn well better provide some provably practical results."

He looked first at me; then, head slowly turning, he looked around the entire table as he continued. "But I want to say to Mr. Morley and to everyone else but Dr. Danziger, who has always understood this, that while decisions vitally affecting this project cannot be his alone, which is probably unfortunate, this is still as it always has been very much his project. He runs it, he is the boss, only the board can overrule him, will seldom do so, and when rarely it does, it will happen after only the most intense and serious consideration of his views. So that now, Mr. Morley" —he smiled at me—"I'll turn you back to him." He stood up, stretching his shoulders as he rose, and then everyone slowly got up, general conversation beginning, and the meeting was over.

In Danziger's office I spoke first. He, Rube, and I walked along through the corridors together after finally breaking away from the conference room, talking about nothing of importance till we reached Danziger's office. There Danziger sat down behind his desk, got out half a cigar from his top drawer and looked at it, obviously thinking about lighting it. But instead, once more, he put it into his mouth unlighted. I sat waiting till he'd done this; then I sat forward in my chair, leaning across the desk edge toward him. Rube sat facing me, off to Danziger's left and slightly behind him, chair tilted back against the wall. I said, "Dr. Danziger, I don't even know who Colonel Esterhazy is. For all I know to the contrary, he's a colonel in the Ecuadorian reserves." Rube smiled; he liked that. "Whoever he is, I didn't pledge allegiance to him and whatever he may or may not stand for. You and Rube recruited me, I'm working for you, and I'll do what you say."

Danziger was grinning broadly by the time I was through, very pleased. He said, "Thank you, Si. A very great deal." He sat comfortably back in his swivel chair, pulled out a bottom desk drawer, and put his foot on it. "You know, until we actually had a success, yours, things went routinely. Wonderfully smoothly, in fact." He smiled. "My reports were accepted without comment, the board considered whatever problems I brought up, usually having to do with a little more money. Which they generally produced, though not always as much as I asked. We often met with barely a quorum, adjourning in half an hour or so. I doubt that most of the board had any real faith in the project at all; most of them were assigned to it." He nodded several times as he continued. "So maybe I did get to thinking or at least feeling that this was my project solely and entirely." Dr. Danziger took his half cigar from his mouth, studied it, then replaced it, and sat forward, clasping his hands on the desk top. "But of course Esterhazy is right. This isn't just our toy; we've got to show some practicality. And I know it. I'd prefer to go very very slowly. But, really, I'm as convinced as the others that we are most probably proceeding quite safely. 'Probably,' I say: I'd prefer taking no risk whatsoever if I had my druthers.

"But I agree with the decision: What I want you to do is what we all want you to do; there's no conflict. And what we want you to do reminds me in a way of our first space capsule." Again he sat back. "The first tiny one weighing—what? A few pounds. Everyone wanted space on it, remember? The biologists wanted a few mice aboard to see the effects of cosmic radiation. The botanists had some seeds; the geographers, weathermen and military wanted space for a camera; the broadcasters, the entire communications industry, and Lord knows who and what-all had their requests and even demands. So they worked up a package, or tried to, that would give them all a little something, at least in token.

"It's the same with us, Si. That's why the board decided to let you have a look at your man with the envelope. In some sort of way he is apparently connected to a fragment of history, to a minor adviser of Cleveland's. What is his connection, we naturally wonder. Well, our historians want to know whether the project can really help them: Is it true or not that we can actually increase historical knowledge in a way never before open to us? The sociologists have similar questions, the psychologists have theirs, and of course the physicists, of whom I'm one, have a million of them. Your man, somehow connected with a little footnote to history, makes an acceptable first tiny package. If you can cautiously study and watch him, and if you should get results that seem to justify it, we can carefully move on to larger more ambitious matters about which we need additional knowledge.

"So this is what we want, Si. Still observing, still very cautiously—as much as possible the mouse in the corner, the fly on the wall—we want you to observe him. Learn what you can; the purpose being to discover what's possible in this line. It increases, certainly, your interference with old events, but"—he hesitated, then shrugged—"minimize that all you can. Well? You know where he lives: Can you return and find a way to do that for us?"

I started to nod, but before I could reply Rube said quietly, voice perfectly friendly but without smiling, "Alone. This time alone. This time friend Kate is to stay where she damn well belongs."

My mouth opened but I didn't have any words ready. I just sat there with my mouth open for a moment, and now Rube did smile a little. He said, "Don't bother to answer; I'm fairly sure I can guess how it was, and you can't really be blamed, I suppose. And apparently no harm was done. But we've got enough to worry about without adding sightseers."

I nodded. "All right. I'd have told Dr. Danziger, and you can believe that. But how did you know?"

"We know. There's a lot to this project beside you, a lot of drudgery and detail. You've got the glamour part, and we don't bother you with the nuts and bolts. But we're watching out for the project in every way we can, and nothing else and nobody else matters but that. Okay?"

It was a warning and maybe a threat, and I accepted it because it was deserved. "Okay."

He grinned then, the really great smile that had made me like Rube from the start. Then he tipped his chair forward, the front legs striking the vinyl tile hard, and stood up. "Then it's back to the Dakota. Come on, you lucky bastard, I'll drive you."

12

_____

THIS TIME, walking out of the Dakota onto Seventy-second Street, carpetbag in hand, I knew. I turned left immediately, toward Central Park just across the street ahead, and there was no difference in the park that I could see, but—I knew. And a moment later when a wagon full of baled hay, drawn by two horses, crossed the intersection just ahead, I felt no surprise.

But I'd remembered something, and at the corner I didn't cross the street into the park; I turned north. I remembered the incredible open space I had stared across from the balcony outside my apartment window several nights ago: the dark emptiness I'd seen between the Dakota and the Museum of Natural History five blocks ahead to the north. Now I wanted to see it in daylight, and thirty seconds later when I'd walked the block along the face of the Dakota, I suddenly saw it and stopped, staring and flabbergasted; then I began to laugh.

I don't know what I'd expected—anything but this—and still smiling, shaking my head, I dug a small sketch pad out of my carpetbag as I walked along. Then I made a rough but detailed and accurate sketch, which I finished up later. The opposite page shows it. Standing a dozen yards off the sidewalk and facing the Dakota, just south of the corner at Seventy-fourth Street and Central Park West, this is what I saw, except that I've given the trees a few leaves so that you can see them. Those people were _farming_—I mean it—raising actual crops and livestock, living in shanties and sheds that they'd obviously made themselves.

Here they are—the farmers and livestock raisers beside the elegant Dakota doing their chores, the kids playing, the animals foraging for whatever they could find among patches of half-melted snow.

I could hardly believe it, and when my rough was done, I walked on a block or so toward the Museum—now, in daylight, I could see that it was only a single building—and I stared out over a strange astonishing view of farm after tiny farm clear to the Hudson. Even stranger, the streets were all here; in places they were a great raised gridiron of block after block of new streets all graded up to uniform level, the land between the streets lying far below. And down in those uniformly rectangular block-square hollows lay hundreds of acres of farmlands. From here at street level I could see the regular lines of old cultivations under the thin layer of snow. On a few of these miniature farms, people were desultorily scratching at the wet ground with hoes, I don't know why. I sketched that scene, too, of course:

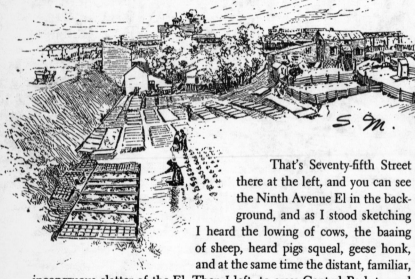

That's Seventy-fifth Street there at the left, and you can see the Ninth Avenue El in the background, and as I stood sketching I heard the lowing of cows, the baaing of sheep, heard pigs squeal, geese honk, and at the same time the distant, familiar, incongruous clatter of the El. Then I left, to cross Central Park toward the Third Avenue El, then on downtown to Gramercy Park.

Nineteen Gramercy Park was a house I'd seen before. It still exists, far into the twentieth century, and I'd occasionally walked past it and the other fine old houses around the little square of park. As well as I could remember, it looked the same now: a plain three-story brownstone with white-painted window frames and a short flight of scrubbed stone steps with a black wrought-iron railing. In a corner of a first-floor window a small blue-and-white sign said BOARD AND LODGING.

I stood on the walk looking up at the house, holding my packed carpetbag, and I was like a man on a diving board far higher than any other he's ever dared. I was about to begin something much more than addressing a few words to a stranger and moving on. However cautiously and tentatively, I was about to participate in the life of these times, and I stood looking at that sign, enormously excited and curious but not quite able to find the nerve to start.

I had to move; that door might open, and someone step out to see me loitering here. I made myself step forward, climb the stairs quickly, and before I could hesitate I reached out and twisted the polished brass knob at the center of the door, a bell jangled on the other side, and then I heard steps. I'd done it now; for better or worse, I'd joined this time.

I watched the knob turn, saw the door move back as it opened, made myself look up. In the doorway, looking inquiringly at me, stood a girl in her early twenties wearing a gray cotton dress and a long green apron; a white dustcloth folded into a turban covered her upswept hair, and she held a cloth in her hand. "Yes?"

Once again the wonder of what was happening seized me, and I stood staring at her. She started to frown, about to speak again, and I said quickly, "I'm looking for a room."

"And board? That's all we offer."

"Yes. And board." I made myself nod and smile.

"Well, we have two vacancies," she said doubtfully, as though not sure she shouldn't get rid of me. "One at the front overlooking the park at nine dollars a week. The other's at the back; it's seven dollars and twenty-five cents. Both with breakfast and supper."

I said I'd like to see them, and she stepped aside to gesture me into the black-and-white-tiled hall; it was wallpapered and dominated by an enormous hatrack and umbrella stand, the middle section of which was a full-length mirror. In it, as she turned to close the door, I glimpsed the slim back of her neck and a wisp of dark hair escaping her turban. Nervous as I was, I smiled; there's something innocent and appealing about the back of a girl's neck when her hair is up. She was pretty, I realized.

I followed her up the carpeted stairs at the end of the hall. In order to climb them, she gathered her skirts at the knees, raising them to the

147

ankles, and I saw that she wore black button shoes with slightly run-down heels, and thick cotton stockings striped blue and white. I glimpsed her calves, full and rounded, and, in spite of the handicap of those shoes and stockings, realized that she had very handsome legs. *She's dead, you know*—the thought spoke itself in my mind. *Dead and gone for decades past.* I shook my head hard, trying to force the thought away; then she turned at the top of the stairs to gesture me into a room, and as I walked past her she smiled, and I saw—very close—the living reality of her complexion, the slight crinkles at the corners of her eyes, the split-second motion of her eyelashes as she blinked, and she was so clearly young and alive that the thought lost all meaning.

I stood looking around the room, and she waited, standing just inside the doorway. It was big and clean, well lighted from two tall rectangular windows at the front. The room was furnished in an old-fashioned . . . but of course it wasn't old-fashioned. The wooden rocking chair, heavy carved-wood bedstead, the little table between the windows with a green felt tassel-fringed cloth, were probably no more than a dozen years old. There was a green-and-pink carpet, worn in a few places, and patterned with huge roses or cabbages, take your choice. Under one window was a window seat cushioned in red velvet, and the windows were hung with starched lace curtains, mended here and there. A gilt-framed engraving of a shepherd in a smock, knee-deep in sheep, hung beside the door, and the wallpaper was a ferocious brown-and-green pattern of tormented doodads. There was a dark-wood dresser with porcelain knobs and a white marble top on which stood a pitcher in a bowl. The bathroom, shared with other roomers, was down the hall, she said. I said, "I like it. Very much. I'll take it, if I may."

"Would you have references?"

"I'm awfully sorry, but I haven't. I just arrived in New York, and don't know a soul. Except you." I smiled but she didn't smile back. She stood hesitating, and I said, "It's true that I'm an escaped convict, an active counterfeiter, and occasional murderer. And I howl during the full of the moon. But I'm neat."

"In that case, welcome." Now she smiled. "Your name?"

"Simon Morley, and very pleased to meet you."

"I am Miss Julia Charbonneau." She was suddenly reserved, almost cool, but I knew we were friends. "This house belongs to my great-aunt;

you will meet her at suppertime, which is six." She turned to leave, hand on the knob to pull it closed behind her; then she stopped, and turned to look back at me. "Since you're from out of town, remember these are gaslights"—she nodded at the globed overhead lights, and at the gas jet projecting from the wall over the bed—"not kerosene or candle. Don't ever blow them out; turn the flame off."

"I'll remember." She nodded, stood looking about the room for a moment longer, found nothing more to add, and turned toward the doorway. "Miss Charbonneau." She looked back, and for a moment I had nothing to say, then I found something. "Please excuse any ignorance. This is my first visit to New York, and I don't know the customs."

"I don't expect they're much different from anywhere else." She smiled again, a little mockingly now. "Anyhow, you don't look as though you'd stay a greeny for long." She walked out, pulling the door closed.

Over at the window I stood looking down at little Gramercy Park a story below, its benches, bushes and grass covered with snow. I couldn't recall when it was that I'd seen the park last, and couldn't tell whether it looked the same; it seemed to. Around the park three sides of the square were just as I'd always seen them; old old houses of brownstone, brick, gray stone. But on the fourth side, Twenty-first Street, there were no apartments now, just more old houses. The sidewalks and paths of the park were shoveled clear, but the snow was piled high in the gutters at the far sides of the street beside the park. It was speckled black with soot; this was still a dirty city, especially in the winter, I supposed, with tens of thousands of coal and wood fires pouring carbon into the air. At least it wasn't radioactive. Before every house stood hitching posts of black-painted cast iron; the tops of some were horses' heads with rings through the noses. Before each post stood a broad stone block for stepping up into carriages, every one clean of snow and ready for use. Otherwise it was the Gramercy Park I was used to.

A movement caught my eye across the square, and I located it through the intervening bare black branches: A door had opened, and a woman stepped out. Now she was pulling the door closed. Now she reached for the railing and, cautiously for fear of ice, walked down the steps. She turned left on the walk, and at Twentieth Street turned the corner, walking toward me. Free of the intervening trees, I saw her clearly now. Her shoulders, under a dark cape, were hunched against the cold, her hands deep in a glossy fur muff; her pillbox bonnet was tied under her chin; her brown cutaway coat was edged with a broad band of black lamb's wool; and the tips of her shoes appeared and disappeared under her skirt hem as she walked. And once more the truth welled up in me; this was New York City, January 1882, and I was here and a part of it.

In almost that moment it began to snow, the flakes tiny and scarce. But within half a minute, in only the time it took the woman walking toward me to reach Irving Place and turn into it, disappearing from my sight, the flakes had thickened. Then they flew fast, swirling, beginning to cover the walks, the paths, the stone steps and stoops, beginning to mound on the heads of the iron horses.

It was too much, I can't really say why, and I turned from the window and lay down on the long single bed, careful to keep my feet off the plain white bedspread. And I closed my eyes, suddenly more homesick than any child. It occurred to me that I literally did not know a single person on the face of the earth, and that everything and everyone I knew was impossibly far away.

For an hour, maybe a little less, I was asleep. Then occasional voices, the sounds of doors opening, closing, and footsteps in the hall pulled me awake. The room was dark now, but the slim rectangles of the windows beyond the foot of my bed were luminous from the new snow outside. I knew where I was, swung my legs to the floor, and crossed the room to the windows.

Streetlamps glowed around the square, the snow sparkling in the circles of light at their bases. To my right and just around the corner of the square a carriage door slammed, and I turned to see the reins flick on the backs of two slim gray horses. Then the carriage started toward me, its sides shiny-black in the light of its own side lamps. Almost immediately, its high thin wheels leaving blade-thin tracks, it entered a cone of lamplight, bursting into black-enamel and plate-glass glitter. Through the glass of my windowpane I heard the faint jingle of harness and the muffled *clippety-clop* of shod hoofs in new snow. The carriage turned the corner, and I stared down at the foreshortened figure of the driver, high on the open front seat, neatly blanket-wrapped to the waist, reins and whip in his gloved hands. Horses, driver, and carriage passed directly under my window; I looked straight down onto the harnessed gray backs, the jiggling top of the driver's silk hat, and the dull black of the carriage roof. Once again horses and carriage moved glitteringly through a cone of yellow light, and I watched their shadows thin to nothingness on the new snow. The shadows reappeared, thickened, turned solidly blue-black, then raced on ahead of the carriage, lengthening and distorting. Now, in the oval rear window, two heads were framed, a man's under a top hat, and a woman's bare head; I saw her hair bound up in a bun at the back. The man turned to the woman, said something—I could see the movement of his beard—then the carriage turned the corner, and I saw its side light, saw the horses disappear; then the carriage itself was gone, except for its thin double tracks. And an exultance at being here in this time and this city raced through me. I swung away from the window, pulling off my coat, walked to the dresser, poured water from pitcher to bowl, and washed. I put on a clean shirt, tied my tie, combed my hair, and walked quickly to the door, the hall, the house, and its people.

A thin young man in shirt-sleeves carrying a shallow pan of water came walking along the hall toward me from the bathroom. He had dark hair parted on one side, and a brown Fu Manchu mustache. The instant he saw me he grinned. "You the new boarder?" He stopped. "I can't shake hands"—smiling, he gestured with his chin at the pan he held—"but allow me to introduce myself. I'm Felix Grier. Today's my birthday; I'm twenty-one."

I congratulated him, told him my name, and he insisted I come to his room and see the new camera his parents had sent him for his birthday. It had arrived yesterday, and with a light stand he showed me—a horizontal gas pipe on a stand, punctured for a dozen flames and backed by a reflector—he'd taken portraits of everyone in the house, and even photographed some of the rooms by daylight. He developed and printed his own films; there were a couple dozen of them strung out on a line like a washing, drying, and I saw that he'd printed them in circles, rectangles, ovals, and every other style, having a great time. I looked his camera over, a big affair weighing seven or eight pounds, I judged, holding and examining it. It was all polished wood, brass, glass, and red leather, wonderfully handsome. I told him so, said I was a camera bug, too, and he offered to lend it to me sometime, and I said I might take him up on it. Then he made me pose, and took my picture—a shorter exposure than I'd have thought, only a few seconds—and promised me a full set, too. I didn't particularly want them then, though I was glad to have them later. I left Felix washing more prints, and that night when I got back to my room I found a full set under my door; everyone's portrait including my own, plus some of the house.

This is one of them, Felix's own picture, and a good likeness except much more sober than I saw him; he was grinning and excited every moment I talked to him.

While I'm at it, I'll include the portrait he made of me: the one below. I'm not sure how good a likeness it is, but all in all I expect that's what I look like, beard and all; I never said I was handsome.

I left Felix, and went downstairs into the big front parlor that opened off the hall; a fire was moving behind the mica windows of a large black nickel-plated stove standing on a sheet of metal against one wall. Surmounting the stove stood a foot-high, nickel-plated knight in armor, and I walked over to look at it, reached out to touch it, and yanked my hand back; it was hot. Behind a pair of sliding doors I heard the clink of china and silver, and a murmur of voices. One was Julia's, I was sure, the other an older woman's. I imagined they were setting a table, and I coughed.

The doors rolled open, and Julia stepped in. She was wearing a maroon wool dress with white collar and cuffs, not the one Felix had photographed her in. This is his portrait of her, and tonight she wore her hair as you see it here, loosely arranged, covering the tops of her ears, and arranged at the back in a bun. Behind her I saw an oval table partly set; then a slim middle-aged woman stepped into the parlor after Julia.

This is Felix's portrait of her, and a very good one; this is just how she looked.

Julia said, "Aunt Ada, this is Simon Morley, who arrives without reference or much luggage. But with an abundance of soft sawder with which he is most generous. Mr. Morley, Madam Huff."

I didn't know what "soft sawder" was, but learned later that "soft *solder*" was the phrase and that it meant exaggerated speech or flattery or both. Smiling at what Julia had said, her aunt actually curtsied; I'd never seen it done before. "How do you do, Mr. Morley."

It seemed only natural, as though I'd done it always, to bow in response. "How do you do, Madam Huff. Miss Julia leaves me nothing to

reply except that I'm happy to be here. This is a charming room."
Listening to myself, I had to suck in my cheeks to keep my face straight.

"May I show it to you?" Aunt Ada gestured at the room, and I glanced around it with genuine interest. This is the view Felix took of

part of the room with his birthday camera; it doesn't show all of it by any means. It was carpeted and wallpapered, and at the windows, in addition to white lace curtains, there were purple velvet drapes fringed with little balls. There were two large brocaded settees, two wood-and-black-leather rockers, three upholstered chairs, a desk, gilt-framed pictures on the walls.

But Aunt Ada was walking to a glass-fronted whatnot in a corner, and I followed. "These are some of the things Mr. Huff and I brought home from our tour of Europe and the Holy Land." She pointed. "That vial contains water from the River Jordan. And those are marble fragments we picked up at the Forum." She gave me a brief account of everything on the shelves: a tiny folding fan from France that was a souvenir of the

Revolution, a little gilt slipper enclosing a velvet-covered pincushion she'd bought in Belgium, a seashell her husband, "my late husband," had picked up from the beach at the English resort at which they'd stayed. And she ended with the prize of her collection: a daisy, brown and pressed flat, from Shelley's grave.

Young Felix came bouncing down the stairs and into the room. He had a clean collar on now, and a tie, vest, gold watch-chain, a short black coat, and black-and-white-checked pants. When he saw I was being given the tour, he caught my eye and winked. Then he sat down at the front windows and began to read a newspaper he'd brought with him, the *New York Express*. Julia was back in the dining room, setting the table, and Aunt Ada and I moved to the white marble mantelpiece and a row of Christmas cards there. On cards as shiny as though they'd been varnished, there were frowzy-haired little-girl angels extending flowers; a few thin Santa Clauses in red-and-white garments like monks' habits, with attached hoods, and skirts to the ground; and quite a few humorous cards, one of them, for example, showing a Christmas dinner at which a quarreling family was throwing plates and glasses. I was even more startled by the "agony" cards, her name for them. One showed a sobbing little girl lost in a howling blizzard; another offered us a child's footprints in the snow, ending at the edge of a river; another a dead bird flat on its back, claws in the air, the caption reading *Hark! hark! the lark at heaven's gate sings!* I didn't know how I ought to react till Aunt Ada cued me. She said, "They're absurd, of course, ridiculous, but all the go nowadays," and I smiled.

A man in his middle thirties came down now, and Aunt Ada introduced us; this is Felix's photo of him. He was a tall thin man named Byron Keats Doverman, and he wore a mustache, the tips of which flowed into little explosions of whiskers overhanging his jaw. His hair was thick, wavy, red-brown.

He sat down, congratulated Grier on his birthday, borrowed part of his newspaper, and ignored the tour, which continued. I inspected and admired a bamboo easel on which stood a framed painting of some fruit and a dead rabbit. Aunt Ada led me to a small table with porcelain casters, then stood waiting, hands demurely clasped, while I bent over to examine a large sepia photograph propped against a vase filled with cattails. It was a full-length portrait of a woman in tights and wearing a peaked felt hat from which trailed a long feather; she had an elbow planted on a marble pillar and, chin in hand, stood in profile staring off into space. The caption, in gilt script, was *The Jersey Lily*, and in the opposite corner was what I took to be the name of the photographer, Sarony.

She saved the best for the last. Beside a small handsome organ of dark wood, on the mantelpiece of the fireplace, stood a yard-high set of plaster figures that must have weighed a hundred pounds. The title, cut into the base, was *Weighing the Baby*, and the figures were of a bearded frock-coated doctor and a mobcapped midwife examining the reading on the balance arm of a scale, in the scoop-tray of which lay a wailing baby. On one side of this plaster tableau stood a glass dome under which sprouted a formal bouquet of strange flowers. Looking closely, I saw that they were made of dyed feathers.

Aunt Ada had to leave before we were finished; supper was nearly ready, and Julia signaled her. But there were plenty of other things to see: family portraits, framed pictures, a giant fern in a corner by the front windows. I told her I liked her parlor very very much, which was true. I think it's the most pleasant room I've ever been in. Sitting there waiting for supper, then—Felix Grier handed me a section of his paper, and I glanced at it but didn't read it—I sat looking around that crowded, interesting room again, listening to the crackle of the fire in the stove, feeling the heat of it on the side of my face, watching the wind fling an occasional scatter of snow past the front windows, and I felt at peace.

I sat facing the stairs, watching for the man I'd come to see, and presently Miss Maud Torrence came down and joined us: a small, plain, sweet-faced woman of about thirty-five. She wore a blue-serge skirt, a white blouse buttoned high around the neck, and a small gold watch on a necklace chain. She worked in an office, I learned later, and this was the way she dressed for work. Byron Doverman introduced us, then she stood by the windows watching the night outside, and I saw a wooden pencil stuck into the bun of tight-rolled hair at the base of her neck. She asked me politely if I didn't think the weather had been "fierce" lately, and I agreed but said it was what you'd expect in New York at  this time of year; then Julia spoke in the doorway behind us to say that supper was ready.

I was too excited to eat much, too conscious of being here at this table under the almost silent hiss of the gaslights of the overhead chandelier, and beginning to feel worried because my man hadn't appeared. We sat, six of us, with one empty chair, Aunt Ada at the head of the oval table carving the breast of a turkey, then passing our plates to us. For a time we were silent except for murmurs of thanks as dishes were passed. I sat looking around a little, not too obviously. There were half a dozen large framed pictures on the walls. One was a sepia head-and-shoulders of a stern middle-aged man, a family portrait, I supposed; the others were black-and-white engravings of the Roman Forum, pastoral scenes, and the like. Then, all of us served, we began eating, and Byron Doverman tossed in the conversational ball by announcing that he'd just finished reading *Ben Hur*. Julia and Felix said they were surprised he hadn't read it long since. There was a little talk about *Ben Hur* then, especially about its "message," and Aunt Ada asked if I'd read it. I never had but I'd seen the movie, so I said yes, adding something or other about the excitement of the chariot race. Then Byron Doverman said casually that he'd once seen the author, General Lew Wallace, ride past his regiment when he'd been a soldier encamped near Washington during the war. As

I stared across the table at this still-young, reddish-brown-haired man whose face was almost unlined, it took me a moment to realize that he meant the Civil War.

"Heard the latest about Guiteau?" Felix was asking the table in general. "Someone took a shot at him through his cell window—"

"That was in the papers," Julia said.

"Yes, but this wasn't—the story was all over town this afternoon. The bullet hit the wall and flattened into an absolutely perfect profile of Guiteau as the wretch looks when frightened."

I glanced cautiously around the table but they were all nodding soberly, accepting this as fact without a smile. Then I realized that Aunt Ada was speaking to me, asking my opinion about the trial verdict. I sat looking thoughtful, as though considering, trying to remember what little I knew about Guiteau. I hadn't read much about him, but knew he'd been found guilty, and executed. I wasn't here to reform social attitudes, and I told Aunt Ada that since he was clearly guilty I felt sure he'd be hanged.

Down the table Felix was discussing the ice crop; they'd begun cutting near Bordentown, New Jersey, he said. Then there was a little talk about the Metropolitan Elevated scandal, whatever that was. I smiled at Julia and said the turkey was wonderful; I've always thought of turkey as dry and nearly flavorless but this was succulent. It was wild turkey, Julia said, and when I looked surprised, and asked where she'd got it, *she* looked surprised. "At the market, of course." I asked about that, and found that they also sold quail, grouse, partridges, tame squabs, wild ducks including canvasbacks, redheads, and mallards, and hares and rabbits. I'd always thought hare was another name for rabbit, and started to ask about that but didn't; Julia's eyes were narrowed, and she was staring across the table at me wonderingly. I turned to Felix beside me, and just to be saying something asked if he were interested in baseball.

He said he was, a little. He'd gone to the polo grounds a few times last summer when they weren't playing polo, to see the Mets play. I said, "Who?" He said, "The Metropolitans." I nodded, and said I thought that's what he said. "How did they do?" I asked. He said, "Not so well; they had bad pitching," and I said I wasn't a bit surprised.

For dessert we had a birthday cake, Felix blowing out the candles. And then we had a birthday party! Julia and her aunt stayed in the dining room, closing the sliding doors, to clear the table. In the parlor Maud Torrence sat down at the organ and began looking through the sheet music on the rack. Felix Grier and Byron Doverman stood behind her, and when I sat down with the paper, they called me, and I knew there was no escape, and walked over.

I was able to join in on the first song, "I'll Take You Home Again, Kathleen," and when we finished young Felix said, "If only Jake were home we'd have a quartet!" That was my chance to ask, "Jake who?" and Felix said, "Jake Pickering, our other boarder," and now I knew his name, and felt I'd made some progress.

The next number was "If I Catch the Man Who Taught Her to Dance," or something like that, and all I could do was try to follow along. Then Julia and her aunt came in, and we all sang "In the Evening by the Moonlight" and "Oh, Dem Golden Slippers." Aunt Ada did pretty well, but Julia was a little off the beat occasionally. Byron Doverman said, " 'Cradle's Empty, Baby's Gone!' " Julia said, "Oh, no," but the others insisted. Maud found the music, and—all reading the words over her shoulders—we sang what is probably the most lugubrious song I've ever heard, about this poor dead baby, and including lines like "Baby's gone to join the angels, peaceful evermore." Julia smiled at me, shrugging; she seemed to think it was ridiculous. But when Maud finished she turned from the organ saying she'd played enough, and her eyes were bright, she was on the edge of tears, and I remembered that this was a time when babies died easily; maybe the song meant something to her.

The doorbell rang, and again I wondered if it were my man. But Julia answered the bell and came back sorting through four or five envelopes, one of which she handed Byron; the others were birthday greetings for Felix. It was a mail delivery at very nearly seven in the evening, and when I said I was surprised, Julia answered with a touch of big-city smugness that mail was delivered five times a day in New York City. "Byron," she said then, "will you favor us with some magic?" He nodded, took the stairs to his room two at a time, came back down just as fast, then walked around the room pulling coins from our ears, and asking people to "pick a card, any one at all." The truth is that he was pretty good, and everyone, including me, actually enjoyed the performance.

He finished, put the deck in his pocket, and sat down. Aunt Ada said, "My uncle sent me a fan from China, and I fan like this." She began waggling her hand under her chin as though fanning herself, and everyone copied her. At her right, in a chair next to the windows, Maud Torrence said, "My uncle sent me a fan from China, and I fan like this." With her left hand she began waving an imaginary fan at her left ear, and—our right hands still waggling—we all did the same. It was my turn and I said, "My uncle sent me a fan from Czechoslovakia and I fan like this." I exposed my teeth as though I had a fan in my mouth, and began nodding my head, everyone imitating. Felix was next and he ended the game with twin fans from the Sandwich Islands, lifting both feet from the floor and fanning away. As we all copied the movement everyone burst into laughter, and it *was* funny, all of us reared back in our chairs, heads, hands and feet simultaneously waggling away.

Aunt Ada said, "Where is Czechoslovakia, Mr. Morley?"

"Why, I believe it's south of Germany."

She nodded, accepting this, and I think Maud Torrence did, too. But the two men and Julia were looking at me. I knew what was wrong; there was no Czechoslovakia, wouldn't be for decades yet, and I grinned to show I'd only been joking.

Felix's face was flushed, his eyes bright; he was having a great twenty-first birthday, and he said, "Julia? *Tableaux vivants!*"

"All right." Whatever it was, she liked the idea. "Shall I choose first?" He nodded, and she said, "Then I'll need you and Byron." They walked into the dining room, pulling the sliding doors closed after them, and Aunt Ada got up and turned the lights of the parlor chandelier very low. Then she and Maud sat smiling expectantly at the closed doors of the dining room, and when they glanced at me I was doing the same. Julia called, "Ready!" and Aunt Ada, who was nearest, got up and rolled open the doors.

The dining-room lights were turned up high and bright, and the three of them stood in the doorway almost silhouetted as though on a stage; they were posed and motionless. Byron and Julia were facing Felix, who stood on one foot, the other slightly raised. Wedged under one arm he held a long stick of some sort like a crutch; his mouth was open as though speaking, his eyes wide. Julia's head was thrown back, her mouth open, her eyes as wide as Felix's. Byron looked stricken, too, the back of one fist pressed to his forehead.

They stood there, swaying slightly; we all sat and stared. Then Maud, voice frustrated, said, "Oh, I *know* it, I know it so well!"

Suddenly, triumphant, Aunt Ada cried, *"The Soldier's Return!"* and the *tableau vivant* broke up, chattering, heads nodding in confirmation. Aunt Ada stood; apparently it was her turn now. "I'll need you, Mr. Morley," she said, and I followed her into the dining room, closing the sliding doors behind us. "Do you know *The Slave Auction?*" she said eagerly. I stood frowning as though trying to remember, then said I was afraid I didn't. "Never mind, I'll pose you. We'll need a gavel." She stood looking around the room, then hurried to a cabinet against one wall, opened a drawer, and brought out a big soup ladle. "This'll do; hold it like a gavel." She pulled a straight-backed chair up to the closed doors, turning its back to the door. "Climb up; this will be the auctioneer's stand." I got up on the chair, facing the doors. "Raise your gavel; you're saying, 'Going, going, gone!'" I did, and Aunt Ada knelt before the chair facing the parlor, crossing one wrist over the other as though her arms were bound. "Ready!" she called, all excited, then she dropped her head, chin on her chest.

The doors began sliding open, and though I didn't move—gavel hand upraised, my mouth open—I felt my face flush. But they all knew this one instantly, yelling, *"The Slave Auction!"* almost simultaneously. Then they were gabbling congratulations, the gist of them being that they'd guessed instantly only because we'd done it so well.

By the time we'd had a couple more *tableaux vivants—The Wounded Scout* and *Lovers' Retreat*—I found out through various references what we were doing. We were imitating the poses of figures in statuary groups made by a man named Rogers who duplicated them in plaster by the thousands. Apparently every home had a Rogers group—*Weighing the Baby* on Aunt Ada's mantelpiece was one—and everyone was familiar with most of them. I sat like the others, trying to look as though I were recalling titles that might match the poses in the dining room. Across from me Maud sat absently scratching her initials in the frost on the windowpane beside her. It occurred to me that I hadn't seen genuine frost on a windowpane since I'd written on my grandfather's farmhouse window when I was a child. In the final *tableau*—Julia was one of the lovers, sitting on a bench and looking sad—I saw her flick a glance at me, and I thought I could read her mind; I was the only person in the room who hadn't once been able to call out a title, even a wrong guess.

Byron suggested charades next; I could tell from his manner that he must be good at them. But Felix—and I thought maybe he wasn't so good—said charades were too much like *tableaux vivants*. Julia was sitting over by the whatnot cabinet now, still looking at me a little curiously, and now she said, "Perhaps Mr. Morley will entertain us. It's your turn, Mr. Morley; we're all agreed!" Everyone else did agree instantly, and I nodded. In Julia's voice, I thought, there'd been a hint of challenge as though she were saying, *Who are you? Prove yourself!* Well, I wanted to, and sat wondering what to do, and felt a sudden flicker of panic. I looked over at Julia again; she was waiting, smiling a little mockingly.

Then I grinned at her and held up both hands, palms toward her, thumbs touching, framing her head and shoulders. "Hold still." She sat motionless, eyes suddenly bright with interest. "Turn your head only; just a little. No, the other way, toward the cabinet." She turned her head slowly, and when the light from the overhead chandelier slanted across her face, side-lighting it and silhouetting her profile against the dark wallpaper just behind her, I said, "Don't move, don't breathe." I'd already found the key to my Dakota apartment in my vest pocket, and now I turned to the window beside me, and scraping through the thin white layer of frost with a sharp corner of the key, I set down the outline of her cheekbone. I glanced back at Julia, then in one swift clean curve put down the angle of her jaw. The lines showed up well, the blackness of the outside night sharply exposed against the rime, and I worked fast. Everyone else was on his feet now, standing respectfully beside my window to watch.

It turned out well, a good sketch; in no more than two minutes I'd caught the likeness. The prominent cheekbone, the slightly too-sharp jawline, a suggestion of the small firm chin—all were there in three quick lines. The precise tilt of the eyes and—I even managed this—a feeling of the faint shadows beneath them lay there on the white of the windowpane in a few sure-handed squiggles. So did the dark straight brows and fine straight nose. I nodded, releasing Julia, and she hurried over to join the others.

She didn't like it. She didn't say so, and after a long few moments, bent forward to stare at the sketch on the windowpane, she began to nod, pretending politely to be pleased. But the nods were too rapid, and she didn't look up at me, and I knew she was hiding disappointment in her eyes. The others, too, were only murmuring polite approval. "What's wrong with it?" I said quietly.

"Nothing!" She looked up at me now, eyes widening, simulating surprise at the question. "It's beautiful! I'm astonished!"

But I was shaking my head. This was an ability I took pride in, and I wanted to know. "No, tell the truth. You can't fool me; you don't like it."

"Well." She straightened, and stood looking at the floor, a finger at her chin as though thinking; she was embarrassed. "It is not that I don't like it, but . . ." She glanced at the sketch again, then back at me, her eyes distressed, sorry she'd begun this. "But what *is* it?" she burst out, then quickly added, "I mean it's not *finished*, is it? I can see it's a face, or would be if it were finished, but . . ." I was nodding rapidly, eagerly, cutting her off; now I understood what was wrong. We're trained from infancy to understand that black lines on white can somehow represent a living human face. I've read that savages can't do it; they make no sense of a drawing or even a photograph until they're taught to translate it as we do. And this sketch on the frosted window—quick suggestive fragments, allowing the mind to fill in the rest—was a technique of the twentieth century as incomprehensible here as though it had been in code, as in fact it was.

To Julia I said, "Stand right here, don't move, give me five minutes, no more." I didn't wait for an answer but stepped quickly to the middle window and, working as fast as I could go, began sketching with my key point in a technique I'd occasionally tried for the fun of it, working with Martin Lastvogel. It was the technique of the woodcut, every line there, nothing omitted; the entire shape of the face, eyes, nose, lips, all fully drawn, then carefully shaded in a firm delicate cross-hatching. I was taking up the entire pane; with this technique I needed the space. The glass was frosted completely except for the upper corners. These were clear, as shiny black against the night outside as a mirror. But working this close, I could see through them, see the streetlamps, the snow-covered walks and street, the vague black bulk of Gramercy Park's shrubbery and trees. And now suddenly, walking briskly along the walk toward the house, I saw him; the short, stout, familiar hurrying figure, stubby plug hat on the back of his head. I paused, my hand motionless, watching him. Then he turned onto our steps, disappearing from my view, and I glanced over at Julia to continue the sketch.

As well as she could while holding the pose, she was watching what I was doing; now as I looked over at her she lifted her arms, fumbled at the back of her neck for a second, then her hair tumbled down, falling to below her shoulders, and her chin lifted slightly and there was a flash of pride in her eyes.

Her hair was dark dark brown, wonderfully thick now that it was released, long and lustrous. It was magnificent, and so was she. I'm certain my face showed what I felt, and I murmured, "Beautiful, *beautiful*," and saw her lips quirk with pleasure, and she flushed. No one else had noticed, but because I'd been expecting it I'd heard the small sounds of the opening and closing front door, and from a corner of my eye had seen him stop in the hall doorway. Now, not really even attempting to catch the splendor of Julia's hair but at least suggesting the length and weight of it, I quickly finished my windowpane sketch.

But the kind of drawing I'd attempted takes longer than I'd given it and more practice than I'd had, and of course it didn't turn out well. I stepped back, studying it as the others crowded around, and all you could really say was that it showed the face of a girl—that was clear enough—who was pretty and had long hair. It was any girl, not this one in particular, though it bore a vague generalized resemblance.

But Julia stood studying it for five or six seconds, which is a long time, then she cried out with unmistakably genuine pleasure. "Oh, it's lovely!" She swung around to me, delighted. "Do I really look like that? Oh, of course not! But it's beautiful! My goodness, you *are* talented!" Her eyes were shining, she stood looking at me now with genuine admiration, even a little awe, and I responded: The feeling leaped up in me like a flame and I wanted to kiss her; it was all I could do to keep from stepping forward and grabbing her.

I saw her eyes flick to the doorway. She'd suddenly seen him, and her

164

face flushed instantly. But her voice seemed calm, she sounded fully at ease. "Jake, we have a new boarder! And a very talented one, it seems! Come see what he's—"

"Put—your—hair—up," he said between his teeth, giving each word the same cold and equal emphasis.

"But, Jake, we—"

He spoke softly. "I said . . . put it up," and Julia's hands moved quickly to the back of her neck to obey.

I'd turned to the doorway—everyone had—and now Pickering walked toward me, his brown eyes so drained of expression they were as menacing as the empty gaze of a shark. He stopped before me, and for a long moment, as long as three or four seconds, we stood staring at each other, the room entirely silent. I was fascinated: Here he *was*, the man who'd actually mailed the long blue envelope.

Then suddenly he smiled, his face alight with friendliness, eyes warm and welcoming—an instantaneous transformation—and his hand moved out to shake mine as he spoke. "I'm Jacob Pickering, a boarder here like yourself." He was shaking my hand vigorously, his face entirely amiable, and all the time his grip was tightening. I smiled back just as amiably, tightening my own grip with all the strength I had. We were fighting, there in that pleasant room, no one else knowing it, our forearms beginning to tremble slightly as we stood smiling at each other while I spoke my own name in return, our gripped, white-knuckled hands moving slowly up and down as though we'd forgotten to stop. Then my grip reached its maximum strength but his continued to grow, and I felt the long bones of my hand coming together. My fingers flew open in his fist, suddenly strengthless; I was hanging onto my smile, teeth grinding silently, and I knew I was going to have to cry out but wouldn't and didn't. Then, literally just short of actually fracturing the bones of my hand, he suddenly let his grip relax, gave my hand one final quick excruciating squeeze, and still smiling warmly he nodded toward my windowpane drawing. "You *are* talented, Mr. Morley. Talented indeed." He had turned and was walking quickly toward the window. "But I hope it hasn't scratched Madam Huff's pane." He leaned forward and, his open mouth an inch from the glass, drew quick deep breaths, expelling them full force, and at the center of the pane a melting circle grew quickly to the size of a plate. Except for its outer and now meaningless portions the drawing was gone. "No," he said, examining the clear glass, "fortunately it isn't scratched at all." He gave an utterly contemptuous glance at the sketch on the other window, then turned, his back to the windows, and smiled around at us all.

Julia said, "I didn't like that, Mr. Pickering. I didn't like that at all." She turned to me. Her eyes were blazing, her hands still busy at the back of her neck, putting up her hair. "Perhaps you will do another of me, Mr. Morley?" she said. "On paper. One I can keep. I'll be pleased to pose for you at any time!"

My hand was in my pocket, hiding it. I knew it must be red and starting to swell; it hurt badly. "I'll be glad to, Miss Julia. Very, very glad." I was turning my head as I spoke so that I finished while looking into Pickering's eyes. "In fact, I insist on it."

He only smiled: at me; at everyone. "Perhaps I was wrong," he said, dropping his head a little in mock humility. "Sometimes I . . . act precipitately." Then he raised his head to look me in the eye. "When my fiancée is concerned."

Aunt Ada, Maud, Byron, and Felix began talking, almost chattering, covering and burying an awkward incident. Julia turned and walked quickly into the dining room and on into the kitchen, where she made tea. Byron Doverman said something to Pickering, who responded. Aunt Ada came over to me, and I asked her about something in the whatnot cabinet: a thin glass vial stopped with a cork. It turned out to be sand from the Sahara Desert.

We had tea, Julia carrying it in on a large wooden tray. Sipping it, we all talked for a few minutes, finishing the evening with a semblance of propriety, though neither Pickering nor I spoke to or even looked at the other. Then everyone shook hands with Felix in final birthday good wishes, and the party was over.

Upstairs in my room, standing in the dark unbuttoning my shirt and staring down into the empty darkness of Gramercy Park, I knew that Rube, Oscar, Danziger, Esterhazy, and I had forgotten the obvious: that simply being with people is to become involved with them. I was to have been only an observer here, strictly enjoined from interfering with events, and certainly from causing them. Yet I'd done just the opposite. About to pull off my shirt, I stopped and stood motionless, staring down at a hitching post mounded with snow. It might be that I ought to leave as fast as I could. That I ought to pack now, sneak downstairs, out, and back to the Dakota before I could do any more harm.

But my mind was yelling, *Thursday! Tomorrow is Thursday!* Tomorrow "at half past twelve," said the note I'd seen Jake Pickering mail, "appear in City Hall Park." I had to be there, *had* to; somehow invisibly, and interfering with nothing, but I *had* to be there. *Just one more day; half a day!* I was saying to myself. For only those few hours I could certainly retreat to the role of observer only, couldn't I? Lifting my hand into the faint light reflected up to my window from the snow outside, I looked at it, then compared it with the other, my hands side by side. The right hand was puffy, and all four finger knucklebones ached steadily. Staring at my hand, I flexed it slowly, then tried closing it into a fist. I couldn't do it, but as it began to close, an involuntary picture popped up in my mind in which that fist was punching Pickering in the mouth.

I had to laugh at that, silently, and I dropped my hand; but it worried me. Yet it was a fact that I needn't even encounter Pickering in the morning. I could wait to come downstairs till he'd left the house, and then never see him face to face again. As for Julia—well, what about Julia? After a few moments I nodded; in a way I wasn't able to analyze, I was somehow involved with her, too. But that didn't matter, either; we were of separate times, and I'd be leaving hers very soon.

I tested something; I thought about Kate, and stood there in the dark examining my feelings about her. Nothing had changed. As soon as I returned, I knew I'd want to see her, and I felt a sense of relief, and then started to wonder about that. Instead, I turned away from the window, unbuttoning my shirt—it buttoned only partway down, the lower part being a single wide shirttail—undressed, and got into my nightgown.

Lying in bed, I smiled; it had been quite a day. Then, within a minute or so, I fell asleep, knowing I might be terribly wrong to stay here but knowing also that I was going to; that I had to see what happened in City Hall Park at half past twelve, Thursday, January 26, 1882—tomorrow.

13

I HAD BREAKFAST alone in the morning, all the other boarders gone. I'd lain in bed listening for them, counting them off as they'd come down the hall and gone down the stairs, all within a few minutes of each other. Then I'd dressed, and sat watching by my window till I actually saw Jake Pickering leave.

Walking into the parlor now, I saw that it was swept and dusted, and I turned to look at the windows. They were almost entirely clear, wiped or washed clean of frost and drawings both, a new film of frost beginning to creep up the glass again. Turning toward the dining room, I wondered again if I could have avoided the trouble last night. No, and now in the daylight I saw that it didn't matter as much as I'd thought. A man so jealous that a casual stranger evokes it must have done other similar things and would do them again. I hadn't really interfered with the past; something of the sort would sooner or later have happened anyway involving someone else, if I hadn't been here.

I sat down at the long dining-room table, and Aunt Ada—listening for me, I think—came in from the kitchen wearing her working clothes: a plain dark cotton dress and a white bib-apron tied in a big bow at the back. She welcomed me, very sweetly and genuinely, asking how I'd slept and if my room were satisfactory. Then, still smiling, anxious not to offend me, she said this was the only morning I could expect breakfast after eight, and I said I'd either get down earlier or do without.

She served breakfast then: a fried chop, fried eggs, toast with three kinds of jam, coffee, and the morning *Times*. Setting these down on the table while I watched, she glanced at me, hesitated, and then—genuinely anxious about my welfare—suggested that if I were looking for work I ought to begin getting up earlier. With the backs of her fingers she felt the base of the silver coffeepot which she'd set onto a thick knitted square, then filled my cup and left, and I opened the *Times*, and began to eat.

The big story of the day was GUITEAU FOUND GUILTY, in the left-hand column of the front page, but I skipped that and read the fourth-column story, THE CHOCTAW RAILWAY GRANT. HOW GOULD AND HUNTINGTON HAVE KILLED OFF COMPETITION WITH THEIR NEWLY ACQUIRED ROAD, though it was a little hard to follow. I did get the idea, though, that a group of "alleged representatives of the Indians," who didn't want a railroad run through their land, was soon replaced by "accredited representatives," who thought it was a great idea.

And I was fascinated by ARCHBISHOP PURCELL'S DEBT, just below the Choctaw story. For reasons the *Times* didn't explain—it seemed to be a continuing story, and I think you were assumed to have previous knowledge of it—Archbishop Purcell apparently had five thousand creditors claiming he owed them $4,000,000 and there was some prospect that to settle these claims a number of "houses of worship would . . . be sold to the highest bidder." Cardinal McCloskey seemed upset, to say nothing of the congregations, and the *Times* said, "The case is now ready for trial, and will be one of the most interesting in the history of American jurisprudence," and I thought so, too.

Eating my toast and sipping coffee, I was reading a McCreery's ad for "evening shades of Nun's Veiling in white, cream, light blue, ivory, and pink" when Julia came downstairs. We said good-morning as she passed through the dining room; then, as she carried in her own breakfast from the kitchen, I had time to look at her. Today her hair was wound into a soft coil piled on her head, and I thought possibly, though I wasn't sure, that she was wearing makeup or at least powder. Watching her, I realized that she was dressed to go out, in a marvelous dress of purple velvet, the skirt gathered up at the front in a series of scallops, and trimmed at the front just below the waist with a lavender bow that must have been eight inches across. And it had a bustle.

But if that dress sounds ridiculous, it was not; she looked great, and I had to recognize as she sat down, picking up her napkin, smiling at me, that every needle on every dial was jumping, and that maybe Jake Pickering hadn't been entirely mistaken last night. I could smile at myself, though, accepting the fact of this girl's appeal clinically and with detachment, because it didn't matter; in a few hours I'd be gone. "I see you are consulting the advertising pages," Julia said conversationally.

I'd already decided I'd better get out of the house for the rest of the morning, so just for a reply I said, "Yes, I need some new clothes."

She smiled. "Well! You'll be a hummer with new duds! I had noticed that you brought very little."

I couldn't resist. "Most of my clothes would look a little strange here. Can you suggest a good store?"

Bringing a piece of toast with her, Julia got up, came around to my side of the table, and began turning the pages of my paper, scanning the ads, while I sat back watching her. She moved gracefully, her fingers quick and accurate in taking the page corners. She stopped at a page nearly filled with ads, leaning forward over the table beside me, to search through them. And—this was absurd, I thought, a poor joke on me carried on too long—there was a perfumed scent from her, from her hair, I think, and I felt a flare of excitement so intense it affected my vision, piling up behind my eyeballs, and I leaned away to one side.

All the ads were one column wide and set completely in type, and now Julia said, "Here," her fingertip touching one of them. "Macy's has some gentlemen's clothing for sale." Trying to ignore the perfume, I leaned closer to read the ad; it said Macy's was selling shirts made to order at ninety-nine cents, which sounded ridiculously low but which I knew was not in a place and time where an able-bodied unskilled man earned two dollars for a day's work of twelve hours. Collars were six and eight cents, said the ad, cotton half-hose eighteen cents a pair. When I reached the bottom of the ad and read, "Our customers may rest assured that we will not be undersold by any other house," I felt a little stab of pleasure at this ancestor of Macy's familiar slogan.

"Or you can go to Rogers Peet," Julia said, turning to look at me; our faces were only inches apart, and she stood quickly erect. "They have a brand-new and larger store," she said, walking back to her side of the table, "and will surely have whatever you need." There was a cool note of dismissal in her voice, and I thought I understood; a man's clothing was a subject too intimate for lengthy discussion. I said, "Okay, I'll try Rogers Peet"—people did say "okay," I'd noticed last night—and picked up my coffee cup for a final sip, and to put a period to the subject.

And as I raised my cup, Julia saw my hand. It wasn't so red this morning but it was bruised blue at the middle knuckle and even more swollen than last night. She stared but said nothing—I think she knew or guessed the cause; maybe Pickering had done this before—and her face flushed. I didn't know why for a moment, then I saw her eyes: She was furious. She looked from my hand to my face. "Do you know where Rogers Peet is?" she said very quietly. I could only say no. "It's at Broadway and Prince Street, opposite the Metropolitan Hotel, and if you've never been in New York before, you don't know where that is, either." It was true, at least, that I didn't know where Prince Street was, and I'd certainly never heard of the Metropolitan Hotel. I shook my head. Julia nodded, and stood up. "Well, I'm going to the Ladies' Mile," she said, "and I'll take you." I began shaking my head quickly, hunting for a reason to say no, and she watched me for a moment, then said softly, "Are you worried about Jake?"

"No, I'm not worried about Jake. But he did say 'fiancée.'"

"Yes." Julia stood staring past me. "And has said it before." She looked at me again. "But as I have said to *him*, I am no one's fiancée until I've said that I am. And I haven't done so yet." She turned toward the living room and the closet in the hallway. "Are you coming?"

I knew I wasn't going to say no and let her think Jake had scared me off. And if I was going to say yes I thought I ought to sound as though I meant it. "You bet!" I said, something else I'd heard more than once last night, and I went upstairs to get my hat and overcoat. In my room I took a small sketch pad from my bag and a couple of pencils, one hard and one soft. I caught a glimpse of my own movement in the dresser mirror, and looked quickly at my face. It was pleased and excited, emotion ignoring logic, and I shrugged; events had simply picked me up and carried me along, and if I couldn't help it I thought I might as well enjoy it.

Julia was waiting in the hall in a flowered bonnet tied under her chin, a dark-green coat, and a short black shoulder cape, wearing a tiny black fur muff shoved up onto one wrist. When she heard my step she looked up and smiled, looking great, and I could only grin and shake my head.

Lord help us all, what New York City has lost through the years! We walked north to Twenty-third Street, Julia eager and excited; she was about to show me the sights and was enjoying it, and I felt touched, she seemed so innocent. At Twenty-third we turned west toward Madison Square and the Fifth Avenue Hotel a couple of blocks ahead at Broadway and Fifth, the beginning, Julia said, of "the Ladies' Mile." Suddenly I said, "Oh!"—an involuntary sound of pure delight at what I saw ahead—and Julia turned her head to search my face, smiling at the intended effect.

To me, living and working in New York City, Madison Square had meant very little; a sun-dried, brown-grassed emptiness of park benches and paths in the summer, filled only at noon, with office workers moodily eating lunches from paper bags, deserted much of the rest of the time except for a few derelicts; in the winter even dirtier, emptier, and more forlorn; and at night in all seasons automatically avoided like every other New York park. At most it provided the relief of empty space from the miles all around it of narrow corridor-streets between high building walls. It didn't seem to have much other meaning or purpose: a drab and pleasureless place.

But now at the sight of it I exclaimed in simple delight, because the square ahead was alive and a joy. Under the winter trees and still-glowing gas mantles were countless children: girls in bonnets tied on with shawls; boys in square little lamb's-wool caps with attached earmuffs; girls and boys in pompommed tam-o'-shanters with plaid bands and ribbons down the back; boys in miniature long-pants suits with heavy mufflers around the neck; girls in long shaggy fur coats; everyone in boots or button shoes, half the girls wearing brightly striped stockings, some of them carrying tiny muffs. Strange little winter outfits, but they were still children in the snow, running, falling, throwing, dragging each other on high wooden sleighs whose runners curved gracefully up into bird's-head ornaments, belly-flopping onto low wooden-runnered sleds. On the paths nannies walked in nurselike outfits pushing baby carriages with tall wooden-spoke wheels. And adults were strolling, just *strolling* through Madison Square, the snow, and the winter for the simple pleasure of it as though being outdoors were something to be enjoyed for itself. Dogs barked, romped, rolled, and cavorted, excited by the snap in the air and the snow. And all around that living, moving square rolled the most glittering parade of carriages you could hope to see.

These weren't just black. There were marvelous rich maroons among them, a deep olive-green, and one had a magnificent body of canary-yellow, the wheels and fenders shiny black. Most were enclosed but a few were actually open, and Julia named some of them: fine names like *Victorias, five-glassed landaus, barouches, phaetons,* and *light rockaways.* Liveried men drove them, top hats taking and revolving the light, polished boots and white pants displayed under the buttoned-back skirts of silver-buttoned outer coats, which in some instances matched the carriage bodies in color. On more than one, carriage footmen, often a pair of them, sat up behind, arms folded in splendid uselessness.

And the horses *pranced,* slim and magnificent, their harnesses and curried bodies shining, heads reined high, manes braided, knees lifting to chests; a lot of them were in matched absolutely identical pairs: black, brown, gray, white. And inside those carriages sat the most stylish, splendid, exciting-to-look-at women I'd ever seen. They were going shopping after a few turns around the square, Julia said—along the Ladies' Mile that stretched down Broadway to the south.

We were closer now, and I grinned with pleasure to see that these weren't like the women who sit back, obscure and hidden, almost cowering into the deep corners of expensive, drably chauffeured automobiles; these ladies sat erect and far forward, smiling, showing themselves off behind the glittering glass, looking regal and utterly pleased with themselves. It was absurd, garish, a blatant open display of money and privilege; and it was so innocent it was charming, and I wanted to laugh out loud for joy in it.

Now, less than half a block away, we could hear, too: the thin, open-air screams of children, the *jink-jink-jink* of harness bells, the sharp haughty *clip-clop* of expensive hoofs on the Belgian-block paving of wood. And today, I saw now, there *was* someone controlling traffic at Broadway and Fifth: a giant policeman in tall helmet and white gloves, guiding traffic with sharply graceful motions of a slim baton like a man conducting an orchestra—making sure those carriages leaving the square were delayed very little by cruder traffic.

It was a marvelous scene, and off across the square through the branches of the winter trees I could see the white façades of strange hotel after hotel, and could read their signs: the Fifth Avenue, Albemarle, Hoffman House, St. James, Victoria, and to the north the Brunswick. It was like nothing in New York I'd ever seen, and I grinned at Julia, and said, "It's Paris!"

She was smiling, her face reflecting my own excitement, but she was shaking her head. "No, it isn't," she said proudly, "it's New York!"

We walked on to Madison Avenue, stopping at the curb to watch for a break in the circle of carriages, and I nodded toward Broadway just ahead. "How far down does the Ladies' Mile go?"

"To Eighth Street." Then, chanting it, " 'From Eighth Street down, the men are earning it. From Eighth Street up, the women are spurning it! That is the way of this great town, from Eighth Street up and Eighth Street down!' " and I could have kissed her. There was a break in the double line of circling carriages, and I grabbed Julia's hand, and we ran across Madison Avenue and into Madison Square. Through the etched branches of the trees I saw something far across the square and ahead to the north, or thought I did: a structure of some kind, but no, not really a structure, something else; an almost familiar shape. We'd entered a path curving ahead to the north and west, and my head was moving from side to side, eyes narrowed, trying to make out what I was glimpsing through the trees and constantly moving people on the path ahead.

I had Julia's hand still, after our run across the street, and I stopped so abruptly I yanked her arm, swinging her around to face me, surprised. I was standing motionless, staring across the square. I knew what I was seeing now, and it was impossible.

What I saw off across the paths beyond the people, the benches, snow, and still-lighted lamps *couldn't be there* but was; and I turned to Julia open-mouthed, my arm rising full length to point. "It's the arm," I said stupidly, then almost shouted it, a man turning to look at me. "My God," I said, "it's the Statue of Liberty's *arm!*" and I turned from Julia to stare at it again across the square.

175

I wouldn't have been surprised if it had vanished during the instant I'd looked away, but there it was still, solidly and impossibly *there:* The erect right arm of the Statue of Liberty was standing on the west side of Madison Square holding the lighted torch of liberty high above the surrounding trees.

I couldn't believe it. I walked so fast it was just short of running, Julia hurrying along beside me, her arm under mine, baffled at the intensity of my interest. Then we were there, stopped directly beside it, my head thrown back to sight up the length of that tremendous arm sprouting from a rectangular stone base. I'd never known it was this big; it was gigantic, an enormous forearm ending in a tremendous clenched right hand with fingernails big as a sheet of letter paper, and the great copper torch gripped in that hand was itself as tall as a three-story building. Far above, leaning over the ornate railing surrounding the base of the flame at the tip of the torch, people stared down at us. "The Statue of Liberty," I murmured to Julia, smiling incredulously. "The Statue of Liberty's *arm!*"

"*Yes!*" She was laughing at me, bewildered, amused. "It's been here for some time, brought from the Philadelphia Centennial Exposition." She glanced up at it idly. "The entire statue is to be erected in the harbor someday," she said without interest. "If they should ever decide where. And manage to collect enough money to do so. No one seems interested in paying for it; some say it will never go up."

"Well, I predict that it will!" I said exuberantly, recklessly. "And I'd say Bedloe's Island is just the place for it!" Then I stared again, delighted that the arm wasn't the aged and permanent acid-green I was used to, but new, the copper still coppery and only beginning to dull, the winter sun glinting dully from the knuckles and from the curved edge of the overhead railing, and at the tip and down one side of the torch.

We went up into the arm then, climbing the narrow little circular staircase inside, edging past people coming down, then stepping out onto the railed and circular walkway around the base of the torch. I looked out over Madison Square, that wonderful, joyous, wintertime square; looked out over the far-off helmet of the mustached, white-gloved, giant traffic cop toward a still-nonexisting Flatiron Building;

looked down onto that narrow Fifth Avenue and strange, strange Broadway, and suddenly I had to close my eyes because actual tears were smarting at the very nearly uncontainable thrill of being here.

The Ladies' Mile was great, the sidewalks and entrances of the block after block of big glittering ladies' stores crowded with women—the kind of women we'd seen at the square, their carriages waiting for them at the curbs now, and every other kind and age of woman. The display windows were low, down to within a foot or so of the walk, a lot of them guarded by waist-high polished brass bars, and the protection was needed. Women stood shoulder to shoulder at some of them, staring at the displays, and when one turned away another was usually waiting behind her to slip into her place. I tagged along with Julia and looked at a few of the displays, and actually they weren't much: mostly ribbons and yard goods unfolded from bolts onto supporting stands. It took me a few stores to realize that we hadn't seen any dresses in the windows, and when I said so to Julia she looked puzzled. "But dresses are made at home," she said.

Hats seemed to be in separate stores, and so did gloves. I stood with Julia looking at a window full of them, some lying in flat shallow boxes, others on plaster display arms. One group of them on display arms were for evening wear, buttoning from wrist to elbow, and some even higher. I nudged Julia and pointed at one pair dyed purple. "Eighteen buttons," I said. She nodded, then stood, lips moving very slightly as she counted; then she pointed to a black pair. "Twenty." I looked the row over, picked a lavender pair, began counting, but Julia interrupted, pointing to another black pair. "Twenty-one." I nodded, began counting the lavender buttons again, and there were twenty-two buttons from wrist to biceps, and we both laughed when I announced this, turning away. "I'm the champ," I said, and Julia said, "Of course."

The street life as we walked, slowly—the only way you could move on those thronged walks—was fantastic: Boys, working against the flow of pedestrian traffic like fish fighting their way upstream, shoved advertising throwaways into every hand that would accept one; and men and women, walking, or standing in doorways, sold everything you could think of, and a lot you never would. I made a few sketches along the way, later on working them up a little. I've included some of them here:

This girl of about sixteen stood in a doorway holding a wooden board on which boutonnieres of artificial flowers were fastened. She must have seen me looking at her, because when I glanced up from her board to her face she was waiting to meet my eyes; she smiled hopefully, and then of course I had to buy one. They were ten cents, and when I handed it to Julia she thanked me, looking as though she were wondering what to do with it; she tucked it into her muff.

In the same block a man stood at a doorway, a basket at his feet, holding out something in his palm for anyone's inspection. When I looked I saw it was a tiny spitz puppy no more than five inches long. There were six more in his basket, whimpering and squirming, and he was offering them for sale. I turned from him, and two men were walking toward us in the crowd, one passing out leaflets, both of them wearing identical sandwich boards and very high-crowned peaked hats. Each of the two hats and sandwich boards was identically lettered

2 ORPHANS, and though I reached for a leaflet I didn't get one, and never did find out what that pair was all about.

At Broadway and Twentieth, passing Lord & Taylor's, we had to stop abruptly to let a procession of two sail past us toward the curb, a really magnificent dowager in a little flat hat tied on with a ribbon in a big bow under her chin, and a long fur-trimmed coat, and followed by a bareheaded man—store manager, floorwalker?—in a morning coat, wing collar, striped pants, and obsequious smile, carrying her packages, the footman of the waiting carriage leaping down to take them.

At Nineteenth we passed a magnificent store of white marble, and I glanced at a brass sign—one was set into the lower edge of each of the long row of display windows—and it said ARNOLD CONSTABLE & CO. Beside the store, a middle-aged woman selling toys from a basket sat on a tiny folding campstool next to a flight of stairs. We passed a man in a dark-blue

army overcoat, wearing a blue forage cap—the flat Civil War kind—and he was working his way upstream of the traffic flow with a wooden trayful of apples hung from a leather sling round his neck. We passed an elderly woman selling pressed ferns from a basket; I have no idea what they were for. We passed a one-armed middle-aged man, also wearing a blue forage cap; he had a grind organ hanging from his neck by a strap and supported by a single leg; he was turning the handle with his one arm, cranking out—I listened to be sure, and yes, it was—"Hail, Hail, the Gang's All Here!"

We were never out of sight of one or another of the great clocks set high above the crowds on elaborate iron pedestals; only the well-off carried watches, I remembered Martin's saying; they were expensive, to be passed on to sons and grandsons after them; no Timexes here.

I noticed at least half a dozen women in mourning, and I mean complete mourning, everything a solid black; two of them wore heavy black veils besides. And I saw many more lame and crippled people, and people on crutches, and people with pockmarked and birthmarked faces, than I'd ever seen on the streets before.

We walked under a huge wooden pair of pince-nez glasses hanging out over the sidewalk to identify the upstairs office of an optometrist; it must have been six feet long, gilded, and with enormous blue eyes painted behind the lenses.

A man stood at a portable table with a sign tacked to its edge. The sign was a bird drawn with incredibly ornate and involved pen flourishes and holding a wide curling ribbon in its beak. The words of the sign were written on the ribbon, so fancifully you could hardly read them, and they said the man behind the table would write your name in the same fancy script on a dozen calling cards while you waited, for ten cents.

And there were jewelers, confectioners, drugstores, and we passed a restaurant called Purcell's and another called Maillard's. There were quite a few cigar stores, and we must have passed five or six hotels between Madison Square and Union Square, each with cigar-smoking, top-hatted, important-looking men endlessly passing in and out. There were still other signs hanging over the walk; gilded wooden watches from the jewelers, a wooden boot from a shoe store, and before every cigar store stood a life-size wooden figure holding a bunch of cigars. A couple of the figures were Indians, but one was a beautifully carved and painted Scotch Highlander, and I saw a baseball player, Uncle Sam, and a terrific goateed, broad-brim-hatted figure that I took to be Buffalo Bill. Two of the hotels had below-street-level barbershops, and at the curb before each stood ten-foot-high wooden barber poles striped red-and-white and surmounted by great gilt balls.

At the north end of Union Square, as we crossed the street toward it, what Julia called "a German band" stood playing: five men playing a clarinet, a trumpet, and three brass horns including a slide trombone. They played well, really well, and just as we passed all but the trumpeter paused while he played a series of rising and falling trills that were great. I dropped several coins into the felt hat that lay bottom up at the feet of one of them.

Up ahead I saw a horse edge in to the curb out of the Broadway traffic and begin to drink from a stone horse-trough. At Broadway and Fifteenth on the square we passed Brentano's Literary Emporium, and I'm not certain of this but I thought a far-off sign read TIFFANY'S. I turned to ask Julia, but she was looking at me curiously, and spoke first.

She said, "How did you know what it was?"

"Know what what was?"

"The Statue of Liberty's arm."

I had no answer for a moment; how *could* I have known? "I saw a photograph of it."

She didn't doubt me. "Oh? Where?"

Well, where might I have seen it? "In *Frank Leslie's Illustrated Newspaper*. I just didn't realize it was here in New York."

She nodded, then frowned. "A photograph?"

"Yes, of course. I'm certain the woodcut was made directly from a photograph." She nodded, satisfied, and I said, "Look!" not quite sure at what, but changing the subject. Then I saw a little cluster of people standing before a shopwindow and nodded toward them. We walked over; it was a photographer's shop, Sarony's, and they were looking at a display of sepia photographs: actors and actresses in costume, including tights; long-haired, mustached and bearded politicians, writers, poets, Civil War generals. But the little knot of people—some leaving it, others joining it—was staring in at the most prominent part of the display, a long enlarged photograph mounted on a display easel, a vase of daisies standing before it.

It was a familiar face, I was certain I knew it: a bareheaded young man with shoulder-length hair and the beginning of a smile, wearing a long black winter coat with a huge shawllike fur collar and foot-long fur cuffs, holding a pair of white gloves. "Oscar Wilde!" I said, and Julia and one or two other people looked at me pityingly. As we turned away Julia said smugly, "I heard his lecture, you know."

"What lecture?"

"You *are* a goose; I thought everyone knew. His lecture at Chickering Hall a couple of weeks ago."

"Oscar Wilde lectured here? You heard him? You were actually there? What did he say?"

"Oh, his subject was the English Renaissance. I don't suppose I paid attention as closely as I should have; Jake was annoyed. But I was annoyed at *him*; nearly everyone laughed when Mr. Wilde appeared, Jake as loudly as any."

"At what?"

"The way he was dressed: a clawhammer coat, knee breeches, bows on his shoes. And he wore white kid gloves. He has a *very* large face."

"But what did he *say*? You must remember something."

"Well . . . he was speaking of Byron, Keats, Shelley, the pre-Raphaelites. And he said, 'To know nothing about these great men is one of the necessary elements of English education,' and everyone laughed. I believe he liked that, because then he said, 'They had three things which the English public never forgive: youth, power, and enthusiasm,' and there was loud applause. Then he said, 'Satire paid them the homage which mediocrity pays to genius.' "

"You heard him say that?" I grinned, and shook my head. "You actually heard Oscar Wilde say that?"

"Of course," she said absently, without interest; she was staring at an old man standing beside a glass case set on a barrel at the curb.

He had a stubby white beard, a wooden leg, and wore a short-billed officer's cap, the braid turned green. Walking toward him, we could see a ship model behind the glass under full sail in a sea of cloth waves. On top of the case a hand-lettered sign said ALL THE WORK OF A POOR OLD SAILOR.

We stopped to look, and the old man turned to the case, began working a wooden knob in its side, and the ship started to toss, and the waves moved, alternate layers in opposite directions. He stared patiently ahead so as not to seem to beg, but there was a wooden box with a slot beside the sign, and I dropped a quarter into it and felt Julia's arm under mine tug hard. As we turned to walk on, she whispered fiercely, "He is said to own an entire block of fine houses in Brooklyn!"

As though she owned it, Julia showed off to me an enormous block-long store between Ninth and Tenth on Broadway, called A. T. Stewart's, and we stopped so that I could stare. I knew about this store; I knew it was going to survive on into the 1950's as Wanamaker's, but I hadn't realized it was white marble. Stepping closer, I saw that it wasn't marble but cast-iron painted white. In the same block was something called Bunnel's Museum, thick with hand-painted signs: FAT WOMEN, SKELETON, MIDGET! ZULUS! DR. LYNN, THE VIVISECTIONIST! HE CUTS MEN UP! HE MAKES PEOPLE LAUGH! And opposite Stewart's, Jackson's Mourning Store, its windows filled with black clothing, men's, women's, and children's, and including silk hats banded with black crepe that hung down at the backs. A sign in the window said they were OFFERING REDUCED PRICES PREPARATORY TO TAKING STOCK, and I made a small joke about this being a good economical time to die, and Julia looked startled, then laughed as though it were a brand-new kind of joke to her, as maybe it was.

A shabby-looking man walking toward us had a cigar box full of little pellets of some kind, and he started to speak but Julia said no so sharply she cut him off, and we left him standing. He was selling "grease erasers," Julia said, to take spots out of clothes, and they didn't work; she'd bought one for a dime once and tried it. Another man was walking slowly toward us, the fingers of both hands flying. Up closer I saw that he had a little contraption in his hand, a needle threader, and he was threading and rethreading the same needle in endless demonstration. Pinned to both lapels were dozens more of them, and as he walked he said, "Ten cents, ten cents, ten cents," over and again. Not far behind him a Turk in red fez, red gold-trimmed vest, white knee breeches, and curled-up red slippers was selling tonka beans from a tray. Before he reached us, I'd turned suddenly aside, pulling Julia along; in a window before which half a dozen people stood staring, sat a baby—it couldn't have been more than two—suspended in some sort of PATENTED BABY-SWING, according to the signs pasted on the window

and on placards behind it. It sat there apathetically, holding a rattle, a living window-display, and it occurred to me that it might be doped up with one of the laudanum preparations I'd seen advertised in *Harper's*.

But it was a fine and exciting Ladies' Mile, doped-up baby or not, and before we reached the end of it we passed several more old friends: I remember Revillon Frères just below Ninth Street, and W. & J. Sloane between Third and Bleecker. And we watched a lightning calculator with his blackboard, doing any kind of mathematical problem anyone called out to him, with really unbelievable speed. He was a marvel. A cigar box with a few coins in it was at his feet, and I dropped a quarter into it, wondering who he could possibly be—or had been.

At Bleecker Julia stepped to the curb beside a lamppost, out of the way of pedestrians, to point down past Houston to what she said was Prince Street, a couple of blocks off, and a new brick building on the northwest corner. That was Rogers Peet, she said; she'd leave me here to go on back and do her shopping. I wasn't sure whether to shake hands with her or not, but I did, and she gave me her hand. I said, "Julia, it's been one of the best times I ever had in my life."

She smiled at what seemed like an enormous exaggeration, and said she'd enjoyed it, too, smiling beautifully. Something about the moment, a deceptive intimacy, gave me a sudden courage and I said, "Julia, you can't possibly be seriously considering marrying Jake."

She stared. "And why not?"

She seemed genuinely puzzled, yet I couldn't believe in it. "Why . . . he's far too *old* for you. And too fat, too homely. And just too all-around *ridiculous*, Julia!"

After a long pause she said, "It is you who are ridiculous. He is a fine figure of a man. Far from too old. And he will be an excellent provider." She reached out, put a hand on my arm, and smiled. "A woman must consider these things, you goose. Better to be practical than a spinster." She turned quickly and walked off, up Broadway.

I stood watching her: Except for a goodbye later today with whatever excuse I invented, this was the last time I'd see her. Once I'd have thought a girl actually wearing a bustle would look foolish to me, but Julia didn't; she looked graceful, she looked absolutely fine, and I realized that the clothes of all the people passing steadily by, even the shiny silk hats, already looked natural to me.

Up ahead Julia was almost lost; there was a final flash of her purple skirt, then she was gone completely, beyond the intervening pedestrians, and I walked on.

It was a dozen blocks or so to City Hall Park, and I walked, but still I arrived much too early. A little wind had come up, and it was too cold to sit in the park and wait; I couldn't risk Pickering's seeing me waiting here anyway; I'd have to move on. But for a few moments I stood beside the little park looking across it at City Hall and at the Court House behind it, marveling at how very much they looked as I remembered them. As well as I could recall, the entire park looked just as it did in my own time, and I brought out my sketch pad, stepped into the park, and sketched it for reference: City Hall and the Court House, the paths, benches, and winter trees. I stood looking at my sketch for a moment, and it could have been done in the latter half of the twentieth century.

But now I sketched in a few hurrying pedestrians, and then some of the traffic: a carriage, a waiting hack-line of two-wheeled hansoms at the Broadway corner, an enormous green-and-yellow mail truck pulled by four horses on its way to the post office. I looked across the park at Centre Street, and stood remembering how it looked whenever it had been that I'd seen it last—how it was *going* to look, that is; how the traffic there now would be driven from the streets by the automobile that would follow it. And I sketched that into my scene, too: the automobiles, the enormous diesel buses, the huge trucks that were going to choke this and every other New York street; and I faced them all the same way as though they were not only following but driving the horse-drawn traffic off the scene.

I walked on; this was the business and office section of lower Broadway, the area Kate and I had been in, and I crossed the street and walked on along the west wall of the huge, absurd-looking main post office, remembering to look up at the enormous pennant reading POST OFFICE fluttering very stiffly, just now, from a cupola. Just ahead to the south on the other side of Ann Street, I noticed that everyone passing glanced into what looked like a seven-foot-high, extremely narrow sentry box with a gabled roof. It stood at the curb in front of a drugstore in the Herald Building called Hudnut's Pharmacy, and when I passed it I looked in, too. Inside it hung a tremendous thermometer, the biggest I've ever seen, sheltered in the hut from the wind. The temperature was 19 degrees, and I was pleased to know the exact temperature, a lot more interested in the weather somehow than I remembered ever being before.

Here in the daylight I was very much aware of what Kate and I hadn't seen in the dark: the incredible profusion of telegraph wires. Like a rube, I walked along for half a block staring up at a gray winter sky actually darkened, or so it seemed, by literally hundreds and hundreds of black telegraph wires on both sides of the street and running across it in bunches of sometimes several dozen, an astonishing mess. Every few yards wooden telegraph poles sprouted from the walk, some of them—I stopped and counted—with as many as fourteen crossarms loaded with wires, each pole, I noticed, marked with the name of whatever competing company had put it there.

Traffic was very heavy, rumbling and pounding along on the cobbles, and it occurred to me that this wasn't a very broad way; it was a narrow street, actually, which didn't help the congestion any. There were a great many flat-bedded or low-sided drays hauling barrels or boxes. One dray labeled MARVINS' SAFE CO. carried a crated safe, and I could see it through the slats, brand-new, black and shiny, a freshly painted little scene—cows in a field—on the upper half of its door. As I watched, a boy ran up behind the dray, scaled the low back gate, and sat down astride it, hitching a ride. In the same block a loaded moving van rolled by, an immense red-painted box on wheels, its driver high up on a seat over the rumps of his team. On the side of the van, under the gilt-painted name BUTLER BROTHERS, MOVING, there was a large painted scene in a wildly ornate gold-painted frame. It was no pastoral scene but a cannon-flashing duel between full-rigged ships, labeled in an oval inset at the bottom THE BATTLE OF LAKE ERIE. The Broadway stages, dozens and dozens of them constantly trundling up and down the street, sometimes three or four in a row, were very much like the Fifth Avenue buses only they were painted red, white, and blue, and *they* had scenes, too, painted on the sides; mostly pastoral, and pretty much daubs. But they were all different, and I liked this whole idea of scenic decoration of ordinary things. The twentieth century's diesel monsters, I decided, would be improved by some of the same.

There were a great many light, single-horse delivery wagons, and in among the commercial traffic an occasional fine carriage moving uptown, toward the Ladies' Mile, I supposed. And everywhere I looked, there were signs, the names of firms occupying the buildings on which the signs hung. Most were black letters on white, or gold letters on black, and they hung out over the sidewalks or were wired to building ledges just below rows of windows, slanting slightly downward so they could be read from the street.

I liked the street; it was varied, interesting to the eye. The entrances to some of the buildings were four or five steps above street level, the wide flights of stairs often separated by a brass railing into incoming and outgoing sections. Generally there'd be more offices or a barbershop or restaurant or something in the basement section, half below street level, the stairway down to it protected by black iron guard railings with a row of points along the street-level railing to keep loafers from sitting on them. The buildings were constructed from every possible material; there was plenty of brick and wood; there were some whose entire fronts were of cast iron, often as high as three or four stories; there were marble and granite, brownstone, wood, and even stucco. And they were of mixed periods; between newer four- and five-story stone office buildings I passed a lot of small, modest houses of an obviously earlier time, with old-fashioned dormer windows in the upper stories, but the lower stories turned into shops with plate-glass display windows. At one such display window eight or ten men were standing, and I joined them. A girl, looking very prim and a little embarrassed, and never glancing at us, sat demonstrating a typewriter. It was a strange-looking contraption, high and almost completely open, exposing its works, and decorated here and there with gilt-and-red arabesques. Stuck to the window with little dabs of paste were samples of her work, praising the machine, its speed, and its superiority to handwriting. We all watched till she finished what she was doing, a short, sample business letter. Then she stuck that to the window and began a new sample. A man beside me said, "They'll be all the go soon; you watch." But I shook my head and said, "No, they'll never catch on; they lack the personal touch," and he looked thoughtful.

I turned away from the window; the walks were crowded, mostly with men. Were there far more portly and even fat men now than you'd see in the late twentieth century? I thought so. Dozens of boys—why weren't they in school?—darted through the crowd in messenger uniforms, the day's equivalent of the telephone, I supposed. There were occasional other boys, not much older, carrying canvas sacks of what seemed to be actual money; I heard the clink of coins inside them. And there were younger boys, some no more than six or seven, often literally in rags, their faces and hands permanently dirty. Some of these were selling papers. I saw all the morning papers—the *Herald, Times, Tribune, Sun, World*—and the first afternoon editions of a lot of the others: the *Daily Graphic, Staats Zeitung, Telegram, Express, Post, Brooklyn Times, Brooklyn Eagle,* and still others I can't remember. Every one of them carried column headings about the Guiteau verdict, and I heard Guiteau's name mentioned often by passersby. Others of the smaller boys shined shoes and boots from portable stands carried by straps slung over their shoulders. These were the boys, it suddenly occurred to me, that Horatio Alger wrote about; he was alive now, I recalled, maybe writing *Tom, the Bootblack* at this moment. But the bright, eager, cheerful faces he wrote about weren't down here. These faces, even the six-year-olds', were intent and knowing, shrewd and alert, as they had to be—I thought I could see this in their faces—if they were to eat tonight. Several men suddenly stopped on the walk, stepped to the curb, pulled out their watches and then stood, heads thrown back, staring up and across the street, watches still in hand. Even while I was wondering about it, more men stepped to the curb, dragging watches from their vest pockets. And within less than a minute hundreds of men lined the curb of Broadway for blocks, glancing from the open watches in their hands to the roof of one of the tallest buildings along here.

The roof was a shingled many-gabled complexity of windowed pyramid-shaped towers of various sizes; rising from their center, and highest of all, was an ornate square tower surrounded at its base by a fenced walk. WESTERN UNION TELEGRAPH CO. was painted in a circle on the side of the tower, and now I saw that a great many of the wires lining the street originated from this rooftop. A flagpole rose from the roof of the tower, an American flag fluttering rapidly from it; and at the top of the pole directly behind the flag I saw a large bright-red ball. The ball was made with a hole through it apparently, like a doughnut; it surrounded the pole and must have been visible up there for miles around.

I didn't know what was going on, but I got out my watch—two minutes to twelve, it said—and stood like the hundreds of other men all up and down Broadway as far as I could see. Suddenly, and there was a simultaneous murmur, the red ball dropped the length of the flagpole to its base, and the man next to me murmured, "Noon, exactly." He carefully set his watch, and I did the same, pushing the minute hand forward. All around me I heard the clicks of the covers of gold watches snapping shut. The hundreds of men at the curb turned and became part of the streams of pedestrians again, and I was smiling with pleasure: Something about this small ceremony, momentarily uniting hundreds of us, appealed to me mightily.

Now, just past the stroke of noon, music—chimes—had begun somewhere behind me, and I knew the tune: "Rock of Ages." I turned to look back, and smiled. I'd seen the source of the sound just down the street: it was an old friend, Trinity Church, its chimes clear in the winter air, and I hurried along to it. Then, a couple of dozen steps past the church, my back against a telegraph pole out of the stream of pedestrians, I made a quick reference-sketch which I finished up much later. I'd sketched Trinity before, but this time, incredibly, its tower rose black against the sky, higher than anything else in sight. I finished, making notes in the margins for the final job, stood looking at it, and a messenger boy in a brass-buttoned blue uniform stopped for a moment, looked at my sketch, nodded at me, and walked on. This is the finished sketch and it is absolutely accurate except that I added leaves to show the fine old trees more clearly. This is the Broadway I walked along—in the middle distance at the left you can see the Western Union Building and the time ball which had just dropped to the base of the pole a few minutes before.

Walking back, glancing down at my rough sketch, I was tempted to stop and add the ghosts of the tremendous towers that would someday surround Trinity, burying the tower at the bottom of a canyon. But I was passing the church entrance now, and four or five men hanging around on the sidewalk before it, sizing me up correctly, called, "Visit the steeple, sir! Highest point in the city! Best view in town!" There was just time, and I nodded to the one who looked as though he needed the money most.

Inside he led me up a steep endlessly winding stone staircase, on up past the bell-ringing rooms, then past the bells, clanging so deafeningly here that you couldn't make out the separate notes. Finally, at the top, we reached a wooden-floored ledge running under several narrow open windows. My knees felt the climb, and I was trying to hide my puffing. I reached out and tried one of the stone windowsills, making sure it was solid, and the guide laughed. "I was waiting to see whether you'd try that sill; they all do. Not one man in ten will lean up against it till he's sure it'll hold. I've had men up here wouldn't stand within two feet of it when the windows was open. And I've had ladies get sick the minute they looked down." He kept up the chatter while I looked out: The steeple was 284 feet high, he said; it was the highest point in the city, 16 feet taller than even the Brooklyn Bridge towers, and the church stood

S. Mosley

on a higher piece of ground besides. At least 5,000 people visited this steeple every year, and probably more, but very seldom a New Yorker alone; no one had ever tried suicide by jumping; and so on and on, while I stared out at the entire upper Bay.

The sky was steel-gray, the air very clear, everything sharply etched. Over the low rooftops I could see both rivers, the water—of the Hudson especially—ruffled, gray as hammered lead. Lining South Street off to my left were hundreds and hundreds of masts; I watched the ferries, great paddle wheels churning; I stared out at the church spires high over the rooftops in every direction; I saw the astonishing number of trees, to the west especially, and thought of Paris again; and I looked down at the walks onto the heads of passersby in Broadway, the tiny circles which were the tops of silk hats tilting and winking dully in the clear winter light. At an opposite window I looked uptown, across the roof of the post office toward City Hall Park. Beyond it, off to the east and sharp against the winter sky, stood the great towers of newly cut stone supporting the immense cables from which the roadway of Brooklyn Bridge would hang; now I could see workmen moving along temporary planking laid here and there across great open gaps of the unfinished roadway, the river far below clearly visible.

It was a great view of the city from what was, of course, the day's sightseeing equivalent of the Empire State Building far in the future. But there was nothing laughable in the comparison, I thought, staring out at the city; this *was* the highest view in town just now, however lost among incredibly higher buildings it was going to become. And if someday I'd have to go up ninety-odd stories to get a murky, smog-ruined view of New York instead of this brilliantly defined closer look at a lower and far pleasanter city, then who should be doing the laughing? I wanted to sketch the view, but it would have taken hours just to rough it in, and now I had to hurry. Downstairs I gave my guide a quarter, which made him happy; then, moving fast, I walked back toward City Hall Park.

14

At TWENTY-FOUR MINUTES past noon, standing at a first-floor rear window of the post office, I stood looking across the street to the north at the little wintertime park and the people moving along its crisscrossing paths, and the strangeness of what I was doing took hold of me. Staring out that soot-dirtied window, I was remembering the note I'd seen in Kate's apartment, the paper yellowing at the edges, its once-black ink rusted with time. And the meeting in this park, arranged by that note, became an ancient event, decades old and long since forgotten.

Could it really be about to happen? I wasn't able to believe that it would. People, strangers, continued to walk out of and into the park and along the walks all around it. Just ahead and across the street to my right, Park Row, stood the five-story New York Times Building I'd seen the night Kate and I walked to the El station, and again it was strange knowing it still stood in twentieth-century Manhattan. Now in daylight, I read the long narrow signs, suspended just below windowsill level, of other lower-floor tenants of the building: FOREST, STREAM, ROD & GUN . . . LEGGO BROS. . . . The Times Building shared a common wall with another five-story stone building right behind it almost directly across the street to my right. It was nondescript, with tall narrow windows, its front—like the Times Building beside it and like most other such buildings in this area—hung with narrow gilt-on-black or black-on-white signs suspended just below the windows of the tenants. Then my eyes dropped to the street-level entrance, and Jake Pickering was standing in it.

I was inside the post office, across the street from the south end of City Hall Park. The doorway in which Jake Pickering stood was recessed, several yards back from the street and up two or three steps from street level; it was almost directly to my right so that I could see him, but from the park ahead I knew he couldn't be seen. And he took care not to be seen, standing on the steps close beside the stone wall of the recessed doorway. He was searching the park across the street from him and ahead. Then, satisfied, he stepped quickly out, moved across the walk, and dodging through the traffic, he crossed Park Row and walked swiftly into the park, and directly to the center, where most of the walks converged. There he stood, hat on the back of his head, outer coat unbuttoned, hands jammed into his pants pockets, his jaws clenched on a cigar, angling it upward, and he waited.

Five minutes passed. I could see Pickering's breath; it was cold out there, and he felt it and began strolling slowly back and forth, a dozen yards each way from the center of the park. But he didn't button his coat or take his hands from his pockets or his cigar from his mouth. From time to time he puffed the cigar, its blue smoke mingling with the white vapor of his breath, and I realized that he was posing, offering a picture of a man at ease. And succeeding: His posture and slow walk, everything about him, said that he was relaxed and content, that he didn't even notice the cold.

Five minutes more passed; the City Hall clock across the park said twelve thirty-five. And when I looked down from the clock the second man was well inside the park walking swiftly toward its center from the west. And I knew that the fleck of blue in his gloved hand (the event was no longer ancient; a chill moved along my spine at knowing that here I stood watching it begin) was the envelope I'd seen Pickering mail, held in the other man's hand now as a symbol of recognition.

Pickering had seen him and was walking toward him; my breath was clouding the dirty pane, I was leaning so close, and I stepped back a grudging inch or so. Now Pickering was smiling, and the two men stopped, facing each other. As the second man tucked the blue envelope into an inner coat pocket, Pickering removed the cigar from his mouth, and I saw his beard move as he spoke, then the slight waggle of the other man's beard as he answered. At this distance they might have been black-bearded twins standing there on the path, each in shiny silk hat, dressed virtually alike, each with the portly figure of the day. Their heads turned as they glanced around, searching the park, and I resisted an impulse to duck from sight. Then Pickering pointed, and they angled across the park, toward me and toward a bench protected from the wind by the high stone base of the statue against which it stood. They reached it, and sat down almost hidden from my view by the statue's base, only the left knee and shoulder of one of them in my line of sight.

I had to hear them, *had* to, and I walked swiftly out the rear doors, ran across the street behind the tail gate of a brewery wagon piled with wooden barrels, then walked into City Hall Park to the base of the statue. I turned around, and with my back nearly touching the base I stood frowning a little, occasionally glancing irritably along the·path as though waiting for someone who was late. ". . . don't understand why," one voice was saying reasonably. "It's below freezing, turning colder momentarily, and there is a wind besides; no one sits in a park on a day like this. If you have no office of your own, there's the Astor House lobby just across the street; I'll stand treat at the bar."

"Oh, I have an office of my own," Jake Pickering's voice said; there was a fat chuckle in it. "Not much of an office. Nothing like *yours*, I'll warrant. But still, you'd like to see it, wouldn't you? You won't, though. Not yet. No one sits in a park on a day like this; true. But that's why we're going to sit here; what I have to say is strictly between the two of us. The subject is Carrara marble; it brought you here. On the run. And it'll keep you here. In the cold. Andrew Carmody, the ever-so-eminent millionaire."

"It brought me here," the other man replied levelly. "But not to be played with. So keep your remarks about my eminence to yourself, and say what you want without further ado, or I'll stand up, walk off, and be damned to you."

"Good enough. You'll have to forgive me, but I have reached the culmination of several years' work and am enjoying my little triumph."

"What do you want?"

"Money."

"Assuredly. As who does not? Get to the point."

"All right. Cigar?"

"No, thank you; I'll smoke my own."

There was a silence, the strike of a match, the sound of cigars puffed into life; then Pickering spoke again. "I work in City Hall where I am a clerk, the lowest of the low. Yet I sought the job, sir! Leaving employment much more remunerative. Now, why? *Why*, you ask."

"I didn't"—I heard Carmody puff at his cigar—"but continue."

Pickering's voice lowered. "Tweed is my reason; are you surprised? He is dead in prison; the Tweed Ring is smashed and already half forgotten. Yet only a few years ago no day passed—remember?—that the *Times* did not speak of 'the slimy trail of the Tweed Ring.' Well, who stole more than thirty millions from the city? Was it only Tweed? Or Sweeny, Connolly, and A. Oakey Hall? No. Tweed had hundreds of willing helpers still undiscovered, each of whom took his share of the swag, large or small. So why have I spent two years at unsuitable employment, a *filing clerk* at City Hall?" Pickering's voice lowered even more, dramatically. "Because that's where the slimy trails *are*."

I was alert, intent, breathing shallowly, not missing a word. Yet something nagged at the back of my mind, and when I recognized it I had to smile. In the way Pickering used his voice, in the words and phrases he chose, there was just a little more than drama; it edged toward melodrama. I think all of us generally act as we think we're supposed to. I had not one but two professors at college who would lean back in their chairs, listening and fitting their hands together fingertip to fingertip, professorially. I had a friend, a compulsive gambler, who often stood casually flipping and catching a coin, his face expressionless. And now Pickering and Carmody were acting their roles in a time when the melodramatic conventions of the stage were largely accepted as representing reality. Deadly serious, meaning every word, each of them, I think, was also appreciating his own performance.

"The slimy trails," Pickering was saying, "wind through aisle after aisle of filing cases. I realized that!" he said proudly. "I understood that Tweed Ring corruption was so widespread and with so many ramifications that the evidence could never all be destroyed. It must exist still, I knew, buried among literally tons of old records, if only I were cute enough to recognize it when I came across it, and to fit its pieces together like a Christmas puzzle. So I became City Hall's most industrious clerk!"

"Commendable. If you're looking for work, see my head bookkeeper."

I heard a sound I'd come to recognize: the metallic snap of the gold protective cover of a watch lifted to reveal the face, then the very slightly different sound of its being snapped shut.

Pickering said, "Yes, you're a busy man of affairs. But you have nothing more important, Mr. Carmody, *nothing*, than to listen to what I have to say. At whatever length I wish to say it!" There was a pause, then Pickering continued quietly, "I've spent endless hours during month after month in the file rooms, hunting those trails through the dust of the years. Discovering and following them as they emerged, losing them, rediscovering them days or weeks later among tens of thousands of false invoices, canceled bank drafts, padded receipts, incriminating messages, memoranda, and letters. The very best of those trails, sir, I have preserved; removed complete from City Hall! A paper or two at a time, you understand, slipped into my pocket and taken to my modest office during my half-hour lunchtime. Or simply mailed to it, to be added to my files during many and many a long evening I've spent there at my desk studying and assembling those files.

"Yet most of what I've learned proved useless! The evidence full and complete! Irrefutable proof of the most blatant corruption. And then I'd find the rascal had died a month or so before. Others I didn't find at all; probably moved to the territories or Canada. Others I found still alive, still here in New York. But no longer rich—broke! While in still other instances the evidence I had assembled, although clear enough, remains insufficient. And search though I did, I could never supply final proof. So all those slimy trails, Mr. Carmody, come down to a very few. And to one above all: the obscure contractor who was paid to supply and install nothing less than Carrara marble to adorn the corridors, rooms, and anterooms of our Court House. *Tons* of magnificent Carrara imported from Italy—at least that is what the invoices and properly stamped customs receipts I have found say. Along with paid labor bills for dozens of workmen, listing their very names and addresses, who are said to have spent weeks installing and finishing it. Would you like to see one? Here is an invoice."

I heard the crackle of paper, there was a silence of several seconds, then Carmody said, "So I see."

"No, keep it, sir! As a souvenir. I have many many more."

"I have no doubt of that, which is why I offer the return of this."

"I don't want it. Are you thinking I might return it to my files? While you follow, and discover where they are kept? I assure you, sir, I will not return to my office except for a final visit. That will be for the purpose of handing over his entire file to the contractor of whom I speak."

There was a pause of a moment or so; then Pickering's voice dropped as he said, "For modest though they were by Tweed Ring standards, his profits made that contractor rich. Because he took them into New York real estate, and now only a few years later he has millions, *millions*. And a wife who, I am told, enjoys each dollar of those millions and the assistance they render her pretensions to society. Mr. Carmody, walk over to the Court House with me, if you care to." Pickering, I'm sure, had nodded toward the Court House just behind City Hall. "And we'll search it together, room by room. Just as I have searched it: sometimes sitting in court rooms as an apparent spectator at trials, my eyes roving the room for marble; or standing in bureau offices waiting my turn to ask a question, my gaze searching every surface of the room. I've examined it floor by floor, corridor by corridor; even the very janitors' closets and the accommodation rooms. And if you can point out to me one single square inch of that Court House which you covered with Carrara or any other marble, contractor Carmody, then I give you my word I'll trouble you no more."

The reply was an expressionless monotone. "What do you want?"

"One million dollars," Pickering said softly, his lips enjoying the feel of the words. "No more, no less; it is all I need to take the road you followed to far greater wealth."

"Not unreasonable, I suppose. When?"

"Now. Within twenty-four hours. . . . *Don't shake your head, sir!*" Pickering cried out angrily. "You have it, and more!"

"Not in *cash*, you idiot." Carmody's voice was quietly furious. "I have it, yes. And I'll pay it. If you can produce and hand over the evidence you claim. But my money is in property—*all* of it. I have no idle cash!"

"Of course you haven't. That is as I should expect. But the solution is simple: Sell some of that property."

"It is *not* simple." He said it through his teeth. "To extract a million in cash from my holdings *cannot be done* just now. Whether you understand that or not. In every way this is the *wrong time*. My money is tied up. In a large, unfinished French flat, a bargain but upon which work is necessarily stopped for the winter; even the plastering must await warmer weather. And in nearly a dozen sites for commercial buildings, the old houses upon them to be pulled down in the spring. In mortgages good as gold, and some better, but not yet due. In empty lots up north of the Central Park, waiting for the city to reach them. In a word, sir, I am overextended! Spread dangerously thin! If I were to attempt to raise a million now, I couldn't get ten cents on the dollar. And now you know more of my affairs than any other living man." There was a silence of several seconds, and when Carmody spoke again his voice was different, quiet and contained, almost friendly, as though he'd welcomed the other man into his confidence and now they were very nearly partners. "I will tell you a secret, known to no other. My greatest fear has been that somehow I would die during the next few months; for if that melancholy event should occur, I believe my wife would quickly be penniless. They'd be onto my fortune like wolves, ripping it asunder, and off to the four corners with the fragments. She knows nothing of finance, nor can a woman legally act in such circumstances with the speed, ability, and fine judgment required. I shall profit by the risk, and soon. But at this moment my affairs are balanced on the point of a pin: I don't dare take a journey these days! I should be afraid to become ill for as long as a week! Do you understand me, sir? The structure would collapse if demands were forced on it. And then *all* would be lost, everything. Wait," he said in an actually friendly tone. "Contain your patience, as you have done thus far, for a little longer. And in the spring—Don't *you* shake your head at me, sir!—I'll pay it! I've said I would! I'll pay more; a million and a quarter in the spring! But you must give me—"

Pickering chuckled, a comfortable sound. "Nothing; I'll give you nothing. Oh, you are a wonder! You must have talked yourself into that fortune! But I know a bluff when I hear one, and I'll give you till Monday, no more. I can't wait for months, and you know it! Did you think I would not know that? Or did you suppose the friendship between Inspector Byrnes and the wealthy men of this city was a secret from the rest of us? I'd end up in Sing Sing! On what charge I don't know, but there I will surely be if I allow you the time to arrange it."

Carmody's voice was strained with rage. "You may end up there yet. I *am* acquainted with Inspector Byrnes!" There was a pause, while he almost literally swallowed his rage. "From time to time I've been able to render him some small service, and I warn you—"

"No doubt you have. Every wealthy man in the city knows him; he is said to be rich through the market tips of Jay Gould alone. But I know him, too; do you know I was once turned back at the Wall Street deadline?"

"Were you indeed!" Carmody burst into harsh angry laughter.

"Yes, I was," Pickering said quietly. "Several years ago when I was without employment, and perhaps a little shabby in consequence, I was walking down Broadway toward Wall Street where I hoped to find work as a clerk. But at the Fulton Street deadline a copper stopped me."

"As he should have if you looked like a pickpocket or beggar; everyone knows Byrnes won't have them in the Wall Street area. And quite properly."

"I was no pickpocket or beggar! And said so! It was a young copper and he listened. Then someone spoke from a carriage at the curb. We looked over, and it was Byrnes's head out the window. 'If he argues, jug him,' he called, and the young copper's hand went for his billy, and I swung round on my heel and turned back. Don't smile! That moment will cost *you* a million! I turned back, Mr. Carmody, and my face was white; I could feel it. I could hardly see through the mist before my eyes. But it was then I knew, *knew*, that someday I'd come walking back to the deadline and the coppers would touch their helmets to me! Because I *belonged* on the other side with the Fisks and the Goulds and the Sages and Astors. It was on that day, though I didn't know it then, that I began the search for *you*."

There was a sudden change in the location of Pickering's voice; he'd stood up, I realized, probably turning to face Carmody. "I am very far from ignorant of financial matters, whatever you may think. You will need, certainly, several business days to raise the required sum. This is Thursday, and I am giving you through Monday, two and a half business days. Three, counting Saturday morning. Come back Monday night. Here. To this very bench. At midnight, Mr. Carmody, when the park and the streets of this area are deserted; I intend to be certain no one follows us. Be here with the money in a satchel or I'll expose you. I won't wait even an hour. Within that time I will be in the offices of the

Times"—there was a moment's pause and I imagined he was nodding toward the building across the street—"with my documents."

There was a silence of six, eight, ten, twelve seconds; then I knew they were gone, and I walked out, around the base of the statue, and onto the path before the bench. They were walking swiftly out of the park along the angled paths, one to the east, the other north toward the Court House, and I stood watching them go, certain that neither would look back.

15

IT WASN'T CERTAIN, I supposed, that Pickering's private office was in the building I'd seen him come out of earlier. But it seemed likely, and I walked across Park Row and stood on the corner of Park Row and Beekman Street looking up at it. It had no distinction; just a plain, tired-looking, flat-roofed old building with storefronts on the street floor, and above them four identical stories of narrow, closely spaced windows. The storefront windows were dirty, and a lot of them had torn and faded summer awnings folded back against the wall; the bottom halves of some were protected by rusting metal grillwork. In lower Manhattan many a drab building just like it has survived into the second half of the twentieth century.

It was depressing to look at. In the windows of the New York Belting and Packing Company lay stacks of gray cardboard boxes and piled-up coils of leather belting; next to it was a dingy-looking stationer's: Willy Wallach. Jumbled together in another window stood big glass jugs in protective wooden cases; they were labeled POLAND WATER, whatever that was; OWEN HUTCHINSON, AGENT, it said on the window. And there was S. Gruhn, tailor, and Rodriguez & Pons, cigar dealers, and I don't know what all.

Under many of the upper-floor windows hung the usual long narrow signs, tilted downward so they could be read from the street. They were of varying lengths; as long, I supposed, as the office space rented by the business firms whose names were painted on them. TURF, FIELD AND FARM, said one under a row of fourth-floor windows; another said THE SCOTTISH AMERICAN, and another THE RETAILER. I saw SCIENTIFIC-

AMERICAN under a row of third-floor windows, and down at the far end of the same floor hung a sign I glanced at as casually as at the others, and which—I mean this literally—I later saw in nightmares, and still do. THE NEW-YORK OBSERVER, this one said.

I walked up a few wooden steps that needed painting, into the recessed entrance, and pushed through a pair of heavy wood-and-glass doors into a vestibule lighted only by the daylight from the street behind me. The building was worn out; inside there was no hiding it, and no one had tried. The wooden floor stretching on into a gloomy interior was worn, the nailheads shiny, and it was filthy: covered with tobacco spit, cigar butts, and permanent ground-in dirt. So was the wooden staircase at my left, the treads so worn they were scooped out at the centers. On the dark-green plaster wall, patched in soiled-white places, was a directory of tenants. The index finger of a large, carefully painted hand—each finger distinct, the sleeve cuff shadowed to seem rounded—pointed ahead into the gloom; behind the cuff was lettered a list of tenants' names and office numbers. An identical hand was painted on the wall of the staircase, pointing up, another longer listing of names behind it. On both lists some of the names had been professionally lettered, but they were faded now, sometimes chipped; these were the older tenants, I imagined. Newer names were often crudely lettered, paint dribbles actually running down from the letters of one of them. A good many names were scratched or painted out, others written in above them. Some of these were only scribbled; one was simply penciled longhand. And none of them read "Jake Pickering."

A man and then a messenger boy had come in after me and gone up the stairs, and I heard sounds back in the first-floor gloom. Now I heard steps coming down the stairs, then a middle-aged or early-elderly white-bearded man appeared, wearing an overcoat and a round cloth cap with earmuff flaps. He glanced at me, and I said, "Is there a building superintendent somewhere?"

He said, "Ha!"—a short bark of disgusted laughter. "A building superintendent! In the Potter Building! No, sir, there is no one here with either the title or office; there is only a janitor." I asked where to find him, and he said, "A question often asked, but seldom answered with any certainty. He has a den, a lair, under the Nassau Street entrance, and is sometimes caught there. There's Ellen Bull"—he pointed ahead into the building, and I saw a vague bulky figure silhouetted down the hall-way. "She'll direct you." I thanked him, and he said, "If you find him, which is doubtful, tell him, pray, that Dr. Prime of the *Observer* reminds him once again that his offices are much too warm for com-fort." He smiled pleasantly, gave me a short nod, and pushed through the doors to the street.

I walked into the building and found Ellen Bull, a tall very large Negro woman who must have weighed over two hundred pounds; she wore a bandanna tied over her hair and carried an empty pail and a mop. The janitor's cubbyhole, she said, was directly under the Nassau Street stairs to the basement. I thanked her, and she smiled, her teeth very white in the gloom; she was about forty-five, and as I walked on, it occurred to me that she had probably been a slave. I passed heavy paneled-wood doors, a few of them numbered, most of them not. Some were ajar, most were closed. Some were labeled with carefully painted names: AUGUST W. ALMQUIST, PATENT AGENT; J. W. DENISON; W. H. OSBORN, LAWYER. Others bore only a square of paper or cardboard, handwritten with a name and tacked to the door panel. In the middle of the building the hall was lighted dimly by gas jets behind globes, the gas turned low; nearer the entrances whatever light there was came from the street.

In the Nassau Street vestibule, under the stairs leading up into the building, a second narrower flight led to the basement, and I walked over and looked down it; it was completely dark. From somewhere overhead I heard the steady rasp of a handsaw and the nerve-jarring squeal, endlessly repeated, of deeply driven nails pried loose. "Anyone there?" I called down into the basement. Only silence; I'd have been surprised at an answer. I walked halfway down the stairs, but no farther; I wasn't going to blunder around down there in the blackness and break a leg. Overhead the squeal of the nails and the sound of the saw con-tinued, and I cupped both hands at my mouth, and called again; more silence. Then I yelled "Anyone *down* there?" and got a distant squeak of a reply from somewhere below and far back. I walked up to the vestibule again, stood waiting, and presently heard feet shuffling along a floor for a dozen steps before they sounded on the wood of the stairs. I looked down and saw a skinny old man emerging from the basement darkness, his hand on the railing as he slowly climbed up. At first I saw only a bald head, freckled on top; then blue eyes lifted to squint up at me, needing glasses, I supposed; then wide green suspenders curving over the shoulders of a white shirt appeared; and finally the rest of him moved into view out of the darkness, knees slowly lifting as he climbed, pants much too big at the waist, hardly touching the old man, in fact.

I gave him Dr. Prime's message as he climbed the last few stairs up into the light, and he began nodding sadly. "I know. I know. Everyone's complaining. It *is* too warm!" He stepped up into the vestibule, sighing, and nodded toward the plaster wall beside me. "Feel!" I put my hand on the wall and nodded; it was pretty warm. "Flue goes up through there, and we're burning wood these days." He rolled his eyes up toward the squealing and sawing. "Cutting an elevator shaft through, and the owner's burning the old flooring," he said contemptuously. "Saving coal. Makes a hot fire, and a lot more work for me."

I listened, making sympathetic grimaces, then said I was looking for a tenant, Jacob Pickering. He sighed, and said, "Well, Mr. Pickering, what's *your* complaint? If it's too hot, I can't—"

"No, I'm not Pickering; I'm *looking* for him. Which is his office?"

But that was too much; he was shaking his head again, turning back toward the basement. "*I* don't know; how should I know? I know the *old* tenants; I knew every tenant when the paper was still here! Now the paper's gone, building's gone downhill. *Potter* Building it is now," he said contemptuously. "All the old tenants are leaving fast as their lease expires. Full of fly-by-nights now. They come and they go, some even sublet and don't tell me *or* Mr. Potter. *I* can't keep track of them; have you been upstairs?" I said no, and he shook his head at the impossibility of describing it. "Rabbit warren. Chopped up into new little offices with matchboard siding; you could spit through the walls! Even new hallways up there now, and be still more of them pretty soon, up on the top floors where the paper was. Who knows who's up there?"

I was stuck for a moment, then I thought of something. "How do they get their mail if you don't know who's where?"

He mumbled, his head ducked, starting down the stairs. "Oh, I manage; I always manage somehow."

"I'm sure you do, but how do you manage?"

I had him now; he had to stop and look back and say it. "I keep a book."

I'd guessed that. "And where's the book?"

"Downstairs," he said irritably. "Way back somewhere; I'm not sure where I—"

I had my hand in my pocket. "Well, I realize it's a lot of trouble." I found a quarter, remembering that it was more than an hour's pay for this man, and handed it to him. "But I'd be very grateful—"

"You're a gentleman, sir; glad to oblige. Be back in a minute."

It was more than a minute, but he came back upstairs with a pocket notebook, the cardboard cover curling back, the upper corners of the pages splayed out; it had a hole punched through a corner, a piece of dirty white twine tied through it in a loop. He opened it, scanning the pages as he turned them slowly, wetting a thumb each time. I stood looking over his shoulders; at least half the names had been scratched out, other newer ones overwritten. He mumbled all the time: "Ought to be torn down, build a new one. Elevator ain't finished; been like this for weeks, and won't help anyway. I can't keep track; somebody moves in, it's up to him to tell me his name if he wants his mail." He chuckled; in his old voice it was nearly a cackle. "And he generally does! Or if he moves out, and wants his mail sent on. And he generally does! Here he is: Pickering. Third floor, Number 27. That's right up above, next to the new shaft; can't miss it. He'll be complaining once the elevator's working, if it ever does; they're noisy devils, you know. I was on one."

I climbed upstairs, and on the second floor the door of the office immediately to my right beside the staircase stood open. The steady sound of the sawing and the regular shrieks of pulled nails came from the doorway, and I walked over and stood looking in. Two carpenters in white overalls knelt on the floor, their backs to me. One was sawing through the wooden floorboards between the joists, allowing the short sections of sawed-off tongue-and-groove boarding and wider subflooring to drop straight through to the basement—where the old janitor, no doubt, had to gather them up and burn them. The second carpenter was methodically prying loose the short stubs remaining nailed to the joists, using the claws of a hammer, and letting them drop through to the basement too. The two men were gradually working their way backward toward the doorway I stood in. Between them and the opposite wall the flooring was gone, the big wooden joists fully exposed. Presently they'd be cut off and burned, too, I supposed.

On the third floor, the heavy paneled-wood door of the room directly above the carpenters was fastened with a newly installed and very big padlock; painted on the door in red was DANGER! KEEP OUT! SHAFTWAY! The door of the next office was stenciled 27, and was locked: I tried the knob cautiously, after listening at the door crack. There was no one else around. I was standing in a short corridor that branched off the main corridor at a right angle, and now I quickly dropped to one knee to look through the keyhole of Room 27. Straight ahead across the office I saw a tall dirty window, gray-white with winter daylight; directly under it stood a rolltop desk and a chair. My view to the left was blocked by something standing directly beside the door, so close it was out of focus. To the right I could see one edge of what had apparently been an open doorway connecting this office *en suite* with the padlocked office beside it. But now the connecting doorway was heavily boarded across, and it occurred to me that the carpenters cutting the elevator shaftway must be working upward so that each floor, as it was cut away, could be dropped through to the basement.

I'd learned all I was going to learn, and probably all I needed to learn, about Jake Pickering's office. For half a minute or so I stood there in the corridor—till I heard someone's footsteps coming down the stairs. I knew why I hated to turn and walk away; now my mission was completed, and I wished it weren't.

I walked back to the main corridor, then turned away from the staircase to walk on through the width of the building, passing the doors of Andrew J. Todd, lawyer; Prof. Charles A. Seeley, chemist; The American Engine Company; J. H. Hunter, notary. Then I came to the *The New-York Observer* offices facing onto Park Row, and the staircase to the street. Walking downstairs I was suddenly aware of how hungry I was.

I had lunch at the Astor House, across Broadway as Carmody had said, catercorner from the post office. But I almost turned around and left when I stepped into the lobby. It was packed with men standing in groups and pairs, talking, nearly every one of them wearing his hat, and the marble floor was covered, and I mean covered, with tobacco juice, as I knew they called it. Even as I stood in the entrance looking around, four or five seconds at most, a dozen men must have turned, each with a swollen cheek, to spit more or less expertly and more or less carefully at porcelain cuspidors scattered all over the big lobby floor; some didn't even bother looking. Trying to think of something else, I walked the length of the lobby past an enormous stick-and-umbrella stand, a railway ticket office, telegraph office, newspaper and cigar stand, and into an enormous, fantastically noisy counter restaurant, with a big oak-framed sign reading NO SWEARING, PLEASE. But I had two dozen Blue Point oysters fresh that morning from New York Bay, and they were absolutely great, and I was glad I'd come.

I took the El back to Gramercy Park. I'd noticed the station just east of City Hall Park, got on there, and it curved north through Chatham Square, and turned out to be the old Third Avenue El. I was used to people now; already, in my mind, the other passengers were dressed as they ought to be. But at Chatham Square a family got on that I couldn't look away from. They must have arrived from Ellis Island within the hour, and—incredible to a man of the twentieth century—I could tell where they were from by the way they were dressed. The father, who wore a huge drooping mustache, and the ten-year-old son, both wore blue cloth caps with shiny black peaks; short, double-breasted, porcelain-buttoned blue jackets; short scarves tied at the throat; pants that flared far out from the waist and tapered to the ankles; and although the father wore boots, the boy—I was fascinated, and had to force my eyes away—actually wore wooden shoes. The mother was stout, crimson-cheeked, wore two dozen skirts, and exactly the kind of bonnet you can see on the label of a can of Old Dutch Cleanser. On the floor at the father's feet was a carpetbag, and up on the seat beside him a big cloth-wrapped bundle. They looked happy, amiable, peering out the windows and commenting in what must, of course, have been Dutch. They were marvelous. They looked like a chocolate ad. And I realized that at this moment—almost the last moments—the world was still a wonderfully variegated place: that soldiers in Greece were probably still wearing pointed shoes, long white stockings, and little ballet skirts; Turks were in fezzes, their women veiled; plenty of Eskimos hadn't yet seen their first white man or caught his diseases; and Zulus were still happy cannibals in an unbulldozed, unpaved, unpolluted world.

I knew we must be getting close to my stop, and looked away from the Dutch family long enough to glance out over this strange low New York, its church spires the highest things on the island. It was weird to be able to look straight across the city and see the Hudson, and astonishing to see how many trees there were. Most of the cross streets seemed lined with them, and there were a good many on the avenues. Some were fine big ones, taller than the houses around them, and I realized that the greenery of all these trees would give the town a rural look in summer almost like a large village, and I wished I could see it then.

We were approaching my stop, and for an instant, down a cross street to the west—Seventeenth? Eighteenth?—I caught a glimpse of a fine and splendid-looking five-story apartment building with a mansard roof. I was almost certain—it was red brick with brownstone facings—that I recognized it as the Stuyvesant. A friend of mine, an artist, who had lived in it till they tore it down, sometime in the fifties, I think, had a watercolor he'd done of it on his living-room wall. He still missed the place, it was such a magnificent, high-windowed, enormous apartment. It actually had twenty-foot ceilings and four wood-burning fireplaces; New York's first apartment building, he said, known as "Stuyvesant's Folly" while they were building it because people said no New York gentleman would ever consent to live with a lot of strangers. He liked to talk about it, and I was glad to have had even a glimpse of it.

I got off at Twenty-third Street, walked back to 19 Gramercy Park, and Aunt Ada heard the front door open and came in from the kitchen, her hands and forearms white with flour. I asked if Julia were home, and she said no, but that she ought to be here any time now, and I thanked her and went on up to my room.

It had been some day and I'd walked more than I had in a long time, so I was glad to stretch out on my bed and wait. Now and then, outside my window as I lay there, I heard children in the park cry out, their voices high and thin in the cold outdoor air. I heard the already familiar hollow clop of horses' hoofs and the chink of their harness chains. I didn't want to leave this New York; there was so much more to see in this strange yet familiar city.

I fell asleep, of course, and awoke at the sounds of Julia's return: her voice and her aunt's in the hall. I got up quickly, pulling my watch out. It was just past four thirty, and I put on shoes and coat and trotted down. They were still there in the hall, looking up at me, Julia still dressed for the street; she was showing her aunt some things she'd bought.

We all went into the parlor, Julia untying and pulling off her hat, and I told them the story I'd composed, astonished at how guilty I felt to be looking at these two trusting women and lying. I'd gone to the post office, I said, to cancel the box I'd rented until I got permanent quarters. But I'd found an urgent letter in the box. My brother was sick, and while he'd recover, I added quickly—I didn't want condolences—they needed me meanwhile to help out on my father's farm, so I'd have to leave today; right now in fact. I was suddenly afraid they might ask questions about farming, but of course they didn't. Those two nice women were sympathetic, genuinely. And they said they were sorry I was leaving, and it seemed to me that was genuine, too. Aunt Ada supposed that I wouldn't leave till after dinner, at least, but I said no, I ought to leave right away; it would be a long train trip. She offered to refund part of my week's lodging, which I refused.

Then Julia, suddenly remembering, said, "Oh, *no!* My portrait!"

I'd forgotten it completely, and stood looking at her, my mind scrambling for an excuse. Then I realized I didn't want one. I wanted to do this portrait very much; it seemed like a particularly good way to say goodbye. So I nodded and said that if she'd sit for it now—I wanted to avoid Jake—I'd do it right away, then leave. Julia hurried upstairs to get ready—I asked her to keep on the dress she was wearing—and I followed to get my sketchbook from my overcoat pocket.

Upstairs I packed my carpetbag, stood looking around the room—ridiculously, I knew I'd miss it—then walked out, carpetbag in one hand, sketchbook in the other, and I flipped the cover back to look over the day's sketches.

As I turned toward the stairs Julia stepped down off the enclosed third-floor staircase, almost bumping into me; her hair was freshly coiled on top of her head now. "Oh, may I see!" she said, reaching for my sketchbook. I might have made an excuse, but I was curious and gave her the book. Walking slowly down ahead of me, she looked first at my reference sketches of the farming near the Dakota; they weren't really sketches yet but more like a set of notes to myself, and she didn't comment on them, but turned the page to my sketch of City Hall Park and the streets around it.

I think I might have guessed the kind of response she made; I knew this was an age of absolute and almost universal faith in progress, and very nearly a love of machinery and its potentials. We were downstairs, and now she stopped in the parlor and said, "What are these, Mr Morley?" Her fingertip lay on the paper at the cars and trucks I'd sketched onto Centre Street.

"Automobiles."

She repeated it as though it were two words: "Auto mobiles." Then she nodded, pleased. "Yes: self-propelled. That's an excellent coinage; is it your own?" I said no, that I'd heard it somewhere, and she nodded again and said, "Perhaps in Jules Verne. In any case, I'm quite certain we *will* have auto mobiles. And a good thing; so much cleaner than horses." She was already turning the page, and now she looked at my rough of Trinity and Broadway. Before she could comment I took it from her, and very rapidly sketched in the enormous buildings that would someday surround the little church. I handed it back to her, and after a moment she nodded. "Excellent. Wonderfully symbolic. The highest structure on all of Manhattan to be eventually surrounded by others far taller: yes. But you're a better artist than architect, Mr. Morley; to support buildings this tall, the masonry at the base of the walls would need to be half a mile thick!" She smiled, and handed my pad back. "Where shall I sit?"

I posed her at a window in a three-quarter view, making her let her hair down, and worked with a very sharp hard pencil to force the best delineation I was capable of; no obscuring faulty draftsmanship with a fine thick dash of a line. The hard pencil also allowed the finest shading and cross-hatching I was capable of.

It was turning out well. I had the shape of the face, and I had the eyes and eyebrows, the hardest part for me, and I was working quite carefully on the hair: I wanted to really catch the way it was. But I was slow: Young Felix Grier came home, and I dragged out my watch and saw that it was just before five. He stood watching for a few moments, not saying anything. He smiled when I looked up at him, and nodded a quick polite approval, but his eyes were worried, and I knew why. I was worried, too—that Jake Pickering would come in and raise hell once again, and it was no part of my mission here to make trouble. I stepped up my speed, trying to hang onto my control; I wanted this good. It seemed unlikely that he'd be home from a job at City Hall before five thirty or six, and I expected to be finished and gone within minutes now.

It was my fault, of course, for not thinking of the obvious: that a man like Jake Pickering, hating his job and status as a clerk, would walk back to City Hall and quit his job after seeing Carmody. And now—this time I didn't see him approaching the house—the front door opened, closed, and there he was standing in the hall doorway again. But now he was swaying ever so slightly, and his tie was undone. His overcoat was unbuttoned, his hands shoved into his pants pockets, and his plug hat, far back on his head, had a streak of dried mud at the crown and along one curled rim.

He wasn't out of control; he was drunk but knew what he was seeing. Julia and I staring at him, his eyes moved from her face to the lines on my pad, back to Julia's face, back to the pad. There have been primitive people throughout the world who would not permit a likeness to be made of themselves; they believed it took something of the living person away. And it may be that this man, not realizing or understanding it, had some of that nearly instinctive feeling. Because my sketching of Julia enraged him as though in his mind my eyes on her face, my moving pencil taking her likeness, were a kind of deep intimacy. As it is in a way. In any case, it was somehow unbearable to him; more than rage, it was emotion past thought: berserk. His eyes lifted from the pad to my face. They were very small now, the whites reddened, and they were absolutely implacable. He lifted his arm to full length, and his lips parted to bare his teeth like an animal as he pointed at me wordlessly; I don't think there were words for the fury he felt. Then the arm swung in a short arc to point at Julia. His neck looked swollen and his voice was so thick it was hard to understand. He said, "Wait. Stay here. Wait. And I'll show you." Then almost nimbly—the swaying vanished—he swung round on his heel and was gone, the front door opening and slamming an instant later.

I finished the portrait: why not? After the door slammed I looked at Julia, and my mouth opened to say something but all I did was shrug. Nothing to say, except *Well, well, well*, or something just as inane, occurred to me. And Julia forced a smile and shrugged, too, but her face was white and stayed so. I'm not sure why: fear, anger, shock; I don't

For Julia
Affectionately,
admiring by
Simion Morley

know. But she was defiant too, her chin unconsciously lifted through the rest of the sitting, another ten minutes or so.

She liked the portrait: I could tell that she really did by the way she looked at it again and again; and some color came back to her face. My drawing was fully detailed, very literal; it could have been a *Leslie's Illustrated Newspaper* woodcut. But this one was also a good portrait. Not only did it look like her; I was a good enough artist to manage that, given the time and incentive, but it also caught something of Julia herself, of the kind of person she was, so far as I knew. Maybe it *did* capture something of Julia's "soul."

Anyway, it was good. The others had come into the house; Byron Doverman just as I was finishing, and then Maud Torrence, each stopping to admire and praise before going on upstairs. Aunt Ada came in from the kitchen to call upstairs, saying dinner would be on the table in five minutes. She admired the drawing too, and then insisted, since I was still here, that I stay for dinner. And unless I wanted to look as though I were running from Jake, leaving Julia to face him alone, I had to stay, and I said I would; the harm, if any, was already done. I was afraid, I realized—I didn't know *what* the hell this guy might do—but I was curious, too. Still admiring her portrait, Julia looked up at me and asked me to sign it. I took it, fumbling in my pocket for the pencil, trying to figure out what to say: I couldn't just write my name and nothing more. Then I thought, "In for a penny, in for a pound," or whatever the saying is, and I wrote "For Julia—Affectionately, admiringly," mentally adding, *And to hell with you, Jake,* and signed my name.

In the time I'd been here I'd thought almost not at all of Rube Prien, Dr. Danziger, Oscar Rossoff, Colonel Esterhazy, or even the project itself; they were motionless in my mind, at the small far-off end of the telescope, dwindled and remote. But at dinner they turned real again: what were they going to think of what I'd have to tell them? That I'd disturbed and interfered in events with inexcusable clumsiness? Probably; and maybe they'd be right, yet I didn't know how I could have avoided it. The talk at dinner was all of Guiteau, with a little weather, and I wasn't interested. For me now, Guiteau was once again only a name in an old book; tried, executed, and long forgotten, the world I was preparing myself for hardly even knowing his name anymore. I sat eating mechanically, trying to look as though I were interested, responding when spoken to. But as the project and the people in it returned to life in my mind, I began to recede from this time and place.

I was jerked back into it. We were finishing dinner, Maud Torrence already finished, politely waiting for the others before leaving the table; Felix finishing his bread pudding; Byron holding a cigar, ready to light it as soon as he stood up; the rest of us drinking coffee. We didn't hear the front door open but we felt the draft, the invisible balloon of cold air touching our ankles. I saw Julia, her aunt, and Felix across the table suddenly look up into the parlor, and I turned, with Byron and Maud, to look too.

He was standing in the center of the room directly under the multiple flames of the chandelier, staring in at us—confronting us like a bear on his hind legs. Still wearing his unbuttoned overcoat, his top hat still far back on his head and shining dully under the overhead light, he stood with his arms dangling straight down, fingers limp, shoulders deeply bowed, head thrust forward. He just *stood* there, swaying a little again, and we had time to see that he'd been hurt, apparently; that his tie was gone, his shirt collar open and slightly torn, that the first couple of studs below it were gone too, and that across his chest the soiled white of his shirtfront was speckled with blood. We even had time—sitting there motionless, staring across the tabletop or turned in our chairs—to see that the speckles of blood were growing, small spots enlarging, bigger ones expanding, then joining. He was still bleeding—it took a moment or so to understand and formulate the thought—then Julia cried, *"Jake,"* her voice frightened and concerned, and she stood up so quickly the back of her knees knocked her chair over backward, and I noticed, foolishly, that it made very little sound toppling onto the carpet.

She started around the table toward him; now we were all pushing chairs aside, getting to our feet. But Jake flung both hands up and out, fingers spread like claws, halting us, freezing us where we stood—Julia motionless at a corner of the table, the rest of us half standing or sinking back into our chairs. Through a moment or two he looked at us, his teeth bared, yellow and strong-looking. Then his hands moved to his chest, each hand gripped an edge of his shirtfront, then pulled the bloody shirt apart, exposing his chest. It was hairy at the sides, black and matted, but more sparsely at the center, the skin there very white and visible under the separate hairs. He wasn't wounded or hurt; not accidentally, that is, and not very much. The blood swelling out of his skin in slow drops that, no longer blotted up by the cloth of his shirt, enlarged now and rolled down out of sight came from dozens and dozens and more dozens of needle pricks.

Incredibly, his chest was newly tattooed; with five blue-black letters at least two inches high. I wanted to laugh at the absurdity or protest or squeeze my eyes shut and pretend this wasn't happening; I didn't know *what* I wanted to do or what I felt—but the tattooed letters on his chest spelled *Julia*. He said, "All my life now, I will bear this," and he tapped his chest. He said, "Nothing can ever remove it. Because all of my life you will belong to me, and nothing can ever change that." He looked at us, his eyes moving across all our faces; then he turned, and with absolute dignity walked toward the hall and the stairs to his room, and I didn't want to laugh. It was an absolutely absurd gesture, an almost inconceivable action in the century I was used to. But not here. Here and now, there was nothing absurd about it. There couldn't be: This man *meant* it.

Julia was hurrying across the dining room, paler than ever now; then, running a little, she crossed the parlor, and we heard her running steps up the carpeted stairs. I'd left my packed bag in the hallway, my coat and hat hanging on the big mirrored stand there, and I didn't stay; I wasn't needed. I turned to Aunt Ada, said I had to leave immediately, and she smiled distractedly, shaking my hand across the tabletop, and murmuring good wishes. I said goodbye to the others, who replied with their eyes flicking toward the staircase in the hall. And then I was outside, walking toward Twenty-third Street.

At Lexington Avenue I took a hansom cab and sat back with my eyes closed. I had no interest at all just now in anything outside. I paid off the cab at Fifty-ninth and Fifth Avenue, where Kate and I had come out of Central Park. And now I walked back into it, and then along the paths, under the occasional lights, heading north and west through the dark unchanging park; and presently, ahead, I saw the gabled bulk of the Dakota, its gaslighted windows, and the flickering candle and kerosene lights of the truck farms beside it.

16

I GAVE MYSELF a vacation next day. I convinced myself I deserved it and I knew I needed it: needed a transition between the two worlds and times. I'd slept in the Dakota apartment, and while I doubted that I had to do this anymore, I induced a light hypnosis just before going to sleep. Lying in the darkness in the big carved-wood bedstead in the same nightgown I'd worn at 19 Gramercy Park, I knew that far downtown the old post office stood, its lobby lighted by a few globed gas jets; that the big thermometer in its narrow wooden sentry-box stood before Hudnut's Pharmacy in the darkness of lower Broadway, probably registering close to zero with no one to look at it now; that a few tiny locomotives were following the beams of their kerosene headlamps along the El tracks over the cobbled late-at-night streets of New York. But in the morning, I told myself, I would awaken back in my own time. I began to wonder how I'd feel about that this time, but you're entirely relaxed in self-hypnosis, more than halfway.to sleep, and before I could really begin thinking I was asleep all the way.

In the morning, lying in bed for a few moments after opening my eyes, I felt certain I knew where and when I was, and several seconds later had proof. I heard a sound I knew but couldn't place for an instant: a far-off, high and faintly ominous whine. Then I said it aloud— "A jet"—but I hadn't really needed that sign: I already knew I was back, I could feel it.

Walking out of the Dakota onto Seventy-second Street half an hour later, I turned west, on my way to the warehouse and project, I thought. And then without any previous thought and without knowing why, I swung around, walked back to the street corner, and turned south.

I walked for block after block after block then, down through modern Manhattan—looking no different in my round fur cap, long overcoat, and my beard, mustache and long hair, than many another man I passed. I knew I ought to at least phone the project, and Kate. But instead I did what I wanted to do: I walked downtown, pausing momentarily at curbs to wait for flashing red DON'T WALK signs to turn green and say WALK; and I looked around me at today's streets, buildings, and people.

There is an astonishing amount left in New York of other times. You don't think so of New York, but once you're out of midtown Manhattan it's true. And presently, below Forty-second Street, I began to recognize buildings, and whole groups of buildings, that had survived from the eighties and earlier. But these weren't the similarities I was hunting for now; I was looking for them in people's faces, and I'm obliged to say I found hardly any.

I'm certain it wasn't a matter of clothes, of makeup or its absence, or of hair styles. *Today's faces are different*; they are much more alike and much less alive. On the streets of the eighties I saw human misery, as you see it today; and depravity, hopelessness, and greed; and in the faces of small boys on the streets I saw the premature hardness you see now in the faces of boys from Harlem. But there was also an *excitement* in the streets of New York in 1882 that is gone.

It was in the faces of women moving along the Ladies' Mile and into and out of those splendid lost stores. Their faces were animated, they were glad to be just where they were, alive in that moment and place. It showed in the faces of the people I saw in Madison Square. You could look at their eyes as they passed and see the pleasure they felt at being outdoors, in the winter, in a city they liked. And the men of lower Broadway hurrying along the walks, conscious of time and money, stopping at noon to check the precision of their big watches with Western Union's red time-ball—well, their faces were often abstracted; some were worried; some were greedy or anxious, others complacent and going-to-live-forever. All sorts of expressions just as today, but they were also interested in their *surroundings*, pausing to check the temperature at Hudnut's giant thermometer. And above all, they carried with them a sense of purpose. You could see that: They weren't *bored*, for God's sake! Just looking at them, I'm convinced that those men moved through their lives in unquestioned certainty that there was a reason for being. And that's something worth having, and losing it is to lose something vital.

Faces don't have that look now; when alone they're blank, and closed in. I passed people in pairs or larger groups who were talking, sometimes laughing, occasionally more or less animated; but only as part of the group: They were shut off from the street around them, alien and separate from the city they lived in, suspicious of it, and that's not how New York was in the eighties.

I tested my impression. At Twenty-third Street I turned west, and walked to within half a block of Madison Square. Then I stood on the curb out of the way of pedestrians and looked at it, up ahead. From here it looked the same, physically. And people passed through and around it. But no one, and I'm certain you could see this, took any particular pleasure in it. New York *was* once a different place, and in many many ways.

Except for its uptown side, which was all solid apartments now, Gramercy Park was precisely the same, and so was Number 19. Once more now I stood on the walk looking up at it. There were lowered venetian blinds in the first-floor windows but no other change I could see, and it seemed impossible that Julia and her aunt weren't somewhere inside it doing their morning's work. For once I let myself act on impulse before it had a chance to fade. I ran up the steps, and—another difference, but I shut my mind to it—pushed the electric bell. After fifteen seconds or so just as I was changing my mind, a woman opened the door and stood looking at me, brows lifted questioningly. She had thick white hair tied back off her forehead by a band; she was in her forties, I thought, but with a girl's figure, and she wore orange-colored pants, a matching turtleneck sweater, and a vest of some sort of silvery cloth. She looked very nice, and I pulled off my hat, and said, "I'm sorry, but—I knew the people here once. Some years ago. A Miss Julia Charbonneau and her aunt. But I can see they don't live here now."

"No," she said pleasantly. "We've lived here nine years, and the people before us were here for four; and their name wasn't Charbonneau."

I nodded, as though it were to be expected, as it certainly was. I was postponing the moment of leaving so that I could look into the hall, and she very politely stepped aside a little so that I could see better. The walls were papered in a fragile-looking blue pattern on white, and a magnificent crystal chandelier hung from the ceiling. The hall looked expensive and utterly different, except for the black-and-white-tiled floor; that was the same.

She didn't ask me to look at the rest of the place, of course; not in New York. And I smiled and nodded to show I'd seen enough, thanked her, and left. I don't quite know why I went there; I just wanted to see it, that's all. I walked back to Twenty-third Street, and took a cab to the project.

In nearly every possible way the atmosphere at the project was different this time. The man at the door in the tiny street-level office was Harry, or so it said in red stitching over a breast pocket of his white-coverall Beekey uniform. He sent me up alone in the elevator to Doc Rossoff's office, as instructed, he said, if I should show up here. But there was only Oscar's nurse when I arrived, the big good-looking woman with the gray in her hair. She smiled and greeted me and asked the usual questions but I detected a lack of real interest, I thought; probably to be expected. She had me wait in Oscar's office; she'd phone him, she said, and he'd be here very quickly.

As he was, walking swiftly in four or five minutes later, his hand moving out to shake mine, greeting me just as he had done before, congratulating me, asking questions, his voice eager—except that it wasn't the same either. He was abstracted, I realized after I'd talked for a minute or so, only half listening to my answers, sometimes nodding absently before I'd finished a reply. I soon had the feeling that he wanted to get rid of me, anxious to hurry back to whatever he'd been doing. Because he hustled me off to the "debriefing" room without even an offer of coffee, which wasn't like him, and there'd been a Silex half full on his office hot-plate.

The differences continued. This time none of the others had come hurrying into Oscar's office to see me. And Oscar left me at the door of the debriefing room, asking me to dictate a brief but complete account of this last visit, gave me a clap on the shoulder, and hurried off. Inside the room there was only the technician who ran the recorder. He was threading in a new roll of tape, and he just said hi, and nodded. A moment or so later the girl who made the transcript on the electric typewriter came in, smiled at me meaninglessly, and I sat down and talked an account into the little microphone on my chest of what had happened with me during the previous two days, making it brief but omitting nothing. That done, I began reciting my random list of names, facts, and anything else that might be verifiable that came into my head.

After twenty minutes I asked where everyone was, and the guy who sat watching the recorder reels, occasionally fiddling with the dials, said they were having a big meeting; it had begun yesterday, and continued today. That both explained and did not explain, and I realized I was experiencing a childish feeling of neglect.

He kept me at the debriefing twice as long this time. After forty-five minutes or so I said I'd run dry but he said he'd been instructed to ask me to keep at it, if I could, for a couple of hours—an hour and a half at least. We all three got some lousy instant coffee from a machine just outside in the corridor, then stood around for a few minutes forcing it down, talking over the weather lately, about which I wasn't much help. I had the impression that they'd been told not to question me about this visit because they didn't mention it, and after five minutes we resumed the debriefing. I kept it up for over an hour and a half, though with longer and longer pauses. For as long as two or three minutes, after a while, I'd have to search my mind for something else to add. About every twenty minutes or so the tall bald man who'd done this before came in, and took away whatever the girl had typed.

Finally Oscar Rossoff came back. I was nearly finished, scraping the bottom of the barrel. When he opened the door I was just speaking the name of a boy I'd last known in seventh grade when he'd moved away and whom I hadn't thought of again till this moment. Oscar sat down— he looked tired, his shirt collar unbuttoned, his tie pulled down—and sat waiting, staring morosely into a corner of the room. I said that Arizona had been admitted to the Union as a state in 1912; then I stood up, stretching, and said I was finished absolutely.

The girl typed the last of what I'd just said, and pulled the sheet from her machine. The recording technician stopped the tape, snapped and broke the tape between the two reels, and took off my reel. Oscar said, "Tell Freddy to wait till he's completely finished before he reports, okay?" And they nodded, and left.

He gestured to a chair beside him, I sat down, and he said, "We're in a meeting, Si; a great big fat one. It looks as though we may wash out the whole project, I don't know yet. We want you in the meeting but I have to brief you first; no need to interrupt it for that. It's simple enough. We haven't bothered you with this, but other attempts have been going ahead, too, both during your own and before. The Vimy Ridge attempt failed. There's a section of battlefield there left untouched since World War One: Franklin Miller came out of a dugout where he'd waited in the mud with an infantry platoon through a four-day simulated artillery bombardment, and fighting body lice. Real ones. But what he came out onto was nothing but a great stretch of empty fields, the barbed wire rusted and the trenches caved in, half a century after Armistice Day. He's already back home in California.

"To everyone's surprise and even astonishment, the Notre Dame attempt may have succeeded. For something less than even a full minute, before he lost his mental grip on the situation and was instantly back in the here and now. But we *think*—I'll tell you all about this sometime—that during the space of maybe half a dozen deep excited breaths he was standing on the banks of the Seine at three o'clock one morning in the winter of 1451; Jesus. And the Denver attempt succeeded absolutely. Ted Brietel stood in the little corner grocery store drinking a bottle of pop he'd bought, chatting with the proprietor. Then he walked out into Denver, Colorado, 1901, no question about it; just like you. And he was debriefed like you after half a very careful day there. That's what the meeting is about, Si; we were at it till one thirty last night, and back at it by eight forty-five this morning." Oscar frowned, squeezed his eyes shut, and dug the heels of his hands into his eye sockets, trying to rub away a headache or a bad night's sleep or both.

He looked at me, blinking, then said, "Because there's something doesn't jibe, Si. In the debriefing, I mean. He named a friend he went to college with: Knox College in Galesburg, Illinois. Ted's seen him a few times since. He lives in Philadelphia where Ted does; listed in the phone book there. Except that now he isn't. No one ever heard of him at the place he worked. He is unlisted in Social Security records. There is no record of him at Knox. He doesn't exist, you see." Oscar kept his voice matter-of-fact. "Except in Ted's memory, and Ted's alone. Because whatever Ted did and saw and however circumspectly in Denver, Colorado, in midwinter of 1901, it affected an event or events there: Something changed, and therefore so did subsequent events deriving from it." Oscar shrugged a little. "So that now that particular guy was never born, that's all. As for what else may have changed, what else may be different about these times now, things Ted Brietel *doesn't* happen to know about—well, who can say? Maybe a lot, maybe nothing else at all." We sat staring at each other for a moment or so; then Oscar stood up abruptly. "That's what the meeting is all about; come on."

People glanced up at us when we entered the big conference room; it was crowded now, nearly every chair filled. Some nodded at me abstractedly, smiling a little, but immediately returning their attention to Dr. Danziger, who was speaking quietly. I watched him, too, as Oscar and I pulled out chairs and sat down. He looked at ease, which is more than most of the others did; most coats were off, most ties pulled down, people weren't bothering to try not looking tired, and there was a lot of smoking, a lot of doodling on scratch pads. But Danziger sat well back in his chair, his brown double-breasted suit coat open, his tan sweater-vest buttoned, legs crossed comfortably, one arm resting on his chair back, his big veined hand dangling limp and relaxed. ". . . knowledge we now have susceptible of prolonged study," he was saying. "You don't have to bring up the entire bottom of the ocean and into the laboratory. To fully analyze the core from a single boring and consider the implications of that analysis takes months, even years. This is how we must treat the knowledge, the borings if you will, of our three successful attempts. They'll be studied and can yield new knowledge for years. But there can *be no more of them*"—his posture didn't change but his voice deepened into a tone of authority I wouldn't have cared to challenge—"because it is not true, it is simply not true, that we ought to continue doing something just because we've discovered we can. It is becoming more and more certain, as science uses an almost brand-new ability to pull apart the deepest puzzles of the universe, that we need not and should not necessarily do something only because we've learned how. In company such as this I don't have to spell out obvious examples and consequences of failing to understand that. The lesson is clear. And the danger of even one more attempt is just as clear. We dare not ever again step into the past. We dare not ever again interfere with it in any least possible way. Because we don't know what *is* the least possible way. We don't yet know the consequences of Mr. Morley's most recent visit, but if we should seem to have escaped any very serious consequences of the few cautious successes we've had, it's only blind good luck. A man of no apparent importance, though I'm sure he was important to himself, no longer exists. Never *did* exist, in a very strange yet true sense." The tall bald man came in, actually tiptoeing. Colonel Esterhazy saw him right away, raised his arm, and the man walked quickly to him, handed him a little sheaf of paper, murmured something into Esterhazy's ear, who nodded, and the man tiptoed out again. Danziger continued. "Otherwise our world seems essentially unchanged. But next time might be different; unimaginably, catastrophically different. To continue this project would be the grossest kind of utterly selfish and reckless irresponsibility. I think we had to have this meeting; we had to talk this out in absolutely full detail. But there can be no question of our decision; there is no choice to be made."

He stopped, and looked around the table as though wondering if, although doubting, there might be a question. Half the table's length away a man started to raise his hand, lowered it, then lifted it again. I'd forgotten his name; it was the young history professor from one of the eastern universities who looked more like a television comic to me. Danziger nodded at him, frowning, and the man's face pinkened. Sounding like a professor, at least, he said, "Of course you are entirely right, Dr. Danziger. And I certainly don't dispute it. I haven't attended all these meetings, haven't been able to, and I don't pretend to understand a great deal of what we've done. I am only wondering—I really hate to give this up, if this is at all possible—if a way couldn't be found to introduce what I'd call the absolute spectator. Unknown, unseen, affecting no event whatsoever. A man hidden, utterly concealed, at the first performance of Hamlet; my God. Concealed far in advance of audience and actors, remaining hidden long afterward. Or an absolute spectator at—well, there's at least one of Disraeli's meetings with his Cabinet that I'd give my soul to know all about; no one really knows, and it's important. Could this possibility of the absolute spectator be studied, is all I'm asking. In search of a way . . ."

But Danziger had begun shaking his head slowly, and the man's voice trailed off. Danziger said, "I understand what you're saying. And I understand the temptation because I feel it, too. But there could *be* no concealment that was absolutely certain; I'm sure you see that. And if it isn't absolutely certain, the risk is still there. And the risk can't be taken; we have learned that, and it can't be argued away." He sat waiting. But no one else said anything, and presently Esterhazy spoke in a mild conversational way.

He said, "I think I could almost repeat word for word what Dr. Danziger has said; that's how closely I've listened. As I hope all of you have. The wisdom of Dr. Danziger's advice simply isn't debatable." He made an apologetic little gesture with his hand. "We haven't *quite* talked this out, though," he said as though hating to contradict Dr. Danziger about even this small point. "Not in full detail yet. Because I have some information now we didn't have a few moments ago." Rube was sitting beside Esterhazy, in a white shirt, his tie pulled down. He had the typed pages that had been brought in a few minutes ago, and was reading them, slumped in his chair, and Esterhazy nodded at the typescript, saying, "We've just received the report of Mr. Morley's debriefing: both a full summary of what happened, which is absolutely fascinating, and of the test result. The carbon is being Xeroxed now, and we'll soon have copies for everyone. Meanwhile, and this is what's important, we know the full result of his debriefing analysis. Mr. Morley was gone not just for hours this time, but during two days, and this time his contacts were far more than casual and momentary. It was a calculated risk; we took it, and now we have the result." Rube glanced up at him, and Esterhazy nodded to him. Rube glanced down at the typescript in his hand, then summarized what it said.

"No change whatsoever," he said in a flat, factual monotone. "Absolutely everything checks out okay."

Esterhazy nodded almost imperceptibly, and almost a little sadly; it was a gesture suggesting that facts being facts, neither of his making nor within his control, there was nothing he could do but accept them. "That being so," he said in a voice to match the gesture, "I'm sure it's plain that we simply wouldn't be doing our full duty—to Dr. Danziger, to the project itself, nor to anyone—if we didn't also discuss the meaning of that." He glanced around the table as though inviting discussion, and Rube spoke immediately.

"Okay," he said as though accepting an invitation to start things off, "what are the facts? No result, no changes, no harm from what we think was a visit, however brief, to the city—the village, I suppose—of Paris, in 1451. And if any chain of events had been altered, it's had a long time to grow. No result, no changes, no harm from Si Morley's first brief visit. None from his second visit which was quite extensive, involving a trip half the length of the city and on which he had company. And now: no result, no changes, no harm at all from a visit of two days during which he lived in a house full of people, and not only interfered with but actually precipitated events which"—he nodded at the typescript on the table—"I'd find hard to believe if I didn't know what feeble powers of invention he has." He grinned down the table at me, and there was a murmur of mild laughter.

His grin fading, Rube shrugged the big muscled hump of one shoulder, and said, "To sum up: Brietel caused a change, yes. But a slight one." He looked quickly over at Danziger. "Important to the man it affected, certainly, but—"

"And who was not consulted," Danziger said, "about whether he cared to make the sacrifice."

"That's true, and I'm sorry. But compared with the potentially enormous benefit to the rest of the world, I repeat—and I think it's realistic—the change was slight. Even more important, the effect of all of our other successful attempts, of far longer duration and involvement, was zero. Nil. Suggesting that Brietel's result was simply a long-shot accident. So that in considering whether to continue, and with absolute respect for Dr. Danziger's opinions, I suggest that a case can also be made out for the calculated risk."

"*God damn it!*" Danziger's fist slammed down onto the tabletop and an ashtray jumped, made a half turn in the air, and fell face down on the table, scattering butts and ashes and spinning like a coin till it clanked to a stop. Over its sound Danziger was saying, "*What* calculation! I despise the phrase! Risk, hell, yes! Plenty of risk!" He swung around in his chair to glare at Rube, leaning far over the tabletop toward him.

"But *show me your calculations!*" There was a long silent pause, Danziger glaring at Rube, during which Rube did not turn away or avert his eyes, but he blinked benignly several times to show no hostility and that he wasn't in a contest to stare Danziger down. Then Danziger leaned back and said quietly, "What do we know? We know that in one out of four or possibly five successes we have affected the past. And therefore the present. And that is *all* we know. That next attempt could be disastrous. There is no case at all, Rube, for a calculated risk. Because there is *no calculation*, but only risk. Who has given us the right to decide for the entire world that it should be taken?" He stared at Rube for a moment longer, then looked slowly around the table as he spoke. "As the head of this project and as its originator, I say—I'll order it if I have to—the project must be discontinued, except for study of what we already have. There is no one who could possibly hate this necessity more than I do. But it must and it is to be done."

There had to be a pretty long silence after that, and there was. When Esterhazy finally spoke it was so tentatively and regretfully that it clearly seemed very painful to him. He said, "I . . ." and stopped, swallowing. "I . . . simply cannot bring myself to dispute anything at all that Dr. Danziger might have to say about this project. The urge to suggest that we adjourn for a time, and think about all this, reflect on it, is strong. But many of you have come a long way. And no one expected to have to spend this additional day; I don't think we *can* wait. And so, since this has been brought to a head, I'm obliged to, not dispute but *remind* you—I have to *do* this, Dr. Danziger!—that any vital decision affecting the project must be made by a majority of four senior members of this board, the President himself casting a fifth deciding vote if necessary. Of these four members Dr. Danziger is, of course, the first, the others being Mr. Prien, Mr. Fessenden, the Presidential representative, and myself. I'm certainly not going to make any sort of formal issue of this, but of course it's clear what Dr. Danziger feels, just as clear what Mr. Prien and I think. So, Mr. Fessenden, what about you? Have you reached a decision yet?"

I didn't know who he was till he spoke, or rather cleared his throat preparatorily. He was about fifty years old, pretty bald, though with a skein of gray-brown hair combed straight over the top of his head from the side, concealing the baldness from himself, at least. His face was pretty full below the cheekbones, and he wore glasses with metal rims so thin they almost looked rimless. If I'd ever seen him before, he'd made no impression on my memory. He said, "I'd want to consider my vote, if it ever came to that. At length. Sleep on it. But in fairness, I ought to say that I feel I would join with you."

Esterhazy opened his mouth to say something, but Danziger spoke first. "That's it, then? That's the decision?"

Esterhazy began, "I don't think there's any formal—" but Danziger cut him off, brusquely, rudely. "Quit fooling around; that's the decision!" He waited a moment, then barked out the word. "Well?"

Esterhazy pressed his lips together and shook his head; a painful moment. "It has to be, Doctor. It simply has—"

"I resign." Danziger stood up, turning to shove his chair back so he could get away from the table.

"Wait!" Esterhazy stood up. "We simply can't let this happen this way. I want to talk to you. Alone. In just a few minutes."

I had to give the old man credit: I hadn't ever seen him in an undignified moment, and I didn't now. No stalking out, no violent refusal; that kind of drama was distasteful to him. He did hesitate for a moment, then he said, "Of course. But it has already happened: No one will change or go back. I'll wait for you in my office, Colonel." Then in a complete silence he walked to the door and was gone.

"I don't like it," said a voice down the table, and we all turned to look at him. It was a young but plump and bald man, from one of the California universities, I thought I remembered. He looked intelligent, and he looked mad. He said, "I don't have a vote, much of a voice, or even much of a stake in this; I'm a meteorologist, here mainly to report to my own university. But I'm not going to leave without asking how we have the nerve to do anything but accept Dr. Danziger's opinion and decision."

"Hear, hear! As the British say," someone else called out, his voice sounding pleased, the kind of guy who really enjoys a fight as long as it's between two other guys.

I'd thought Colonel Esterhazy would reply but Rube stood up; slowly, entirely at ease and taking his time, and completely—this popped up in my mind—in command. He said, "How? Because you don't turn back. Not ever. You don't spend billions preparing to send a man to the moon, and then decide not to. Or invent the airplane, look it over, and decide to uninvent it because someday someone might use it to drop a bomb. You just don't *stop* something as enormous as this; the human race never has. Risk? Yes, maybe. Yes, *certainly*. But who did that ever stop? Anyone whose birthday has become a national holiday? We are *going ahead*. We—"

"Who's 'we'?" an angry voice called out; I never did know who.

"All of us," Rube said quietly, leaning forward over the table, supporting his weight on his knuckles, "who have put in endless time and enormous effort on this: an important part of our lives. *Think*, goddammit! Can you actually imagine this being stopped? Dropped? Forgotten? It just ain't gonna happen, gents. So why sit around and clatter our teeth about it?"

That ended it, really, though the talking went on for a while. Copies of my report and test result arrived, and were passed out; each one was numbered, and had to be read and returned before the board left the room. A fair number of people glanced up from their copies to look at me, smile, and shake their heads in amazement, and I managed to grin back at them. The discussion continued through this, some agreeing that the project should be cautiously continued, some questioning or at least wondering aloud about it. I think more than one man there hadn't previously understood how little his presence on the board had to do with making its policies. The meeting ended with Esterhazy reminding the members, most tactfully, that everything they knew about the project was very strictly classified information. They'd be notified, he said, when the next meeting was to take place; meanwhile he thanked them for coming.

Rube knew I had a decision to make, and he was right at my elbow when I left the conference room. In the corridor he invited me to come out to a bar on Sixth Avenue we'd been in once or twice, and where we could get some lunch. I said I wanted to see Dr. Danziger first, and we walked along together to his office. But Danziger's girl said Colonel Esterhazy was in with him, which I don't think surprised Rube, and that it looked as though he'd be there for quite a while. I was starved, so I went out with Rube, and we had lunch: a big bowl of vegetable soup and a pastrami sandwich each, with a couple of steins of beer. We sat in the last booth in the back corner, a brick wall beside and behind us, no one near enough to overhear.

I won't detail every word we said. We gave our orders, and then Rube pointed out very factually and low-key that while they hoped I'd continue with the project—new candidates weren't easy to come by, and training them was a long slow job—I was nevertheless not essential to the project. If I didn't continue, it would distress them but I could eventually be replaced. I knew that, of course. At least I knew it was a real possibility, if not quite the certainty Rube was trying to make it sound. And it gave me a little chill to hear it said, because there was no way I could deny to myself that the thought of never going back would be hard to accept. But all I did was nod and say, Sure, but that continuing with the project wouldn't help my conscience if I decided it was wrong.

Our sandwiches came, we began to eat, and Rube was halfway through his and enjoying it, before he put it down on the cardboard plate, and leaned over the table to answer me. His voice inaudible a yard away, he said, "Si, Dr. Danziger is an old man. Recognize that. And what's happened so far on the project is enough—for him. For him it's a culmination; he achieved what he set out to do. And if that should be all there is, he could be content. I love him; I really do. But he's an old man obsessed with risk. Listen to him long enough, and you'll think that if you sneezed too loud back in January 1882, you might somehow set off a chain of events that could blow up the world. But it wouldn't; it would have no more effect than it would right here and now. Try it, Si!" He grinned at me, and picked up his sandwich again. "Go ahead! There are a couple of dozen people in here; sneeze. And not a goddam thing will happen. Hell, people don't get married or not married or do anything else of any importance because of the routine trivial action of some stranger. You didn't even set off this guy Pickering. That's obviously his nature, it's how he acts, and he'd behave accordingly with or without you. And it doesn't matter anyway; really important events aren't casually brought about. They're the result of so many intertwined important forces that they're inevitable, no one thing causing them. Unless you went back and deliberately did something so vital that it *had* to alter a large event, you aren't going to affect much of anything. You want some dessert?"

I said no, and Rube ordered apple pie and another stein of beer. I didn't say much or argue with him. I sat looking doubtful, and probably confused, because that's how I felt. Rube ate quickly, a quarter of his slice of pie at a bite, followed by a fourth of his stein of beer. Suddenly, impulsively, he grinned at me, a wonderfully likable guy, and said, "Si, stay with us, for crysake. You haven't done a damn bit of harm so far, it's affected nothing at all, and we have the proof of that. And that's how it'll be from now on if you're careful."

We talked a little more of what had happened to me at 19 Gramercy Park, while Rube sat comfortably back in a corner of the booth with a cigar; and I told him something of what I felt about New York then and now. And he listened and asked questions, absolutely fascinated. He said, "I can't do it, you know. I tried long before I met you, and I just can't achieve it; Lord, how I envy you." He glanced at his watch, then sat up reluctantly; he started to slide out of the booth, then suddenly reached across the table and put a hand on my forearm. "I don't really have to argue with you, Si, because you see it as well as I do: The project can't be dropped, it just can't. And since you want to stay with it, there's just no sense in not staying." I didn't nod or murmur any sort of agreement, but I didn't say no, either. Rube slid out of the booth, I stood up with him, and on the way back to the warehouse we talked football. Even now I feel ashamed; I have no excuse. I just could not give up the chance to go back, I knew it, and that's all there was to it.

When we got back Danziger had already left, for good—as I might have guessed, and probably had. But his girl gave me his address and phone number; he lived in an apartment building in the Bronx. I used her phone, and called but got no answer; he probably hadn't had time to get there yet, and might not have gone straight home. When I hung up, I stood with my hand on the phone for a moment or so longer, but didn't dial Kate; was I postponing getting in touch with her?

A little later, walking across town toward her shop, I thought about it. I'd been too busy, I started to tell myself, with hardly a moment to phone Kate. But while that was true, it wasn't the whole truth. Was the reluctance—it had been there, I had to admit it—connected with Julia?

Well, the electricity had flowed faster whenever I'd been around her, that was true, but I didn't think it was Julia.

Maybe it was the news I was going to have to give Kate: that Ira's father had been, simply, a crook; a swindler and grafter. But he was dead long before Kate was born, was no relation anyway, and the news couldn't hurt Ira. I didn't *know* what it was, and just moseyed along through the streets till I got to her shop.

Kate was there; she was just coming into the shop from the little back workroom when I opened the shop door and the bell jangled. She'd been stripping layers of old paint from a chair, wearing blue denims, an old blouse and an apron, and her hands were full of the gunk she was using. So we just leaned toward each other for a little peck of a kiss, and in the workroom I sat on a little keg she had there while she worked on the chair, telling her all about everything. And that was fun, she was so completely enthralled.

After Kate closed the shop we walked a block to the supermarket where she bought a steak and some butter; I went to the liquor store a few doors away and got a bottle of whiskey, then came back and picked up some soda. And when we were upstairs in Kate's little apartment, having our second drink, potatoes boiling in the kitchen, I couldn't understand why I'd hesitated about getting in touch with her. This was the only place I wanted to be, and the hours of being here that still lay ahead all looked very good to me.

Kate had a special interest, of course, in what I had to tell her as we had our drinks and during dinner; she'd seen the time and place I was talking about, had seen or at least glimpsed Jake Pickering. And when I told her about Carmody she hardly moved, just sat with her lips parted, fascinated. When I told her about Danziger, Esterhazy, and Rube, and what I'd decided, she listened, then made a few careful and minimal comments, anxious not to interfere with my decision; I knew she was glad, she couldn't help it, that I was going back.

She got up from the table, went to her bedroom, and returned with her red-cardboard accordion folder, untying the red-string bow as she walked. And once again we looked at the strange little black-and-white snapshot of Andrew Carmody's gravestone. There it stood, mysteriously, among the gone-to-seed dandelions and sparse grass; a cartoonist's gravestone, the top a perfect half-circle, the sides straight, the whole stone sunk low in the ground and a little off kilter. And on the stone, sharp and clear, the strange design: no word, name or date, only the nine-pointed star inscribed in a circle, made from dozens of dots tapped into the stone; the design we'd seen, incredibly, impressed in the snow at the base of a lamp standard, on Broadway, New York, January 23, 1882.

We looked again, marveling, at the blue envelope and the black ink of its address, its ferrous content showing rusty through the black. Kate shook the note from the envelope and read aloud the top portion above the fold, in black. " *'If a discussion of Court House Carrara should prove of interest to you, please appear in City Hall Park at half past twelve on Thursday next.'* " She lowered the note to look at me. "And now we know," she said, her voice awed. "We *really know* what happened in the park. I'm glad Ira didn't." She lifted the note again, and read the portion below the fold. " *'That the sending of this should cause the Destruction by Fire of the entire World'*—oh, *what's* the missing word!—*'seems well-nigh incredible. Yet it is so, and the Fault and the Guilt'* "—she paused to indicate the second missing word or words— " *'mine, and can never be denied or escaped. So, with this wretched souvenir of that Event before me, I now end the life which should have ended then.'* " Kate slid the note back into its envelope. "Do whatever it is they're sending you back for, Si; but find out for *me* what that note means. That's why you're ignoring Danziger, isn't it? You've got to go back; you can't help it." And I nodded.

Esterhazy had the good grace in the morning not to have taken over Dr. Danziger's office. We met in Rube's little cubbyhole, Rube in shirt-sleeves behind his desk, tilted far back in his swivel chair, hands clasped behind his head, grinning at me. Esterhazy half sat, half leaned against a corner of Rube's desk, very neat, almost military in a gray gabardine suit, white shirt, and dark tie. I sat on the one chair facing both of them.

I was to go back and resume, was about all they had to say. They wanted to know whatever else I could learn about Andrew Carmody and what happened between him and Jake Pickering: The historians especially wanted to know, Rube said; they already had a team of two historians with a couple of postgrad student assistants at the Library of Congress digging up whatever they could on his relationship with Cleveland, and a second similar team at the National Archives. Anything I could learn might expand or illuminate whatever they should find out.

The end result of this pilot test project, it was hoped, would be a workable method for enlarging our entire knowledge of history.

On my way back to the Dakota—Rube drove me over—I told myself I was doing the right thing, the only thing; that there was no defect in the arguments I'd listened to and had made myself. But if that was true, I had to wonder, why did I *feel* I was doing wrong? And why, if I was so sure of what I was doing, hadn't I talked to Dr. Danziger? There'd been time to phone him; there still was. But I knew I wasn't going to.

17

IT HAD BECOME habit, leaving the Dakota, to walk out and back into the winter of 1882. I was used to the process now; there were no longer any doubts that it would happen lingering in my mind. Without questioning it I simply knew I was back and accepted it. So it seemed natural, stepping up onto the curb into Central Park—it had snowed during the day—to see horse-drawn sleighs, dozens and dozens and endless more dozens of them gliding along every park roadway as far as I could see.

It was a great sight, and walking along the path I felt that every sense was stirred and I was suddenly keenly aware of the winter actuality of it. My face felt the sharp clean air press onto my cheeks as I walked, and my lungs tasted it, clear and cold. Nearly every passing horse carried harness bells, and the winter air was bright with their sound, the drum of hoofs and the hiss of runners electrically exciting. And there was a special quality, a happy nostalgia, in the sound—high and faintly muffled—of voices outdoors in new snow. A maroon-enameled sleigh, passing close, had side panels painted with winter scenes, some of the horses wore whisks of dyed horsehair or feathers, and I swear that the eyes of every man and woman and child who jingled past me were smiling with the pleasure of the moment.

I stopped on the path and made a quick sketch of the scene. Much later I finished it, working very carefully in the style of the period because it seemed appropriate. It's on the next page. You can see the Dakota in the background, and I wish you could hear the silvery sound of the wonderfully elaborate harness bells mounted on the horses' backs.

Off across the park as I approached they were skating on the pond, and everywhere the park swarmed with kids, belly-flopping onto low wooden sleds, smaller kids bundled to the ears on high spraddle-runnered sleds pulled by older sisters, brothers, or adults. One such passed me pulled by a white-bearded man whose clothes—gaiters, very skinny pants, a strange dull-silk top hat that flared out at the top—were years out of fashion. He must have been far into his seventies, pulling that sled through the snow, and he was smiling; like everyone else I could see in the entire park, he was having *fun*. So was I, and I was suddenly happy to be alive here in this place at this time and moment; I was happy, I realized, to be back.

But I didn't look forward to returning to 19 Gramercy Park; this was Sunday, and Jake Pickering could be home. So I stopped at a saloon on West Fifty-seventh Street—its front door was locked, in deference to the Sunday closing law, I learned, after following two men in through a side door. There I had some soup and two huge sandwiches; I wanted to keep the greetings and questions and especially my first encounter with Jake as brief as possible, going up to my room immediately afterward, and saying I wasn't hungry at suppertime. But when I turned the corner, two big sleighs stood before the house. Felix Grier and a girl I didn't know sat in the front seat of the first one, Felix holding the reins, the girl with Felix's new birthday camera cradled in her lap; Byron Doverman was just helping a young woman into the rear seat. Julia was coming down the steps, carefully because of a layer of new snow, and right beside her Jake, in top hat and dark overcoat with a lamb's-wool collar, held her elbow. Maud Torrence was just behind them, and up on the stoop Aunt Ada stood locking the front door.

They saw me before I could turn away; calling and beckoning. Felix, out of his mind with excitement—over the girl, I imagined—yelled down the street at me. "Welcome home! Just in time for the sleighing party! Mr. Pickering's rented two sleighs!" Waving back feebly, trying to smile as I walked on toward them, I was slamming together an excuse in my mind: tired out; long train ride; coming down with *la grippe*. Because of course I couldn't ride, the fifth wheel, with the two bachelors and their dates; and to ride in the other sleigh, Pickering glowering, then doing God only knew what crazy thing, was impossible. They surrounded me then, Felix leaping out of his sleigh to grab my free hand, the questions popping—how was my brother, how was my family?—welcoming me back, Byron grabbing my hand next, everyone so plainly glad to see me that I felt my eyes smart.

And then my hand was grabbed again, and Jake was pumping it, happily grinning at me! I was trying to respond: My brother was unexpectedly much better; all was well at home; glad to *be* back! But I was staring at Jake, astounded: His big brown eyes were warm and friendly and his smile as he stood shaking my hand was real, as obviously sincere as the others. Julia was smiling at me, so really pleased my heart jumped. She shook my hand, so did Maud, and when Aunt Ada took my hand, she leaned forward and kissed me on the cheek.

And with that, I suddenly *wanted* to go with these people, wanted nothing else more. Aunt Ada took my bag, to unlock the door and set it inside, and Byron and Felix introduced me to their dates: Felix's very young and pretty; Byron's older, and though her face was pocked, an attractive woman, looking quietly intelligent. They politely asked me to ride with them but before I could reply Jake was saying no, I had to ride with *them*, taking me by the elbow, urging me to climb in; and when Julia suggested I ride up front with them, Jake agreed enthusiastically, asking if I wanted "the ribbons," meaning the reins, I realized. I simply gave up trying to figure out what was happening. Jake, I assumed, was a manic-depressive, an emotional pendulum, and I was glad and relieved to let it go at that.

He took the reins after I refused with thanks; the horses would have turned and laughed if I'd tried to drive them. Maud and Aunt Ada sat in back, Julia in front between Jake and me. There's something keenly intimate, I discovered, in being pressed snugly against a girl, waist to knees, underneath a robe. Tucking the robe in on my side, I glanced at Jake but he was grinning, hands on the reins ready to go. It wasn't quite comfortable, pressed shoulder to shoulder, and I brought up my left arm and laid it along the back of the seat behind Julia. But I was careful not to actually touch her; there was no point, no future, in dwelling on how nice it was this close beside her, and I made myself think of the scene, the snow-mounded black-iron fence and trees and shrubbery of little Gramercy Park beside us.

"Ready?" Felix yelled over his shoulder, and Jake exuberantly shouted back that he was. Their reins snapped simultaneously, both teams dug in, and the harness bells came to life. The runners sliding easily, the horses eased back; then at a second snap of the reins as we rounded the corner onto Twenty-first Street, they tossed their heads, snorting jets of warm breath, and began to trot, obviously enjoying themselves, and now the harness bells sang.

All I can really tell you about the rest of that day and the evening is that it was magical. A dream. The white streets of Manhattan were filled with sleighs; the air everywhere was alive with the music of their bells. And if that sounds overly lyrical I can't help it. The weekday wagons and vans were gone, even the horse-drawn buses and cars were rare; the streets and sidewalks were given over to people.

On the walks they were pulling kids on sleds, throwing snowballs, making snowmen; children, adults, old men and women, laughing, calling to each other. And in the streets we passed and were passed by every kind of sleigh, and we called to them and they to us. We raced them sometimes; once, going up Fifth Avenue, we raced three teams abreast, drivers on their feet, whips cracking, girls shrieking, for nearly two blocks before—sleighs coming the other way—we had to fall into single file cheering and shouting. Heading north somewhere in the Fifties, Felix's sleigh half a block behind, Jake turned impulsively into a cross street just as a sleigh coming south swung in, too. Bells jingling, we trotted along side by side, grinning at each other.

It was a big, green-enameled swan's-neck affair, a beautiful sleigh. They were five kids in their late teens and early twenties, and one of the girls, in a red-and-white knitted cap tied under her chin, began singing: *Dashing through the snow! In a one-horse open sleigh! O'er the field we go!* And then all ten of us, everyone but me knowing all the words, came in on *Laughing all the way!* To the exact rhythm of our horses' hoofs and the jounce of our bells, we lined it out: *Bells on bobtail ring! Making spirits bright! What fun it is to ride and sing*—and it was; oh, Lord, it was—*a sleighing song tonight!* Then we roared it: *Jingle bells, jingle bells! Jingle all the way! Oh, what fun it is to ride in a one-horse open sleigh!* For two blocks—people on the walks calling out to us, kids throwing snowballs at us—we sang. Beside me Julia's voice was high, a soprano, very clear, very sweet and lovely, the white mist of her breath punctuating every phrase. Maud was nearly inaudible, Aunt Ada surprisingly youthful and good, Jake a rumbling baritone; and I guess I was a sort of lost-in-the-shuffle tenor. At the corner the kids swung south. Waving and yelling at each other, we headed north toward Central Park, both sleighs continuing to sing as long as each could hear the other.

Felix caught up with us, and in the Park he took the lead, and we all flew along the curving roads with hundreds of other sleighs. Fast as we moved, sleighs raced past us, hoofs drumming, the runners on one side sometimes actually lifting from the snow on the curves. Some of the drivers carried what the others said were fish horns: brass horns they occasionally raised and blew into, producing a single mournful yet somehow exciting blast of brassy sound that hung in the air for a moment afterward. Ahead, Felix pulled over for a shot of the roadway, and we waited behind him as he focused the big red-leather-and-varnished-wood camera, the brass fittings gleaming in the winter light. It came out good, and when I saw it later I asked him for a copy, which he gave me. This is it, and I can't even look at it without smiling with pleasure.

Half a mile farther on Felix saw another shot he wanted, and as we waited behind him and I saw what he was taking—the shot below—I agreed; he had a good eye. They didn't notice us; the mother was getting out a handkerchief for the boy on the sleigh; and I heard the child in the carriage call the older woman "Nanny."

While Felix was taking the shot I walked over to their sleigh. When he finished I told him I'd seen an apartment building across the Park at Seventy-second Street that I admired, and asked if he'd take a picture of it for me. "The Dakota," he said. "Sure! Only *you* take it," and he handed me the camera. I hesitated, but I did want to use it and thanked him, and he showed me how to load in a new dry-plate.

Halfway across the park I asked Jake to stop, and—Felix helping—I took the photo on the opposite page. I like it; it shows how alone the Dakota was. But I didn't allow too well for reflected light from the ice, and, embarrassingly, it's overexposed. There was a man in the middle foreground, for example, wearing a silk topper, and I don't know if you

can see him. We moved on, closer to the Dakota, and—it was a simple camera, really, and a good one—I set it on a stone pillar for a time exposure because the light was failing, and I got a beauty: this one. I couldn't do better with a Leica, Graflex, or anything else, in fact.

On through the park then, and out, and far up past it out into actual open countryside—astoundingly, still on Manhattan Island—until finally we stopped at a big wooden inn called Gabe Case's. It was full dark now, the inn brilliant with light, shining out on the snow in long quartered rectangles, and the place was filled; there were surely fifty sleighs in a great outside shed, the horses tethered and blanketed.

Inside, every table was occupied, the place jammed, the roar of voices and laughter so loud it was almost impossible to talk. Felix had called to me, and I worked my way over to his group, losing mine. We had sandwiches and hot wine, standing up—there wasn't a table empty— talking a little over the roar, but mostly just grinning at each other out of sheer sparkling excitement and joy.

It was an extraordinary afternoon and night, worth a news story in the *Times* next morning, headed "ON THE ROAD" THOUSANDS OF MERRY REVELERS ENJOYING THE SLEIGHING, and it said:

Those persons who owned cutters, ancient sleighs, old piano-box sleds, or any kind of a conveyance on runners, and those who could afford to hire them and were able to sit in them yesterday behind high-bred trotters or horses of low degree, had an opportunity to enjoy themselves after a fashion of their own over the driveways in the Central Park or on the splendid avenues leading out of it. The sleighing was good through Broadway, Fifth-avenue, and all the avenues in the city where there are no street car tracks. The snow-fall gave to the roads the best covering of the season for sleighing, and thousands took advantage of it. A large number of noted horses were on the road, and merchants, bankers, politicians, and professional horsemen passed each other in jolly good humor.

Commissioner of Public Works Hubert O. Thompson, in a delicate cutter, was an object of much interest as he drove in a gentle manner a powerful horse. Commissioner of Jurors George Caulfield, driving a sorrel horse, showed Mr. Thompson the way into Gabe Case's shed, and the latter stepped from his cutter, and seemed to thank Mr. Caulfield for saving his life. Police Justice J. Henry Ford flew over the snow in a stylish cutter drawn by a fast horse, and was not persuaded to stop. John Murphy, the professional driver, sat behind his bay mare Modesty, and flew by like the wind. He was followed by Frank Work, with his team Edward and Swiveller; Joseph Doyle, with his wonderful mare Annie Pond; William Vassar, with Red and Black and Keno; John De Mott, in the most handsome cutter on the road, drawn by the bay gelding Charley; Samuel Sniffen, with his Blackwood Queen; Gen. J. Nay, with his Garryowen; Salvine Bradley, with his team Jack Slote and Hen Seaman; Ike Woodruff, with his Dan Smith; James Kelly, with his brown mare Codfish; Robert J. Dean, with a party in a large sleigh; and John Barry, with his sorrel gelding Gossip.

After dark, when the whole country was white and bright in the moonlight, and the street lamps for miles around seemed like so many lightning-bugs on parade, the fun was at its height, and great sleighs, crowded with laughing and singing young men and women, were rapidly moving in all directions. . . .

We drove home through that night—the others had been waiting for me when we came out of Gabe Case's—and though a wind had come up and it was turning colder, we were snug under our robes, and we sang softly, "The Spanish Cavalier" and, very softly and slowly, "Bring Back

My Bonnie to Me." In the park the snow sparkled, and below it the buildings of Fifth Avenue were awash and mysterious with moonlight, and we drove down through the city marveling. One scene we passed stayed in my mind, and much later I made a watercolor of it; on the opposite page is the scene as I remember it, and I wish I could really show the wonderful actuality of it.

Past the great walls, presently, of the reservoir at Fifth and Forty-second where someday I knew, but the others did not, that the main Public Library would stand; down Fifth, past Madison Square and—I wished there had been light enough for Felix to photograph it—the right arm of the Statue of Liberty, the knuckles of the hand and the tip of the flame mounded with new snow. Then we swung east on Twenty-third Street toward Gramercy Park, and I said, "Mr. Pickering, thank you; it's been one of the finest evenings I ever spent."

He nodded; he was smoking a cigar now, and whenever he puffed, the smoke flowed in a long thinned-out ribbon over one shoulder. He said, "You're welcome, Morley. It was by way of a celebration, you know."

Yes, I know, I thought; *celebrating your chance to get rich through blackmail.* Politely, I said, "No, I didn't."

He nodded again, and leaned forward to get a good look at me across Julia's lap, and I saw something smug and self-satisfied in his eyes. "Yes," he said slowly. He'd postponed this deliberately for most of the evening, I realized later, prolonging the anticipation; now he was tasting the pleasure of saying it. "We looked for you at Gabe's; I wanted you to join us in a toast." The cigar in one corner of his mouth, he grinned at the puzzlement in my face, waiting so long to answer it that Julia—impatiently, I think, though her voice didn't show it—said it instead.

"Mr. Pickering and I have become engaged to be married."

After a moment I said the right things, forming the proper facial expressions. Smiling, I reached across Julia to shake Jake's hand, congratulating him. Still smiling, I agreed with Aunt Ada and Maud that it was wonderful news. Then I grinned at Julia, but as I said, "I hope you'll be very happy," I felt the grin disappear from my eyes, and Julia saw it, and merely nodded shortly, her lips compressing angrily. I asked when and where they were to be married, and sat as though listening to Jake and Aunt Ada respond, but I didn't hear them.

Instead, during the few minutes before we pulled up at the curb

before 19 Gramercy Park, I thought about several things. I thought about the tattooed letters still healing on his chest that marked Jake for life with Julia's name. I'd never been a threat to his future with Julia; that wasn't possible. But he didn't know it, and maybe I might have been if things had been different; that much he'd sensed. Now—his chin and beard lifted high, grinning complacently, cigar smoke trailing over his shoulder—Jake finally had her. To him, I understood, this engagement was a binding contract; she was safe from all threats now, forever his. He really *had* been glad—triumphantly glad—to see me.

But more than Pickering, I thought about Julia, silent here beside me. I didn't believe she was a girl who wanted to be possessed the way Jake thought he possessed her. And I knew, *knew*, she couldn't live out her life and be happy with the kind of degraded human spirit that is able to blackmail. Yet I had to let it happen. Knowing what I knew about Jake Pickering, I had to smile and act pleased, and let this warm, lovely angry girl beside me marry him, and—it would happen—destroy her life. *Dr. Danziger!* I said silently, across the years that separated us. *Do I have to?* But I knew what the answer was: You cannot interfere.

It wasn't possible to just walk into the house, when we reached it, and go upstairs and to sleep. I hopped out of the sleigh to help Julia, her aunt, and Maud Torrence down, and they walked up the stairs calling good-nights. Felix snapped his reins, and he and Byron left in their sleigh to drive their dates home or wherever they were going. Jake stayed in his sleigh to return it to the livery stable, and I think the women assumed I was riding with him. But when the door closed behind them, I made a little saluting gesture of farewell to Jake, and turned toward the stairs. When Jake flicked his reins and drove off, I turned back and walked quickly on to Third Avenue.

I didn't know where I was going, I only knew I had to think, and I walked along down Third, dark and very nearly deserted, for several blocks. But the wind was much stiffer now, the temperature sharply lower and still dropping, I thought. It was snowing again but now it was a hard pelletlike snow, nicking into my face with the wind, gritty underfoot. It wasn't a good night for walking, and at Sixteenth Street I looked back over my shoulder, and a streetcar was trundling along toward me, the horse's head bent to the wind, the kerosene lanterns flickering at the front of the car.

It stopped for me, I got on the front platform, and the horse leaned into his collar, his metal-shod hoofs slipping and sliding heavily in the snow till we got rolling again. Tonight, in this kind of weather with very few passengers, it was a bobtail car, a term I'd heard Byron Doverman use, meaning there was no conductor. Here on the open platform where the driver could watch it hung a fare box, and I dropped in my nickel, opened the door, and stepped in, closing the door against the wind. There was only one other passenger, a derby-hatted, walrus-mustached man reading the *Evening Sun*. I walked down the aisle, crunching dirty wet straw under my feet, and sat down. The tin-shaded lamp hanging from the ceiling smoked badly, and the kerosene smell was very strong.

We rolled along through the windy night and I sat staring absently out at the shabby little Third Avenue stores, a few with dim gaslights far back in the interiors, many with hitching posts and tin-roofed canopies over the walks; some of the blocks we passed through looked like sets in a Western movie. I'd seen all this before and in a way it wasn't much to look at. And yet I stared, never really tired of looking at, never entirely losing the thrill and wonder at being here in, this strange New York.

I once talked with a friend who'd spent a vacation in Paris; like most people he'd loved the city, walking it every day till his legs trembled, pleased with nearly everything he saw. But it wasn't till he'd been there nearly two weeks that one morning Paris and its people suddenly became something more than a background for his vacation. He was sitting in a café, out on the walk, having a tiny cup of Paris-tasting, Paris-smelling coffee, watching traffic stream by, pleased as always with the countless people on bikes expertly threading their way between and around the cars and buses and trucks. Then a traffic light changed, the stream stopped and waited, and a man on a bike, one foot on the pavement, lifted his arm and wiped his forehead with the back of his hand. And he turned real. In that instant he was no longer a quaint part of a charming background; he turned into a real man, tired from pumping that bike, and for the first time it occurred to my friend that there was a reason so many people picturesquely rode bikes through the heavy traffic, and the reason was to save bus fare and because they couldn't afford cars. After that, for the few days that were left to him there, my friend continued to enjoy Paris. But now it was no longer an immense travel poster but a real city, because now so were its people.

Here in the Third Avenue car, my feet ankle-deep in dirty straw but still cold, toes a little numb, I caught a glimpse—through the window of the closed door ahead—of the driver as he drew back on the reins to bring the car to a stop. A middle-aged woman, her face as Irish as an anti-Irish cartoon on a back page of most any *Harper's Weekly*, climbed aboard. She wore a heavy knitted shawl over her gray hair that covered her shoulders too; she had no other coat; she carried a basket on one arm. As she opened the door, the cold air rolling in and stirring the straw in the aisle, I heard the horse's hoofs slipping and clattering for a purchase, heard the crack of the driver's whip, and just as the door closed I saw the driver's body move as he stamped his feet, hearing the muffled sound of it, and he suddenly turned real for me as I understood how cold he must be out there on that open platform.

And then the city, too, turned real, this car no longer a quaint museum piece of the future, but of the here and now: solid, scarred, uncomfortable, dirty because the straw on the floor was stained with tobacco spit, driven by a harassed overworked man and pulled by a badly treated animal. It was cold out on that platform, I knew that, but I got up, walked up front, slid open the door, and stepped out, pulling the door closed behind me. I had to talk to this man.

I had the sense not to start right in. I stood there at his right staring ahead over the horse's swaying rump down the cobbled street under the gloom of the overhead El tracks. My eyes were squinted against the steady pressure of air from our forward motion, and it was so cold they instantly began watering. There were frequent little gusts of a nasty crosswind, and I watched it sift little creeping skims of hard snow onto and off the car tracks. The driver had glanced at me suspiciously; why would I come out here when I didn't have to? And I'd glanced back at him, smiling slightly. He wore a flat-topped round cloth cap with a flap that covered his neck and ears, and over it a ragged knitted tan muffler tied under his chin; he had an immense drooping mustache. He wore a heavy tan cloth coat, very worn; one big pocket, in which a bandanna was stuffed, was half torn off. He had heavy boots, heavy encrusted mittens, and as many clothes, obviously, as he could fit under that coat, so that his body was shapeless. The wavering light from the lanterns hanging from the front of the car shone upward onto his face, and it took me a minute or so after I'd glanced at him to realize that he wasn't old; but his face was permanently gorged, threaded with tiny broken veins, the color of uncooked old beef.

He just stood there, reins loose in his hands most of the time, facing the cold; I couldn't understand why the platform should be *open*. Ahead, a light delivery van with a lighted lantern hung under its rear axle trundled onto Third from a cross street, and, its wheels finding the smoother going of the tracks, settled down into them. It moved a bit slower than we; the car driver clanged his foot bell, and the wagon speeded up.

"Cold," I said then, hunching my shoulders momentarily; it wasn't really a stupid comment but just a word uttered aloud in recognition of his presence.

"Yep. It's cold," he said sardonically.

I was silent for half a dozen hoofbeats. "Do you ever get used to it?" I said then. "After a while? I don't think I could stand it myself."

"Used to it? Well, I should smile." He thought about that for a second or two. "Nah, you don't get used to it. You just get so you can stand it, that's all. If you want to get an idea of what real cold is, just hire yourself out to drive a streetcar in winter. If I was getting up an expedition to the North Pole and wanted a lot of men who could stand the climate, I'd take them from the drivers on the surface roads. Because a man who can stand this sort of service can stand anything." It was a burst of talk; I had the feeling I was the first passenger in a while to give him the chance. We stood silent for half a block; then at a cross street a blast of wind just shrieked across the platform, so impossibly cold the horse actually staggered, and I simply turned my back to it, shoulders hunched, and suffered; I didn't think I could take it, and wanted to go back inside but didn't.

It made him smile a little, made him talk again, when he saw I wasn't going in. "Feels pretty cold, don't it? I see you stamp your feet, and put your hands in your pockets. You stay here very long, and you'll be pretty well frozen out, and glad to get near a stove to warm yourself. But I have to do this all day long; stand out here and face the wind and sleet till my hands are frozen so stiff I can't feel the reins, and my nose has no more feeling in it than an icicle."

"How long do you work?"

"Fourteen hours a day is my working time, and sometimes longer, after the car is washed out and everything attended to. Don't give a fellow much chance to see his family, does it?" I said no, it didn't, and he nodded, and said, "How much do you think we make?" The dam was gone now, the torrent loose; I just shook my head. "A dollar and ninety cents a day. Or a little more for the long routes to Harlem; that is the best we can possibly do. We're supposed to make seven trips a day at twenty-seven-and-one-seventh cents a trip. If the cars are blocked and we don't make so many trips, it is so much out of our pay. You just think about supporting a wife and children on a dollar and ninety cents a day. Most of us work on Sundays; poor people can't afford to rest on the Sabbath in a great city like this. Sometimes when I do have a Sunday off I go to church and take my wife and the children. It seems respectable, somehow, to go. And then the minister gets up and talks about the gratitude we ought to feel to God for all the blessings he gives us, and how thankful we ought to be that we live through his mercy. It may be very true as far as he is concerned, but I often think—and I don't mean to be ungrateful or irreverent—that most people in this world have very little to be thankful for, and very little reason to thank God for life at all. Nine tenths of the people in New York find scarcely a moment in their lives which they can call their own, and see mighty little but misery from one year's end to the other." He was troubled, deeply; his voice showed it; there was an almost inadmissible yet inescapable contradiction he couldn't get out of his mind. "How is it possible for me to thank God in my heart for the food he gives me and for life, while every morsel I eat I earn with my toil and even suffering? There may be a Providence for the rich man, but every poor man must be his own Providence. As for the value of life, we poor folks don't live for ourselves at all; we live for other people. I often wonder if the rich man who owns great blocks of stock in the road and reckons his wealth in the millions does not sometimes think, as he sits at his well-filled table and looks at the happy faces of his children, of the poor car driver who toils for his benefit for a dollar and ninety cents a day, and is lucky if he tastes meat twice a week and can give the little ones at home warm clothes and blankets for the winter.

"Cold, you say. Well, people can get used to anything, I suppose, and we get so used to the cold after a while that maybe we don't mind it much. They used to let us sit down, but a couple of winters ago a man was frozen to death. The car came into the depot, and the driver was found on his stool stiff and stark, with one hand on the brake, and the reins in the other. He had dozed off, and he never woke up. He was a lucky man. The worst place he could go to was warm at least, though I've heard the Eskimos think hell is a cold place. Anyway, he never was obliged to drive a car again at a dollar and ninety cents a day. After that what did the company do: close in the platforms? No, that costs money. A rule was passed that employees should not be allowed to sit down, lest they go to sleep and freeze to death. They say it's a very pleasant way to die, and I believe it, for more than once I've felt myself dozing off and becoming insensible to the cold. But I roused myself and stamped to keep awake, for I thought of the little ones; at least they don't sleep in the hay barges, as they might have to if I was gone."

"Hay barges?"

He looked at me angrily for not knowing. "Where do you think the boys—and yes, the girls, too—who shine your shoes and sell you papers in the daytime sleep at night? They're orphans, most of them, or kids nobody wants, and left to shift for themselves. A few of them sleep in the newsboys' homes and the like, but most sleep anywhere they can. Go down to the East River right now, and shine a light on the hay barges, hundreds of them, tied along the docks and shore. And you'll see the boys—some say thousands, and I think so, too, though nobody rightly knows—curled up in little nests they scratch up for themselves, and some of them not five years old. So I learn to stand the cold for the sake of my own. Sometimes I try to keep warm by an occasional dram of whiskey, but I find the reaction makes you feel all the colder afterward."

Up ahead a man in a derby, wearing a heavy pullover sweater, the top of his gray winter underwear visible at the neck, came running out of a saloon toward the car stop at the corner. As the car slowed for the stop, I decided to get off, and stepped down onto the boarding step wondering what to say to the driver: Good luck? I didn't think so; I didn't think he was ever going to have any. The car stopped, and I looked back over my shoulder at the driver. "Goodbye," I said, and he nodded. "Goodbye."

During my time in the army I was taught how to use your eyes at night; you don't look directly at what you're trying to see. Instead you look off to the side at something else; then, from the corner of your eye, what you really want to see will come clearer. Sometimes the mind works in the same indirect way when you let a problem alone, not forcing an answer. I walked over to Broadway, found a hansom at the Metropolitan Hotel, and by the time I got back to Gramercy Park I knew what I had to do.

It was a long ride up the dark deserted business section of Broadway, but I was out of the wind, wrapped to the waist in a heavy fur robe that was a little mangy, a little smelly, but after a while cozy and warm. The steady unvarying *clap*-clop, *clap*-clop, *clap*-clop of the horse's hoofs, muffled by the steamed-over window glass, was hypnotic, and the thoughts rose in my mind without effort. The city had been a magical place earlier this evening, filled with sleighs and the sound of singing and genuine laughter. But now late at night I understood that it was also the city of the streetcar driver I'd just talked to. And that while I'd been dashing through Central Park in Jake's sleigh, countless lost children were hunting places to sleep at the bottoms of East River hay barges. And now the city was no longer only an exotic background to my own strange adventure. Now it was real, and now I finally understood that I was really here in these times, and that these people were alive. And that so was Julia.

Observe, don't interfere: It was a rule easy to formulate and of obvious necessity at the project . . . where the people of this time were only ghosts long vanished from reality, nothing remaining of them but odd-looking sepia photographs lying in old albums or in nameless heaps shoved under antique-store counters in cardboard boxes. But where I was now, they were alive. Where I was now, Julia's life wasn't long since over and forgotten; it still lay ahead. *And was as valuable as any other*. That was the key: If in my own time I couldn't stand by and allow the life of a girl I knew and liked to be destroyed if I could prevent it, I finally knew that I couldn't do it here either.

Would it be destroyed? I thought about it, and the cab swung off Broadway at Union Square, toward Fourth Avenue, and I wiped the mist from the window with a sleeve, and saw a theater sign under glowing yellow globes: TONY PASTOR'S NEW 14TH STREET THEATRE, it said, and on easel posters at every entrance PATIENCE; OR, THE STAGE-STRUCK MAIDEN. SEE MISS LILLIAN RUSSELL! A GRATIFYING SUCCESS; AN ARTISTIC GEM, and I had an impulse to stop and see the last of the play, but I had too much to think about. Even though I'd known Julia only a matter of hours, actually, I was certain I knew something about her. If you have the ability to make a true portrait of someone, you will learn more about her in the making of it than you otherwise might over days and even weeks of casual acquaintance. I've always appreciated the story you read now and then about the psychiatrist—he would have been called an alienist then—who stood staring at a portrait painted by Sargent or Whistler, I don't remember which. It was a portrait of a man who had been his patient, and after the alienist had studied it for twenty minutes he nodded, and said, "Now I understand what was wrong with him." Well, I'm not Whistler or Sargent, I haven't their talent or insight. But to capture the person on paper or canvas you must observe more than the camera can see. And—yes, I *did* know that for the particular person who was Julia Charbonneau, a life as the wife of Jacob Pickering would change the face I drew into one of permanent bitter unhappiness, and I simply was not going to allow that.

The consequences to the future of interference with the past? I shrugged: There were always consequences to *any* future of every act in the past. To affect the course of an event in my *own* time was to affect still another future unimaginably, yet we all did it every moment of our lives. And now the future which was my own time was going to have to take its chances. Because now I knew that I just wasn't going to let Julia go down the drain as though somehow she didn't matter but we did. I swayed as the cab turned onto Twentieth Street, and then a block later onto Gramercy Park. And as it slowed and stopped before Number 19, I was smiling: I knew now that I was going to find a way somehow to break Julia's engagement to Jake Pickering; and who could say, it had occurred to me, that the consequences to my own time, if any, wouldn't be an improvement? It was a time that could stand some.

18

I was out on the streets in the morning right after a breakfast I could hardly sit still long enough to eat. Aunt Ada served it, along with the *Times*, but I didn't even try to read; I couldn't do anything, really, but think over and over, *This is the day*. Tonight at twelve Pickering and Carmody would meet in City Hall Park. Nothing could keep me from being there too, and I felt I knew intuitively that I was finally going to know what the note in the blue envelope meant. ". . . *the Destruction by Fire of the entire World*. . . ." The words were senseless, they didn't mean *anything*, only—they did: On a day far in the future Andrew Carmody would put a bullet through his head because of them.

I don't know how I could have been so stupid—so just plain *dumb*—but it seemed to me I had nothing to do but fill in the day somehow till it was time to leave for the meeting in the park. I went upstairs and got Felix's camera from his room; he'd said I could, urged me, in fact, and last night at Gabe Case's had repeated the offer. The camera used dry plates which he kept in a box in his closet. He had two dozen of them, so I filled his little varnished-wood carrying case with them. It held ten, and I put another in the camera; there were pictures all over town that I wanted.

Manhattan Island is small; you can cover it from one end to the other in a day, so I took the El down to the Battery first. There was a wait for the train, and I got all focused; the camera had a sliding bellows of red leather, very nice to adjust. I stood waiting for a train then, and out of nowhere a sudden stab of worry pricked my mind: Was there something I ought to be doing, of the utmost importance, instead of this? But the platform was trembling minutely, far down the tracks a train had appeared—from downtown, but it didn't matter to my shot—and I had the camera up, holding it steady till the train moved into focus. This is the shot I got, and by the time I had it and had changed plates, the unresolved doubt had drifted from my mind.

Battery Park was pleasant; a lot of snow, but the paths had been cleared. I saw a scattering of newly arrived immigrants there, getting

their first look at the country, and I couldn't resist a shot of them.

I took the El up to the Brooklyn Bridge then—a real tourist—and climbed the tower by a set of wooden ladders, careful never to look down till I stepped out onto the top of the tower. Without giving myself any chance to think, I started right on across a little temporary wooden suspension bridge strung high over the unfinished permanent roadway. But the thing swayed! The handhold was nothing but thin cable-wire, and there wasn't a thing, if you tripped, to keep you from falling off and down, down, down. It was impossibly high, swinging in a chill winter breeze. With my eyes on the wooden planking along which my feet shuffled, hardly daring to lift, I couldn't help looking between the cracks—at the lead-gray river infinitely far below and the horribly empty spaces of the roadway. Ten steps, and I couldn't go on. I turned around, and two men were walking toward me. There was no room to sidle past them and back to the tower; if I tried I knew I'd fall.

Over a period of time that went on and on and on forever, I forced myself through step after step, the thin handhold sliding through my

clenched hand till my palm was raw and black with dirt. Then finally I stepped off onto the top of the Brooklyn tower, wonderfully solid under my feet, beautifully wide; and I stood swallowing, feeling the sweat of imminent disaster drying on my face.

This is the shot I got up there and I'm proud of it. The two men who had been walking across the bridge behind me, I saw, had stopped in the middle for the view, one of them actually leaning back against the wire handhold; I could hardly look at him. But isn't it a tremendous view? That's Trinity off in the distance to the far left. I felt great now, very glad that I'd—bravely, I tried to tell myself—made the trip across. But I took the ferry back to Manhattan.

And within fifty yards I was deep in the slums and within two blocks had seen far more than I wanted to see; the one photograph I took there will show you why. The sidewalks were clear of snow, but were filled with trash barrels as though there hadn't been a collection in weeks, as I expect there hadn't. And the streets were worse, the gutters piled with snow that was almost completely covered with mounds of garbage and refuse, dirt, and filth of all kinds. Here's the shot I took. We don't care

very much about what happens to our poor, but the nineteenth century cared even less, it seems to me.

I suppose it was cowardly, but there was nothing at all I could do about this, and it was too depressing; walking fast, I headed straight across town toward City Hall Park; I wanted out of there. When I reached Park Row, I glanced left, saw the Times Building and directly beside it the building in which Jake had his secret office, and at the sight of it the thought flared up in my mind like a rocket: *They won't stay in the park!* For a moment I stood motionless on the walk. How could I have missed it? What kind of woolly-headed lack of thought had made me picture Pickering and Carmody sitting across the street there in the park—in the dark of midnight!

I turned onto Park Row toward the Potter Building. And I knew it was true. Jake wouldn't bring whatever documents he had into the park—to be possibly taken by force by whomever Carmody might have hiding there. And he'd want to count the money besides. As for Carmody, he wouldn't be handing over the money till he'd actually examined Pickering's documents. *They'd go to Jake's office for this transaction; they had to. There was no way for me to overhear the meeting.*

I stopped on the walk and stood staring up at the building; I wasn't thinking of photographs now. The building hadn't changed: The upper stories were four identical rows of narrow arch-topped windows that had nothing to say to me; the storefronts of the street level were dirty-windowed as ever, their summer awnings ripped and torn, folded back to the wall, the grillwork protecting the windows' rusting and flaking paint; they had no hope for themselves, and none to offer. I glanced up at the long narrow signs identifying the offices of the chief tenants, which hung under some of the upper-story windows like those on the faces of most lower-Broadway buildings. They hung tilted outward, to be read from the street, and as I had once before I read them again. TURF, FIELD AND FARM, said the raised gold letters on the long black-painted background hung under a row of fourth-floor windows; THE RETAILER, said another, and THE SCOTTISH AMERICAN, a third. Under a row of third-floor windows hung SCIENTIFIC-AMERICAN, and—with no more interest than I had in the rest—I glanced again at the sign I would never forget: THE NEW-YORK OBSERVER.

For no particular reason except to see the other faces of the building—which looked the same as the first, I found—I walked around the building, along Beekman Street, then turned into Nassau Street, and I entered through the Nassau Street entrance. This time when I stepped into the vestibule there was no sound of sawing or pulling of nails, and when I climbed the stairs to the second floor the doorway of the office

I'd seen the carpenters in was closed. Not only closed, but now the doorway was solidly boarded across, floor to ceiling, and painted with warnings; obviously they'd finished removing the floor in there. Climbing to the third floor, I thought they might be working up there now, or about to begin, and that somehow this might give me the chance I needed.

But everything looked the same on the third floor. If they'd been working up here since my last visit, they weren't now; the door was padlocked as before, the same red-painted warning across it. Once again I tried the door to Pickering's office, but without hope, and it was locked.

Nothing had changed; I squatted down, looked in through the keyhole, and once again I saw the rolltop desk and the chair across the room before the tall thin window; and the connecting boarded-up doorway to the right. Then I straightened, and just stood there in the hall, helplessly. There was simply no way to get in. Yet I had to. I stood trying to think of everything I'd ever heard about breaking into a locked room. Slide a strip of plastic or celluloid into the door jamb and it could push back the lock, said stories I'd read. But that was a kind of lock not in use yet; this was a different kind with no spring to push back. There *was* no way to get in; I stood in that narrow corridor, lighted by a single open-flame gas jet, staring angrily and stubbornly at that locked door. Someone came up and someone went down the staircase off to my right, and each time I turned—camera at my side, hanging by its strap now—and walked toward the main corridor as though I were leaving. When the footsteps receded I returned.

I couldn't leave; I was hypnotized. I thought wildly of such things as coming hand over hand down a rope from the roof to the window of Room 27 or the closed-up room next to it. Or of somehow climbing up into the half-finished elevator shaft to the underside of the third floor, and then . . . then what? I didn't know.

I heard the preliminary rattle of a door about to be opened in my corridor, and turned swiftly, walking to the stairs ahead of whoever came out of an office behind me. I went up the staircase, he went down, then I turned and came back and once more stood helplessly and stubbornly in the corridor. A minute passed, I suppose; I knew I might as well leave, but couldn't.

Soft shuffling footsteps—carpet slippers, so that I didn't hear them before they turned the corner into my corridor—sounded directly behind me, and I whirled around. The old janitor was walking slowly toward me, head ducked as he squinted at a little stack of letters he was shuffling through his hands. He hadn't seen me yet, but the moment he raised his head he would; the corridor was much too narrow for me to sneak past him, and there was no other place I could go. I had time to arrange a pleasant smile, then he looked up, stopped, and stood frowning at me; he'd seen me before, he knew that, but he couldn't place me.

Then suddenly he remembered, and nodded. "Morning, Mr. Pickering; no mail for you," and he walked on past me, sliding envelopes under some of the numbered doors. Nothing happened inside my brain. During the fifteen seconds or so it took him to reach the end of the short corridor, turn, and come back, I just stood looking at him. Again he looked up at me, and now he was irritated. "What's the matter; forget your key?" he said, and before I could reply he was shaking his head in angry refusal. "Got no duplicate, not for that door! Supposed to have, and used to have; yes. But it's gone now. I can't help you! You'll have to go home and get your own. I got no time—"

I was grinning, genuinely, when I interrupted him. "Yes, you have," I said softly. "You've got a duplicate, and you know it. But it's a long way off, isn't it? Clear down in the basement." I had my notecase out, and I took out a dollar bill. "But it's not as far as I'd have to go to get my own." I handed him the dollar. "Come on," I said, "I'll go down with you, and save you the trip back up again."

Two minutes later, climbing the stairs from the basement, I had the key with a dirty paper tag labeled 27 in my hand, but I didn't go upstairs with it. I walked straight through the building, out onto Park Row, and next door in the Times Building I found the locksmith whose sign I remembered, near Nash & Crook's Restaurant in the basement floor. He charged me ten cents to cut a duplicate, and I walked back tying the paper tag back onto the original key. Fifteen minutes after he'd given it to me, I handed it back to the janitor whom I found distributing the second-floor mail.

Walking up to the third floor, I realized that I should have tested the duplicate first; but it worked fine. It rattled into the keyhole, caught the tumblers smoothly, revolved; then I turned the knob and stepped into Jake Pickering's secret office.

It was filled with filing cabinets, thirteen of them—I counted—set side by side around the four walls. They were of yellow oak, three drawers high, each drawer with a vertical metal handle. They were scratched and worn, bought second- or third-hand, it occurred to me. Together with the desk and the chair under the window, they filled two thirds of the little office's floor space. I'd taken the key from the lock and closed the door behind me; now I stood listening for a moment. All quiet, and I locked the door. Then as quietly as possible I began pulling file drawers open at random.

Some were very heavy, completely full or nearly so. Most were at least half or a quarter filled; one or two contained only a few inches of papers, and in one of these there was also a pair of rubber overshoes, and in another lay a half-full quart bottle labeled *Eagle Whisky*. The files were extremely neat, no dog-ears of paper sticking out at the tops or sides, and they were separated by tabbed dividers that were very carefully, almost beautifully, printed in either black or red ink. Mostly these markings were combinations of letters or letters and numbers such as *LL4*; *D*; *A 6, 7, 8*; *NN*, and so on. There was no consistency I could detect; every drawer held a dozen or more such tabs, and with no understandable relationships in the markings. I also saw a tab marked *Repeat*, another said *Undiv. Both*, and another was marked *???*. Without lifting any of the papers out, I looked at some of them. Just as Pickering had told Carmody, there were invoices, a lot of them, hundreds and maybe thousands in the thirteen cabinets. And there were reciepts and memoranda. There were occasional letters, some on business letterheads illustrated with black-and-white drawings of home offices, or of factories proudly pouring black smoke from every chimney. And there were what looked to be actual signed contracts, folded and tied with red tape. I couldn't tell how the papers were grouped; every file I looked at, no matter how labeled, contained papers bearing dozens or scores of dissimilar names.

The desk's rolltop was up, and I sat down and looked into the pigeon holes and the small upper drawers, touching nothing, just looking. There was a bottle of Daly's Best Bookkeeping Ink, red, and another of black; a little round cardboard box of steel pen nibs; three wooden penholders, all of them chewed at the ends; a scrap of red-and-black-stained rag obviously used as a pen wiper; five unused long blue envelopes; a tan rectangle of chewing tobacco marked with a red metal star; and a folded sheet of paper. This I did touch, taking it out and spreading it flat; the name *Jacob Pickering* had been written on it in black ink some thirty or forty times, one under the other in a double column. All were clearly in the same handwriting yet greatly varied in style, some much larger and more flowing than others, some very legible, others in a dashing scrawl. He'd been practicing his signature, searching for one he thought most impressive, and I was touched and felt ashamed to be sitting here searching through the man's belongings.

I didn't stop, though, or consider it. I looked through the lower drawers on each side of the kneehole, and saw a cardboard box half filled with unused file dividers; a tumbler of very thick glass which I suspected had been stolen from a restaurant; a pair of leather slippers; two folded newspaper pages which I opened to find a couple of grease spots, some crumbs, and a dry peach pit; a paper sack containing some bread crusts, four or five soda crackers, and an apple going bad; and there was a head-and-shoulders sepia photograph mounted on stiff cardboard of Julia. I touched that, too, taking it out to hold up to the light from the window. It was good; it caught the shine and thickness of her hair, and the knowing, faintly mischievous look her eyes often had even in repose.

I put it away and sat back, looking around the room. Squares and rectangles slightly cleaner than the rest of the wall marked where framed pictures or documents had once hung, and there was an upside-down banjo shape where a pendulum clock had been. Now the walls were naked except for an advertising calendar, marked JUNIUS ROOS & SON, PRINTING INKS, and bearing only the last leaf, for December 1880. From the high ceiling hung an upside-down metal T-shape from the ends of which two gas jets projected. The floor was bare wood; beside my chair stood an extremely battered brass spittoon. And that was the office, with absolutely no place to hide.

I walked over to the doorway that led into the next room. It was in the middle of the wall and completely boarded over with half-inch pine boards five or six inches wide and cut fairly neatly to proper length. But they were ordinary pine with plenty of knotholes, and were only roughly spaced with gaps of an inch or more between the boards. The nailheads had been left protruding an eighth of an inch for easy removal. I'd seen a hardware store on Frankfort Street a few doors down from Park Row, and I left now, locking the door. In ten minutes I was back with a hammer, and I slid it through the gap under the bottom board into the empty room, then pushed it just out of sight around the corner. I knew now how I was going to not only overhear but actually see tonight's meeting—only hours away now—and I left.

There was one picture I wanted above all; it was the real reason I'd thought of taking Felix's camera along this morning. And now I took the Sixth Avenue El to Twenty-third Street, walked a block east to the intersection of Broadway and Fifth, and out in the street, protected by a marvelous candelabrumlike streetlamp—*Why was it ever removed?*—I set my camera on the rim of a large horse-trough, and took this time exposure to eliminate the heavy street traffic. And there it is, in the background at the right, the arm of the Statue of Liberty rising high over the trees of Madison Square.

Here is an enlargement Felix made for me that shows the Statue of Liberty's arm more clearly.

It was nearly noon, I was hungry, and I saw a saloon a dozen steps down Twenty-third Street. I went in, and it looked exactly the way I thought it ought to: a long bar and brass rail, an ornate mirrored back bar, and a table at the rear filled with food. There were stacks of bread, sliced meat—including ham, chicken, turkey, wild duck, and roast beef—potato salad, a big glass bowl filled with dozens of hard-boiled eggs, and pickles, relish, horseradish, mustard, and I know I've missed plenty of other things: sliced pickled beets, for one. It was all free with a five-cent stein of beer, which I ordered, and which tasted different from today's beer. There was much more taste to it, of malt or hops, I think, I'm not sure which. Sipping the beer, I stood eating all the lunch I could manage, and I read a big oak-framed sign over the back bar: gilt letters against a black background on a shiny mirrorlike glass surface. It read:

> *It chills my blood to hear the Blest Supreme*
> *Rudely appealed to on each trifling theme.*
> *Maintain your rank, vulgarity despise;*
> *To swear is neither brave, polite, nor wise.*
> *You would not swear on a bed of death;*
> *Reflect! Your Maker now may stop your breath.*

Apparently I was the only one in the place who read it; no one else, including the bartender, gave a goddam for its sentiment, judging from their speech, and I think it was up there solely for its anti-WCTU propaganda value.

There was a New York City Directory lying at the end of the bar, and I pulled it over: Who was alive in New York City just now? Well, for one, I remembered from a college class in American Literature, there was Edith Wharton; she'd be a young girl of nineteen or twenty now, still unmarried, her family name Jones, observing the New York society she'd eventually write about. But there were four pages of Joneses, of course, and if I ever knew her father's first name, which I doubt, I didn't remember it now. Franklin Roosevelt, I knew, was born in 1882, or at least I thought so. But not in January, and not in New York City, but I looked up "Roosevelt" anyway, and found a dozen or so, including an Elliott and a James. Al Smith, an old-time politician my father used to rant about, was a boy somewhere on the lower East Side now, but I didn't bother looking up "Smith." I found Ulysses S. Grant, listed as living at 3 East 66th Street. Walt Whitman wasn't listed; did he live in Brooklyn? I couldn't remember. But General Custer's wife, Elizabeth B., was listed as "widow" and living at 148 East 18th Street—the Stuyvesant apartment building, maybe?

I finished my lunch, and was turning to leave when I remembered one more name, and I looked it up. It was there, all right: "Melville, Herman, inspector, h. 104 E. 26th." I walked on up to Twenty-sixth, and found 104 between Fourth and Lexington, on the south side of the street. It was a house, old and even now old-fashioned-looking. I hung around outside it for a few minutes, walking slowly up and down Twenty-sixth Street. I knew he was undoubtedly at work, somewhere in a customs shed along the river, and I didn't really know what he looked like anyway. I just had an idea that if he came along I'd somehow know him, and I'd tell him that I liked *Moby Dick* very much, which would have been an exaggeration though not entirely. This was sheer foolishness, and after a turn or two in front of the house, I left. I thought of taking a shot of the house, but it was nondescript, uninteresting, and I didn't have much film left; I'd have liked a picture of the man, though.

At Thirty-fifth and Fifth a bus just like the one Kate and I had ridden

was approaching, and I had to take this shot of it; especially since I also got the A. T. Stewart mansion (there at the right) and the twin Astor houses off to the left. This is where the Empire State Building was to go up later. It's a pretty typical view of Fifth Avenue; the wrought-iron railings there in the lower left corner all guard the stairways to the basement levels of a row of New York brownstones absolutely identical to similar rows that survive unchanged in the latter half of the twentieth century.

A thought broke the surface of my mind like a log breaking loose from the bottom of a lake, and floating slowly up to the top: *Julia*. Well, what about her? I walked north on Fifth; it was almost warm out now, a lot of blue sky showing through the gray. There was no problem about Julia; I'd settled that in my mind last night, and it was a decision I wasn't going to change. Yet a feeling of nameless worry persisted.

I'd used over half my film but when I reached Forty-second Street I had to have a photo of the Croton Reservoir. There was a set of rust-flecked iron rungs set into the stone wall at the corner of Fifth and Forty-second, and while I doubted that it was allowed, I climbed to the top; after the bridge it was nothing. Up on top, standing at the corner looking south, I took the shot below; the reservoir there on the right, more brownstones on the left, exactly like those I mentioned, further south. I think this view gives an even better idea of how narrow Fifth is. Was. Notice the sidewalks; they're of cut stone, not concrete.

For a dozen seconds I stood there on the Croton Reservoir staring down at the carriage stopped at the curb in the lower left of the photo I'd just taken, but I wasn't really looking at it. There *was* something I was neglecting, and it *was* about Julia. But nothing happened in my mind, and when a woman came out of the house—the mansion, really— to enter the waiting carriage below me, the liveried driver hopping down to open the door for her, I sighed, slung my camera over my shoulder, and climbed carefully down.

At Forty-fourth Street I took this. I feel certain that Ye Olde Willow Cottage was a relic of colonial times. Inside Tyson's, entire carcasses were hanging, though in too much shadow to show on my film.

In the fashionable Fifties the crowds were heavier, but I got a shot of William K. Vanderbilt's mansion—that's it in the center, looking

brand-new, and built of dazzling white limestone.

I walked clear up to the Seventies, alongside Central Park, before turning back; I was in the area of small truck farms again, still largely unbuilt upon, and I knew from yesterday's sleigh ride that there was nothing much ahead but more and more open country.

For variety on the way back, I walked over a block to Madison Avenue, turned south to walk back, and at Seventy-first Street I stopped and took this, once again because—I'm not sure why this interested me

so—I felt sure the farmhouse was a colonial relic still in use on Manhattan Island. That's the Museum of Natural History off there across Central Park, very clearly visible from here at the corner of Seventy-first Street and Madison Avenue of a strangely rural New York City.

I had one plate left, and I used it down in the Forties, back in the built-up city again, and, for me anyway, it's the best of all. Madison was a far quieter street than Fifth, but like Fifth it had been promptly cleared of yesterday's snow, and every single stoop and inch of sidewalk—all these houses had servants, I'm certain—was long since shoveled and swept clean.

It was so quiet I could hear my own footsteps, and in the afternoon warmth of this brief late-January thaw, feeling the clear sunny air on my face—the sky almost entirely blue now—I strolled along that peaceful, residential long-ago Madison Avenue momentarily as happy as I've ever been. At Forty-first Street a set of stone pillars flanking the stairs to a brownstone was flat on the tops, and I set Felix's camera on one of them. Taking my time then, focusing carefully, I took a picture that for me captures the quality I've tried to describe, of peace and tranquillity and better times. Here it is: Forty-first Street and Madison Avenue, an

utterly different place and world in the latter twentieth century. But I like it this way. I took my picture and walked on, and I can still hear the *clip-clop* behind me of the horse-drawn car you can see in the middle distance, and the footsteps on that cut-stone walk of the long-skirted woman under the umbrella a block away. In those moments, the moments of this picture, I was in the one place in all the world that I wanted to be.

And then, like a computer finally producing the right card, my mind said, *How? How will you make Julia break her engagement? How can you explain what you know about Jake?* And there was no answer. I began walking faster as though that would help, down toward Gramercy Park and Julia. But I slowed again. It was an easy decision last night, but now: What in the *hell* could I say to her? *Don't ask any questions, but . . . Julia, just take my word for this, but you can't marry . . . Please don't ask me to explain, but . . .*

In the parlor at 19 Gramercy Park before dinner—the day ending, a winter chill coming back into the air with the beginning darkness—I sat with Byron and Felix, trading sections of Felix's *Evening Sun;* Felix was delighted that I'd used his camera, flatly refused to accept payment for the plates I'd used, and said he'd develop and print them after supper. Maud Torrence came down, and finally Jake; Aunt Ada and Julia were setting the table in the dining room, and Julia twice caught me staring at her as I sat wondering how I could possibly do what I had to do.

I began to get mad. Looking over at Jake who was sitting by the big nickel-plated stove reading his paper, or trying to—he kept glancing up as though it were hard to sit still, frowning, and twice he wet his lips—I knew I would not, *would not,* let him marry Julia. And I didn't know how to stop it.

At the table during dinner he was almost directly across from me, and I wanted to needle him, wanted to get *at* him; I couldn't help it. Maud Torrence was talking about a Professor Peirce who had just read a paper before the New York Academy of Sciences on the advantages of establishing national and international time zones. Listening, I discovered there was no standardization of times anywhere in the country or world; any little town was free to pick its own time and often did, so that the time in towns a few miles apart might vary; eleven minutes maybe, or seventeen, or thirty-one. Railroad stations had clocks showing the times in different places, and Byron remarked that railroad timetables on long east-west trips were almost impossible to write because there were some seventy-odd different times used in the places the trains went through. Professor Peirce suggested time zones to be called Atlantic Time, Mississippi Time, Rocky Mountain Time, and Pacific Time, and I considered making a prediction but I was more interested in Jake.

And when Maud finished I said, truthfully, "I was up at the Central Park today, and"—a lie—"I was talking to a man who said he thought he'd seen Inspector Byrnes ride through a little earlier. He sounded as though he'd seen"—I almost said *a celebrity* but suddenly doubted that the word existed yet—"an important personage. Who *is* this Inspector Byrnes?"

It worked just fine: Jake's mouth clamped so tightly shut that his mustache and beard merged, and his eyes turned hard as he flicked a glance at me. As usual when you try something mean and succeed there wasn't really much triumph in it. I felt a little low and unworthy, not pleased with myself, yet with a little room left for a kind of sneaky gladness. Because the topic sprang to life; at least three people had answered simultaneously, and it was obvious that the name "Inspector Byrnes" had a powerful magic.

"That man!" Aunt Ada said, her eyes flashing with disapproval. Maud was murmuring something I couldn't hear except for the word "disgraceful." And Byron had said, "Well, I'll tell you," and he did. "He may not follow the letter of the law all the time"—Byron had put down knife and fork both, leaning over the tabletop, he was so interested in his own words—"but you can't kick about that; he gets results! He's got the pickpockets on the run! *And* the bank robbers. Isn't that right, Jake?"

Jake had gotten out a cigar, and though he didn't light it at the table, he sat chewing it, rolling it in his mouth, not even pretending to eat anymore. He didn't answer Byron, just nodded shortly.

"He invented the third degree," Felix told me, anxious to exhibit his knowledge.

"That's hardly to his credit!" said Aunt Ada.

Maud said anxiously, "It means beating people, doesn't it?"

Julia hadn't said anything, and I glanced at her to find that she was watching me, her eyes curious, speculative. It occurred to me that she might have realized something of what I was doing in bringing up Byrnes. I just grinned at her, not denying it, if that's what she was thinking.

"Oh, no," Byron answered Maud. "At least that's not all it means. I don't expect he minds knocking a man about a little when he knows he's guilty. As why shouldn't he? I don't think we need have any niminy-piminy fancies against that. Would you have him let a criminal go scot-free, to society's peril, for want of a little persuasion? The man's not vealy, he's the most experienced policeman in the city! He's unscrupulous, true, and often acts beyond his authority and legal powers. And it's a known fact that he accepts—if not money, stocks or bonds—inside information from the Wall Street millionaires he's befriended. He's said to be rich as a result. But we should think of him as like a good first sergeant; if he runs the company properly, you mustn't inquire too closely into his methods. And if he receives a few perquisites not found in regulations, it's only right and proper, else why should he take the trouble? He's far more than a crude bully, and if I'd seen him pass in his carriage, as did your acquaintance in the park, Mr. Morley, I'd have touched my hat brim. His famous 'third degree' is usually more than merely beating a confession out of some ruffian; have you heard how he solved the Unger murder case?"

"Yes!" said Felix with such anxiousness to tell the story that Byron smiled, and said, "Go ahead, Felix; you tell it."

"Well, sir, Byrnes tortured the suspect, actually tortured him"—Felix glanced around the table to see if he'd had an effect—"without placing so much as a finger upon him. For three days he kept him locked in a cell almost in complete darkness; the only light came from a window far down at the end of the corridor outside it. No one spoke to him. Nor did he even see a human face; food was slid under his cell door while he slept. He had nothing to do but pace his tiny gloomy cell or lie on the lounge which was its only furnishing. Just before dawn of the fourth day, the prisoner's spirit at lowest ebb"—Felix glanced around the table again; he had his audience's attention, all right—"Byrnes silently took his place at the barred door of the prisoner's cell. And now, for the first time, he lighted the lantern hanging from the ceiling just outside the cell door. The unaccustomed light shone upon the face of the sleeping wretch, and he awoke with a start. Byrnes stood motionless, staring at him, and they say that the coldness and menace of his gaze can burn holes through a man. Blinking in the light, the prisoner caught sight of those two cold eyes staring in at him, and sat up with a cry. And precisely as Byrnes had foreseen, he now caught sight, for the first time, of the lounge on which he had spent the greater part of three days and nights. It was spattered—stained in great smears—with dried gore! *This* was the lounge on which he had murdered his sleeping victim! With a great cry the prisoner sprang from it and fell to his knees before Byrnes, his hands clutching the bars of his cell, begging to be released, and confessing everything! Byrnes had a stenographer waiting with a notebook, and not till the prisoner had dictated and signed his complete confession was he led from the cell with the bloodstained couch into

275

another. A month later, soon after his trial, he was hanged."

"Horrible. *Horrible*," said Aunt Ada, and Julia and Maud nodded, while Byron shrugged.

"That trick may just possibly have been a violation of his civil rights," I murmured, but no one paid any attention to that.

Jake took the cigar from his mouth, and said, "I have heard he is not above arranging false evidence, if he can't get proof any other way."

"Possibly." Byron shrugged again. "It's generally acknowledged that he is without moral purpose or even the comprehension of it. But the boys in Wall Street have not been heard to complain."

"No," said Jake. He nodded thoughtfully, and I felt certain he was thinking that after tonight he'd be one of those boys himself. I thought of asking whether Byrnes had had any success in apprehending blackmailers but didn't bother. We talked a little more about Byrnes; then about Guiteau, as always; and finally everyone but me joined in a thorough condemnation of Mormonism. From several references I learned that apparently polygamy was still going strong out on the Utah prairies, and no one here approved of that, though Byron seemed more amused than incensed. Then Julia and Aunt Ada passed around winter-apple pie for dessert.

It was a horrible evening; for me and for Jake. He was up and down, picking up a magazine or newspaper and reading for a few minutes, then hopping up to cross the room and talk to someone, hardly listening. For a while he sat alone at the dining-room table playing solitaire. Twice he went up to his room—for a drink, I suspected—and came right down again.

I was physically quieter but my mind was screaming. Twice I had to beat down the nearly irresistible temptation to get up, walk out to the kitchen where Julia and her aunt were washing dishes, and tell her everything I had to tell—about where I'd come from, why I was here, and everything I'd learned about Jake.

I just didn't know what to do, and I don't remember whether I even tried to read. A little after ten—his mind, I was certain, filled with what was about to happen—Jake couldn't stand it anymore: he said an abrupt good-night to Julia, who was sitting at the dining-room table now, mending a towel, and went upstairs. Maud went up to her room a few minutes later, and within another five minutes—this was an early-rising household—Byron and Felix, who'd been sitting in the parlor matching pennies, had gone up, too. Aunt Ada came in from the kitchen, and when I heard her in the hall locking the front door, there was nothing left for me to do but say good-night, too, and go on up to my room. As I climbed the stairs, Julia and her aunt were turning out lamps and discussing the breakfast menu.

In my room I stood in the dark with my ear at the door crack, heard Aunt Ada and Julia go up to the third floor to their rooms, heard their good-night to each other, listened a few moments longer, and heard no one out in the second-floor hall. Then—now or never—I opened my door, stepped out, closed it silently, and climbed quickly and without a sound to the third floor. Julia's room faced the street, I knew, and there was a crack of light under her door. I walked to it and rapped very lightly with a fingernail. Julia opened the door, and I said, "I waited till you came up here; I have something to tell you that no one else must know."

She hesitated only the fraction of a moment, then nodded. "Come in." I walked into a small room with a single dormer window, a window seat underneath it, a cot with a white spread, a small desk, a rocking chair. Julia motioned politely to the chair, but I said, "No, you take it," and sat down on the window seat. Julia took the chair, facing me, and with her wrists crossed on her lap, smiling at me pleasantly, she sat waiting.

I said the only thing I'd been able to think of during that long long evening, and maybe it was the best thing I could have said, because it was uncomplicated. "I'm a private detective," I told her, and in her nod I thought I could see a kind of satisfaction as though this answered a question. "I'm here to investigate one of your boarders, I'm sorry to say." I waited a moment, then added, "For blackmail." Her eyes grew bigger; she knew I wasn't talking about Felix or Byron, and I nodded in confirmation of what she was thinking. "When this will become generally known, I'm not sure. Perhaps it never will be. It might even be successful; I'm not from the police." I hesitated, then said, "Julia, I couldn't let you marry him; I *had* to tell you this."

Her voice level, neither disputing nor agreeing, she said, "And whom do you say he is blackmailing?"

I told her; the name meant nothing to her. But then in almost his own words I described Jake's preparations of over two years, his real reason for working at City Hall; and watching her face, I suspected it had the sound of plausibility to her, that some old questions in her mind had just been given a possible answer. I told her about the meeting planned for tonight, that I was going to eavesdrop, and how. Then for quite a while, as long as three or four minutes, which is a long time in those circumstances, Julia sat silently considering what I had said. Before her bed lay an oval hooked rug, faded from many washings, and she'd stare at that, glance up at me appraisingly, then down at the rug again. I sat leaning back against the window, feeling the coldness of the glass through my coat, looking around the room; it was very neat, very spare. There were a couple of framed pictures on the wall, of no consequence, and half a dozen books and a church paper stacked on the window ledge; I couldn't see the book titles. The walls were papered to within a yard or so of the ceiling; clean white plaster after that. The single gas jet, directly over the head of her painted iron bedstead, was fitted with an opaque white globe.

This was a comfortable enough room, an acceptable retreat for a busy person who didn't spend much time in it. But it had a temporary owner-less character, almost deliberately so; looking around it, then glancing again as I did now at Julia—her lower lip was caught under her front teeth, and she was frowning at the rug, moving it slightly with the toe of one buttoned shoe—I thought I could guess what she might be think-ing. This was an intelligent forceful girl who helped her aunt run a boardinghouse for a living. There must have been some rough times in that; she'd have a feeling for reality. She'd thought about her own future, and it wasn't in this room but in marriage. Yet as soon as she heard what I'd said about Jake, she knew it might be true.

Was she thinking about marrying him anyway? Warning him about me? Maybe, but I didn't think so. It was a risk I had to take. I didn't know what she'd felt about Jake when she'd agreed to marry him. It was hard for me to believe it was love, but who ever knows about that, or even what the word means to anyone else? She'd felt something for him; she may have been calculating to a degree—forced to be—but she wasn't ruthless. She felt something for Jake but she was also real-minded about herself and her future; she wasn't simply accepting my word against him, but she wasn't denying the possibility either. I don't know whether I saw a movement from a corner of my eye—probably I did—but I turned my head to look down at the street, and Jake was just stepping off the bottom step of the front stoop, buttoning his coat, and I stood up quickly to get out of sight in case he looked up.

Julia knew instantly what I'd seen. She stepped to a curtain, moved it a half inch from the wall, then stood—I was behind her now, looking over her shoulder—watching Jake walk quickly to the Twentieth Street corner and out of sight. I think Julia would have decided as she did anyway, but this cinched it. She stood staring after him for a moment or so after he'd gone from sight, then turned and—not asking, just telling me—said, "I'm going with you tonight."

I nodded. "All right. Meet me in the front hall in two minutes."

19

JAKE was in his office: it was eleven thirty-five and Julia and I stood in the darkened doorway of the Morse Building directly across Nassau Street from the Potter Building entrance, and I counted floors and then windows; on the third floor up from the Nassau Street entranceway the second window to the right was a tall rectangle of yellow light. It was Jake's office, the only room lighted in the entire dark face of the old building. Ten minutes later it lowered, flickered redly for a moment, then was out.

Julia's arm was under mine, and I felt it tighten. To herself she murmured, "He's leaving," and I nodded in the darkness. There was a three-quarter moon out, very high in the sky, but we stood far back, deep in the complete darkness of the doorway. I pictured Jake . . . locking his office door now . . . walking down the short hall in the faint light from outside, perhaps using a match, though I could see no light. Down the stairs then, a hand on the banister. And now, just about now, he'd be turning to walk through the long hall the length of the building toward Park Row and City Hall Park. Crossing the street toward it, he'd glance up at the City Hall clock; it would say ten or eleven minutes to twelve. Perhaps far across the park in the moonlight Carmody, too, would be entering it, a heavy satchel at the end of one arm.

I pressed Julia's arm to step forward, and—you can never entirely anticipate what anyone else will do—Jake stepped out of the entrance directly across the street onto the sidewalk, and stood looking carefully around in every direction. Was he listening, too? We'd instantly frozen motionless, not breathing. Could my pounding heartbeat actually be audible in the complete silence? Had our feet shuffled and made a sound? Across the street, Jake walked on past our doorway to Beekman Street and then across Beekman, on down toward Ann Street, his footsteps loud and echoing between building walls.

Of *course* he hadn't left by the Park Row entrance to be seen by Carmody and whoever else might have been waiting and watching just across the street in the park. Instead, he would come toward City Hall Park now, walking north on Broadway and entering it from the west, keeping the location of his office a secret till he was ready to lead Carmody toward it himself.

We waited, listening, watching from our doorway. I saw Jake reach Ann Street and turn west out of sight, the sound of his steps instantly cut off. Then we hurried across Nassau Street—we had minutes at most—and up the moonlit stairs, and down the short hall to Jake's doorway. I had my key out, found the lock, turned the key, and the door opened. I struck a match and walked, shielding it with my hand, to the jet over the desk, turned it up, touched the match to the tip, and it popped redly into flame. I lowered it to steadiness, then actually ran across the room to reach under the bottom board of the covered-over doorway, and find my hammer.

There was nothing to do but accept a certain amount of squealing protest from the nails as I pulled them. But I drew slowly with an even pressure, keeping the noise down; and as soon as they were loosened, I pried the board off silently with the hammer claws. Two boards off, then a third, leaving a foot-and-a-half opening a couple of feet above the floor; I helped Julia as she ducked, her hands on the board just below the opening. She got one leg through, then lowered her shoulders, ducked her head under, and cried out in fright. I looked through the opening: The room was lighted dimly by moonlight through its single tall window, and most of its floor was gone, nothing but black space below.

They'd worked, the carpenters, since I'd seen them last; finishing the second floor below, then moving up to this one, and sawing out the floor boards up here, exposing the long joists. They'd worked—possibly this afternoon—from the far wall, back toward the doorways, and now there was left only a corner of the floor, an approximate triangle from this boarded-over doorway to the door to the hall.

There was enough left to stand on, perhaps to sit, and after a moment longer and keeping a tight grip, Julia crawled on through. I followed as fast as I could move. We'd lost a few moments we might need if Carmody had been waiting in the park and they'd started right back. They could be in the entranceway now, starting to climb the stairs.

I had to take the risk, accepting the noise and hoping. Holding the last of the three boards I'd pried off back in its place, nail points fitted into their original holes, I was able to hammer it back precisely in place, plenty of room for my arm to swing, easily able to see. I had the second board in place, feeling a little cramped now, but my projecting arm still able to swing the hammer. My arm was actually raised, ready to come down, when I remembered.

I dropped board and hammer clattering onto the floor of Jake's office, and then—squeezing, forcing, not worrying about a ripped-off coat button so long as it fell on our side, scratching my face from cheekbone to ear—I fought through the two-board opening, stumbled into Jake's office, nearly falling down, then ran the two steps toward his desk, my arm reaching out before me. Then my fingers were on the gas-jet key, twisting, the light popped out as Jake had left it, and in the new darkness I scrambled back, forcing my way into the empty, nearly floorless room. Julia had my hammer and the dropped board ready for me, and blinking my eyes, trying to speed up their adjustment to the dim moonlight, I fitted the nails into their original holes, and pounded them in to their original depth. I remembered to lay my hammer on our side of the doorway, and as I picked up the third board we heard the City Hall clock, very faintly, the bulk of the building between us and it, begin to slowly bong out the hour. We didn't wait to count; it leisurely sounded twelve times while Julia and I, each with our fingers curved around top and bottom of an end of the board, pulled it into the last opening, and—by trial and error, sliding it around—we found the nail holes, finally, the points dropping into place. Each with our hands at first one end of the board, then the other, we pulled it in toward us with all our strength while I prayed silently to somebody or something not to let us slip and shoot backward into the dark emptiness behind and below us. The final slow bong sounded, the board was as secure as we could get it, and with my fingers through the cracks above and below the board, I felt for the nailheads. They projected a good half inch, and when I tried the board it wobbled. But it was firm enough, I told myself, and would look all right from the other side.

We had a minute or two, it turned out, and it may have been as long as three, to get settled. As comfortably as we could, our outer coats folded as cushions, we sat in the nearly dark room facing the boarded-up doorway. We sat, knees drawn up, arms around our ankles, as close as we could bring our eyes to the cracks without showing the tips of our shoes at the opening below the bottom board. I reached out to touch Julia's knee and patted it reassuringly; at least that was the intention.

We heard nothing of them out in the hall, no footstep, voice, or even the creak of a floorboard. A key rattling suddenly into the lock of Jake Pickering's office was the first sound of them, and Julia's hand shot out and gripped my forearm. Then they were in, a confusion of footsteps on the wooden floor, and, sounding terrifyingly inside the room with us, Carmody's voice said, "What's this!" its sound hollow in the empty space we sat in, and Julia's hand on my arm squeezed down hard.

The gaslight in the next office rose high, projecting in knotholes and slits of light onto the far wall of our room the wavering shape of the boarded-up doorway, and down its center was the shape of a man peering in. In the open few inches at the bottom of the doorway the tips of a pair of boots almost touched mine, and beside them on the floor was the silver tip of an ebony cane.

"It's nothing; an elevator shaft," Pickering's voice answered impatiently. We couldn't see past Carmody standing less than six inches from our eyes. "Let's have the suitcase." For a moment or so Carmody, suitcase in hand, staring into the room over our motionless heads, didn't move. "Floor's gone," he murmured to himself then, and turned away.

Except for the narrow fuzzy-edged bars and small circles of projected light on the wall behind us, and a yellow parallelogram of light at our feet, our room was shadows and blackness, the high moonlight slanting down through the narrow window only a pale wash of light disappearing into the darkness below. On the other side of our barricade I could see almost the entire office except for the near wall, a strip of floor, and a strip of ceiling just outside and above our doorway. My shoulders moved in a shudder of guilty excitement and apprehension at watching people in secret that I hadn't felt since childhood.

"Up here," Pickering was saying. He stood beside his desk, facing us, pointing at its top. Suitcase in hand, Carmody stopped before the desk, and we heard him grunt as he swung the case up onto the desk top. Both men had their hats off, hung on nails by the door, but wore their outer coats. We watched Carmody's busy hands, heard the creak of straps unfastened, the metallic clicks of fasteners snapping open. Waiting beside his desk, facing us, Pickering stared, eyes wide.

Then Carmody opened the suitcase flat on the desk top and it was filled with paper money, greenbacks and yellowbacks bound into thin stacks by brown-paper ribbons. We heard Jake Pickering exhale, saw him lean forward to stare down. Then, grinning slowly, he lifted his eyes to Carmody, and they were friendly, happy, as though both of them shared the pleasure of the sight on the desk top. "It's all here?" he said slowly; his voice was awed. Carmody nodded, and Jake grinned again, very fond of Carmody now, everything forgiven.

Still nodding—I watched the gleam of his dark hair as his head moved—Carmody said, "Yes: it's all there. All you're going to get: ten thousand dollars."

I was holding my breath, and I had to give Jake credit; he hung onto his grin. But his eyes narrowed and in the slight flicker of the gaslight they glittered at Carmody, hard and menacing. He didn't say anything; he placed the knuckles of his fists on the edge of his desk and leaned forward on his stiffened arms over the suitcase toward Carmody, and waited, staring at him till Carmody had to speak. "The public is tired of Tweed Ring scandals!" he said angrily, but his voice was defensive. "As a minor nuisance you and your information"—he nodded at the suitcase before them—"are worth that much but no more. The Ring is dissolved and Tweed is dead, like most of the witnesses." With the silver head of his cane—it was molded in the shape of a lion's head—he gestured at the filing cabinets around the walls. "And all your papers can't send me to prison."

"Oh, I know that." Jake didn't alter his position. "Your money will keep you out of jail; I always understood that. But I'll destroy your reputation, and your money won't ever bring *that* back."

Carmody laughed, a snort through the nostrils, and began pacing the room. Gripping his cane at the middle, he waggled the head, gesturing as he spoke. "Reputation," he said scornfully. "You're a clerk. With a clerk's mentality. Did you believe that anyone who matters would think the less of me because of your information? Hardly a rich man in the city who hasn't done all that I have, and most of them worse!" He stopped at Pickering's desk and with the head of his cane contemptuously touched the suitcase full of money. "Take this, and think yourself lucky."

But once more Jake was grinning. "You're right; Carnegie wouldn't care. He'd merely think you a fool for getting caught. And Gould wouldn't care. Or Michaels or Morgan, Seligman or Sage, or any of the rest of them. The men wouldn't care at all." He reached across the stacks of money into a pigeonhole of his desk, and brought out a long newspaper column torn carefully down both sides. It was folded in half, and he opened it, turning so the light would catch it; I could see that it was a long printed listing, apparently printed in a double column. " 'Mrs. Astor,' " he read from the top of the list, his voice supplying the quotation marks. "That is all it says, because we all know *which* Mrs. Astor, don't we? And *she* would care, Mr. Carmody. 'Mrs. August Belmont' would care. 'Mrs. Frederic H. Betts, Mrs. H. W. Brevoort, Mrs. John H. Cheever, Mrs. Clarence E. Day'—*they* would all care. And 'Mrs. Stuyvesant Fish, Mrs. Robert Goelet, Mrs. Ulysses S.—' "

"What are you reading?" Carmody said harshly.

"A few names at random. From the list of managers of the Charity Ball at the Academy of Music tonight. 'Mrs. Oliver Harriman, Mrs. J. D. Jones, Mrs. Pierre Lorillard, Mrs. Thomas B. Musgrave, Mrs. Peter R. Olney, Mrs. John E. Roosevelt, Mrs. A. T. Stewart'; *they'd* all care! And 'Mrs. W. E. Strong, Mrs. Henry A. Taber, Mrs. Cornelius Van—' "

"That's enough."

"Not quite." Pickering looked up from his list. "There is one name I passed by: the most important of all. She would care the most of any on this list, because never again would her name be included in such illustrious company." Pickering's forefinger moved to the top of the list, began to slowly slide down it, and stopped almost immediately. " 'Mrs. Andrew W. Carmody,' " he read, and the silver lion on Carmody's cane smashed down onto his head, and he dropped like a stringless puppet, striking the desk chair, sending it squealing across the office. Julia had gasped; more than a gasp, it was a choked cry, but the shrill of the chair covered the sound, and as she tried to rise I grabbed her shoulders, holding her down, my lips at her ears whispering, "No! No! He's not really hurt!" though I didn't know that.

Carmody stood staring at Pickering crumpled on the floor; then he looked at the blood-reddened head of the cane in his hand. He looked at the open suitcase full of money, then down—not at Pickering now but at the newspaper fragment in Pickering's hand, because he suddenly stooped and snatched it from Pickering's fingers. He stood reading it then, scanning it, rather, rapidly searching for a name. He found it, and murmured aloud, " 'Mrs. Andrew W. Carmody.' " For a moment longer he stared at the printed list, then again looked down at Pickering motionless on the floor. Suddenly he crumpled the clipping in his hand to a ball, and threw it hard at Pickering. He threw his cane to the floor, and actually ran the two steps necessary to reach the desk chair. He pulled it to Pickering's side, stooped, gripped him under the arms, and dragged him limply up into the seat of the chair. There, head lolling, Pickering would have slid off the seat, but Carmody shoved down the back of the chair, tilting it so far that only Pickering's toes touched the floor. Carmody reached down, unfastened Pickering's belt, and yanked it from its loops. Then he threaded it through the slats of the chair back and brought the ends together across Pickering's chest and upper arms. They wouldn't meet, and with one upraised knee Carmody held the chair tilted, removed his own belt, and fastened an end to the buckle of Pickering's. Then he looped the double belt around Pickering's chest and upper arms just above the elbows. With the buckle at the back, he cinched it so tightly we heard leather and wood creak, and I wondered if Pickering could breathe.

But he could: He was stirring as Carmody finished, mumbling, a long thread of saliva swaying at his mouth corner as, eyes still closed, he struggled to lift his head. Carmody stepped back, picked up his cane, and walked swiftly around to the back of Pickering's chair. Jake's head lifted, I saw his eyes open, focus, then squeeze tight shut as the pain of the concussion struck him. His head must have throbbed agonizingly because I saw his face go dead-white; then his cheeks puffed and his shoulders hunched as he fought against nausea. For a few seconds he didn't move. Then he very slowly lifted his head again, and opened his eyes a little at a time, accustoming them to the light. His shoulders convulsed once again, then he was able—blinking a lot—to keep his eyes open, and the color began to return to his face.

He stared down at himself for a few seconds. Then his hands moved up to the belt. But the most they could do, bent as far as they'd go at the wrists, was brush the leather with the tips of his fingers. Carmody walked around the chair to face him. They looked at each other: a narrow almost perfectly straight ribbon of drying blood ran down Pickering's temple, and another down his forehead to the corner of one thick, black eyebrow. Carmody said, "You've created an impossible situation. You found the key." With the tip of his cane he touched the little crumpled ball of newsprint, then flicked it toward the boarded-up doorway where it shot under the bottom board, rolling past me, and I saw it drop down the shaft. "This season is the first in which my family has taken its place among New York's society. It won't be the last; I'll see to that." He closed and strapped the suitcase, then swung it to the floor, setting it beside the door. "You should have taken this much when you had the chance. Now it will be nothing." Carmody took off his coat, tossed it to the desk top, unfastened his tie and collar, unbuttoned his vest, then took a cigar from a vest pocket, and lighted it carefully. When it was going good, he shook out the match, dropped it to the floor, and stepped on it. Then he walked to a filing cabinet and pulled open the top drawer.

For a few moments he said nothing, just stood there, cigar in his teeth, staring down at the coded file-markings. Jake Pickering could revolve his chair, and had turned to watch him. Carmody glanced at him over his shoulder, apparently about to speak, but did not. He turned back to the file, and beginning at the front of the cabinet he began to look at every paper in it, flicking through them with a steadily moving forefinger. He glanced at perhaps a paper every second, his hand seldom pausing in its steady motion, though occasionally he touched the extended forefinger to his tongue and occasionally he removed the cigar from his mouth to tap the ashes to the floor. He rarely removed a paper, merely glancing at each as he flicked past it. But occasionally he stopped to read at greater length, taking the paper from the files. Twice he set such a paper aside, on top of the cabinet. The others he didn't trouble to replace, crumpling and dropping them to the floor.

But I suppose there were three or four thousand, maybe as many as five thousand sheets in the two-foot depth of that wooden file-cabinet drawer. The City Hall clock bonged once; it was one o'clock. Carmody was less than halfway through the drawer, and on top of the cabinet he had set aside only two papers. Pickering said, "I've waited so that you could see for yourself; it will take you hours to search through that one cabinet alone, and there are thirteen of them all together, an unlucky number for you."

Carmody walked to Jake's desk and dropped his cigar stub into the cuspidor on the floor beside it. He walked back to the open drawer, placed his hands in position to resume his search, and smiled at Jake over one shoulder. "I have all night," he said pleasantly. "And if that isn't enough, all the next day. And as much more time beyond that as may be required." His forefinger resumed its steady motion, the continuous small sound of the flicked corners becoming almost a part of the silence.

I leaned very close to Julia, and when my lips touched her ear I whispered on the exhalation, almost soundlessly. I said, "Lie down; rest. We're going to be here a long long time." I could see her face clearly; as she nodded, a stripe of yellow light from the other room moved up and down her forehead. She nodded, and so slowly it was soundless, she lay back on the floor along the wall. In the doorway I carefully leaned a shoulder and the side of my head against the jamb, and with one eye watched Carmody through a crack. Nearly motionless, he stood before the open file drawer, head bowed, only his arm and hand in steady monotonous motion.

When the clock outside bonged twice, Carmody was about a third of the way through the middle drawer, and now Pickering spoke again. "By now you will have observed that no complete filing is to be found in one place. To assemble all of yours—scores of documents scattered through every drawer of every case—would take me twenty minutes, perhaps. The system for discovering them lies in my head. But you've found only two in two hours! Isn't it time you understood that you must deal with me?"

Carmody didn't pause or even glance up. He said, "All night and even all the next day for a million dollars is satisfactory wages to me," and the steady, endless riffling past sheet after sheet continued.

I watched, dreamily; there was no way to measure passing time till the clock struck again. Presently, without pausing in his work, Carmody slowly lifted one foot and moved his leg up and down, flexing the muscles, revolving his foot at the ankle. He did the same thing with the other leg, then stood, feet a little wider apart than earlier, riffling past paper after paper. I continued to stare out at him, neither awake nor asleep. After a time Carmody paused for a moment, thinking, then slid the entire drawer out of the cabinet, and, his feet shuffling under the weight of it, carried it to the desk top. Sitting on the edge of the desk facing the drawer, he resumed his search, and Pickering laughed at him. "I wondered when you'd think of that," he said. "If you're tiring, let me offer you my chair." But Carmody didn't even move his head in acknowledgment, and his fingers never stopped.

I lay back beside Julia. We were in darkness here, and I couldn't tell if she were awake, and and was afraid to whisper unnecessarily. I wished I had a cup of coffee, and in the moment of thinking of it I wanted it so badly it seemed impossible that I couldn't have it. Something to eat, I thought then, and was instantly famished. I forced a smile but I wondered how long we could possibly stay here; I'd anticipated nothing like this. Could Carmody possibly mean that he might stay here all of tomorrow? It was impossible; he'd have to go out for food, he'd have to rest. And so would Jake; if only both of them were to sleep, Julia and I might ease our way out of here. I was drifting to sleep, and made myself pop my eyes open in the dark. I didn't dare sleep; a few feet to my right the floorboards ended; I could roll off and fall three floors to the basement. I sat up; Julia was sleeping, I knew; I could just barely hear her slow regular breathing. I couldn't move back to the doorway, I realized; she might roll to the right, too, to fall or to be heard in the other room. I had to stay here beside her, ready, if she began to stir, to ease her quietly awake.

For two hours I sat not daring to even lean a shoulder or the side of my head against a wall. My head endlessly drooping and jerking upright again, I kept awake and heard the clock outside strike three; in the next room the tiny flickering sound seemed never to stop.

An unbelievably long time later the clock again began to strike and as it started I stood up under the cover of its bonging. My legs were terribly stiff, and I had to reach quickly across Julia to the wall beside her and steady myself. Then, very slowly and completely silently, I stretched every muscle—arms, legs, back, neck—counting the slow bongs; it was four o'clock. I stepped to the doorway, and found a crack to peek through. Jake was asleep, head on his chest, snoring very faintly. Carmody still sat on the edge of the desk, but now his upper body lay along the length of the file drawer on the desk top before him: the top drawer, I saw, of the second cabinet. He slept silently; I had to watch closely to see the tiny motion of the back of his vest. I assume most people are tempted—at least the impulse stirs—to occasionally commit the outlandishly impossible: to whistle in church, to say something wildly inappropriate to a situation. It popped up in my mind to yell "Boo!" as loudly as I could, and then watch the wild scramble in the next room. I smiled, and sat down beside Julia, and knew she was awake, I'm not sure how.

I lay down beside her to bring my mouth to her ear. I had to put an arm around her in order to get closer and to get oriented; I didn't mind. "You awake?" Her hair brushed across my nose as she nodded. I whispered the situation then, and told her the time. She asked whether I'd slept, then made me change places, and she sat doing guard duty while I fell almost instantly to sleep.

The first daylight on my face and the slow bong of the City Hall clock awakened me. I opened my eyes; Julia's hand was hovering an inch from my mouth, ready to close over it if I started to speak. I lifted my head and kissed her palm, and she yanked her hand away, startled, then smiled. She made a pointing gesture toward the next room, then placed her finger across her lips, and I nodded. I'd been counting with the clock; it was seven, and when it stopped I heard once again what I seemed now to have been hearing forever—the steady *flick-flick* of paper in the room beside us.

We moved silently to the boarded-over doorway and sat down as before. Except that the room was now gray and shabby with daylight—a powdering of new snow had appeared on the outside windowsills—nothing had changed. Carmody sat on the desk top flicking steadily through the inches of paper in, I saw, the bottom drawer of the third cabinet. Jake had turned in his chair to watch; there was a huge swollen lump on his head nearly the size of a fist, and his face was haggard, his eyes red, the skin below them drooping into wrinkles, and his mouth hung open a little. He was in pain, I thought—from the blow on his head, perhaps, or the inability to alter his position. But Carmody's face looked almost as tired, his eyes dulled and staring, and I wondered if he were still able to fully comprehend the blur of paper passing endlessly before them. There were five sheets now, lying on top of the second filing cabinet.

Something had to change soon; that was obvious. In the new daylight, very white from the fresh snow, I glanced at Julia beside me, and she looked rested, and she smiled at me. But just the same I knew that neither she nor I could stay here much longer. And neither could Carmody. He might be willing to leave Jake Pickering just as he was, but he himself would have to leave soon if only to get some food, and return. If he left, he'd have to gag Jake, I supposed. Jake didn't dare shout now and take another blow on the head, but he'd surely shout if Carmody left, until someone heard and investigated—which wouldn't take long. The city was fully awake, Julia and I could hear the steady roar of it outside our windows. The building was awakening, too; twice I'd heard the sound, coming up the shaft, of footsteps on the building staircase. What should we do, I wondered, if Carmody left? We couldn't push our loosened boards aside and walk out through Jake's office without his seeing us. I leaned back out of the doorway to look down. Beside and behind me the floorboards were gone and I could see far below into the shaft, lighted at each floor by the windows facing east on Nassau Street. The joists of the floors below us had been removed, I saw; there was no way at all for us to get out of here by way of the elevator shaft.

And I was tired. I ached from hours of sitting or lying on wooden floorboards. I was thirsty and hungry, and Julia must be the same. But if there was anything to do but continue to sit here, staring into the next room, I couldn't think of it. I simply repeated to myself that something had to change soon, something had to give; and when Julia glanced at me I smiled reassuringly.

After half an hour or so Carmody stopped. He got to his feet, revolving his shoulders, rotating his head as he bent his neck, working the stiffness loose. He stood looking speculatively at Jake, and I thought I could read his mind; he was wondering if he dared leave him for a time, and how best to do it. But then he thought of something I hadn't; he turned, and began opening the drawers of Jake's desk one after another.

I'd once searched these drawers, too, and I remembered what he was going to find.

He reached the bottom left-hand drawer, opened it, lifted out the paper sack, looked into it, then looked over at Jake, and smiled. He sat down on the desk top and ate the four or five big white crackers, holding his cupped hand under his mouth to catch the crumbs, which he tossed into his mouth last. There were soft brown spots on the apple, but he ate it all, including the core. He wasn't deliberately taunting Jake, but Jake sat watching him, and when Carmody stood up again, dusting the last crumbs from his hands, he was grinning. He opened a file drawer, brought out the half-full bottle of whiskey, pulled the cork, and tossed down a good belt. The cork still in hand, he looked consideringly at Jake for a moment. "Want an eye-opener?" he said, and Jake hesitated, then shrugged a shoulder, unwilling to say yes, unable to refuse, and Carmody walked over and, a little contemptuously, held the bottle to Jake's lips, watched him swallow twice, then took it away. Then—I clutched my head in both hands, and rocked back and forth helplessly—Carmody went back to work.

For over two more hours we sat in a semi-stupor; the snowstorm was heavier now, snow piling up on the window ledge, lying flat against the glass. We'd been here sitting or lying on a hard floor too long, and I knew we couldn't take it much longer. Most of the time Julia sat simply staring at the floor and so did I; after a while I put my arm around her shoulders and made her rest against me, her head on my shoulder. It occurred to me that Jake Pickering looked to be in pretty good shape; his color was better now, probably from the whiskey. But he'd also had more sleep than any of us; and his arms, while bound, were protected by a considerable thickness of cloth, and the leather binding was broad and flat; they wouldn't be numbed. Still, he hadn't been able to stand or move about for over nine hours; I thought he must be in pretty severe discomfort, and I had to admire the calmness of his voice when presently he spoke.

We'd heard the clock strike nine half an hour or so before, and now Jake—voice a little dogged, an edge of doubt sounding—said, "A financier is bound to be skilled at figures: Here is a problem to test you. If a man can search through two and a half file cabinets in nine and a half hours, how long will it take him to hunt through thirteen?"

Without turning to look at Pickering Carmody had stopped to listen, hands lying motionless on the compressed paper in the drawer before him. It seemed a mild enough taunt; I expected Carmody to smile or shrug, reply in kind, and resume work. But I'd found myself automatically responding to Pickering's "problem" by trying to work out the arithmetic of it in my head, and I think maybe Carmody did the same. He sat for a few moments apparently thinking; and I believe that something about the inescapable answer to the question—the forced realization of the immensity of what still lay ahead, the long sickening blur of concentration he'd already gone through being only the beginning—got through to him. Because he suddenly broke. He whirled to stare at Jake, who grinned at him, and Carmody spun back to the drawer and plunged his clawed hands into it to snatch up an immense thickness of paper. Arms rising high, he whirled back to Jake and slammed the whole sliding mass of paper down into Jake's face.

The force of it rocked Jake back in his chair, the metal springs creaking, the paper cascading down his chest and off his shoulders, separating into sheaves and sheets, fluttering to the floor, sliding down off his lap. But when Jake rocked forward again he was still laughing, and Carmody gathered up the rest of the file, an immense wad, stood, and smashed it down onto Jake's swollen head. But Jake never stopped laughing, and then Carmody went wild.

He yanked a top drawer straight out of a file cabinet, it fell, cracked open, and spilled half its contents, and Carmody booted the smashed drawer to spill out the rest. He yanked out half a dozen more drawers as fast as he could grab their handles, and every one crashed, shaking the entire floor, and burst. Then Carmody waded through the sea of paper kicking, and the paper flew in a waist-high storm. He stood panting for a moment or two, looking wildly around the office—for a way to get rid of the spilled paper, I think, because he suddenly began shoving it with the side of his foot straight toward our doorway. Then he booted a heap of it through under the bottom board past Julia and me, and we heard the flutter of loose sheets, then the distant plop of most of the mass of it landing at the bottom. He shoved out half the paper on the floor like that, under the boarding and down the shaft, before he had to stop for breath, facing Jake and glaring at him, his shoulders heaving, his breath sighing; and Jake never stopped grinning.

The wild spontaneous action did Carmody good, I think, because as he got his breath back he began to grin, too. And then for a few moments, strangely, there was almost a companionship between the two men. Carmody reached into the inside pocket of his coat lying on the desk beside a file drawer, and brought out a cigar, raising it toward his mouth. But instead he looked at Jake for a moment, then extended the cigar to him, and Jake leaned forward, nipped off the end between his front teeth, and spat it to the floor. Still grinning, Carmody put the other end of the cigar into Jake's mouth, saying mildly, "What the hell are you laughing at?"

He turned to get a second cigar—they were in a protective leather case—and as Jake replied, Carmody bit off the end of his cigar, listening, nodding. "Because you can kick my files all over the building," Jake said. "You can cause me a hell of a lot of work getting them together again. But you can't eat them, Carmody. Somewhere in this mess, up here or down the shaft or both, are a little handful of papers that are still going to cost you—one million dollars." The cigar in a corner of his mouth, Jake grinned lopsidedly at Carmody who nodded, brought out a big wooden kitchen match, and expertly snapped it to light with his thumb nail. He held the flame for Jake, who puffed the cigar end to a red circle; it made my stomach queasy to watch, before breakfast. Then Carmody lighted his own cigar, leisurely, enjoying the process, the way a cigar smoker does. He breathed out a round puff of blue smoke, then took the cigar from his mouth, and holding it between the tips of his four fingers and thumb, inspected the glowing end satisfiedly. For a moment he watched the glowing end film over with ash. Then he bent his wrist to flick out the match, but he didn't. Wrist still bent, his eyes moved to the flame which was halfway down the wooden length of the match now, the blackened curling head protruding beyond it. He stood staring at the steady orange flame, his thumb and forefinger crawling to the end of the match to avoid being burned. Then he opened them, thumb and forefinger, and simply allowed the match to fall to the floor, the flame fluttering.

It might have gone out before it reached the floor. Or it might have dropped onto bare wood and burned itself out. But the match end fell, the charred end breaking off, onto the edge of a sheet of flimsy. The room was utterly silent, motionless, except for the tiny wedge of flame;

Carmody standing, Jake leaning forward in his chair as far as he could go, cigar gripped in his teeth, both staring at that match. It seemed to go out, a thread of blue smoke suddenly rising, but no. A tiny pale flick of flame showed, held motionless, then suddenly there was a yellow-edged ring on the face of the paper, turning immediately brown. It grew, a ragged hole in the paper, a circle of expanding char ringed by flame. Then it was audible, a tiny crackling, the flame reddening and jumping, the paper brightly afire. The enlarging ring of fire crawled toward the edge of the sheet, touched an overlapping sheet, and now it was afire, too.

I didn't remember standing up but of course we were on our feet, Julia and I, her hand clenched on my wrist, her eyes burning a question. I hesitated, standing there at the boarding, my eyes pressed to a crack. If either Jake or Carmody, now, had glanced at the bottom of the doorway, he'd have seen our stockinged feet and ankles, but of course neither did. The flame grew slowly, sliding across the sheets, and I knew that it could still be stamped out, that I could shove a shoulder to the loosened boards and have the fire out in seconds. I put on my shoes to be ready, and Julia put on hers. Then I picked up our coats and hats, and we put them on, our eyes at the cracks. I felt alert, ready to move the moment the fire got out of hand, and I smiled at Julia; I was apprehensive but not frightened, and neither was she.

But Jake was tied, helpless. I think he tried to hold in the words, his teeth clenched down on the cigar in his mouth, but he couldn't. "Jesus," he said, "no!" Then he looked at Carmody, and now his eyes were pleading; hating it, but pleading.

Carmody glanced at him. Then, fascinated, his eyes were drawn back to the plate-size ring of very slightly crackling, slowly crawling flame. "It's the answer, isn't it?" he said softly. "*Burn* your goddam files! And that's an end to it; I simply never thought of it."

"Carmody. For Christ's sake." Jake's voice was level, then it burst out. "Undo me!"

"Why?" He wasn't taunting him; it was a serious question.

"Carmody, you *can't*. What about other people in the building? Strangers who never did anything to you!"

"They'll escape; there are plenty of stairs. And the building's past its usefulness; Potter will be glad to have the site cleared." He grinned at

295

Jake, picked up his coat from the desk, and put it on. The flames, I saw, could still easily be stamped out, there was no question of that, and I waited. If Carmody left, I'd have to shove through the doorway, stomp out the flame, and we'd unfasten Jake. I still hoped Carmody didn't mean to leave Jake—and he didn't. He gave him a very bad few moments while he got into his coat. Then he grinned. "I'll let you loose. In a minute. We'll walk out yelling 'Fire!' and clear the building. No one will be harmed." Then he stood, waiting. But paper lying flat—and this was a thick carpet of overlapping sheets—doesn't burn too easily; to flare up fast it needs air from underneath. For a time the ring of flame expanded in almost a perfect circle. Then we watched it turn into a charred-edged distorted oval. My restraining hand still on Julia's arm and shoulder, we stood motionless, silent, watching. The importance of not interfering was strong in my mind; so long as they left soon, Julia and I could leave the building at a walk. I wasn't here to alter events, least of all to save a decrepit old building.

But Carmody was frowning and impatient now; he stooped, picked up a double handful of paper, and began crushing and twisting it into spills, tossing them onto the flames one at a time, heaping them, and now the flame and smoke suddenly flared, crackling like a bonfire, and Carmody swung to Jake, his hands busy at the buckle at the back of the chair. It was all I could do to stand still, and while Julia obeyed my hand on her shoulder, her eyes were growing frantic.

Then the buckle was undone, Jake springing from the chair, staggering after the cramped hours of sitting—and he actually fell forward into the flames! But he *hadn't* fallen; he'd thrown himself onto the fire and was rolling like a madman, and the smell of singed cloth and hair filled the office! He was putting it out, he was going to succeed! Then Carmody had him by the foot and ankle, dragging him from the fire on his back, Jake's arms and hands flailing for something to hang onto. He yanked his leg loose, rolling onto his hands and knees, scuttling back toward the flames, but Carmody ran past him. He thrust the side of his foot and ankle directly into a still-burning wad, and with a sudden thrust of his leg he kicked the flaming mass under the bottom board of our doorway, Julia and I instinctively stepping aside, and it slid across the floor between us and dropped. Instantly we heard it roar with new life as it fell through the air, and I turned in time to look down the shaft and see it hit in a ball of flame, shatter, subside for an instant; and then the mass of paper at the bottom of the shaft burst into fire like an explosion. It was no crackle now; the sound of the fire was the roar of a waterfall, and tongues of flame leaped a third of the way up the shaft—we could feel the beginning heat of it!

There was no stopping this, there could be no more waiting; I turned the point of my left shoulder to the boarded-over doorway, shoved hard with my right leg, and crashed through, sending the loosened boards flying into the office. I grabbed Julia's hand, and we stepped over the last two boards, still in place. Jake, on hands and knees, had Carmody's foot and ankle in both hands, Carmody hopping frantically on the other fighting for balance. Their faces turned, staring at us in absolute astonishment. For a frozen moment they were motionless, a tableau, Carmody on one leg, Jake on his knees holding the other leg at the ankle.

"Leave!" I yelled. "You've got to leave! *Look*, for Christ's sake!" I pointed through the doorway to the shaft; there were no flames visible but you could hear the roar and see the shiny heated air tremble and swirl. Then Jake yanked Carmody's leg with all his strength, and the other foot on a layered mass of slippery paper shot out from under him, paper flying, and he crashed to the floor, shaking it. From his knees Jake leaped forward like an animal onto Carmody, and they began rolling over the floor. I don't know whether Jake didn't understand that the fire had gone down the shaft and that it was far beyond putting out, or whether he'd lost all ability to think at the sight of everything he'd put his hopes in about to be lost. But out in the hall I heard running steps and somewhere else a man yelled "Fire!" A frantic rush of steps pounded down the staircase from the floor above, and a woman screamed chillingly. More shouts of "Fire!" and now it was Julia who counted. The rolling wrestling pair on the floor had been warned, they were free to leave, too, and I turned to the door, Julia's hand in mine, but she was yanking her arm trying to break free. She yelled, "Jake! *Jake*, for God's sake, leave!" I was hanging onto her hand so hard I was afraid I would splinter a bone, and now I dragged her to the door and opened it. I ducked behind her, grabbing her other wrist to keep her from hanging onto the door frame, and shoved her through; then I forced her down the short hall toward the stairs.

All over the building we heard screams, and yells of "Fire!," pounding footsteps, shouted names. My left hand on Julia's right wrist now, I was half a step ahead of her, pulling her along, and I swung us onto the stairs, running hard, feet flying, alert not to trip—then suddenly I grabbed the banister, braking us to a stop. These stairs were all right, and—we could see over the railing down the stairwell—so was the landing and the next flight of stairs to the second floor. But from the second floor to street level, the stairs directly beside the elevator shaft were completely gone from sight, a mass of solid orange flame and thick rolling black smoke writhing up toward us. A man in shirt-sleeves, a pen still in his hand, and two girls, their skirts lifted to mid-calf, were slowly backing up the staircase toward us, staring fascinated at the roaring black-and-orange mass below. Suddenly they whirled and ran up toward us.

We ran back up the stairs ahead of them, and then as fast as we could go, all out, down the long hall that ran the length of the building toward the Park Row staircase. Julia tried to slow at the short hallway branching off to Jake's office but I had her wrist, and I yelled that they were probably out and gone. Then we were past, our feet pounding the wooden floor toward the other staircase ahead. But fast as we'd moved we were still too late.

At the stairwell we looked over the rail, and the Park Row stairs were ablaze from first floor to second, the flames climbing the steps as we stared. Obviously the fire had flashed through the entire lower floors; the whole lower part of the building must be ablaze. The man and the two girls running behind us had come up, and just as we all turned to look back the way we'd come, the flames appeared at the head of the stairs far behind us. They shot higher, touched the underside of the next flight up, and then those stairs, too, were afire, and now I realized that the floor under our feet was hot.

I grabbed at the knob of a door beside us leading into one of the offices on the Park Row side; it was locked, and I turned—Julia's hand still in mine—and we ran down this hall along the row of doors to one I saw standing ajar at the very end. THE NEW-YORK OBSERVER, it said on the door when we raced up to it, and we ran into a large room of rolltop desks, wooden tables, file cabinets. A window stood open, its green shade flapping, and with Julia I ran directly to it. If there was to be any exit from this building for us it had to be through this window, and I was inwardly chilled with fright. Because I remembered the building's exterior. There were no ledges running around it, only windowsills, and we were three stories up, three very tall-ceilinged stories; we couldn't jump.

There were footprints in the new snow on the windowsill. Had someone climbed out and jumped? I looked out; no one lay sprawled on the walk below. But I saw that a crowd was already gathering along the east wall of the Post Office Building catercorner across the street, and in City Hall Park directly across. The crowd grew as we stared; I could see people running to join it along all the park paths. Directly below us in the street the first fire engine had stopped, two firemen running with a hose toward a hydrant, another uncoupling the horses. Bells were clanging, and down Park Row came another engine, white steam jetting from the tall brass cylinder behind the driver, its pair of white horses running all out, manes flying, hoofs striking sparks. And far across the park on Broadway a hook-and-ladder truck pulled by four gray horses made the obtuse-angled turn into Mail Street toward us.

All this I saw in a split-second glance; then I looked back to the window ledge, and saw the sign I'd once read from the street, THE NEW-YORK OBSERVER sign directly under the ledge. It was fastened to the wall at its lower edge, but the upper edge hung out a foot or so, held by rusty wires. I had no idea whether it would take our weight; I knew it wasn't meant to. It might take Julia's weight; she had to go first before my weight weakened the sign or tore it loose. I said, "Out, Julia! Onto the sign! Crawl to the Times Building!" But she shook her head, closing her eyes, and her face went white. Eyes still closed, she stood shaking her head, and I understood that it was impossible—there are people who simply can't take the fear of falling—for her to make herself crawl out onto that sign alone. I'd slammed the office door behind us to keep out the fire when it came. I turned to look at the door and black smoke was curling underneath it.

There was no other decision left to make now, and I stepped up onto the windowsill, crouching. I put my left foot down and out onto the top edge of the slanting sign, and slowly transferred weight to it. It held, and holding to the sill with both hands, I lowered my right foot into the trough between sign and building. Then I slowly stood, letting go the sill, easing my full weight onto the sign, the wind flicking hard-edged snowflakes into my face and eyes, and ridiculously, in spite of an agony of fear that the sign would tear loose and drop me, I was glad of my fur cap and overcoat. The sign groaned but it held, and I turned to the open window beside me. In her dark coat and bonnet, Julia stood petrified, staring at me, and before she could back away I shot out my right hand, grabbed her wrist, and pulled so hard and quickly that she had to get a knee up onto the sill or be dragged right across it. I kept up the pressure, pulling her forward, and now to keep from actually falling out she had to bring up the other knee and I kept tugging—sharp little yanks now—and with no volition of her own, but to keep from pitching out headfirst, she had to swing her legs over the sill, and then she was out, just ahead of me, half standing, half crouched on the THE NEW-YORK OBSERVER sign, a hand up before her eyes fending off the whirling snow. I saw a small kink in a wire just ahead of Julia straighten under the strain, then I was shouting at her: "Don't look down! Don't ever look down! Just *move!*" I pushed her, and then, half crouched—each with a left foot on the top edge of the sign, the other in the trough, our right hands moving along the face of the building—we crawled toward the Times Building ahead to the north, the wind moaning around us, snow and sleet slashing our faces.

This building and the Times Building were constructed wall to wall, touching or almost so, hardly a fraction of an inch between them. The two walls served as a solid, windowless and doorless, double-thickness masonry firewall and it seemed to be working: There was no sign of fire in the building ahead. But from directly below us as we crept along high over the street, a river of heat flowed up past us, partly deflected by the V of the sign, but almost scorching on our hands as they slid along the sign's upper edge. Julia moved more slowly than I did, hampered by her many skirts, and I had to stop, and again I became aware of the street and the park. Fire bells had been clamoring below us, and now I looked down through the haze of falling snow directly into the spark-belching stack of a fire engine; I saw firemen running with ladders and others standing in pairs holding brass-nozzled hoses playing thick white jets into the burning building, and their black rubber coats were already beginning to whiten with new ice. Police with lengths of rope stretched between them were forcing the crowd off the street and up over the curb and walks across Park Row. The crowd there, edging the park, was much denser now, and from here it seemed almost solid black. Strangely, to me, there were a number of raised umbrellas in the crowd against the snow, and for some odd reason the sight of the tops of those black umbrellas made me realize how high up I was. I raised my eyes from the crowd, and far off across the park on Chambers Street, a single-horse black ambulance, a white cross on its side, raced toward us from the west. I thought I heard its bell and I saw the driver, leaning far forward, whipping the galloping horse on; then it disappeared behind the Court House.

It took a second or two to see those things, and Julia had crawled on no more than a yard. I glanced behind and below, before moving after her: Flame shot high, black smoke rolled and coiled from the top of every window I could see on the first floor and from some of the second; and on the ledge of a third-floor window the man and two girls who'd been running behind us stood huddled. He had one arm outstretched across the two girls, keeping them off our sign, knowing it would undoubtedly pull loose and fall from the weight of even one more person. He saw me looking, and gestured wildly, urging me on.

I crawled ahead, trying to hurry, my foot snagged a support wire, and I heard it twang and snap behind me, heard the sign groan, felt it shuddering under our weight. A woman screamed in that instant, very close, and I thought it was Julia. But it came from just overhead, I realized, and I glanced up as I crawled on. The toes of a pair of shoes projected from a window ledge directly over me, and I leaned out over the street to look up. A woman was standing on the ledge, her eyes wide and blank with terror; there was no sign under her window.

Julia stopped suddenly, crouched motionless on the very end of the sign, and I leaned out over the street to look past her and see why she'd stopped. The floors of the Times Building were slightly higher than these, so the sign under its third-floor windows hung a little above ours. The sign was short, running under only two windows, and I could see the white letters on black reading, J. WALTER THOMPSON, ADVERTISING AGENT. There was a foot-and-a-half gap between the two signs, and Julia crouched at the end of ours, frozen—unable to make herself step up and across that empty space.

Our sign began vibrating violently, and I looked back: One of the girls on the window ledge, her face wild with panic, had a foot out on our sign, about to step onto it. The moment she did it would rip loose and fall; I *knew* that. Julia had looked back, too, and she saw and understood what I did. Suddenly she stood upright, and—I was certain her eyes were squeezed shut—she stepped blindly up and out over the gap with her right foot. It struck the wall of the Times Building, then slid down into the trough between wall and sign. She lifted her left foot from our sign, and threw her body forward across the gap, her left foot hunting for the top of the other sign. I never want to see such a moment again—watching Julia's foot plunge down toward the snow-mounded edge of that sign, knowing that if it missed she'd fall out and over its edge. But it struck, slithered an instant in the slippery snow, then her right hand smacked the wall of the Times Building beside her, and she stood swaying for balance. She half stooped, half fell forward, and—even in her terror she remembered me behind her—she crawled on, making room for me to step across, too.

But I didn't. I crept to the end of the sign I was on, and waited: I couldn't be certain Julia's sign would hold us both but now I knew that this would hold two. Looking back once more I saw only the one girl on it, making her way toward me. Julia reached the first window and before I had time to wonder if it were open, a man's coat-sleeved arms shot out, gripped Julia under the arms, and lifted her right off the sign and in through the window, her feet kicking a little as they disappeared.

I stood up then, stepped right across the gap, and moved quickly toward the same window. Just before I reached it I looked back through the snowstorm, and now the second girl was out on the sign, scuttling along it, but the man still waited on the sill, and now an occasional flick of flame moved out past him; the heat must have been terrible. I made a little saluting gesture and smiled, hoping it would encourage him; he had nerve. Then I was at the window, the same man—young and bearded—helping me in, and Julia and I were safe.

I had an arm around her waist, grinning at her, and both her arms were tight around me, her head pressed to my chest. She kept looking up at me, shaking her head, and making a sound that was partly a laugh and partly a sob of relief, murmuring, "Thank God, thank God, thank God." With my free arm I was shaking hands, as he introduced himself, with the man who'd pulled us in. He was Mr. Thompson, and this was his office. It was a fairly large room with a rolltop desk, two wooden chairs, a wooden file cabinet, a drawing board, and a batch of one-column newspaper ads, all type, thumbtacked to a bulletin board. Two men stood smiling, and I recognized one: It was Dr. Prime of the *Observer*, the man who'd directed me to the janitor of the other building several days ago. He and the man with him, he said, had escaped over the sign as we had.

Thompson turned to his window again, to help the first girl out on the sign crawl in, and Julia and I left. We walked down the hall to the building staircase, and a man in shirt-sleeves came hurrying toward us, struggling into a coat. He called out as we turned onto the stairs. He was a reporter from the *Times:* Were we among the people he'd seen escaping into the building from the *Observer* sign? I said we weren't, that they were all back in Thompson's office. Then Julia and I ran down the stairs to the street.

We stepped out into wind and slashing snow, and instantly a voice shouted angrily at us. I looked up; a fireman out by his engine stood gesturing violently, waving us on across the street; red coals from the firebox of the great brass cylinder sifted steadily down onto the melting snow between the big red wheels.

Before we could move, four or five men ran directly past our doorway carrying a long pair of extension ladders from a hook-and-ladder truck just to the north. One of the men, a stocky, angry-faced middle-aged man wearing a dull-silk hat tied on with a blue muffler, shouted straight into my face as he raced past, "Help us!" Julia and I ran with them, they set the ladder down, and I helped them swing it up against the burning building and raise the extension. As we heaved the extension up with a rope-and-pulley system built into the ladder, I had a chance to raise my head and see what we were doing.

Three men in vests and shirt-sleeves, one wearing a green eyeshade, stood on the ledges of three adjoining fourth-floor windows, peering down at us through a curtain of snow. The man in the window nearest the Times was panicked; his forearms upraised, fists clenched, he was shaking them violently up and down, his mouth wide-open and screaming meaninglessly.

Our ladder was too short: Rising between a pair of windows, it touched the building wall just above the third floor, well below the three men on the fourth. I didn't know what to do, and looked around frantically; half a dozen yards behind me Julia stood out in the street staring up at the burning building, and something about her expression made me run out beside her and turn to look, too. And now I saw the entire face of the building.

I have, as I always will, I think, a copy of *The New York Times* of the following morning, February 1, 1882. The entire front page and most of the second is filled by an account of that awful fire. I don't want to put down what Julia and I saw now; instead I will quote directly from the *Times*.

> . . . the upper windows . . . were seen to be full of living forms. Terror-stricken faces of men and women peered down through the smoke upon the thousands of their fellow-creatures below, stretching out their hands for aid, and shrieking loudly for rescue. [I'll see that forever; the way they held out their hands.] The mingled smoke and flames gave to the faces an unearthly hue, and the shrieks, mingled with the roar of the fire and the hoarse calling of the firemen, came to the ears of the surging crowd below like voices from the tomb. The firemen were doing all that men could do, risking their lives fearlessly in the effort to save those of the imprisoned sufferers, but their movements, rapid as they were, seemed slow enough to the suffocating creatures in the burning building. To reach them by the stairway was impossible, so quickly had the fire done its work. The firemen raised ladders, but they only reached to the third story, and time was necessarily consumed in raising the shorter ladders to increase their length. Meantime those in the building saw death steadily and surely advancing upon them from the rear, and the preparations to save them from the outside seemed endless. . . .

Julia screamed, her hand rising to her mouth: The panicked man had jumped, his body slowly turning in a complete somersault as he fell, his legs pumping furiously and instinctively against the air for a foothold that didn't exist. We swung our heads away an instant before he struck the walk.

Two firemen were running toward us from the Times Building carrying a wooden table; the angry little man in the top hat was shouting and beckoning at me, and I ran back to the ladder. We all stooped, gripped the legs, heaved up the ladder, and staggered sideways with it, the top sliding and bouncing along the building wall high above till it rested between and below the windows in which the remaining two men were crouched. Flickers of flame had begun darting out the tops of their windows, and occasional coils of smoke rolled out and up. The firemen had reached us, they shoved their table under the ladder legs, and we set the ladder down on it, and looked up the face of the building.

The ladder top was closer but still well below the two men. But under these two windows ran a sign; I couldn't read it through the snow and the smoke rising from the windows below. Now one of the men crept out onto the sign, crawled to a point over the ladder, turned, and hanging from the sign's front edge, lowered himself, his feet feeling for and finding the topmost rung. He let go, knees bending, grabbed the ladder top, then scrambled down fast as he could go. The little man in charge had been shouting at the second man: "You will be safe in a moment! Remain calm!" And now the second man reached the ladder like the first. As he clattered down, the little man was beaming, grabbing each of our hands, and giving it a shake. "I am Anthony Comstock. My heartfelt thanks! God be praised!" he was saying.

The two firemen stood waiting, each with his hands on the ladder; the moment the man on it dropped onto the street, they began cranking it down. They yelled a thanks to us, told us to get the hell across the street before we were killed, and we all ran across Park Row, ducked under the police ropes holding back the crowd lining City Hall Park, then turned to look back across the street.

I heard a sound from Julia; she was crying, and she slowly turned her head away from the burning building. It was a sight I don't think the modern world ever sees. Only the outer walls of that building were stone; the entire interior—floors, window frames, doors—was wood. So was nearly every object of furniture in all its offices and rooms. Even the walls and ceilings were wooden lath under plaster. And over the years the building had turned gunpowder-dry. The fire had almost literally exploded through the entire street floor, and swarmed up both flights of stairs to the next. Now broad pennants and gouts of flame leaped high, red, and frantic from every window of the lower floors; they actually seemed to be *trying* to climb higher. With those flames, thick sooty smoke roiled and twisted, flowing hotly up and out from the top of every one of those windows. The wind pushed down Park Row in bursts, the air thick with flying snow, and for a long moment or two the flames would bend with a gust of the wind, flickering and trembling, fighting to stand erect and reach up the face of the building again.

Any time I close my eyes and remember, I can see the horrible *color* of it: the dark grimy face of the old building, the terrible orange-red-and-black of the huge wild flames and rolling smoke, the spidery red lengths of the ladders, the people on the ledges mostly in white-and-black but one girl in a long vivid green dress, all of it seen strangely, nightmarishly dreamlike, through a white curtain of swirling snow.

We watched, thousands of us strung along the park edge and the east wall of the post office standing in absolute silence except for the steady pump of the engines, the shouts of the firemen, and the thin cries of the people high on the ledges. Those on some of the third-floor ledges were rescued fast, though the windows over the *Observer* sign were solid flame now. The last of the third-floor people were already climbing or being carried down; one girl hung limp over a fireman's shoulder as he brought her down, her arms swaying loosely down the length of his back. Suddenly the entire crowd moaned; a few of the extension ladders were apparently long enough to reach the fourth floor but as the topmost extensions were cranked up past the third floor now, the thicket of telegraph wires strung above the sidewalks pressed against the faces of the extensions. Without shifting the ladder bases impossibly close to the face of the buildings, the tops couldn't get past the wires.

Half a dozen firemen had lifted one ladder and, using it like a vertical battering ram, were trying to jam it past the wires by sheer force. We saw thin black threads of wire tauten, snap, and fall, the ends flying, and the ladder top burst through. Two more ladders were forced up this way, and we watched people scurry down, sometimes completely disappearing in black smoke. Other ladders couldn't get through, and we saw a man, and then a woman, hang from a ledge, feet dangling, and—at a shout from the fireman on top of the ladder—drop onto it, the fireman balanced, legs wrapped around the rungs, waiting to grab them.

Two men stood on the ledge of a fifth-floor window. Suddenly the glass of the window bulged, a ball of red-smeared black smoke rolled out between them, and I saw the shards of glass fly far out over the street, twisting and falling, splintering the light as they fell through the flying snow. The window gone, the heat was too much and the tail of one man's coat was smoldering and smoking as the men dropped to their knees, turned to face the building, then lowered themselves by their hands from the ledge, feet thrashing as they felt for and then found a toehold on the raised ornamentation set in the building's face over the fourth-floor windows. But now the flames were roaring up from the fourth-floor windows, too, and I'm certain they'd have died in seconds from the heat and combustion gases if a fireman hadn't seen them, lifted the stream of his hose from the third-floor window into which he'd been pouring it, and doused the two men. He kept it up, alternating the stream between the third-floor windows and the two clinging men until a ladder was forced through the wires to the fourth floor. A fireman swarmed up it, and must have shouted, because one of the two men shifted himself hand over hand a foot or so to one side, then dropped squarely onto the ladder, landing just below the fireman. It must have hurt and may even have sprained or broken something because he came down the ladder very clumsily—but alive. The second man, too, swung himself over the ladder, and dropped onto it.

All this in moments, *seconds*, after we'd ducked under the police lines; then Julia was shaking my arm. "Jake! *Jake!*" she was yelling in my ear. "Maybe *he's* at a window! On the Nassau Street side!" I'd actually forgotten Jake and Carmody; they'd been pushed right out of my mind. But Julia turned, and I followed her, struggling straight back through the crowd. We got clear, then ran along the ragged back edge of the crowd through the park and across Mail Street to the post office. There we worked our way to the front of the crowd again, people muttering, turning to glare as we edged past, a few cursing me. We got to the front, at the very edge of the curb, but the rope police-lines were up, and we couldn't cross. Here we saw not only the western Park Row face of the blazing building, but we looked down Beekman Street, too, and saw the entire southern face of the building.

A fifth-floor window facing Park Row and near the Beekman Street corner suddenly broke out, the glass flying. Behind it something was moving, then a woman climbed heavily up onto the ledge. Her face was black—from the fire, I thought for a moment—then I saw the spot of red above the dark face and realized it was a bandanna around her head. This was Ellen Bull, the Negro cleaning woman who had told me days before where to find the janitor. Standing far up there on the ledge now, she began waving her arms wildly about her head; it may have been in panic but I think maybe she was trying to dissipate a terrible heat pouring out from behind her. Because in almost the next moment the flames broke out and seemed to be actually touching her long gray dress. She dropped to her knees, turned, slid off the ledge, and now she was hanging by her hands, her body swaying in the air beneath it. There were no flames from the fourth-floor window just below her yet, the glass there unbroken, but there was no foothold here either. Off to our left two men had ducked under the rope and were running hard toward a wagon just across Mail Street. It had been trapped at the curb by the fire apparatus, an elderly woman next to us said, its team led off across the park by the owner. At the wagon the men were untying, and now yanked off, a gray tarpaulin covering, and they ran across Park Row dragging it with them. Under Ellen Bull's dangling feet five stories above them, they began spreading the tarp, and maybe a dozen men behind the police lines at the corner of Beekman ducked under and ran to them. But no one was in charge. We could see though not hear them shouting at each other, gesturing, yanking the tarp. They got it spread, waving each other to positions, but no one was looking up as Ellen Bull's hands opened, and she dropped.

There was a terrible moan from the crowd, and the men at the tarp looked up, tried to run into position, but she flashed past them and clear over here we heard the awful sound as she struck the pavement. There was a sigh of absolute despair from the crowd, and a woman near us covered her face with her gloved hands, bending double, elbows jamming into the pit of her stomach, and she fainted, toppling sideways but held partly upright by the press of people around her. Ellen Bull was being lifted onto the tarpaulin by the men who'd tried to save her; then four of them carried her the length of the building, and on into the Times Building. The *Times* said next morning that she'd been taken to the Chambers Street hospital, and died half an hour later.

On Beekman-street an aged man was hanging from a fourth-story window [says my copy of *The New York Times* for Wednesday, February 1, 1882—and now Julia and I stood in the silent crowd watching him] and the ready hands of the firemen were hoisting a ladder to reach and save him. He clung with a death-like grip, but the flames were stronger than he. They were seen to burst from the window by the lintel of which he was hanging. The firemen were almost within reach of him, when suddenly a deep groan escaped from a thousand throats, the old man's hand was seen to relax, and his body came tumbling to the hard pavement below. The man was Richard S. Davey, a compositor on the *Scottish American*. The unconscious body was taken to the Chambers-street hospital, where death relieved the man from further suffering in a short time.

From the corner of my eye I saw Julia turn to me, and when I looked at her fully her face was literally the whiteness of paper, and her eyes were enormous. Almost thoughtfully she murmured, "We could have stopped it," then she grabbed my arm in both her hands and shook me so violently I stumbled. "We *could* have!" she cried out at me in a rage. For a moment longer she looked at me, then turned away murmuring, "I can never forgive myself."

I had no answer; I wished I were dead. I had to move, had to *do* something, had to take some action against what was happening. In the line of cops holding the police-line ropes, the one nearest us stood like the others facing the crowd in his knee-length blue coat and tall felt helmet. But also like the others, he turned often to stare back over his shoulder at the fire across the street. This time when he did it I lifted the rope, shoving Julia under and ducking after her. Then we ran hard through the snow and the freezing streams from hose joints and hydrants. On the other side we were cursed by the cops, but we ducked under the ropes, pushing into the crowd, working our way toward the Beekman Street corner just ahead. We could smell the smoke here and hear the crackle and roar of the flames, and—during gusts of wind—feel the heat carried across to us. We reached the corner beside the New York Evening Mail Building, then started to work our way along Beekman Street toward Nassau Street, a short block to the east; I knew Julia hoped to find Jake there. And then I had my chance to do something.

In the next morning's *Times* account there is a paragraph reading:

While the excitement was at fever heat, Charles Wright, a young bootblack, who is well-known to people doing business around Printing House-square, looked up to the burning building and saw three men wildly gesticulating at the windows of the fifth or upper story. From one of these windows a wire rope was stretched to a telegraph pole on the opposite corner of Beekman-street. It had held a banner during the last campaign. A means of escape for the three men shot across Wright's mind in an instant, and in another instant he was engaged in putting it into execution. The telegraph pole was slippery with snow and ice but a dozen strong arms raised the boy and pushed him up until he reached the slight projections which serve as a foothold for the line-men.

The *Times* didn't have it quite right. The boy—a Negro, by the way—turned to the pole, shinnied up a couple of feet, but a sheeting of ice stopped him, and he yelled, "Help me git up!" All of us around the pole saw what he had in mind, and I stooped way down, my back to the pole, got my shoulders under his feet, then stood, boosting him higher. Two men, one on each side of me, each worked a hand between my shoulders and his feet, and shoved him up a yard or so more, and now he could reach the first of the wooden footholds.

Up the pole the young lad "shinnied," as he expressed it, until he reached the wire rope. It was the work of a moment [It took more than a "moment"; it was a good minute or more] to sever its connection with the pole, and the wire then fell to the side of the burning building. The three men on the fifth story seized this rope and slid down it, one after the other, in safety to the ground, although their hands were seriously injured by friction in the descent. Young Wright was received with cheers as he reached the ground, and he became the hero of the day. But for his timely action there is little doubt that the men thus saved would have been consumed before other aid could have reached them.

That part of the account is entirely right. It was beautiful to see that cable smack the side of the building when the boy let go of it; to see it hanging, then, to within a few feet of the walk; and to see the first man swing out onto it, and to see it hold. Each of the next two men kept his head, waiting till the man before him was on the ground. But they all slid too fast, burning their hands. And we did cheer Wright when he got down from the pole. I got a ten-dollar yellowback from my wallet, gave it to him, and half a dozen others gave him money; one man gave him a gold piece. The three rescued men came over, found the boy, shook his hand, and led him away with them, and I'm sure they must have done something for him, too, which he damn well deserved.

Opposite is a page, greatly reduced in size, of *Frank Leslie's Illustrated Newspaper* of February 11, 1882, showing Charles Wright up on the pole unfastening the wire to save the three men.

VIEW OF THE SCENE AT THE HEIGHT OF THE FIRE.

A FATAL LEAP.

ESCAPED BY MEANS OF A TELEGRAPH WIRE.

THE RUINS AFTER THE FIRE.

RESCUE OF THREE MEN BY CHARLES WRIGHT.

NEW YORK CITY.—INCIDENTS OF THE GREAT FIRE ON PARK ROW, JANUARY 31st.—SEE PAGE 431.

Julia and I were working our way through the crowd along Beekman Street, when all around us heads turned to look east. Just ahead, on the other side of a narrow alley, the wooden scaffolding of a big, new, still-unfinished stone building suddenly broke into flame; the fire had jumped clear across the street. The front of the building rose into two towers, higher than anything else around, and now the flames shot up the scaffolding to reach the towers. There it caught the window frames, in which glass hadn't yet been set, and ran up and along the eaves, gabled roof-lines, and the ornate railings of the tower rooftops. It was a sudden weird strange spectacle of burning rings, squares, triangles, and the parallel lines of the railings, like an enormous Fourth of July set piece seen high in the air through a snowstorm, and I think the crowd turned to it, as we did, in relief from the things we'd been seeing.

But while we were watching, a young woman had crept out onto a fourth-story window ledge of the burning building, and when I turned and saw her I wondered if she'd been inside all this time; maybe running from one side of the building to another till she found this one not yet on fire. Just above her, fire roared out of the fifth-story window as though it were fed by forced draft, the tongues and billows of orange flame shooting halfway out over the street like a kind of squirming canopy over her head. She wasn't panicked, though; she closed the window behind her, careful to pull it all the way down. Then she stood, raised her arms above her head, and put a hand on the window opening on each side, supporting and steadying herself. It was an astonishingly calm posture. There she stood, not shouting, not screaming, but simply looking down at us, waiting. She must have known there was no going back: that this window was her last chance, and that there wasn't much time before the fire burst through it behind her.

And nothing was happening, no fireman coming with a ladder below. I suppose they thought, and they couldn't be blamed, that no one else would appear at a window along here at this stage of the fire. The girl stood waiting, in her long black dress, arms outstretched, hands on the sides of the window opening which framed her; she wore a white scarf tied around her neck. Suddenly the glass broke behind her, and a tremendous gout of black smoke filled the entire window, rolling on out and hiding her completely. Near us a woman cried out, anguished, and the crowd stirred, muttering. Down the line somewhere a man was shouting angrily for a ladder. Out on Beekman Street a cop ran past us fast as he could go.

There was no flame in the black smoke pouring out over the ledge up there, and we all—every last soul in that crowd, I'm certain—held our breaths: Would she be gone when we saw the ledge again? Julia didn't know it but she had both hands on my forearm, squeezing, squeezing.

The wind pulled the smoke away fast and she was still there, one hand on the window frame, the other cupped tightly over her mouth; now she struck her chest hard and we could see she was coughing. Then again she stood, arms outstretched between the stone sides of the opening, looking down at us and waiting, and the crowd was murmuring at her calmness and bravery. Minutes passed; a man near us stood staring up at the girl and cursing steadily; he may not have known he was doing it. Then, finally, two firemen came running around the corner from Nassau Street carrying an extension ladder. But at the building wall they stood, still holding the ladder, and talking, one man shaking his head violently. The cop at the police line had run over to them, and now he ran back: "Ladder's too short!" he yelled to us. One fireman began running back the way he'd come, then stopped—I never knew why—and came running back. And now they lifted the ladder up against the building and rattled the extension up fast, the ladder tops bouncing against the wall as it rose.

It was too short. There was newspaper criticism, in days that followed, of the shortness of fire-department ladders in a time when many buildings were four, five, and six stories tall, and newer ones ten. This ladder, raised to its highest now, touched the wall a good four feet below the girl's ledge; and now again a great slow billow of soot-black smoke rolled across the windowsill behind the girl, and covered her completely. She'd have died, I'm certain, lost consciousness and fallen back into the building or out and down onto the street, except for the wind. It snatched the slow roll of smoke and sent it flying in thinning fragments along the face of the building, and we could see the white scarf and the black skirt fluttering.

I want to explain. Since we'd stepped out of the Times Building doorway onto the street and seen the burning building, I'd been silently talking to myself. I didn't really blame myself for failing to burst through into Jake Pickering's office and stamping out the tiny new fire when I could have; no one could have anticipated what so suddenly happened. What ate at me now was this: that by our hidden presence at that old event Julia and I might have changed its course in just the way Dr. Danziger had always been afraid of. Perhaps we'd made a tiny sound, for example, barely heard and hardly noticed by Carmody as he searched through the files. Yet even a tiny, hardly noticed sound might very slightly have affected his subsequent actions. So that he'd dropped his burning match an inch to one side, say, landing it on the paper it set alight. Otherwise, if we hadn't been there to make even the least sound, who could say but what his match would have fallen onto bare wood? And that he might simply have stood, then, and watched it burn out?

I knew Julia must be agonizing through her thoughts, too: these were real people we'd just seen die. And now this incredible girl stood high over the street above us, waiting in silent courage to either die or somehow be saved in what now had to be only a matter of seconds.

I couldn't take one more death; I couldn't have stood it if she'd fallen back into the building or down onto the street before me. I had to do *something*, and—it wasn't bravery, it was simple necessity—I was shoving my way forward, then I'd ducked under the lines and was running across the street. I didn't climb, I just sprang up onto the face of that ladder, then I was racing up toward the top. I hate heights; they make me uneasy and I can feel panic stirring inside me. But now there was no room for it. I was in a kind of exaltation, my head tilted back to stare up those rungs, hands and feet flying, the ledge rushing toward me. I didn't know what I was going to do up there, but when my hand closed on the topmost rung I did know, as though I always had known. Both hands rose, cupped over the rounded tops of the ladder, my feet continuing to climb until I was crouched in a ball, my left foot on the very top rung, right foot on the rung just below. For a moment I hung motionless, getting the feel of my balance. Then in precisely the right moment I lifted my hands free of the ladder and shoved upward with both legs, hard. For an instant I was balanced in the air, then I toppled, forward, and my clawed hands smacked down onto the window ledge, a hand on each side of the toes of the girl's shoes projecting over the ledge; I was looking up, and could see the buttons running down the side of one shoe.

I only had to tell her once: She turned quickly, and half climbed and half slid down my back toward the ladder. Looking down between my feet, I saw a fireman's head and shoulders appear. His hands rose, gripped her ankles, guided them down, and she slid from my back onto the ladder below me. And then—this wonderful girl had already worked out in her mind what to do about *me*. The fireman holding her, she reached up and set her hands on my waist, pressing in hard, and with that support steadying me I was able to let go the ledge, stoop quickly, and find the ladder tops again with my hands. We moved fast then, climbing down in a row, and we weren't even halfway to the ground when the black smoke from the window she'd stood in changed instantaneously to roaring orange flame.

I stepped down onto the street, the girl threw her arms around my neck and kissed me on the cheek. I asked her name; it was Ida Small, and I took her hand for just a moment and felt happy and redeemed.

I won't forget Julia's eyes ever, as I ducked under the line and she stood waiting. Hands were clapping me on the back, people congratulating me, someone yelling something right in my ear; an old man in a top hat, wearing his white hair in an antique length down to his coat collar, tried to give me his gold watch. I thanked him, refusing, then took Julia's arm, getting us out of there, toward Nassau Street ahead.

I could see that, in these moments at least, Julia was in love with me; her eyes were filled with it and all I could do was grin and keep feeling my head, wondering how I'd lost my hat. I felt like a fake because bravery hadn't been involved; I was looking for absolution. And found it: Ida Small, who really *was* brave, still had a life ahead of her.

The *Times*, next morning, said she was "employed as an amanuensis in the office of D. P. Lindsley, author of a work on Takigraphy." She was working alone, which was why she hadn't known about the fire till long after most others.

In the February 11th *Frank Leslie's Illustrated Newspaper* on the next page, the entire cover was given to a woodcut illustration showing Ida Small up on the ledge and "her anonymous rescuer" on the ladder. And while I know I shouldn't, I'm including that cover here, although the face of the man doesn't really look too much like me, and I wasn't wearing a vest either.

FRANK LESLIE'S
ILLUSTRATED
NEWSPAPER

No. 1,377. Vol. LIII.   NEW YORK. FOR THE WEEK ENDING FEBRUARY 11, 1882.   [Price 10 Cents. $4.00]

NEW YORK CITY.—THE ESCAPE OF MISS IDA SMALL, AT THE GREAT FIRE ON PARK ROW, JANUARY 31st.

At the corner we stood watching both the Nassau Street face of the building and the Beekman Street side, but there was no one at any of the windows now and even the ladders had been taken down. Like the rest of the crowd along both streets we just stood in helpless fascination, staring at the streams of water arching in through the window openings of the burning building, at the fountains of heated air and sparks rising endlessly from the stacks of the steam-powered pumpers, at the slanting, whirling curtain of snow.

Suddenly the fire ended: The roof fell in, crashed tremendously onto what was left of the next weakened floor, then the entire interior smashed through to the basement and an enormous gust of sparks, smoke, and whirling burning fragments rose fifty feet over the roof with a sighing whooshing sound that must have been heard for blocks. In moments, the building gutted, the fire was over, and you could see through the window openings on up through emptiness to the sky. In the basement the wreckage still burned but almost feebly, the force of it gone, and the snow fell, whirling prettily, down through the emptiness enclosed by the walls. Above every gaping window-opening of the burned-out building lay a great fan-shaped smear of blackened masonry, and already it was becoming hard to picture this great dead hulk as having once been alive and full of people. It seemed impossible that we'd been in it listening to Jake Pickering and Andrew Carmody only—I pulled out my watch, and couldn't believe it—an hour ago.

The enormous spectacle over, the crowd around us began talking, the sound rising to a steady excited murmur, and I heard a voice say, "It's a blessing the paper moved out."

To Julia I said, "What paper is he talking about?"

"The *World*," she said dully. "Until a few months ago that was the World Building, and most people still call it that. They occupied the entire top floor; scores of them would surely have died up there."

"The *World*," I said slowly, trying the sound of it, and then I understood. *That the sending of this*, the note in the old blue envelope in Kate's apartment had said, *should cause the Destruction by Fire of the entire World*—"Building" *w*as the missing word—*seems well-nigh incredible. Yet it is so*. . . . And for the rest of his life that was to torture Carmody's conscience. I felt the weight lift from my own conscience: Now I knew that nothing Julia or I had done had caused the fire.

I took Julia's arm and worked our way out of the crowd, south down Nassau Street. We heard a shout, a single warning cry, then a vast murmur from the watching crowd, and as we swung around to look, the entire Beekman Street face of the building leaned inward, very slowly, nearly imperceptibly, then faster, faster, and—still nearly all of a piece—it crashed like a felled tree down onto the burning wreckage in the basement. And now, the entire empty interior opened to view and to the storm, the building was truly gone.

We took the El home. Julia sat looking blindly out the window, and I spoke to her now and then, trying to comfort her, but couldn't. It was true, and I knew it, that nothing we'd done had contributed to causing the fire. We'd been invisible spectators influencing events in no least way. And while I couldn't explain why I knew that, the certainty of it sounded in my voice, and I think I persuaded Julia of that truth. But of course she wished that we *had* altered subsequent events; I'd literally forced her out of Jake's office and now Julia had to wonder if we could have helped him by staying. I had to wonder, too, though I wouldn't have changed what I'd done, or most likely we'd be dead too.

At the house Julia went straight up to her room, exhausted. There was no one downstairs, the place silent. It was past lunchtime, and we'd had no breakfast, but I wasn't hungry so much as empty, and I didn't feel like prowling around the kitchen. I went up to my room, took off my coat, and lay down. After the night and morning we'd spent I was very tired but too full of what had happened, I thought, to be able to sleep. But of course I did, within only minutes after stretching out on top of my bed.

It was dark when I woke up from a hunger so intense it made me dizzy. I had no idea what time it was; it might have been very late. But Maud Torrence and Felix Grier were in the parlor reading when I came downstairs. They glanced up and nodded to me casually, and I understood that they didn't know I'd seen the fire. Just as casually I asked if Jake Pickering were home, and Felix, already turning back to his book, just shook his head.

I walked on through the darkened dining room to the kitchen; I could see a light under the crack of the door. Julia sat at the kitchen table with her aunt, eating—cold sliced roast, from dinner probably, bread and butter, hot tea—and as soon as I walked in Aunt Ada hopped up to get me some, too. From her face I could see that she knew all or at least something about what had happened, and she didn't question me. Julia looked up and nodded wanly; there were dark circles under her eyes. I was certain I knew the answer, but had to ask, "He's not back?" Julia said no and, squeezing her eyes shut, dropped her chin to her chest, and sat shaking her head as though trying to deny a mental picture or a thought or both, and I didn't know what I could say to her.

When I finished my supper Julia was still at the table, hands folded in her lap, waiting. I looked at her, and she said, "I want to go back, Si," and I just nodded: I didn't know why, but I had to go back, too.

Outside it was snowing again and there was still a wind. The snow on the walks was too deep for walking now but there were wheel marks in the street, and we walked in those to the El station on Twenty-third Street. And by ten o'clock we were standing against the east wall of the post office, sheltered from the wind, and:

. . . the snow in Park-row in front of the *Times* office and in front of what remained of the old *World* building [says *The New York Times* of February 1, 1882] was disturbed only by the feet of the firemen and Police officers. Lines of hose across the car tracks were buried out of sight in the snow, and the streams of water that played from the nozzles were seemingly wasted. The flames continued as bright as though a great flood could have no effect upon them. The gas supply pipes created much of the glare. Men and women and children huddled close to the walls of the Post Office on the Park-row side. . . . The wind increased to a gale, and the snow beat about with such effect that the crowds were driven to seek refuge elsewhere, and by 10 o'clock the streets in the neighborhood were almost deserted. A few staid persons, who appeared like statues of snow, seemed to think they were in duty bound to be on hand. They rubbed their backs against the sides of the Post Office and kept their eyes fixed upon the ragged Park-row wall of the burned building. The winds howled through Beekman-street, and Park-row, and whipped up Spruce-street into Nassau and Park-row with such fury that those who ventured to turn those corners were fairly lifted from their feet. The City Hall clock appeared as though in a mist. . . . By 11 o'clock the snow had almost ceased to fall, the shrieks of the winds had died away, and the atmosphere was clear and cheerful, but the crowds did not return.

We were among the last to leave, hypnotized by the black hulk across the street. The streetlamps before it were smashed and unlit, and the face of the wall was dark and without detail. But the lower window openings were sharply defined by the steady glare of the flaming gas pipes on the other side, and we could see the new snow mounded on their sills. The wreckage looked centuries old, an ancient ruin, and the dark shapes of the firemen were motionless, the only movement the play of the water arching through the empty windows. Higher up, the walls were touched by the diffused sourceless light that so often accompanies a nighttime snowfall; and we stared up at the smoke-blackened OB-SERVER sign along which we'd crawled, and just beyond it on the face of the Times Building the sign of J. WALTER THOMPSON, ADVERTISING AGENT, onto which we had stepped and saved our lives. Finally we left; as we crossed Park Row into Beekman Street, the City Hall clock said ten to eleven.

The Beekman Street sidewalk had been trampled clear of snow all day and into the evening; now with only an inch of untouched new snow it was easily passable. We looked across the street; here the wall had fallen, and we looked into the emptiness of what had been the inside of the building. The flames of the broken gas pipes roared softly, steadily, white arches of water wetting down everything near them. But the fire itself was over, "the Destruction of the World" complete, and it was already passing into—not even history, but oblivion. At this moment a swarm of artists would be hard at work under gaslight, over at *Leslie's Illustrated Newspaper* a couple of blocks to the west at Park and College Place, and at *Harper's*, carving out the woodcuts of the fire that would appear in a week or so. The girl beside me, and most of the city, would look at their work for a few moments, recreating the sensation. But I understood as they could not how quickly the men now carving those wooden blocks would be gone, together with the entire population that would look at them, incredibly including this girl. Here and there a last few copies would yellow in files, turning into something quaint and faintly amusing; and this vanished building and awful fire would be gone from all human memory. For a few moments, walking along Beekman Street across from the wreckage already being covered over with snow in places, I was overwhelmed in melancholy; human life was so short it seemed meaningless. It's the kind of thought you have, usually, only in the deep middle of the night waking up alone in the world. But I knew a

320

time when this building and fire were as though they'd never been, and so I had the feeling now.

We turned the corner into Nassau Street and—without speaking, each sensing it in the other—we began to hurry, suddenly anxious to leave this place forever. Ahead, just across the street from the Nassau Street entrance to the Times Building, the streetlamp was unbroken, and its circle of yellow light lay sparkling and softly beautiful on the snow of our walk. Here, too, on this walk, the snow was almost untouched, but not quite; a single line of footsteps marked it, disappearing into the darkness beyond the lamp. They began as though someone peering into a window opening of the destroyed World Building had crossed Nassau Street, stepped up onto the curb, and walked on.

We reached the footprints, our own beginning to appear beside them. Then, directly under the lamp, I gripped Julia's arm, and we stopped. Sharply imprinted in the snow, just as I'd seen it once before, lay the tiny shape of a tombstone; within it dozens of dots formed a circle enclosing a nine-pointed star. But this time there were a lot of them. Behind each sole print in the line of footsteps ahead lay the round-edged straight-bottomed tombstone shape. "They're *heel* prints," I said; then I crouched beside one, pointing. "The star and circle are the heads of the nails."

I looked up at Julia, and she nodded, mystified. "Yes, of course; men often have that done when their boots are made, a personal design of some sort." She shrugged. "It's just a good-luck sign."

I nodded; I understood. This was Carmody's sign; he had escaped the fire. And only a few moments ago he was here—to look once more upon what he had done. For a moment longer I stood staring at that strange little print in the new snow. He'd be buried under that sign. Years from now his widow would wash and dress his newly dead body, then bury him under this identical sign. Why? Why? The question still remained.

We walked all the way home. The wind gone, the snow stopped, it was no longer cold; and this late and so soon after the storm, the streets were deserted and we had the world to ourselves. At least the streets we walked on were empty; half lost most of the time, we traveled back and forth east and west, but working always to the north along the old old streets of the old old city of lower Manhattan. The walks were occasionally shoveled clear but generally not, so we walked in packed-down carriage and wagon ruts. As the storm clouds broke up, a half-moon began to appear and disappear, so that sometimes, a block or more from a streetlamp, we moved through darkness. At others we walked in moonlight that, doubled by reflection from the snow, was like day.

Often we walked along, or crossed, silent residential streets precisely like those still existing in great areas of twentieth-century San Francisco. In San Francisco not just isolated relics but entire whole blocks of nineteenth-century houses stand untouched, looking in every way, except for parked cars, like still-existing old photographs of themselves. And now, here in lower Manhattan of the nineteenth century—we often think of it wrongly as having been nothing but block after block of brownstones—were whole blocks and streets of tall, wooden, wonderfully ornate houses exactly like their counterpart streets in modern San Francisco. Occasionally there was a light far back in a house behind a curtained window; someone sick, we supposed. And once in a while, far ahead or down a side street, we saw a moving figure. Occasionally, no wagon tracks visible, there were stretches of knee-deep drifts, and taking her hand, I helped Julia through them; until presently, after one such stretch, we didn't let go. Holding each other's hand, we walked through that silent bright night, and, as I'm certain Julia did, too, I could feel the horror of the fire begin to recede into the past and let go of us. At a long, shiny stretch of hard-packed snow surface, icy at this time of night, we ran on impulse, still hand in hand, then slid along that stretch, balancing in a way I'd done last in grade school. It was late and we didn't laugh or call out, but we grinned. And once or twice we scooped up snow, packed it, and arched it high into the air for the fun of it. It was fine, that walk, and at one point we heard—from a stable somewhere back of a house, I suppose—the sudden high whinny of a horse and I was suddenly aware of the enormous *mystery* of being here, walking the streets of New York City on a winter night of 1882.

We reached Fourteenth Street and turned east to walk a short block to the foot of Irving Place, which led, then as now, straight up to Gramercy Park. Just ahead, the building on the southeast corner of Fourteenth and Irving Place was brilliantly lighted, and we heard music: a waltz. "The Academy of Music," Julia said, and when we reached it the side entrances were open, and we stopped at one of them to look inside.

What we saw was stunning, dazzling. At least a third of the main floor, the seats removed, was covered by a slightly raised dancing platform, waxed and shining, filled by whirling, dipping, waltzing couples. In the gallery a great orchestra played, violin bows in slanted motion, and every box—level after level of boxes curving in a great horseshoe from one side of the stage clear around to the other—was filled with chatting laughing people overlooking the dancers. Still more spectators filled the stage and the entire rest of the main floor. Great urns of flowers stood along the edge of the dancing platform, and high above the stage hung huge letters and numerals made of gas pipe. They were lighted, and the yellow-white letters of flame spelled CHARITY—1882.

The ball was an island of light, music, and excitement in a white and silent winter night; it seemed magical to have come onto it like this. Every man there wore white tie and tails, yet the variety of hair length and style and the even greater variety in beard, mustache, and sideburns kept them individuals, recognizable and interesting to the eye. And the *women* in their long but off-shoulder and often surprisingly low-cut gowns—well, if the daytime dress of the eighties tended to be drab, these women made up for it tonight. I don't know the terminology of women's clothes or the materials they're made of; I'll quote again directly from next morning's account of the ball in the *Times*:

> Mrs. Grace wore cream colored brocaded satin with pearl front. Mrs. R. H. L. Townsend wore blue satin brocaded with leaves and flowers of gold; Mrs. Lloyd S. Bryce wore white brocaded satin flounced with lace; Mrs. Stephen H. Olin wore white watered silk, with pearl and diamond ornaments. Mrs. Woolsey wore black tulle with black satin waist and diamond ornaments. Mrs. C. G. Francklyn wore white silk and diamonds. Mrs. Commodore Vanderbilt wore white silk and diamonds. Mrs. Crawford wore blue silk. Mrs. J. C. Barron wore white satin and lace with diamonds.

My reason for quoting this is that these women, a hall filled with them, absolutely *glittered*.

Standing a few feet from us, a man in white tie and tails but with the look of a cop had been watching us; tolerantly enough, the time for ticket collecting long past. I looked over at him now, and he sauntered over. "I know someone here," I said to him. "Is there any way to locate her?" I narrowed my eyes and pantomimed looking out over the hall; for some reason we treat cops as though they were all dumb. He turned to a little gilt chair, picked up a handwritten list of several pages, and handed it to me. "Proscenium Boxes," it was headed, and under this it listed boxes and their occupants by letters beginning with D, and I looked quickly down a long column of names. "Artist Boxes," said the next column, and these boxes were listed by composers' names, beginning with Mozart, Meyerbeer, Bellini, Donizetti. I looked through the names under these, all beautifully written in a woman's hand; I looked under Verdi, Gounod, Weber, Wagner, Beethoven, Auber, Halévy, Grisi, and then, under Piccolomini, I found the names of four women and their husbands, and one of the four was the name I was looking for.

The guard, or cop, pointed out the Piccolomini box, and it was nearly full; four women and three men sat watching the dancers below. The guard walked off, and I murmured to Julia, "There they are: four women. One of them almost certainly knows that today her husband killed half a dozen people. And nearly burned to death himself. So tell me: Which of those four women is she?"

"There is no question of that, is there?" Julia said. "The woman in the yellow gown."

I nodded; there was no question at all. There she sat, her spine straight, her back not touching the little gilt chair, a strikingly handsome woman in her mid-thirties; and her face was absolutely composed. She'd have been good-looking, very nearly beautiful, except that looking at her face you hardly thought of that; I've seldom seen a face, and never before or since a woman's, of such utter composure, extreme capability, and absolute determination. "Do you see what she's looking at?" Julia said, and I realized that the woman in yellow wasn't watching the dancers.

In the very front of her box, one of the largest and most prominent in the hall, Mrs. Andrew W. Carmody was staring ahead at the great flaming gas letters—CHARITY—1882—that said this was the greatest social event of the year. And I understood why Andrew Carmody had acted, had *had* to act, as he did. "What are you thinking?" Julia said; I couldn't take my eyes off that fiercely beautiful face.

"She scares me. I feel chilled, looking at her. But I'm fascinated, too—sort of illicitly thrilled."

324

"Oh? And why?"

"Because the time will come when that kind of face and person and the kind of high drama she's involved in won't exist anymore; they'll be out of style. Evildoers will be tawdry, committing crimes of violence or bookkeeping in which any sense of drama will be nonexistent. And of the two kinds of people and evil, I'll take those with a sense of style."

Julia was looking at me, her brows raised quizzically. I took a last look at Mrs. Carmody and that wonderful ball; then we turned and walked away, moving past a long line of carriages waiting at the curb, their sidelights flickering, their horses motionless under blankets, the liveried men waiting, and then up the silent street to home, the sound of the waltz dying behind us.

20

I SLEPT very late next day. When I finally came downstairs it was well past noon but I had breakfast anyway, reading the *Times* account of the fire, which covered the entire front page and part of the second. Every other boarder had long since gone, so I sat alone; Julia served me. Looking very pale, violet smudging under her eyes, she brought in coffee when I sat down, and we said good-morning, nothing more.

I had pancakes, Aunt Ada cooking them; I could hear the rhythm of her spoon against the crockery bowl stirring up the batter as Julia stood pouring my coffee. When Julia brought in my first stack, she stood beside the table as I buttered them, I looked up at her, and she said, "He didn't lose a happy life, did he, Si?"

I shook my head. "He was obsessed. Half insane with cravings he would never have satisfied. Nothing would ever have been enough for him, Julia. Once in a while there really is a man better off dead, and he's one."

But Julia rejected that, shaking her head even before I'd finished. "These aren't matters for us to decide. If we'd stayed, if only we'd *stayed*—"

I said, "Listen," and picked up my paper, which was opened to the second page. " 'Assistant Foreman James Heaney, of Hook and Ladder Company No. 1,' " I read aloud, " 'said that his truck reached Nassau-street about two minutes after the breaking out of the fire, and that he was never more astonished in his life. A powder magazine, he thought, could not have flashed up more quickly.' " I looked up at Julia, then back at my paper. " 'Captain Tynan said tonight that in all his experience on the Police force he never saw a fire burn with greater fierceness and intensity.' "

I turned to the first page, ran my finger down a column, and read, " 'The following statement regarding the origin of the fire is made by Mr. E. O. Ball: "I was passing down the rear or Nassau-street stairs . . . and when near the foot of the stairs flames burst up through the new elevator shaft from the basement. Nothing had occurred indicating an explosion up to that moment. The flames rushed up the shaft like a flash of lightning, and almost as quickly up the stairways in terrible torrents of fire, with dense black smoke, which almost instantly cut off all possibility of egress. . . ." ' "

She had a hand pressed to her chest. "It really says that? I haven't looked at the paper; I couldn't bear it."

"Those are actual quotations, word for word, from *The New York Times*, February 1, 1882, anyone free to read it and check up. The paper's full of them, Julia. " 'Edward S. Moore of the Scottish American,' " I read, " 'says that . . . in less than one minute after the alarm of fire was given all means of escape by the Park-row side of the building was cut off.' And there's more of the same from 'John D. Cheever, of the New-York Belting and Packing Company . . . 'Alfred E. Beach of the Scientific-American' . . . and a guy named James Munson who looked out his office window in the Tribune Building, saw the World Building just as usual, then looked out again only five minutes later and saw the entire building aflame. Julia, let yourself alone. You didn't cause the fire, couldn't have stopped it, and couldn't possibly have helped Jake." I tossed the paper to the table, then pointed to a paragraph. "Don't miss this, by the way: It's a full account of Dr. Prime's escape along the *Observer* sign into Thompson's office in the Times Building. The man with him was named Stoddard."

I'd helped Julia; I could see I had. What I'd read was true, and I saw the conviction and sad knowledge come into her eyes, finally, that nothing could have been changed. When I'd finished my pancakes, Julia brought in a second stack, and I read her a couple more items I'd found in the paper. Guiteau's relatives, a brief story said, were planning to refrigerate his body after the execution, and exhibit it, charging admission; I smiled but she didn't. A second item said the Harvard class of 1876 had collected money and had sent one of its members to help a classmate in Denver accused of murder, and Julia did smile a little.

Sometime around midafternoon I was looking through a *Harper's Weekly* by a parlor window, when I saw a cop walk past in his tall felt helmet and long blue coat; there were sergeant's stripes on his sleeve. He turned in, rang our doorbell, and Aunt Ada answered it; Julia was upstairs somewhere. I heard the cop at the door, badly mispronouncing and slow with the syllables as though he were reading the name, say, "Miss Charbonneau? She live here?" Aunt Ada said yes, and called up the stairs to Julia. The cop said, "Morley, Simon Morley. He live here, too?" I was up by then, walking into the hall, paper in hand, before Aunt Ada could answer; the cop stood on the stoop, a small square of paper in his hand.

"I'm Simon Morley."

He nodded. "Come along, then." Julia was coming down the stairs, and he nodded toward her. "The both of you. Get your coats."

Aunt Ada and I both said, "Why?" simultaneously.

"You'll be told, all in good time." Something about the way he'd said *all*, and *you'll*, and *along*, told me he was Irish.

I said, "Well, I'd like to know now. Are we under arrest?"

"You damn soon will be if you don't do what you're told!" His eyes were suddenly furious and vindictive, the way cops so often are if you question anything they do. Julia was patting her aunt's arm and murmuring something soothingly. I knew we weren't exactly in the heyday of civil rights, and for Julia's sake, not to say my own, I shut up.

I got my coat and fur cap from the big mirrored stand in the hall, and Julia got her coat and bonnet from the closet under the stairs, assuring her aunt that we'd undoubtedly be home before long and that there was nothing to worry about.

The carriage waiting at the curb was for us. I'd assumed we'd be walking, but the cop stepped past us, opened the carriage door, and gestured us in. Watching us, a man sat on a little folding jump seat facing the rear. I helped Julia into the wide seat opposite him. Then, stooping, I stepped in between her and the man in the jump seat, feeling the little jounce and sag of the carriage body under my weight. The cop on the walk slammed the carriage door as I sat down beside Julia, and as I looked out at him his arm flew up in salute to the man sitting opposite us; not very smartly but with plenty of respect. The reins snapped, the carriage started up, and the man nodded to the sergeant in calm response to the salute. Then he turned to look us over, and as I saw that formidable chilling face full on I suddenly knew who he was. I'd never set eyes on him before, but I *knew*, and suddenly I was badly scared.

He was big, with heavy square shoulders: This is a picture I found of him, and it's a good likeness, though it doesn't show the bald spot at the crown or the look of those eyes in actuality; it's the eyes that were frightening. They were big, and gray, close together as you see, but alive with his own secret interest in us, moving over our faces and clothes, absolutely without interest in us as human beings. We were something to him, something important, but not as people.

He had the largest mustache I've ever seen, completely covering his mouth. And if that enormous walrus mustache, lying there on his face as heavy and thick as though it were carved out of wood, either looks funny or sounds funny, believe me it was not. I stared back, fascinated, wondering if the mouth behind that mustache was so cruel it had to be hidden.

He wore a black overcoat, unbuttoned now; a black braided suit with cloth-covered buttons; a single-breasted black vest with a heavy gold watch chain passed through a buttonhole; black shoes. He wore a stiff wing collar and a big genuine-looking pearl stickpin—the one in the picture, I think. But it was the face that held me; it moved slightly as those strange gray eyes searched us, frisked us, examined our skins for scars, I could almost believe. I had to drop my eyes to get away from his, faking an interest in my own shoes, and the action made my face flush and made me feel guilty.

This was Inspector of Police Thomas Byrnes of the New York Police Department, its most famous or notorious member by far; and if he had personally come to take us away, then this was no ordinary arrest and I felt a steady thrill of sharp fright. Trying, I suppose, to fight it off, to stand up to this man, I asked a question I meant to sound hard and assured. But it didn't come out that way; it sounded half humorous in intent as though I were ready to claim I was only kidding. I said, "Well? Aren't you going to warn us of our Constitutional rights?"

Nothing changed in his face, but the gray eyes moved rapidly over mine, extracting whatever meaning there might be in this boldness. He saw there was none, and without expression he answered in a ludicrous mixture of half-illiterate speech and a strange broad "a" of what I suppose he took to be upper-class talk. "I'll warn you; keep your half-witted [only he pronounced it "hoff-witted"] remarks to yourself, or I'll show yiz the fat end of a sap." Strange talk from Inspector Byrnes but I didn't laugh, even inwardly.

And then we rode in silence for a dozen blocks, down Third Avenue under the El, rattling and swaying over the cobbles, occasionally lurching or sluing a little sideways through patches of snow. Julia stared out the little round window beside her, angry, refusing to look at Byrnes. I sat, occasionally looking up at him but mostly at the floor or out at the street. The day was overcast and the stores we passed were lighted only

330

feebly, the lights generally far back in the store, yellow and steady if the gas flame was mantled, reddish and flickering if not. A good many stores had permanent wooden awnings built out to posts at the edge of the walks, and once again as I had before, I tried to interest myself in the knowledge that because of this and the frequent hitching posts, Third Avenue in 1882 looked very like a set for a Western movie. But I wasn't interested at all.

We passed Cooper Institute, looking just as I'd seen it last, as far as I could tell, then curved left where Third and Fourth merge into the Bowery. We jounced along a few blocks farther under the El; a train darkened the day even more as it clattered over us, and a little shower of sparks and red embers dropped from the engine, one of them striking the horse's rump and lodging there for a moment, turning gray, but the horse gave no sign of feeling it. "Anything to tell me?" Byrnes said suddenly and I nearly jumped, then shook my head, and so did Julia. A typical Byrnes trick, I thought—the long long silence, then the sudden question that would startle us into talking, if we'd known what he wanted us to talk about. But I was wrong; he was way ahead of me. He had a reason I don't think I could ever have anticipated.

A couple more blocks, then we swung right, onto Bleecker. Three short blocks down Bleecker, then left onto—I saw the painted glass sign around the panes of the streetlamp—Mulberry Street. Halfway down the block we stopped on the left, and I saw two great square lamps flanking the steps leading up into a four-story stone building; the panes of the lamps were green, and I knew this was a police building. The driver was on the walk opening the carriage door, Byrnes gestured, and Julia stepped out. The driver—in derby and tan overcoat, but a cop— was waiting, and as her foot touched the walk he took her arm, firmly. Byrnes motioned me out, and was right behind me, a hand tight around my wrist. Quickly up the steps, and as the plainclothes cop with Julia opened one of the big double doors, I read the gilt letters, heavily shaded in black, on the large plain fanlight over the doors: NEW-YORK POLICE HEADQUARTERS.

Inside, walking very fast, down a wooden-floored hall past a uniformed very stout cop at a desk, I saw worn floors, stained and chipped porcelain cuspidors, dirty dark-green plaster walls, and I smelled the smell, whatever it's made up of, of this kind of much-used building.

Moving just short of a run—why, *why* do cops habitually and meaninglessly act nastily, as though it were a kind of instinct?—we were hustled down a flight of stairs, and then into a dingy, low-ceilinged, brick-walled basement room. In it stood a small table; an ordinary wooden kitchen chair; a perforated gas pipe backed by a reflector and mounted on a stand, and connected to a gas outlet by a flexible tube snaking across the wood floor; and, on a wooden tripod, an enormous camera of reddish polished wood, brass, and black leather.

Three plainclothes cops in shirt-sleeves followed us right in; one was bald, the other two wore their hair parted on the left like the inspector's, and two of them wore walrus mustaches, though smaller than his. At a gesture from Byrnes, Julia and I took off our coats and hats, and piled them on the table by the door. One of the men had walked immediately to the camera and begun fiddling with it. The other two stood waiting at the chair before the camera—to hold me down in it, I realized, if need be.

I had no chance of resisting successfully and I knew it, and yet it was the same Constitution now as in my time, and I had to say something. I said, "I want to know why I'm here. I want to know what I'm charged with. I want to consult an attorney. And I refuse to be photographed before I do."

Byrnes nodded to the two cops. "You heard the gent; tell him why he's here." They grabbed both my arms, one on each side of me, one shot up his knee, kicking me right at the tailbone with tremendous force—Julia cried out—sending me stumbling across the room toward the chair; I'd have fallen if they hadn't had hold of me. They whirled me instantly around, twisting my arms in the shoulder sockets; then, each with a hand on a shoulder, they slammed me down into the chair so hard the wood groaned and the chair slid on the wood floor. My mouth was open in a soundless gasp, the pain forcing tears to my eyes. One of the men bent over to bring his mouth close to my ear, and his voice was gleeful with the pleasure of what he'd done and was doing. He said, "You're here, *sir*, because we want you here!"

I turned fast, spitting the words into his face before he could draw back. "You *stinking* son of a bitch!"

His hand shot forward to grip my throat and hold my head so I couldn't move out of the path of his other fist drawing back fast to strike, but Byrnes spoke quickly. "No, I don't want him marked." After a moment the fist dropped, the hand at my throat squeezed hard, then dropped.

My rebellion hadn't helped, and I'd known it wouldn't. But I was willing to have made it. Beside me the two men stood ready for more resistance, their faces hoping I'd offer it, but once was enough.

The man at the camera had a kitchen match in his hand, and now he lifted one leg and swiped the match across the tightened cloth of the seat of his pants; the match snapped into flame, and I smelled the sulphur. He turned a brass valve, gas hissed from his standing light, then he touched the match to the perforations, and it popped into flickering red flame. He turned the valve, lowering the gas, and the dozens of little tongues shrank to a steady blue, and the light from the shiny reflector behind it was hot on the skin and bright to the eyes, and I squeezed them nearly closed. "None of that!" A hand on my shoulder shook me, a lot harder than necessary so that my teeth clicked. "Open your eyes!" I forced them open, and the man at the camera was stooped under his black cloth. The camera bellows slid forward, stopped, moved slightly back; then I saw his hand squeeze a bulb.

"Got him," he said, and then it was Julia's turn. I was glad to see that no one touched her when she sat down. I might have felt I had to do something if they'd been rough with her, and been beaten to the ground. The photographer squeezed the bulb, and when his head ducked out from under the black cloth, Byrnes's extended arm and forefinger were pointing at him. "*Now*," said Byrnes, and the man murmured a quick yessir, and actually trotted from the room with his plates. One of the other two men had his notebook out, and Byrnes glanced at me. "Twenty-eight to thirty," he said, and the man wrote quickly. "About five-ten, a hundred and fawty," Byrnes said, and the man's pencil flickered. Byrnes described me and my clothes, including hat and overcoat, then Julia and her clothes; and the man with the notebook hurried out.

Byrnes beckoned to me, and I walked over. He said, "Give me your wallet," and I reached into my inside coat pocket for it, feeling I'd never see it again. With my other hand I brought out the little handful of change I had in my pants pocket, and contemptuously held both change and wallet out to Byrnes. "Keep the change!" he said, smiling at his own joke, and the plainclothesman snickered. Byrnes didn't touch my wallet; he shook his head, and said, "Count it first." I did: I had forty-three dollars. When I finished, Byrnes was scribbling in a little notebook, then he looked up. "How much?" I told him, he filled in the amount, tore out the little page, and gave it to me, a handwritten receipt for forty-three dollars, signed *Thomas Byrnes, Inspector.* "We're not petty thieves here," he said, then turned to Julia, and told her to count the money in her purse. He took the bills—she had nine dollars—gave her a receipt, handed the purse back, and Julia thanked him drily and asked why he'd taken our money. "You might try to escape," he said, shrugging. "But you wouldn't go nowhere much without money, would yez?"

Back into the carriage then, Byrnes facing us again, watching, waiting. Over to Fifth Avenue, then we turned uptown. I said, "Where are we going?"

"I think you can guess."

"No, I can't."

"Then wait and see."

Our carriage rolled through Washington Square, looking then as now except that there was no arch; even a lot of the buildings were the same, especially along one side of the square, and for a moment it seemed impossible that in the next second or two I wouldn't see a car somewhere. Block after block then, trundling up Fifth behind the endless *clop-clop-clop-clop* of our horse. From time to time Julia's eyes met mine, and I'd try to smile reassuringly, and so did she. Then I'd look out the windows, trying to be interested in the people and buildings we passed, but the certainty that somehow we were in serious trouble wouldn't let go my attention.

When finally we stopped, between Forty-seventh and Forty-eighth Streets, I'd guessed where we were going—so had Julia, I could see when she glanced at me—but I couldn't possibly imagine why. There it stood across the sidewalk from our carriage door: Andrew Carmody's Fifth Avenue mansion looking almost exactly like the old Flood mansion still standing on San Francisco's Nob Hill, even to the magnificent stone-and-bronze fence around its patch of lawn. The carriage door was open, the driver gesturing us out, waiting to take Julia's elbow, Byrnes reaching for my wrist.

On the wide front porch, the cop rang the bell, and we all stood waiting. Did Carmody think, when he'd seen Julia and me burst out of the boarded-up room beside Jake's office, that we'd somehow been part of the blackmail scheme? Was he going to accuse us of it now?

A maid opened the door; she wore a long black dress with sleeves to the wrists, an enormous white apron, and a complicated white lace cap. She was a girl, no more than fifteen, cheeks as red as though they'd just been scrubbed. "Please come in, gentlemen and miss; you are expected," she said so respectfully she seemed frightened. Neither Byrnes nor the cop said anything as they started us forward, and I smiled at the girl and thanked her, to show up what louts the cops were.

Facing us across a wide hall as we stepped in was a pair of magnificent staircases of dark polished wood, curving in opposite directions. As I followed the maid my head was turning, trying in spite of what was happening to us to see all I could of the immense hall stretching off into the distance on each side of the stairs. I saw tremendous rugs on a tiled floor, walls ornate with molded plaster, globed light brackets, tables, chairs, flowers in vases.

Through a vaulted doorway, down a short hall of polished parquet flooring, through another high doorway, and into a room as different from Aunt Ada's parlor as two rooms could ever be. It was four times as large, with french doors along one side, and its furnishings were entirely French, in the style, I think, of one of the Louis'—graceful, and so light and dainty they hardly seemed usable. The white woodwork and the backs of the two tall doors from the hall were heavy with gilt ornamentation. Framed paintings hung on the walls; white marble busts stood in arched niches. A white-and-gilt grand piano, or possibly a harpsichord, stood near the windows.

It was a beautiful room, all soft colors, and standing in it as though it were a setting for her—posed before a small white-manteled fireplace—stood Mrs. Andrew Carmody in a long loose-sleeved pink dress, holding a folded fan of ivory. Her face was precisely as Julia and I had seen it last night in her box at the Charity Ball, as composed as though she had never in her life had a doubt.

"Good afternoon, Inspector: Mr. Carmody has been told you are here and will be down in a moment." She smiled at Byrnes, as easily unconscious of the rest of us as though she actually didn't see us.

"Good awfternoon, Modom Carmody. I trust he ain't suffering?"

335

"His burns are painful, but . . ." She moved a shoulder slightly, and smiled at him brilliantly in a way that said the conversation was over. Her fan spreading open as she lifted it, she moved it once or twice before her face, and to cover the truth that he hadn't been asked to sit down, Byrnes stepped over to a marble bust of Marie Antoinette, and bent forward to inspect it.

Steps were sounding slowly down one of the entrance-hall staircases, then along the parqueted floor of the hall. They reached the open doorway and as I turned to look, the steps became soundless as the shockingly bandaged man slowly crossed the great rug toward a chaise longue. The white bandages crossed his forehead, covered both temples and cheeks, and wrapped snug around his throat. But the nose and the narrow strips of flesh between it and the bandage edges were so red and swollen, so terribly burned, that whatever film of horribly damaged skin was left seemed hardly enough to hold in check the blood that seemed ready to break through just behind it. His hair was completely gone, burned off, the top of his head swollen and crusted. His eyes were inflamed, and he constantly blinked or momentarily squeezed them shut. One heavily bandaged arm hung in a black sling, and the finger ends protruding from it were swelled huge and split.

At the chaise longue he lay back as though exhausted. He wore black pants faintly striped in white, and a dark-blue braided smoking jacket. A folding table beside the chaise held a glass, a pitcher, an open cardboard pillbox, and a fever thermometer. For a few moments he lay silent, eyes closed, then he opened them, said, "As—" and coughed heavily several times, wheezing deep in his chest. Then he tried again, keeping his voice so subdued in order not to start up the coughing again that it was nearly a whisper. "As you see, I have been burned; in the fire yesterday. I was fortunate to escape with my life." He drew a sudden deep breath, his hand rising quickly to his chest as though he were about to cough, but he swallowed twice and repressed it. For a moment or two he lay motionless, eyes closed. Then he opened them, glanced at Julia, glanced at me, then nodded several times to Byrnes. "Yes," he said, almost whispering it, "it is they. Thank you, Inspector. Please sit down."

"Oh," Byrnes said as though he were standing only because he'd absent-mindedly forgotten to sit. He pulled a small chair to the chaise and sat down. "Now, sir, pray tell what has happened."

336

We stood listening while he told Byrnes about the letter Pickering had sent, and the meeting in City Hall Park. "I didn't doubt he had documents; as a contractor I'd done honest work for City Hall for which there were undoubtedly records of payment. Not everything done for the city while Tweed was in power was dishonest."

"Of cawss."

"And yet his documents had a slight value. I am engaged in certain delicate business negotiations involving millions, which could be upset by gossip and slander, however false. So I had the man followed. Pickering made no attempt to avoid this, and the gumshoe easily learned that he lived at 19 Gramercy Park. I had him ascertain the names of the other occupants, too. For all I knew, some of them might also be involved in this absurd scheme. Yesterday morning I met Pickering, who took me to his secret office in the old World Building; and I brought a thousand in currency, prepared to pay it merely to be rid of the man. If he'd insisted on one cent more, I'd have had you arrest him at his home."

"Quate rate," said Byrnes, and it took me a moment to understand that he meant *quite right*. It was a pretty good story, I thought; altered about as I'd have done, I supposed, if I'd been in his shoes. Stopping occasionally to cough, he went on to say that Pickering reluctantly agreed to accept a thousand dollars, knowing he had no proof of crookedness; that Pickering had explained what the boarded-up doorway was about; and that while Pickering was pulling documents from his files in exchange for the thousand dollars, a fire broke out in the next-door elevator shaft, he had no idea how. To his absolute astonishment we—he pointed at us—had burst through the boarded-up doorway, I had sprung at Pickering and grappled with him, while Julia began stuffing the money in her clothes. He could hear the crackle of flames, see smoke rolling up the shaft, hear shouts of "Fire!" and hear people running; he had to run for his life. He began to cough heavily, and Mrs. Carmody, glaring at us, hurried over, and held the glass of water from his table while he sipped at it.

I could only stare at him; then I turned to Julia as she turned to me, both of us mystified. Why Carmody wanted to involve us I couldn't begin to imagine—and then I thought I might have a hint, because the bandaged head was shaking angrily as he pushed the glass aside, pulling himself upright on the chaise. "I escaped down the Nassau-street stairs," he said in a harsh whisper that was the equivalent of a shout. "One of the very last to do so, I suspect. At the cost of burns about the face and head and of one hand and arm that my physician says"—his voice was bitter— "will disfigure me for life." His face would be distorted forever, he said, and permanently reddened; very little hair would ever again grow on his face or head. "And *they* are responsible!" he said, his finger shooting out at us, and I felt he almost believed it, and that certainly he blamed us for his terrible injuries and hated us.

Obviously, he finished, we'd known about Pickering's scheme. As of course we had; at least I had. Of the people at Pickering's house, we were the only two who matched the descriptions and ages of the pair who'd burst into Pickering's office; that's why he'd had Byrnes bring us over for identification. He lay back in his chair. "And if Pickering is still missing, then they are responsible for his death. Except for their interference, he could have escaped with me."

Byrnes turned to look at us. "Pickering is still missing."

"Then there stand his murderers."

I'd never faced such hate as came from the reddened eyes blazing at us from between the bandages. Was there any use in my protesting the truth: that *he* had started the fire; that he, not we, had struggled with Pickering; that Pickering's death was Carmody's fault? I wanted to yell it out, but in that case how could I account for our hiding next to Pickering's office? By telling Byrnes all about Danziger and the project? There *was* no explanation for our being there.

Byrnes was looking at me. "Well?" he said. "Anything to tell me *now*?" And after a moment I shook my head.

The doorbell rang. We heard steps toward the front door, the door opening, the maid's voice, then a man's. Footsteps approached along the hall; then the maid stopped at the doorway, and the cop we'd left at 19 Gramercy Park came walking in carrying his helmet under one arm. He actually bowed, head ducking humbly, then took a step backward, a finger rising to smooth his mustache. The bandaged head on the chaise nodded regally in return, and Mrs. Carmody graciously inclined her head. The little ceremony actually took several seconds, and if I hadn't known this before, I'd have known now that this was a place of wealth and power and that both these cops understood it. "Well?" Byrnes said then, and his voice indicated *his* standing in this room, far superior to that of the uniformed cop.

"Yes, sor." The sergeant unfastened the two brass buttons of his uniform coat just over his belt. He shoved a hand in; then with the instinctive feeling for drama that everyone of this time seemed to be born with, he walked over to the table beside Carmody's chaise longue. Not till he reached it did he pull out a thick paper-banded stack of greenbacks and slap them down on the table. "Found this, sor, in his room." He nodded at me. "The landlady showed me the room, and the money was in his carpetbag, hidden under some clothes."

I was paralyzed, almost literally; I couldn't move or speak. Byrnes had crossed to the table, to lean over and examine the stack of greenbacks. "And is this your money, sir?"

The bandaged head turned as though it hurt, and the inflamed blinking eyes looked down at the money. "Yes, the bills are marked. My bank will identify them, every one." And Byrnes picked up the packet, turned, and walked over to Julia and me, tucking the bills into an inside coat pocket.

"Well?" He stopped before me almost cheerfully, and for the third time said, "Anything to tell me now?"

"There's nothing to tell." I shrugged. "He's lying, and the money is a frame-up to support the lie." I didn't know whether the word "frame-up" was in use yet, but if not he understood me all the same, and nodded. "We never touched that money—" I stopped suddenly; I'd thought of something. "Have you examined it for fingerprints?" I said excitedly. "You'll find his, all right!" I pointed to the chaise longue. "But you won't find mine or Miss Charbonneau's!"

"Won't find what?"

"Our fingerprints!"

"I don't know what you're talking about."

He didn't. I could see that he didn't. I didn't know when the use of fingerprints as identification was discovered, but obviously it was not yet. "Never mind. He's lying. That's all I have to say."

"Well, that's possible," Byrnes answered. The sergeant walked over to him and whispered in his ear. Byrnes nodded, and the sergeant left. Byrnes looked at me speculatively for a moment, then rubbed his chin as though genuinely considering the possibility that I was telling the truth.

"We have a chawge and a denial. If you two done it, nobody but Mr. Carmody seen you. Tell me this: Were you there at all? Hiding next to Pickering's office? For some innocent reason, perhawps?" He smiled invitingly.

But I'd had time to understand that it was impossible to admit even being there. How could we explain it? If I admitted we were there but couldn't say why, Carmody's charge seemed true. I shook my head immediately. "No. The only connection between Pickering and us is that we lived in the same boardinghouse. We don't know anything about his blackmailing this man. Or whether it's even true that he was. I begin to suspect that maybe Mr. Carmody here killed Pickering. And left him to burn. He's afraid the truth will come out, and wants a scapegoat before questions start being asked. Since we lived where Pickering did, he hides the money in my bag or has someone else do it, and accuses us."

Byrnes was nodding sympathetically. "Quate possible, if you wasn't in the World Building at all yesterday. And you say you wasn't?" I nodded, and Byrnes stepped to the doorway. "Sergeant!" he called down the hall.

Footsteps sounded immediately on the parquet flooring of the hall; then the sergeant stopped in the doorway, his helmet still under his arm like a football. A man walked past him into the room, and I realized that I knew him but for a few seconds couldn't place him. He nodded politely to Mrs. Carmody, then glanced at the bandaged figure on the chaise, but looked quickly away. He stared closely at Julia and me for several seconds, then nodded to Byrnes. "Yes, it is they." He glanced at a pair of photographs in his hand, and I recognized them; they were copies of the police photographs of Julia and me taken earlier. "I recognized them from your photographs," he was saying, handing them to Byrnes. "As Dr. Prime told you, they escaped as he did; I helped them climb into my office." He looked at Julia and me again, his eyes genuinely troubled. "I am sorry if they are in trouble," he said, and it was an apology to us for the necessity of doing what he'd done. Byrnes thanked him, and J. Walter Thompson, into whose office we'd climbed from the burning World Building yesterday morning, nodded around the room and left. In spite of what he'd just had to do, he was a nice man and I almost wished I could call after him, and assure him that his little one-man business was going to succeed, and even grow.

We were deeply in trouble now. *Anything to tell me?* Byrnes had asked in the carriage on the way to Police Headquarters, and several times afterward. And certainly if we'd been in the World Building fire at all, we had something to say to an inspector of police unless we were hiding something. He'd pointedly offered us the chance to speak, I was sure now, in the certainty that it would make any explanation we made after we'd been accused seem like an obvious lie. He'd pinned us nicely, and I knew that in spite of the absurd way he talked this was a dangerous man.

"Congratulations, sir," he was saying, offering the credit to the bandaged man on the chaise. "Appears like you caught a pair of murderers."

"Thanks to you. When I am somewhat recovered, and back on Wall Street, I should like to thank you again. In my office. You still retain your well-known interest in the Street, Inspector?"

"Oh, yas, indeed."

"Splendid; we all appreciate it. Not a pickpocket, not a troublemaker down there since you established the John Street deadline. I will let you go now, Inspector. I know you will be fully occupied in making entirely certain this pair does not escape justice. *Once that is done* . . . come see me at my office."

"Count on both those things, sir."

I was hypnotized, listening to these two bargaining over us. And I was scared. But when I looked at Julia to smile reassuringly at her, it wasn't false; we were in trouble but I knew that for Carmody to prove anything against us in a courtroom, his word against ours, would be a lot different from persuading Inspector Byrnes.

And in less than a minute I learned that Byrnes thought so, too, and I began to feel almost cheerful. We were hustled out of the house, the sergeant between us, one hand gripping an arm of each of us, Byrnes behind us. At the curb Byrnes stepped forward to open the carriage door. But then, a hand on the door handle, he stopped, and turned to look at us thoughtfully. He said, "In the cawtroom, he'd charge and you'd deny. There's the money found in your room and Thompson's identification. But there is the smell of Tweed Ring scandal around Carmody too, isn't there? And he *did* pay blackmail, howsomever small." For a moment he was silent, looking at us consideringly; then he opened the carriage door. "Jump in, Sergeant!" he said, and the sergeant looked surprised but he let go our arms and did what he was told. Then Byrnes turned to us, his back to the sergeant, and spoke quietly; neither the sergeant nor the driver could hear him, I'm certain. "Constitutional rights, you say," he murmured as though the novel sound of the phrase intrigued him. "Well, all right; I think it's too soon to arrest you. I think we have to find more evidence." For a moment longer he stared at us, then seemed to reach a decision. "On your way," he said. "But you're not to leave the city, understand?" We looked at him, not entirely sure he meant what he seemed to be saying. "Be off with you!" he said almost kindly, smiling with a kind of fatherly affection for Julia, at least as well as that hard face could manage.

It was no time to wait till he changed his mind, I thought, and I took Julia's arm, and we walked away, fast, south on Fifth in the opposite direction from the way the carriage was headed. A dozen steps, twenty steps, thirty, and he hadn't changed his mind and called after us. I couldn't resist looking back. He was still standing by the carriage watching us. "Sergeant!" he yelled suddenly, and yanked open the carriage door. Then he pointed after us :"Our prisoners are escaping!"

I stopped, my hand on Julia's arm swinging her around with me, and we stood staring. My mind wouldn't translate what was happening into sense. Because the sergeant's helmeted head had appeared out the street-side window of the carriage, and he was pointing at us, his arm extended, his forefinger aiming. But it wasn't his finger at all, because I saw it flash, heard it roar, felt the *zing* of the bullet split the air near our heads.

Our minds worked then; we were running for our lives, and we heard the explosion of the sergeant's revolver, the high-pitched *zing*, and I saw a chip fly out of the balustrade of the brownstone house just ahead. Again the astonishingly loud explosion of the big revolver, then we were at the street corner, and in the instant of hurling ourselves around it I had to look back once again: Byrnes was in the street, his hand on the sergeant's wrist forcing the gun straight upward; not to save us, I knew that, but because there were too many startled citizens now, stopped and staring, between us and the gun.

We were around the corner on Forty-seventh Street running hard, Julia with her skirt gathered up in one hand, people gaping. Across the street a man on the steps of the Windsor Hotel suddenly ran down and across the cobbles toward us, his hand raised in a "halt" gesture, saying something, I couldn't tell what. But I raised a fist, and he stopped at the curb and watched us tear past. It was a long crosstown block, an endless row of identical brownstones, and halfway down it Julia gasped, "I can't, I have to stop!" We slowed to a walk, and I looked behind. But though people were turned to stare after us, others leaning out of carriage windows or looking back from the drivers' seats of delivery wagons, no one was chasing us and there was no sign of Byrnes or the sergeant, I didn't know why.

We reached Madison Avenue. A horsecar traveling south was just past the far corner, and we stepped out into the street, and I helped Julia up onto the rear platform as it moved past, then swung up after her. It was rolling along about as fast as we could have traveled on foot unless we'd run full speed without letup, which was impossible; and this was a lot less noticeable. I paid our fares, we sat down and stared out the window, getting our wind back and trying to look as inconspicuous as possible. But no one looked at us. People sat staring out their windows at the quiet street. I'd walked along here in the sun, with Felix's camera, day before yesterday. People coughed, yawned, and got on or off the car, crunching down the aisle through the ankle-deep straw that was supposed to keep your feet warm and didn't. At Forty-fourth Street and again at Forty-third, I looked down the short block to our left at Grand Central Station standing exactly where it was supposed to stand, and where I'd seen it countless times. Only now it was red brick and white stone, and only three stories high.

Forty-second Street just ahead was busy, noisy; we could hear the endless clatter of iron-tired wheels over cobble paving, and two cops stood out in the street directing traffic. One was short, the other tall, but both had great protruding stomachs bellying the blue cloth of their long uniform coats. Our tracks curved east onto Forty-second Street, and the tall cop beside the tracks glanced toward our car, then took off his helmet and peered into it.

We drew abreast of him, starting to take the curve, and when he was directly beside our window I leaned across Julia's lap to peer down into his helmet and see what he was looking at. I don't think I've ever been more astonished. There, jammed down into the deep crown of his felt helmet, lay my face looking up at me. Beside it lay Julia's—our police photographs again, mounted on heavy cardboard—and now I understood why Byrnes's photographer had actually run from the little basement room with his plates. From that moment on, as fast as he could work, our photographs were being duplicated. And as we'd jogged block after block uptown in the carriage, as we'd stood listening to Carmody, to Byrnes, to Thompson, these photos were being rushed to very possibly every cop on duty in the city—*the warning to look for us already out while we were still in custody.*

Now in the instant of our passing, the cop on Forty-second Street looked up from the helmet in his hand. And I knew too late that for an hour or more he'd been checking our photographed images with the faces of all the pedestrians crossing before him and of the passengers in each car passing his post; there was probably a promotion for the man who got us. Our eyes met and, a foot from mine, I saw his widen in startled recognition and—this astonished me—in sudden sharp fear. What he'd been told about how dangerous I was, I didn't know, but— we were a car length past him now—I heard the urgency in his voice as he turned and shouted at the other cop. He answered—I couldn't make out what he said—and they both began to run down the middle of the street after us.

They were twenty yards behind, and they didn't gain—running heavily, flat-footedly, heads far back, each with a hand on his jiggling belly. It was a scene in every way precisely like many another I'd seen in old-time silent-movie comedies. They weren't shouting now; they needed all their breath to run. But the short one pulled out the long nightstick hanging from a loop of his wide leather belt, held it high over his head, brandishing it threateningly, and the resemblance to the Keystone Cops—they even wore mustaches—was complete.

Except that there was nothing funny about them. They were absolutely real, and I knew that if they caught us, we could end up in Sing Sing prison. Neither driver nor conductor had seen them, though a couple of passengers had turned as Julia and I had, to stare back at them. At Grand Central Station just ahead the car would stop, I was sure, and they'd catch up with it in seconds. I was sliding from my seat toward the aisle, a hand on Julia's wrist; and looking as serene and innocent as I could manage, I walked on toward the front of the car,

Julia right behind me. We passed the conductor, I smiled at him vaguely, then we stepped out onto the open front platform.

Directly before Grand Central Station, high over the center of the street, stood the little wooden gabled building of an El station, stairs leading up to it from each side of Forty-second Street. It was a spur line apparently, leading to the main line of the Third Avenue El, I supposed, and I had only one vague plan, if it could be called even that. There were four flights of steps leading up to that station, two on each side of the street, and the station stood directly at the end of the spur-line track. Any one of the four flights could be reached through the station, and if we ran up one of those flights we had an exactly even chance— two cops, each coming up one flight of steps after us—of running down one of the other two flights and escaping them.

It was all I could think of, and standing on the platform, I murmured, "Jump off and run when I do," and Julia smiled and nodded as though at a casual remark of mine. I was watching the driver, I saw his mittened hands draw back on the reins, felt my body lean slightly forward as the car began to slow; then I nudged Julia, and we jumped off and ran hard. Down the center of the street alongside the horse, then cutting before him, ducking between two wagons, one of them piled high with barrels, up onto the sidewalk, and then pounding up the stairs two at a time, Julia in the lead and running as fast as I was.

People coming down paid us no particular attention, merely stepping aside to let us pass, and I realized that people running up or down these steps at Grand Central were no unusual sight. I heard shouts behind us, turned at the top of the flight, and saw the taller of the cops hit the first step—he was moving faster than I'd thought—then we ran on into the station. Inside we walked. I put on a smile as we approached the ticket booth, pulling two nickels from my pocket. Julia was tugging at my sleeve, I looked at her, she gestured with her chin, and as we stopped and stood waiting while the man in the booth leisurely tore two tickets from his roll, I looked out and saw a one-car train standing on the track, engine first with its front end nearly touching the station house here at the end of the single track. Inside the car an old man, his clasped hands and chin resting comfortably on the top of his cane, sat quietly waiting till it was time for the train to start. At the far end of the car the conductor sat staring out the window toward the other side of the street.

It was momentarily tempting but as I took our tickets I shook my head at Julia. To be caught inside that car, a cop entering at each end, just couldn't be risked.

We walked quickly out onto the platform, and passing the engine, I turned to look back toward the head of the stairs we'd come up, and saw the helmet rising into view, then the cop's face, and saw his head turn and catch sight of us. Then Julia and I ran along the platform toward the stairs at its opposite end, and as we passed the car, I heard the conductor slam the waist-high metal gate of its open platform. The tiny steam engine behind the car tootled, and I turned to see its miniature drive-shaft move; then the car was rolling past us and Julia moaned—we could have been on it!

But it was too late now. *Chuff-chuff, chuff-chuff*—the engine, moving backward behind the car on this return run down the single track, was picking up speed, the conductor at the back of the car slamming the back-platform gate closed, and the second cop's helmet rose into sight at the head of the stairs we were racing toward. They'd outguessed us. I swung around, and the other cop, belly jouncing, a hand holding his helmet on, was running along the platform toward us not fifty feet away.

I've never really been one of the people who think fast in an emergency. I think fast enough, that is, but usually what I think of is the wrong thing to do. This time, hardly thinking at all, I did precisely the right thing. Both cops running toward us now, I turned to Julia beside me. My arms, swinging in toward her waist like giant claws, gripped her, raised her high off her feet, and dropped her down on the other side of the waist-high gate on the rear platform of the car rolling past us. Then—the short cop grabbing at me, his hand raking down the back of my coat as I turned—I jumped into the open doorway of the engine cab as it passed, swung around fast, and the cop running at me ran his face right into the heel of my hand. He staggered, then stood staring after us as we rolled past the end of the station platform.

Across the little engine cab from me, the engineer, leaning out his window to stare down the track ahead, had neither seen nor heard me jump on, over the rattle and rapid *huff* of his engine. Standing there in the engine's open doorway, I was completely oriented; I knew I

346

was directly above the center of Forty-second Street, moving east just past Grand Central Station. The sketch—just below—is one I've made showing our train just after leaving Grand Central Station and the El platform. Third Avenue, toward which we are moving, is off to the right, and that's Forty-second Street below our train. I looked up and saw only the gray and empty winter sky in the space I'd always before seen filled by the soaring, needle-spired tower of the Chrysler Building. I glanced

down, and where the base of the Chrysler Building belonged stood the round little red-brick-and-white-stone tower you see in my sketch, no more than a dozen feet taller than our tracks. And in that moment—the moment of my sketch—moving through this partly familiar yet utterly strange and now suddenly hostile city, I felt a rush of homesickness nearly overwhelm me; I had to close my eyes for a moment to fight it off.

Within seconds we were slowing down, backing in between the twin arms of the station platform at the other end of the two-block spur line. It wasn't impossible that the two cops could hurry along Forty-second Street for those two blocks, even commandeering a carriage or wagon for all I knew, and I stood in the doorway of the engine cab staring ahead at the Third Avenue line, hoping a train we could transfer to would be just coming in. But there was none even in sight, and the moment the wooden floor of the station platform appeared beside me, I hopped off the engine—I don't think the engineer ever did see me—and let my own momentum carry me trotting forward to the slowing car just ahead. Julia was standing at the gate, the conductor right behind her. "That's against the law, you know!" he said angrily to me. I wasn't sure whether he meant lifting Julia over the gate or riding the engine, and I said I was sorry, and handed him our tickets. Then—I wanted to yell at him to open the gate but was afraid if I did that he'd be deliberately slower than ever—he got out his punch, carefully punched both tickets, handed them back to me, and I thanked him. And only then did he open the gate and let Julia off. Then we ran for the stairs.

I think the two cops could have been there if they'd really tried, waiting for us to step down off the stairs onto the walk at Third and Forty-second. But they'd have had to move faster than they'd done in some years, and no one grabbed us. But across the street a cop walking his beat looked into a saloon over the tops of the two waist-high latticed doors of the entrance, then strolled to the curb at the corner, and stood, skillful as a professional entertainer, bouncing and twirling his club at the end of its thong. I had the feeling that he'd given far more time to club twirling than crook catching, and as we turned and walked south on Third Avenue, moving away from him as fast as we could without obviously hurrying, I was glad that this was his beat. Julia was looking at me questioningly, and I understood. Were our photographs in his helmet, too? I shrugged; if not, they would be soon. Every cop in the city would have them, to be passed on to the next shift, and with extra cops and probably plainclothesmen out, too. The reward Carmody had almost openly offered Byrnes would be big if we were caught and convicted, or "killed while escaping"; it wouldn't matter which. Because Byrnes was clever: Our "escape" and flight, of course, would be accepted as confession.

The cop on the corner was half a block behind now and hadn't even glanced at us. But the next one could be different, and if he wasn't, then the one after that. We simply could not walk through the streets for block after block; we'd be caught within minutes. And any public transportation would be as bad. We had to get off the streets right now: into a hansom, it occurred to me longingly, where we could sit back and move unseen through the streets with time to think. But Byrnes knew the problems of people trying to hide; it takes money, and he had ours.

"Julia, have you any friends who'd hide you for a few days, lend you some money?"

"In Brooklyn, yes; we lived there up until two years ago. But the only friend here I could ask to do that lives at Lexington and Sixty-first, and—"

"Too far, too far!" I got rattled. "Where are we, Julia, Forty-first? What's the nearest bridge? Maybe they aren't guarding them yet, and we can still—"

"Si, there's only one bridge, Brooklyn, and it's way downtown."

I nodded, glancing at store windows we passed, trying to see whether they reflected anyone following or about to challenge us. More than ever before, I was realizing that Manhattan is an island and not a very big one, either; you can walk its circumference in a day. "I don't want us to be trapped sitting on a ferry like a couple of pigeons. We need *money* dammit! To hole up in a hotel where they can supply our meals. Suppose we telephoned your aunt—" I stopped.

"Did what?"

"Never mind."

But she'd heard me. "I don't know anyone who has a telephone. Or who has even seen one."

"I know, I know!"

"We could send a messenger boy; there's an office near here."

"But we'd have to wait there for the reply?"

"Yes."

"When the boy came back, the cop that I'm certain must be watching the house would be right along with him. God, how I wish there were movies! Between us we probably have the price of a cheap one, and we could sit and wait till dark."

"Movies?"

I'd lose my mind if this kept up. I said, "We've got to separate, Julia. Till dark. They're looking for the pair of us; let's not make it easy for them. It'll be dark in forty minutes, an hour at most. And I'll try to sneak in and out of the house then; I've got money in my room. Meet me in a hour and a half at—where's the nearest good place from the house?—in Madison Square. Walk through it as though you're going somewhere, and I'll follow you out. If I'm not there, try again in half an hour. Then give me up, and"—I shrugged—"do your best. Okay?" Before she could answer I looked at the windows of a store we were passing; the entranceway passed between double display windows, one pane of each set at a 45-degree angle to the walk. It reflected the half block or so behind us and I saw a man running silently toward us. He was in plainclothes, wearing a derby and a long topcoat, but nothing could disguise the truth that he was a cop. He was running on his toes without a sound, and he was about the length of a football field behind. Without turning around I spoke quietly and very rapidly. "Julia. You must run. To the corner, and around it, and keep on. Do it now, *now!*"

She didn't hesitate or waste time looking back, but gathered up her skirts and ran. I turned and walked straight out into the street. There I turned to face the sidewalk and stood waiting. And now the man running toward us had a choice to make between me or going after Julia, leaving me behind his back, and not sure what I'd do. He had to choose me, and he did it cleverly, running right past me as though going for Julia, as I thought he was for a moment. Then he whirled in a fast right-angle turn and came at me. But I'd picked a metal pillar of the El tracks to stand near, and I stepped over to it. For a moment or so we stood, both of us balanced on our toes, the pillar between us, trying to outfeint each other. Then he lunged, I shoved off hard from the post, and he was after me.

But he could shoot and probably would if I began outracing him, and at this distance he wouldn't miss. Running on was pointless, and I did the only other thing left to do. I whirled and literally threw myself at his ankles in an action he may not ever have seen before—a football tackle, though this was from the front. I'd played a little football in high school before the players got too big for me. And now I hit his shins with my left shoulder, my arms wrapping tight around his knees in a tackle so illegal it would have drawn a hundred-yard penalty—and he went right on forward over my shoulders and down onto cobbles. I thought my shoulder was broken—the numbness reminded me of why I'd had to quit the game—but I was up right away and running in the opposite direction. I looked back; he was still lying on the street. Fifteen more running steps right down the middle of the street, wagon drivers turning to stare, then I looked back again. He was on his knees, turning to face me and pulling a big nickel-plated revolver from his back pocket. I stayed on the side of the line of pillars opposite him, and kept glancing over my shoulder in a series of fast peeks. Using both hands, he was aiming carefully; he wanted me, all right. I slowed suddenly, then sprinted, trying to throw his aim off; he fired, and the bullet struck a pillar, making a surprisingly loud clang. People stood frozen on the walks, but none of them seemed to want to come out into the street. At the corner I turned and ran east in the direction opposite from Julia's, and the gun roared again, and I mentally examined myself and decided I hadn't been hit.

I was around the corner now, out of his line of fire. He was far behind, probably just getting to his feet, and I knew I'd make it to Second Avenue if my wind held out. I had to walk the last dozen yards gasping, looking behind me, but he was nowhere in sight. At Second I turned south, knowing that—no radios, no patrol cars, hardly any phones—I was temporarily safe again.

Four blocks down I walked into a saloon, ordered a stein of beer, took a couple of sips, then walked back through a dim hallway to the toilet, and killed six or seven minutes just standing there. I came back and had a couple more sips of beer; there were half a dozen men standing at the bar, paying me no attention. Then I walked to the free-lunch table and took a ham sandwich, with two hard-boiled eggs and a dill pickle, back to the bar, and ate them with the rest of my beer. And when I left I had two more hard-boiled eggs, and a thick cheese sandwich, which I'd sneaked into my overcoat pocket.

I spent fifteen minutes standing in an alley in a locked doorway; occasionally, in case anyone was watching from an upper story somewhere, I hauled out my watch and looked at it, as though waiting for someone. Then I walked again, down Second. Twice a horsecar passed but I was keeping off them now; I wanted to be ready to move in any of four directions. At Thirty-seventh Street I saw a cop ahead, and turned off Second and went back to Third, then headed south again. Seven or eight blocks, and a cop came walking out of Twenty-ninth Street not ten yards ahead, looked toward me, said, "Hey!" and began to walk quickly in my direction. I stopped. He was far too close for me to run; I'd have been shot in the back. A few steps ahead and at the outer edge of the walk near the curb, a man and a woman had stopped, too. And now the cop, pulling off his helmet, stopped before them. As I walked past—my steps as quiet as I could make them—trying to shrink myself into invisibility, he took his photographs out of the helmet, and I saw that the couple was young and that the girl's dress, the hem visible under her coat, was the same color as Julia's though not the same shade and the man's overcoat was vaguely like mine. But they matched the description Byrnes had dictated, and as I turned onto Twenty-ninth Street I heard the cop order the man to turn his head, and I knew he was comparing his face to my photograph. As fast as I could without drawing attention, I walked over to Lexington Avenue. There a pair of lamplighters were moving down the street, touching each lamp into light, and before I reached Gramercy Park, at Twenty-first Street, it was dark.

The fenced-in rectangle of Gramercy Park lay between me and Number 19. I stood in the shadows between two streetlamps, and through the bare branches and black iron bars of the fence I looked across its snow-covered grass and bushes to watch the house. The lower-floor windows—parlor, dining room, kitchen—were all lighted, and so were two of the upper windows. I'd seen someone, either Byron Doverman or Felix Grier, pass a front lower window, a newspaper in his hand. And now a light upstairs went out. Then, barely visible through the intervening shrubs, fencing, and trees, I saw the cop on the other side of the square. He was walking slowly past the house.

He walked on to the corner of the square, then turned and walked back just as slowly, on past the house again to the opposite corner. He turned to walk back, and I hauled out my watch and timed him. It took just about a minute and a half to walk past the house once more, up to the corner again, and turn; and it took the same time to walk back. Six times, watch in hand, I watched him walk that beat, back and forth in the same path, and as regular as my watch he did it in a minute and a half each time. If I timed my movements with his, it would be perfectly possible to walk around the corner of the square toward the house, and then—behind his back as he walked slowly past the house—to silently cross the street, hurry up the steps, and with my own key unlock the front door and slip inside before he turned to walk back again. Up the stairs to my room, the rest of my money in my hand within seconds. Then down again, watch the cop through the door crack, then out and across the street behind his back once more.

But I didn't move: Was it really going to be that easy to outwit Byrnes? The man had set a trap for me and Julia, overlooking nothing so far. Was this cop, so easy to sneak past, only what he seemed? I stood watching him, and again he walked his beat in precisely the same way, and then again. Maybe he *was* what he seemed—just a cop, not Byrnes himself; a human being doing a tiresome job and falling into a regular pattern. I moved a few yards along my fence, stood watching again, and suddenly I saw him. Entirely motionless—he must have been chilled through no matter how many layers of clothes he wore—a man sat on a bench inside the park facing Number 19. He was dressed in dark clothes, his coat collar up, and, motionless in the darkness there inside the park, he was almost invisible. There he sat, waiting for me or Julia to cleverly time our movements to the slow metronome of the cop's walk and cross the street as he watched. Then, the street door closing, a low whistle, and the cop strolling the sidewalk suddenly turning to run to the house.

I actually backed away from the park for a step or two, then I turned and walked off. It was only a few blocks to Madison Square, and though I walked them warily I knew now that we were going to be caught. Unless I simply deserted Julia, which I wasn't going to do, Byrnes had us—bottled up, trapped. Without money for food, even holing up somewhere was useless. He had us as planned; as he'd known he would since even before he'd picked us up. Did he want us killed? While "avoiding detention"? Maybe; it would be a simple and very quick way to the meeting in Carmody's Wall Street office. Or did he want us caught? It probably didn't matter to him; our "escape" proved our guilt, or at least disproved any claim to innocence. For two powerful people like Byrnes and Andrew Carmody to actually convict us of a charge of murder after our attempted escape wouldn't be hard in an 1882 courtroom. And all I could do about it was stick with Julia; I had to do that and just hope against hope, I didn't even know for what.

I saw her enter the square from Fifth Avenue, walking briskly, purposefully, along the curve of a path, her long-skirted silhouette sharp against the light from an overhead standard, then blurring in the shadows, sharpening again as she walked into the next cone of pale yellow light. I met her at the downtown end of the park, she smiled with relief when she saw me, and I took her arm, and we walked toward the other end as though we knew where we were going. As we walked I told her what had happened, that we still had no money, and for a moment she closed her eyes, and said, "Oh, God."

"What's wrong?"

"I'm so *tired*, Si; I simply cannot continue endlessly walking." Then she smiled, squeezing my arm under hers, and I smiled back; I had nothing to encourage her about. She'd stopped at a messenger-service office, she said, soon after she'd left me, and sent a handwritten note by messenger boy to her aunt. She was all right, it had said; she'd be away for a time; she'd explain when she returned; meanwhile her aunt wasn't to worry. "Of course she will," Julia said, "but at least she's heard from me, and it was the best I could do. I wish—" Under my arm, hers moved sharply, and I saw the cops, a pair of them, crossing Fifth toward the square, and we turned right around to walk just as purposefully back in the direction we'd come from, hoping they hadn't yet seen us through the trees and shrubs. It seemed useless yet we instinctively postponed being caught.

As we approached the south end of the park and could see Twenty-third Street, I saw a cop standing on the walk ahead. His back was to us, he didn't see us, was probably thinking of anything but us. If we walked out of the park past him, though, he'd see us, and once more we turned on the path. Up ahead, still two-thirds the long length of the park away from us, the cops were walking along toward us, talking. We could turn east or west now, it didn't seem to matter which, and we took the first intersecting path we came to, west toward Fifth. Julia hurried along with me, but when she spoke I knew she was close to crying. She said, "Si, I *have* to stop, I *have* to. Let me just sit down on a bench here, and you go ahead. Come back later, Si, and if I'm still here—"

But I was shaking my head, pulling her along by force, making her walk, nearly running. Something about this path, the look of the trees and placement of the benches here, had become suddenly familiar. I'd walked here before, and—yes. We rounded the bend of the path and there ahead it came into sight, a dark nearly formless bulk obscured by the thick screen of bare trees, but I recognized it. As we completed the curve it came suddenly clear, dimly silhouetted against the dark sky: the immense right arm of the Statue of Liberty, the tip of its great torch high over the trees.

We climbed the winding stairs fast and silently, and then at last we sat down, out on the circular railed platform at the base of the great metal flame. The ornamental railing concealed us but we could look out through it, and for as long as a minute, I suppose, we just sat in silence looking down on the dark city, listening to the sound and watching the dim swaying lights of Fifth Avenue traffic. It was chill. We felt the cold of the metal through our clothes. But for the moment—just sitting, no longer having to walk—being here was enough. If it occurred to anyone to climb up and look for us here, as it might, there'd be no escape. Byrnes had run us, if not precisely to ground, at least into a cul-de-sac. But for the moment we just didn't care. In the faint light from the lamps of the square, I could see the dull, very slightly iridescent glow of the shaped copper against which Julia's head rested and I could see that she was smiling tiredly. "How good," she murmured, "how *good* just not to have to move." She opened her eyes, saw me watching her, and smiling again to show she didn't really mean this, she said, "Now, if we only had something to eat." I remembered, grinned, and brought out the mashed sandwich and mashed eggs, their shells cracked to particles, and handed them to her. She didn't even bother asking where they'd come from, but just shook her head, marveling, and began eating the sandwich. She offered me some, but I told her I'd eaten, and where, and made her eat it all.

We spent the night inside, sitting near the top of the curved staircase out of the little wind that came up. We sat huddled together on the third or fourth step from the top so that, eyes level with the floor of the platform, we could look out under the railing at the city. I sat half facing Julia, my arms around her, her head on my chest. It was cold in here, but out of the wind it was tolerable, and I enjoyed it. Julia slept right away, but for a time I sat holding her and staring out at the city; all I saw was darkness sprinkled with a few dim lights. They disappeared, one or two at a time; presently there were no lights at all, the city outside nearly silent, and then I slept, too.

Twice we awakened, very stiff and cold, and stood up and stretched and flexed our fingers. The second time, careful to make very little sound, we went outside and walked around the circular platform half a dozen times, looking down onto the treetops and the silent lighted paths of the park, looking out over the low dark city. Inside again, huddled together for warmth, my arms around Julia once more, I knew I'd had all the sleep I was going to get for a while on a cold metal staircase. I was still tired but the sleep had helped. Presently Julia whispered, "Awake?" and as I nodded, the side of my jaw brushed her hair so that I knew she could feel it. "Me, too," she said.

And then without planning it, without any thought at all before the quiet words began, I told Julia who I was and where I had come from; I felt that it was time, that it was her due. I told her about the project; about Rube, Dr. Danziger, Oscar Rossoff; about my life in that far-off time. My voice a steady murmur hardly audible beyond her ear, I talked about my preparations with Martin, my life at the Dakota, the first successful attempt, my arrival at her house. Twice she lifted her head to stare up at my face, searching it as well as she could in the barely relieved darkness, then lying back in my arms, and I wondered what she thought. I couldn't tell. I knew I was violating a fundamental rule of the project, and knew that no one in it could ever understand this. But I felt it was right. Finally I finished, and waited.

I could feel her draw a deep breath, then she sighed, and said, "Thank you, Si. You're the most understanding man I've ever known. You've

356

helped me through a long night; I haven't been so enthralled since I was a girl, and read *Little Women*. You should write that story down, and perhaps illustrate it. I'm certain *Harper's* would consider it. And now I think I can sleep again."

"Good," I said, and sat grinning at myself in the darkness: a story made up and spun out to entertain her; what in the hell else was she supposed to think? And within a few minutes, four or five, I think, I was asleep, too, this time in the soundest sleep of all.

I woke up for good, knowing in the odd way you do that this was the last of the night, dawn not too far away now, and I was sorry. Uncomfortable as it had been, it had also been good, here with Julia. Now nothing lay ahead but a day we weren't going to get through. We'd be able to buy some sort of breakfast probably, then there was only more walking, all of yesterday's weariness back in our legs in an hour, until presently we were caught. Possibly, I thought, we ought to give ourselves up right away; at least we'd be warm then, and could stop running.

There was no light, the first sun a long way off, yet the darkness was just faintly diluted. Looking out, I could see the ornate pattern of the railing, and I hadn't been able to do that before. All over again the strangeness of where we were struck me. I had to say it to myself; incredibly we were here, high up in the arm and torch of the Statue of Liberty. And then it occurred to me: Could it be made to happen? I considered it, and thought that maybe it could, and I carefully tightened my arms around Julia, pressing my cheek to the top of her head, holding her very close, making her as much a part of me as I was able. Then, in the technique Oscar Rossoff had taught me, I began to free my mind from the time I was in. For this, too, this great metal hand with its torch, was a part of both the New Yorks I had known, existing in each of them. And in my mind I allowed the twentieth century to come to life. Then I told myself where I was; where *we* were, Julia and I. And I felt it happen.

My arms squeezed, holding Julia even tighter during that moment, so that she stirred and opened her eyes. She looked up at me blankly. "Where . . ." Then she glanced around her, realizing, said, "Oh," and smiled. I let her go, stood up stiffly, and she got up, too, and we walked out onto the platform. The darkness was going, a whiteness and lightness coming into the air, but we couldn't really see; we heard it instead.

I was expecting it and recognized the sound first, glancing at Julia. I saw the look of bafflement come to her face, and she turned to me, frowning. "Waves?" she said. "Si, I hear waves, I swear I do!" Then she sniffed the air. "And I can smell the sea." She was frightened. "Si, what—"

I had my arm around her shoulders, saying softly, "Julia, we've escaped. The story I told you last night is true. It was the truth, Julia; *I've brought you with me into my own time.*"

She stared at my face, saw the truth in my eyes, and buried her face on my chest. "Oh, Si, I'm frightened! I can't look!"

Ahead, the whole sky was light now, pinkening the horizon, the tiny whitecaps in the harbor far below suddenly just visible. "Yes, you can," I said, and took her chin, lifting her head, turning it toward the railing to the east. She looked out across it, saw the water and the harbor far below; then she turned to see the blue-green skin of verdigris, the patina of decades, on the giant copper torch and flame behind us, and began to tremble.

Under my arm her shoulders actually shook with fright—yet she couldn't stop looking. Her head turned endlessly from side to side, seeing it all; and all that she said over and again every few seconds was "Oh, *Si!*" in a frightened, excited, ecstatic wail. Her face was dead-white, and her hand as she raised it to press tight against her cheek was trembling, but she'd begun to smile.

Far out, the first thin edge of sun suddenly touched the rim of the ocean, and now ships were visible. Then, the sun edging up over the horizon as we stared, I took Julia's arm, and we walked around our little railed circle. On the other side Julia stopped to stand stock-still, her breath suddenly caught motionless in her chest as she stared out across the harbor at the astonishing, soaring skyscrapers filling the tip of Manhattan Island, their tens of thousands of windows flashing orange in the dawn.

21

WE TOOK the first sight-seeing boat back to Manhattan, the handful of wintertime tourists who filed off it glancing curiously at Julia's clothes as we stood waiting to board. They ignored me, my overcoat and round fur hat, not much different from plenty of others. This was the one boat of the day returning to New York empty of passengers—except, this time, for us. The next boat would leave its new arrivals and take the first batch back, and so on throughout the day. I was grateful; I didn't feel like being stared at. A little belligerently, the attendant asked where we'd come from. I said we'd missed the last boat yesterday afternoon, and had spent the night on the island. It took him a second or so to decide what he thought about that, then he grinned a little lewdly and motioned us on; our clothes didn't seem to bother him a bit.

The second deck was open, and we climbed the inside stairs to it as the boat nosed out into the channel. Then we moved through the water toward Manhattan, Julia motionless beside me watching the skyscrapers on the tip of Manhattan Island growing impossibly larger and larger. We had a completely unobstructed view of lower Manhattan, and of New Jersey, South Brooklyn, Staten Island, and of the harbor looking toward the Verrazano bridge, and for ten minutes Julia just stared without out speaking. Then, leaning toward me but without for an instant taking her eyes from the immense buildings crowding the tip of Manhattan—beautiful now in the full morning sun—she said, "What makes them stand *up?*" I explained what I knew or thought I knew about steel frameworks, but stopped in mid-sentence. She wasn't listening, hadn't heard a word. She just sat staring, till suddenly she gripped my arm, her face lighting up. "The new bridge!" she said, pointing at the Brooklyn Bridge up the East River, to the right of Manhattan.

A cargo ship heading for the sea was not so much approaching as simply swelling in size, and Julia sat staring at it. When finally it passed, quite close, its steel sides rising up past us forever, Julia shrank close to me, her eyes blinking apprehensively. "Will it tip?" she whispered. "Could it fall?" I told her it was impossible, but as we both stared up at the black clifflike side of the big ship sliding past us, its propellers mumbling, I knew what she felt. It seemed unlikely that anything this big and high out of the water could float, and I wondered what Julia would have said if the new *Queen Elizabeth* had incredibly steamed by.

And then a plane passed, a four-engined propeller plane not too high, maybe ten thousand feet, drilling away up against the gray sky. I was pleased, glad to show off what is probably the symbol of this particular century. I said, "Julia, look"—she'd heard the sound but didn't know where to look till I pointed upward. "That's a plane, an airplane." I waited, a little smugly I suppose, for her to be astounded. But she stared up at it for a dozen seconds, smiling slightly, interested and pleased to see it, but not surprised. Then she nodded at me. "I've read of them, in Jules Verne. Of course you'd have them by now. I should love to ride on one. Are there many?" She'd already turned back to what really astounded her: the windowed cliffs of Manhattan.

"Quite a few." I was laughing at myself; it served me right.

There were no immigrants in Battery Park as we stepped off the boat. When we crossed the little park and reached the street, Julia stopped suddenly, a hand rising to her chest. At first I thought she'd been overwhelmed by the immediacy of the towering buildings and the narrow streets of cabs, private cars, and pedestrians, and by the sound, which was the normal traffic roar plus the ear-numbing chatter of jackhammers. But she wasn't looking at cars or buildings but at the people, the ordinary people walking past us. I looked at her closely, and understood that it wasn't the way they were dressed that had stopped her. I remembered the sudden awe that had come over me once at seeing the actually living, visibly breathing people of 1882, because now I felt certain I saw the same dizzying wonderment in Julia's face. On Liberty Island she'd been so conscious of her own appearance that the boat passengers getting off had scarcely seemed real. But now, as with me once, there they were passing before her, unnoticing—and they were alive, moving, talking!—the people of more than a lifetime after hers. When she turned to look at me her face was pale again, and she could only shake her head, wordless and frightened.

We walked a short block up Broadway, past what's left of Bowling Green, and I said, "Do you know where you are?"

The question startled her as though asked in a foreign city she'd never before seen. Trying to guess, she looked up and down the street, then turned to me, still half frightened by all she saw, but smiling, too. "No."

"Lower Broadway."

"No! It isn't!" Again she looked up and down the street, and now the smile was gone. "Oh, Si, there's nothing I know; nothing! I—"

I said, "Hold it," took her arm, and we walked quickly uptown, two more short blocks. And then Julia slowed, a hand rising to her mouth in shock, staring ahead and across the street. We walked on fifty yards, stopped at the curb, and Julia and I stood staring across the street at tiny little Trinity Church lost at the bottom of a glass-and-stone canyon. Then her chin rose as she slowly lifted her gaze—up, up, and up at the towers that completely dwarfed the highest place on her Manhattan Island.

Finally she turned to me. "I don't like it, Si. I don't *like* seeing Trinity like this!" Then once more she looked across the street and up to the distant sky above the great buildings. And now when she turned back to me she was smiling again. "But I'd like to go up in one of those buildings." Still smiling, she squeezed her eyes shut for a moment, making a mock shudder. "Broadway; at least it's noisy as ever." Again she glanced up and down the busy street. "How strange not to see a single horse." Suddenly she noticed. "Si! Everything's going one way!"

We got a cab at the corner, and I explained one-way streets as we drove east toward Nassau Street. Julia was looking appreciatively around at the interior of the cab, and I lowered my voice so the driver wouldn't hear. "This is an automobile."

"I know!" She lowered her voice, too. "I remembered your drawing of Madison Square; I recognized them the moment we saw them." "I like auto mobiles. This is fun!" She felt the cushion appreciatively. "I wish Aunt Ada could see them. Look!" She pointed suddenly; she'd been glancing around her, and now she'd noticed a tiny red sedan behind us. "How cunning! And the driver is a *woman!* How I should like one, too!" The cab was slowing for the traffic light at Nassau Street; it was turning from green to red, and Julia understood it at sight. "How clever. Now, why in the world didn't we think of that? But of course they are electric-lighted, aren't they, behind the colored glass?"

We got out where Nassau Street meets Park Row, the cab waiting at the curb. I pointed down Park Row toward Broadway. "That's where the Astor Hotel stood, Julia. They built a new one uptown at Forty-fourth Street, and now it's gone, too." I pointed again, at a building I don't think I'd ever seen before either. "And that's where the post office was." Each time I pointed Julia looked obediently, understanding my words and nodding; but I don't think it was really possible for her to understand that that was really where the Astor had been, and this was where the post office had stood.

But then she exclaimed, a sudden little "Oh!" of surprised delight, as she suddenly noticed City Hall and the Court House, both looking exactly as we'd last seen them, and realized that the park across the street was City Hall Park. It, too, was unchanged as far as I could tell; if there were small changes, as there must have been, they weren't notice-able to either of us. Julia stood looking across the street at it, smiling genuinely but tremulously; for just a moment there was the shine of tears in her eyes, then they were gone in the pleasure of what she saw. Very quietly she said, "I'm glad, Si, so glad it hasn't been changed. How good to see it."

Oriented for the first time now, Julia suddenly understood where we were, and looked quickly up at me for confirmation. I nodded, she turned, and—I gestured to the cabby, who followed us along the curb—we walked along Park Row, along the side of what had once been the Times Building, still here though greatly changed. And then we stopped at the site of the building we'd seen burn to the ground. A building as old, now, as the World Building had been then stood in its place. It was equally nondescript, and incredibly very much like it; it looked as though it had probably been built immediately after the fire.

We stood looking at it blankly. In my mind I could easily see the great lashing tongues of orange flame crackling out the window tops of the old World Building; I could still smell the black smoke, still hear the hurricane roar of a fire that was now gone from all human memory, surely, except mine and the girl's beside me, and I wondered what Ida Small's life had been like. I walked forward and placed the flat of my hand against the building wall, and then so did Julia. For a moment we stood with our palms pressed to the actuality of the stone that stood here now, feeling it draw the warmth from our hands, and it should have been real. But Julia looked at me and shook her head, and I nodded. I said, "I know; it's not real for me, either." I put my hand back into my overcoat pocket, and Julia slid hers into her muff.

She walked back to the curb, where our cab was waiting, then turned to the old building and pointed. "That must be about where the OBSERVER sign hung." She glanced at the cabby who was pretending not to listen, then stepped closer to me, lowering her voice. "Si, can you believe that we crawled along that sign only two days ago?" She pointed at the old Times Building. "And there is the very window we climbed through into Mr. J. Walter Thompson's office."

I nodded, smiling at the difficulty of even imagining these things. I said, "His advertising agency still exists. I think it's the largest in the world now, or close to it."

"Oh?" she said brightly, as though at good news from an old friend. "I'm pleased to hear it; he was a very nice man."

We drove on then, block after block, Julia's head constantly turning. It was nearly all completely strange to her, a brand-new place except that she could see the big yellow street signs. And again and again I heard her murmur, "Gone . . . gone . . . gone . . ."

I don't know what the cabdriver was thinking; he was looking at us in his mirror every few seconds now. But when he caught my eye and started to speak, I gave him the hardest glare I had in stock. I don't really like New York cabdrivers. They've been overly publicized, have become arrogant, and I wasn't interested in anything cute this guy was about to say. Julia knew, too, that now he was listening to everything we said, and sometimes when we stopped for a light, people in cars and trucks beside us glanced in at our clothes, then looked at our faces. And of course it had happened even more when we'd walked or stood in the street. Actually I don't think anyone gave us much thought; they'd suppose we were on our way to a rehearsal of some kind, probably for a television commercial. But Julia was very aware of their looks, and when the cabdriver gave us still another inspection in his mirror, she leaned close to me and murmured, "Will we be at your house soon, Si?" and I nodded yes, and told the driver to speed it up.

I made one detour, though. At Third Avenue and Twenty-third Street, I told the driver to head west, and when he started to remind me, wise-guy style, of my original directions, I said, "*West on Twenty-third!*" and he turned.

We drove around Madison Square then, and heading south on Broadway, driving past the west side of the square, Julia grabbed my arm suddenly just as I'd thought she might. "Si!" she whispered. "It's gone! Really gone!"

"What is?"

"The arm! The Statue of Liberty's arm!" The cabdriver was losing his mind with frustration. "It *would* be, of course," Julia murmured, "but . . . now I know that it really happened. And that the entire Statue is in the harbor." Her arm was under mine, and she squeezed my arm tight to her side. "It's scary," she said, and made herself smile at me.

As we waited for the light at Twenty-third Street, Julia sat looking forward through the windshield, no longer caring about the cabby. "The Fifth Avenue Hotel," she said, pointing. "Gone." She looked back over her shoulder through the trees of the square. "All the hotels are gone. Delmonico's, too." At Twenty-second Street, waiting for the light, to turn east, Julia pointed again. "The Abbey Park Theater; gone. And the Ladies' Mile, Si?"

I nodded. "Gone. All gone."

The light changed, we turned east, and I said, "That's Lexington Avenue just ahead; we can turn south there for one block to Gramercy Park. Your house is still there. Do you want to see it?"

"Oh, no!" She shook her head violently. "I couldn't stand that, Si."

Julia was pleased with the elevator in my building, though not with the middle-aged woman holding a poodle under her arm who kept staring at Julia and her clothes all the way up to my floor. I kept a key wedged between the molding of the front doorframe and the wall of the building hallway, where they separated a little about a yard above the floor. With a folded slip of paper, I worked it out now, unlocked my door, and gestured Julia in. She stepped inside, I flicked the wall switch, and—it was almost as much a novelty to me now as to Julia—the living-room chandelier came on.

She grinned like a kid, glancing from chandelier to wall switch and back at least three times. She looked at me questioningly then, I nodded, and—taking the toggle of the switch carefully between thumb and forefinger—she clicked it, the chandelier went off, and Julia stood staring up at it. "How wonderful," she murmured. "Such fine clear light any time you wish it. As easily as this," and she flicked the switch once more.

"I prefer gaslight," I said, but that was so unbelievable she didn't bother answering it. Without taking her eyes from the chandelier, she moved the switch again, and the light went off. I got money from under the paper lining a dresser drawer, and when I went downstairs to pay off the cab, Julia stood, still staring at the chandelier, fascinated, delighted, clicking the light switch on and off, over and again.

I helped Julia take off her coat, and hung it, with her hat and muff, in the closet, Julia's hand rising to push at her hair, and there was a moment or so of awkwardness and constraint between us. I think it was the act of removing coat and hat when she was alone with me in my apartment, something Julia would feel wasn't right, at least in any ordinary circumstance. She covered it by examining my davenport and few sticks of furnished-apartment furniture, a real enough interest actually, since the look of them was new for her. She asked a question or two, then walked to the windows, where I joined her, and she stared down at Lexington Avenue for a few moments, marveling once again at being here.

I remember most of the day in a series of pictures: Julia at the refrigerator while I hunted for things to make up a breakfast, marveling at its coldness, at its astonishing ability to actually create ice, at its freezing compartment, at the light that came on when you opened the door; her astonishment at instant coffee, her pleasure at its fragrance, and her wrinkled-nose disappointment at its taste; her surprise and pleasure in the frozen orange juice I magically took from the freezer compartment, stirred up in a pitcher, and poured over ice cubes.

And countless other pictures: Julia back in the living room, her third glass of iced orange juice in her hand, as she stood looking at the blank face of my television while I stood with my hand on the knob warning her of what was going to happen when I turned it. She nodded quickly, excited by what I'd promised, possibly not believing me or at least not really comprehending that I could mean it literally. Because I turned the knob, and in spite of my warning she was badly frightened, crying out and stumbling as she backed away, spilling a dollop of juice on the rug, as a distorted pattern on the screen suddenly turned itself into the moving speaking face of a woman urging Julia to try a new, improved dishwashing soap. Jules Verne hadn't prepared her for this; television was completely astonishing; she could hardly believe what she was seeing even as she stared at it. Then she babbled, asking how it worked, and she listened to my answer uncomprehendingly, alternately watching my face and sneaking looks back at the screen.

I told her that while what she was now watching was on tape, the machine could also show you distant events while they were happening, thinking this would astonish her even more. But she asked what I meant by tape, and when I told her there was a way of preserving pictures of people in motion together with the actual sounds of their voices, *that* was what astonished her.

I think the television set—and what I told her—was so bewildering that for a few moments she wasn't sure she liked it. But I slid a chair up behind her, touching the backs of her knees, she sat down slowly, and the bewilderment turned to a fascination as absorbing as a child's. With absolute open-mouthed attention to every movement and sound, day-time soap opera or commercial, she sat in rigid straight-backed motion-lessness, having forgotten to even sit back. And when I showed her that you could change the picture by turning a knob, she sat turning the knob around and around at ten-second intervals, from serial to panel show to old movie to Julia Child, and I actually had to tap her shoulder to make her turn and hear what I was saying. I said, "I'm going out for half an hour. Will you be okay here?" She just nodded, her head already turning back to the screen.

In my bedroom I changed to wash slacks, sport shirt, sweater, moc-casins, and put on a short tan car coat. She glanced up as I came back into the living room to say, "Is this how men dress now?" I said that yes, it was one of the ways, and she nodded, her head already turning back to a fascinating Allstate Insurance commercial.

I doubt if she realized how long I was gone, which was more than a half hour, closer to forty-five minutes. Because when I came in, she was sitting back in her chair but still staring at the television set: an old movie, a comedy from the forties that must have been ninety-five percent incomprehensible to her. But it moved and it talked and that was enough.

Of the series of pictures which are my memories of a lot that happened that day, the next is even more memorable than Julia's hypnosis by television. I had to turn off the set to get her away from it; she said, "Oh, no, not *yet!*" as the picture shrank and the screen went dark.

I was laughing. "Julia, there are other things to see! You can look at the television again later."

She nodded, and stood—but reluctantly, looking back at the set—and said, "A theater in your home—*six* theaters! It's a miracle. How can you bear to do anything but watch it?"

"Some people can't. But I don't think you'd be one of them. It's really no *good*, Julia, it's not worth watching, most of it." But of course she couldn't see that, not yet. I'd set the four or five packages I'd brought in on the davenport, and now I picked them up and began piling them into Julia's arms. "I think you'll have to put these on, Julia. You can change in my room."

"What are they, Si? Clothes? Modern clothes?"

"Yep." She hesitated, but I said gently, "People will stare at you otherwise, Julia," and she grimaced, and nodded. I said, "Forgive me for speaking of this, but I have to explain: I think you can keep on whatever underclothes you're wearing; though if you run into any problems, let me know." I was having trouble keeping my face straight. "There's a blouse, skirt, slip, and sweater in the packages. And shoes and stockings. Put them all on. I brought a garter belt for the stockings, which I'm sure you'll figure out. And if anything fits too badly, we'll stop at a store and replace it. Okay?"

"Okay." She nodded shyly, and went into my room, and I opened the last package, a suit box, brought out the street coat I'd bought her, and laid it over the back of the davenport as a sort of final surprise for Julia. It was tan cloth, with wide lapels, a deep collar, and big mother-of-pearl buttons. All these things had been expensive but I didn't care.

Julia was gone longer than I'd thought she'd be, and doors being as thin as they are today, which Julia surely didn't realize, I could hear her little exclamations of surprise and occasional puzzlement. Then I heard her say, "Oh!" in a shocked little tone, and the next picture in my assorted memories is of Julia—following a long wait after the "Oh!"— coming hesitatingly out of the bedroom and stopping just outside the door. Her voice embarrassed, she said, "Si, you made a mistake; just look at this skirt!" and I couldn't hold it in another second, and burst out laughing. The skirt I'd bought her was tan wool, and of a really conservative knee-length. And she had it on all right. But it was tight at the waist because she'd put it on over at least two of her own ankle-length white petticoats.

"Julia, I'm sorry!" I said; she was looking indignant. "But you can't wear those petticoats; wear the slip!"

"Slip?"

"The pink petticoat I brought you."

"I am wearing it!" Her face was shiny red. "Under my petticoats, and it's much too short!"

I'd bottled the laughter up, shoved it way down inside and it was off my face completely but fighting to get out. "No, Julia," I said gravely, "the slip isn't really too short. It's the same length as the skirt; a shade shorter so it won't show." I shrugged. "It's what they wear today. I didn't design them."

She stood for a moment as though thinking about arguing it, while I kept my face rigid at the sight of a good fourteen inches of ruffled white petticoat hanging down below the hem of that skirt. Then she turned abruptly, and was gone for at least ten minutes.

She came out of the bedroom walking like a duck, arms rigid at her side; it took me a few seconds and steps to realize that this strange walk was because her knees were pressed tight together. "Is this . . . how it's supposed to look?"

She stood motionless for my inspection, and I stood staring because Julia looked great. The blouse looked fine at the collar, the chocolate-brown sweater was a snug but not too tight fit, and the skirt looked terrific. As I'd suspected, she had a fine figure, though I hadn't known her legs would be absolutely beautiful. High-heeled shoes, the clerk had reminded me, were out of style right now, but I'd insisted on buying high-heeled brown leather pumps, and now I saw that I was right. In sheer flesh-toned stockings, those high heels emphasizing her fine-boned ankles and full round calves, Julia was stunning. She was a spectacularly handsome girl in this outfit, and her long hair, gathered up in a bun at the back, seemed just right for it. My face, eyes, and grin showed what I thought, and it helped her; she smiled, too, in sudden pleasure and pride, and bent forward to look down at her skirt. Once more she caught sight of its hem, far far higher on those beautiful legs than she'd ever dreamed she'd wear. And her face flushed, she ran two steps to the davenport, snatched up the coat I'd left there, and as fast as she could move, she wrapped it around her waist, the bottom of the coat touching her shoes. "I can't!" she wailed. "Si, I simply *cannot* go out in the street like that!"

I couldn't help it; I was laughing, shaking my head as I walked over to her, and I put an arm around her shoulders, and then on impulse and without thought I kissed her. It was just a quick kiss, and she looked startled. But she smiled, and I got her to put on the coat by telling her its hem would be longer than the skirt—as it was by an inch or so. And that helped. The coat on, she looked down at herself again, and while I think she felt like running to the bedroom again, she made herself stand still. Every woman she'd seen outside, I reminded her, wore a coat just as short, and she nodded grimly, accepting it.

I walked to my room to get a felt hat from my closet, and when I came back Julia stood at the mirror which hung over the little table beside the front door, and she was tying the strings of her bonnet under her chin. This time I didn't even bother trying to hold back; it would have been useless. I laughed for a dozen seconds, unable to stop or speak, and Julia stood looking at me, not angry but baffled; and each time I'd look at her standing there frowning puzzledly in those high heels and short modern coat, wearing that ancient, flat-topped flowered hat on her head, its strings tied in a bow under her chin, the laughter got a fresh start. I didn't mean to be rude or offend Julia, and was relieved that she didn't seem angry; it was just that she'd seemed so modern suddenly that I'd stupidly thought she understood how good she looked. But of course the new outfit was utterly alien to her; she had no way of judging it. To Julia her familiar bonnet looked just fine with these strange new clothes.

But when I told her the bonnet didn't go with them, the woman she was understood instantly that it must be so, even though she couldn't perceive it, and she yanked loose the bow under her chin and snatched off the bonnet. Plenty of women went bareheaded in the street, I told her, especially with long hair like hers. She looked surprised and doubtful about that, and I said if it bothered her when we got out, we'd stop and buy her a new hat. Then I put my hands on her coat sleeves at the shoulder, and stood at arm's length looking her over, letting what I thought and felt show. "Julia, take my word for this; when we go out now, you'll be one of the best-looking women in all New York. And that's the truth." She saw that I meant it, and I watched the pleasure come into her eyes, and saw her chin lift. Then, wobbling a bit on heels an inch higher and much smaller than she was used to but managing it pretty well, she walked back into my room; there was a full-length mirror on the closet door, and I knew she was heading for that. And knew she could face going out now, and that it wouldn't take this girl long to be as pleased as she ought to at the way she looked, and I wished I'd kissed her again before she moved away from my hands at her shoulders.

Downstairs I got Julia into a cab right away, letting her get used to being out in full sight of the world a little dose at a time. Then we drove uptown on Third Avenue so that she could see the street astoundingly without El or even streetcar tracks. At Forty-second Street we turned west to pass Grand Central Station, and Julia said, and I agreed, that it was far more impressive than the little red-brick Grand Central we'd seen here last.

Up Madison Avenue, the charming quiet little street that Julia knew unrecognizable now, of course. And then to Fifty-ninth Street along the lower edge of Central Park, and once more she had the relief and pleasure of finding something familiar essentially unchanged. I hired one of the horse-drawn hacks that wait in a line beside the park on Fifty-ninth Street; I thought Julia would enjoy it. And for a while—*clip-clop, clip-clop* once more—we drove more or less aimlessly along the winding roadways while Julia marveled at the absence of any other horses, and at the swiftness and relative silence of the "auto mobiles." She liked the cars, thought they were far more handsome and much more interesting than carriages, and I realized she'd rather have taken a cab.

Along Central Park West, and I showed her the Dakota surrounded by other buildings now; then we drove back to the hack stand. I paid off the driver, and we walked on toward the corner of Fifty-ninth and Fifth. This was the corner at which I'd had my first real look, on a cold January morning, at the world of 1882, staring in fright and fierce excitement at the horse-drawn bus approaching me, then turning to look south at a narrow, quiet residential Fifth Avenue. I'd been with Kate, but I didn't want to think about that just now. I wanted Julia to see that very same stretch of Fifth Avenue in my world.

Approaching the corner, across the street from the Plaza Hotel, I said, "We're walking along beside Central Park, Julia; and that's the corner of Fifty-ninth and Fifth, so you know where you are." I'd timed this carefully, and now I raised my arm, saying, "So tell me—what street is that?" and I pointed down the length of what may just be the most spectacular dozen and a half blocks in the world.

She gasped, turned a stunned face to me, then looked back, and the magnitude of the change in what she saw, the assault on the senses of that sudden look at today's astonishing structures, was almost too much. "Fifth *Avenue?*" she said weakly, and then, astounded, "*That is Fifth Avenue!?*"

"Yes."

For as long as a minute we both stood looking down its length, remembering what it had been. Then Julia glanced at me, managing a smile, and we walked down Fifth, passing the shining immensities, the breathtakingly handsome and the miserably ugly architectural confections along the mile or so that at least half the people in the world have seen in actuality or on film. Those great smooth-faced buildings and walls of glass are alien even to modern eyes, and I'm not sure Julia was able to apprehend them fully, they were so divorced from anything and everything she knew. It was so nearly impossible, I think, to take in and even try to comprehend, that when she looked across Fifty-first Street just ahead, suddenly narrowing her eyes to be sure she really saw it, she felt as I once had, but even more strongly—she burst into tears at sight of St. Patrick's Cathedral standing almost unchanged in this other world. Across the street from the cathedral at Rockefeller Center— which I don't think Julia ever even noticed—there are stone benches, and I led Julia to one. Then we sat while she stared over at St. Pat's; then she looked up Fifth Avenue, back at St. Patrick's for a reference point; then she looked down Fifth to the south; then once again her eyes swung back to the old cathedral for relief. It helped convince her that she was where she was, its familiarity a comfort and reassurance, and presently we walked on. Here and there Julia found familiar old names; women's stores she'd seen last on Broadway. And we'd stop while she stared at the glittering display windows, drinking it in, fascinated by the jewelry, the clothes, the furs, hats, and shoes. I said, "The Ladies' Mile, Julia," and she nodded.

"I think I like it. I think possibly . . ." She hesitated, then continued, "They're very strange, but I think possibly I'd come to like these things." Once more she looked slowly up and down the length of Fifth Avenue. "Even these buildings." She shook her head. "Who could believe it? Who could ever imagine *this*?"

At Forty-second Street we looked at the soot-marked white building of the main Public Library, and I marveled with Julia at the absence of the great slant-walled reservoir. Then—she needed rest from looking—I took her to a small bar I remembered on Thirty-ninth Street. At first she refused to go to "a saloon," but then she accepted the knowledge that today women did many things they once hadn't done.

We had a table off in a corner away from the bar, only one other couple there, whispering in a corner. Julia had a glass of wine, I had whiskey-and-soda, and Julia relaxed. By tacit agreement we hadn't talked until now about what we'd left behind us; we'd needed relief from it, and had had it, but now again we talked of the fire . . . of Jake Pickering . . . of Carmody's strange behavior, and our flight from Inspector Byrnes. In this room, the sounds of today's New York a part of the very air, the names we spoke sounded odd to me, remote, even faintly comical. To have actually been frightened of walrus-mustached Inspector Byrnes who had never heard of fingerprints seemed absurd; had we really been scared or only participating in some sort of harmless make-believe? That was something of the tenor of my thoughts as we quietly talked over our drinks, and the reason I spoke with a little smile. But Julia was serious, not understanding my smile, and of course I understood that for her we were talking of a world in which Byrnes, Pickering, Carmody, and the fire in the World Building were far more real than this.

We said nothing new; we were only obeying a necessity to talk things over. Julia was worried about what her aunt would be thinking now, and hanging unspoken over everything we said was the question of Julia's future. But that needed time to work out, and I said nothing about it because I had nothing to say, though I had a lot to think about.

I had other things to show Julia, and after a while we left, and found a cab. It was still light, and I took Julia down to the Empire State Building, and we went up to the observation floor. In the elevator during the long long express ride past dozens of floors, Julia watched the floor-number panel, trying to believe we were really moving up this fast and this high, and her hand, holding mine, squeezed tight in the realization that we were. On the stone-railed open-air platform some ninety-odd floors above the earth, she looked out over the hazed city, making herself understand that here high over Thirty-fourth Street the distant greenery far ahead was really Central Park, and that the network of car-filled streets spread out far below us was really the city she'd known intimately but here no longer did. She looked out at the city, the park, the rivers. Then she looked around at the sky and pointed out a remarkable cloud; she'd never seen one anything like it before. I looked, and in a sense I suppose it really was a cloud—it had become one. High in the sky the air must have been windless, and a jet trail, its sharp edges gone, had puffed itself up into an absolutely straight, thin, mile-long cloud touched by the lowering sun. And then I, too, saw it not as a jet trail but as a strange elongated, ruler-straight cloud, and had one more glimpse of the different view Julia had of my world.

She was interested when I told her what the cloud really was; and she enjoyed her visit up here, impressed and excited by it. But presently she turned from the railing, sighing a little, and said, "And now it's enough, Si; this is all I can stand right now. Please take me home."

So instead of a restaurant for dinner—I'd meant to show off one of the nicer places—we stopped at my building's delicatessen, and I picked up some chopped steak and frozen vegetables. The vegetables—corn and some broccoli frozen hard and sealed in transparent plastic, and which I dropped into boiling water in their sacks—fascinated Julia. As we all do, she liked the easiness of preparing them, but of course the taste or tastelessness was something else, though she was polite.

We took our coffee into the living room, and, refreshed and revived, Julia said, "I've seen your world now, Si; I've had a glimpse of it, anyway. Now tell me what's been happening during all the years—it's so strange to say this—between my time and this." She snuggled back into the davenport cushions, looking at me as expectantly as a child about to hear a story.

I suppose I responded to her smile and expectation of pleasure, because—pausing to think. *Where do you begin? How do you sum up decades?*—I found myself hunting for good things to say. "Well, smallpox has been almost eliminated; you never see pockmarks now. And cholera. I don't suppose there's been even a case of it for years. Not in the United States, anyway." Julia nodded. "And polio—infantile paralysis. It's been just about eliminated, at least in all the big civilized countries."

She nodded again; she seemed to have expected this. "And heart disease, too? And cancer?"

"Well, no, not yet. But we're replacing hearts! Surgically removing the damaged heart and replacing it with another one from someone who just died."

"That's miraculous! And they *live?*"

"Well, not too long, usually. It doesn't really work very well. But it will."

"And how long do people live? To a hundred or more, I'm sure. I read a prediction in the *Atlantic Monthly*—"

"Actually, Julia, people don't seem to be living much longer, if at all, than in your time. Matter of fact, there are some new things that, ah—are killing us off and shortening our lives that don't exist in your time. Air pollution, for example. But we have air conditioning."

"What's that?"

"Machines that cool off the air in summer."

"*Everywhere?*"

"No, no; just indoors. I've got one in the bedroom—that thing in the window, if you noticed it. During a hot spell it'll cool the air to seventy degrees."

"What a luxury."

"Yeah, it's pretty nice. And they have them in most offices now, restaurants, movies, hotels."

"What are movies? You've mentioned them before."

I explained that they were like television only much larger, much

374

clearer, and—every now and then—much better. Then I found myself talking about electric blankets, supermarkets, radar, air travel, automatic washers, dishwashers, and even, Lord forgive me, freeways.

Julia finished the last of her coffee, picked up my empty cup and saucer, and took it with hers to the kitchen. She walked back into the living room saying, "But what's been *happening*, Si? Tell me about that." As I thought about it, in terms of actual events, she began wandering about the room, fingering the drapes, looking at the back of the television set, flicking the overhead light fixture on and off a few times. I was stuck for an answer. It reminded me of letter writing; you can fill several pages describing a weekend, but try bringing an old friend up-to-date with the events of the last five years, and it's not so easy. What had happened in more than a lifetime?

"Well, there are fifty states now."

"*Fifty?*"

"Yep," I said as smugly as though I'd created them. "All the territories are states now. Also Alaska and Hawaii. And they've changed the flag; it has fifty stars now."

Julia nodded, interested; she was poking through the magazine rack at the end of the davenport, and now she pulled out a newspaper.

"And, let's see. Well, there was an earthquake in San Francisco in . . . 1906, I think. The city was pretty well destroyed, mostly by the fire afterward."

"Oh, I'm so sorry; it's a lovely city, I've heard." She nodded at the newspaper in her hand. "You have a way to print photographs, I see." She put down the paper and walked to my bookshelves.

"Yes, also in color. There ought to be an old *Life* magazine around somewhere with some color photos. And—my God, how could I forget! We're shooting rockets into space! They carry capsules with men in them. A couple of them have traveled to the moon, and landed. With men in them. And returned to earth."

"Do you mean that? To the *moon?* With men in them?"

"Yes, it's really true." Again I heard the ridiculous note in my voice sounding as though I'd had something to do with it.

She looked delighted. "Have they been *on* the moon?"

"Yep. Walked around on it."

"That's fascinating!"

I hesitated, then said, "Yeah. I suppose so. But not as much as I'd have thought when I was a kid reading science fiction." She looked puzzled, and I said, "It's hard to explain, Julia, but . . . it doesn't seem to mean anything. After the excitement of the actual trip—it was on television, if you can imagine that, Julia; we could actually see and hear the men on the moon—I almost forgot about it. Right away, too; I seldom thought about it afterward. It was unbelievably courageous of the men, and yet . . . somehow the project almost seemed to lack dignity. Because it didn't have any real purpose or point." I stopped because she wasn't listening.

As I'd talked, Julia had been looking over my book titles and presently she'd taken down a novel and begun leafing through it. Now, suddenly, she swung around to face me, and her face and neck were scarlet right down to the white collar of her blouse. "Si. Things like this"—she glanced at the open pages of the book in her hands, horrified—"are said in *print?*" She clapped the book shut as though the words could crawl off the page. "I would never have believed it!" She couldn't look at me.

I had nothing to say. How explain the changes in thought over more than a lifetime? But I was smiling; the novel she'd looked at was really very mild. There were others on the shelves that might literally have made her faint.

Disturbed, agitated, Julia had reached out and plucked another book from the shelves almost at random. She read the title aloud, hardly listening to herself, anxious to bury the subject of the horror she'd come onto. " 'A Pictorial History of World War Eye,' " she said. Then the meaning of the words came to her. "A war? *World* war? What does that mean, Si?" She started to open the book, and as her hand moved I was on my feet and walking quickly toward her.

It's always astonishing to realize later how lightning-fast the mind can sometimes work, what a lengthy series of thoughts and images it can produce within a fraction of a second. It had been a long time since I'd looked through the book Julia was opening. But during two very fast steps to her side I was remembering dozens of the photographs it contained: a destroyed town, only rubble and partial walls, and in the foreground a dead horse in a ditch . . . refugees on a dirt road, the frightened face of a small girl looking at the camera . . . an airplane

376

going down in flames . . . a trench half filled with dead bodies in uniform, their legs wrapped in cloth puttees, the face of one of them decomposed so badly it was mostly skull, though the hair remained. And one photograph I particularly remembered in every detail: On a shelf-like projection shoved into the wall of the trench sat a bareheaded soldier, alive. His feet were ankle-deep in water at the bottom of the trench directly beside a corpse, and he was smoking a cigarette, looking out at the camera hollow-eyed, stupefied, as though he'd never smiled or ever would. These horrors, I had suddenly realized, mustn't be revealed to Julia unless she joined the world that had produced them, and—making myself smile—I took the book from her hand just before she could open its pages. "Oh, yes," I said easily, turning the book to look at the gold letters of the title on the spine, as though to confirm the title. "That happened a long time ago."

"A *world* war?"

"They called it that, Julia, because . . . all the world was concerned about it. It was everyone's business, you see, and . . . they soon put a stop to it. I'd almost forgotten it."

How much sense that made to her, if any, I don't know. She said, "And what does 'World War *Eye*' mean?"

"Well . . ." I couldn't think of anything to say but the truth. "That isn't a letter of the alphabet. It's a number, Julia, a roman numeral."

"World War . . . *one?* There've been *more?*"

"A second one."

She was suspicious. "And—what was it like?"

My mind performed its commonplace miracle again. Hardly pausing before I replied, I was able to consider the four long years of trench warfare of World War I: the battle at Verdun in which a million men had died, unrestricted submarine warfare. Then I thought of World War II and the destruction of cities by the Germans, the killing of women, old people and babies; of the fire-bombings of German cities by the Americans, creating actual hundred-mile-an-hour hurricanes of fire incinerating women, old people and babies. And of a man I have often imagined, a German designer, getting up each morning, having break-fast, going to his office, sitting at his drawing board, neatly rolling back his sleeves, and then very carefully, with detailed india-ink drawings and precise manufacturing specifications, designing false shower heads which would presently loose poison gas to kill people by the millions in what were literally factories of death. And I thought of people killed even more efficiently: instantaneous death for hundreds of thousands in the brilliant flashes of two atomic explosions over Japan. What was World War II like? Unbelievably, it was worse than World War I, and no answer or foolish lie came to mind now.

She guessed. She knew that wars weren't called "world wars" for nothing. She looked at the thickness of the pictorial history I had taken from her; then she looked up at my face and said, "I don't want to hear about it."

"I don't want to tell you." I put the book back in its place, and we returned to the davenport. Julia didn't sit back, though. She sat on the edge of the cushion, her hands folded—clenched together, actually—in her lap. Staring straight ahead, getting her thoughts in order, she was silent for a few moments. Then she said, "During the day I've thought about what I wanted to do. And I've thought about staying here, if it were possible to tell Aunt Ada what had happened. During part of the day, when we walked down Fifth Avenue, I thought I'd made up my mind that if we could tell Ada, I *would* stay." I was sitting beside Julia, and she turned to look at me, managing a little smile. "I never thought I could possibly say this to a man, but I can: Do you love me, Si?"

"Yes."

"And I you. Almost from the first, though I didn't know it. But Jake guessed it, didn't he? Or felt it. Now I know, too. What should I do, Si? What do you want me to do? Shall I stay here?"

I thought that needed thinking about, then realized it didn't. I suppose Julia believed I was considering my answer as I sat looking at her face, but I wasn't. I was talking to her silently. I said, *No, I won't let you stay here. Julia, we're a people who pollute the very air we breathe. And our rivers. We're destroying the Great Lakes; Erie is already gone, and now we've begun on the oceans. We filled our atmosphere with radioactive fallout that put poison into our children's bones, and we knew it. We've made bombs that can wipe out humanity in minutes, and they are aimed and ready to fire. We ended polio, and then the United States Army bred new strains of germs that can cause fatal, incurable disease. We had a chance to do justice to our Negroes, and when they asked it, we refused. In Asia we burned people alive, we really did. We allow children to grow up malnourished in the United States. We allow people to make money by using our television channels to persuade our own children to smoke, knowing what it is going to do to them. This is a time when it becomes harder and harder to continue telling yourself that we are still good people. We hate each other. And we're used to it.*

I stopped; I wasn't going to say any of these things. The burden wasn't hers. I said, "You've been to Harlem."

"Yes, of course."

"Do you like it?"

"Certainly. It's charming; I've always liked the country."

"Have you ever walked in Central Park at night?"

"Yes."

"Alone?"

"Yes; it's very peaceful."

There were horrors in Julia's time, and I knew it. I knew that the seeds of everything I hated in my own time were already planted and sprouting in hers. But they hadn't yet flowered. In Julia's New York the streets could still fill with sleighs on a moonlit night of new snow, of strangers calling to each other, of singing and laughing. Life still had meaning and purpose in people's minds; the great emptiness hadn't begun. Now the good times to be alive seemed to be gone, Julia's probably the last of them. I said, "You have to go back," and reached over to take her hands in mine. "Just believe me, Julia. Because I love you. You can't stay here."

After a few moments she nodded slowly. "And you, Si—will you come back, too?"

The elation at the very thought of it showed in my face because Julia smiled. But I had to say, "I don't know. I have some duties here first."

"And you don't know if you could, do you? For the rest of your life."

"I'd have to be very sure."

"Yes, you would. For both our sakes." For several moments we looked at each other; then Julia said, "I'm going back, now, Si, tonight. Or I'll begin pleading with you to come, too. And to spend the rest of your life in another time is something you must determine alone."

I thought so, too, and I nodded. "Can you go back alone?"

"I think so. I couldn't have come here into a future past all imagining;

you had to bring me. But I can visualize my own time, feel it, and know it is there—far better than you the first time you tried."

Something roared up in my mind that I'd almost forgotten, it seemed so remote from this room and time. "Carmody! You *can't* go back, Julia! Carmody will—"

"No, he won't." She was shaking her head. "Do you remember what I was doing when Inspector Byrnes came for us? You were downstairs in the parlor, reading and I—"

"You were upstairs."

"Yes; in Jake's room, Si. I'd folded his clothes and put them into his trunk. And I was wrapping his boots when I heard you call. This afternoon for no reason I can understand, I remembered those boots. I'd just picked them up when the doorbell rang, and, Si—I saw the heels. The nails formed a pattern, and the pattern was a nine-pointed star in a circle. Jake survived the fire, not Carmody. That was Jake at Carmody's home covered with bandages. And filled with hate."

I knew it was true, and I knew what had happened. "My God, Julia; he walked out of that fire, somehow. Badly burned, yet a plan already forming in his mind. He walked straight to Carmody's, I'm certain, saw Carmody's widow, and—can you conceive of this?—they made a deal! Without Carmody she could lose the fortune, so he *became* Carmody. When we saw her at the Charity Ball, her husband newly dead, she'd already made the arrangement. Has anyone ever wanted money and position more than those two? They really make a pair, don't they!"

"What are you smiling at?"

"Was I? I didn't realize. It's not easy to explain, but . . . I'm smiling because Jake is such a *villain*! It's the first time I've ever even used the word, but it's what he is, all right. Complete. In everything he does. He's a complete man of his times, and I guess I'm also smiling because in spite of everything I like him. Good old Jake, disguised as Carmody, down on Wall Street at last. I hope he corners the market, whatever that means."

"Yes," Julia said, "he was cursed. I hope he finds happiness, though I am certain he will not." She didn't know what I'd meant, of course. To her there was no strangeness or comedy in the word *villain*; it's what Jake was, that's all. She said, "He can't harm me now; I know who he is, and when he understands that, I'm safe. So will you be . . . if you come back." She stood abruptly, and walked quickly to the bedroom to change her clothes.

I rode downtown with Julia in a cab. It was dark now; she sat back from the window, and no one but the driver saw her clothes. Half a block from our destination we got out, well away from the nearest streetlamp. I paid off the cab, then Julia and I walked quickly to the immense granite-block base of the Manhattan tower of the Brooklyn Bridge.

In the deepest shadows I took Julia's hands in mine and stood looking at her. In her long skirt, her coat and bonnet, her muff hanging from her wrist on its loop, she looked right; she looked the way Julia ought to. I said, "I want to come back; I want to spend my life with you, but . . ."

"I know. I know."

We repeated what we'd already said, several times. I took Julia in my arms then, and held her for quite a long time. I kissed her, we looked at each other once more, then simultaneously inhaled, mouths opening to speak. We stood staring, breaths held momentarily, then smiled a little sadly; we'd said it all. Julia reached out and laid her fingers on my cheek for a moment, then shook her head quickly; she wouldn't say goodbye.

She took my hand, and we walked a few paces out from the great granite wall of the bridge tower, then turned to look at it; now it was like an enormous stone curtain shutting out the world. She said, "The time I was born into and belong to are there, Si; far more real to me than the time I glimpsed today. My own world . . . I can feel it very strongly, it's very real; can't you?" I nodded; I couldn't speak. Julia turned, kissed me very quickly, then let go my hand and walked swiftly forward at a long angle toward the corner of that enormous wall. She reached it, hesitated, looked back as though she were going to speak, but didn't. She took the final steps and was gone then, around the corner of the huge base of the tower, the sound of her steps rapidly receding.

Silence. Then I began to walk toward the same corner. I broke into a run, fast as I could move, and was around it far quicker than Julia could have disappeared from sight. But she was gone.

22

"THIS MAY LOOK to you like unseemly haste—and taste," Colonel Esterhazy said to me; with a move of his hand he indicated Dr. Danziger's office. He sat behind the desk; Rube and I had come in and taken the two leather-padded metal chairs before it. Like Rube, Esterhazy was wearing cotton army pants and shirt today, without insignia but as rigidly pressed as though they were made of khaki-painted sheet metal. Rube's were neat enough but the creases didn't look welded in. I had on my blue suit. Esterhazy was saying, "But I'm here only because we're so terribly cramped for space; this was the one empty office. Someone has to head the project, and Dr. Danziger is gone." He moved a shoulder regretfully. "I wish he were sitting here instead of me."

I didn't say anything to that. I'd glanced around the office as we walked in, and it looked about the same only neater. Danziger's photographs and bookshelf were gone and so was a carton filled with papers he'd had on the floor, though now there were half a dozen folding chairs stacked against the far end wall. The desk top was empty except for a pen stand, and I imagine the drawers had been cleared out. Behind the desk now stood a gold-fringed nylon American flag on a standard, and on the wall hung a large framed color photograph of the President.

Rube said to Esterhazy, "The debriefing showed all-clear, as I phoned you. And believe me, that's a relief." He turned to me, smiling. "Because you were a busy fellow this trip, weren't you? Escaping the fire. Escaping . . . what's his name?"

"Inspector Byrnes."

"Yeah. And escaping the girl, too, I suspect. Julia."

I just smiled, and the two of them sat grinning at me for a few moments. I'd spent the morning here at the project, reeling off my list of random facts, dictating a long full report of everything I'd done on this last "trip," as we seemed to be calling them now. Everything except that Julia had come back with me. That had nothing to do with the success or failure of my mission so I just said that in the middle of the night, hiding in the arm of the Statue of Liberty, she'd remembered the nail pattern on Jake's boots. We'd known she was safe then, and at dawn I'd taken her home to 19 Gramercy Park, gotten my money, then hired a hansom up to the Dakota. I said I'd spent yesterday in my apartment sleeping.

Rube said, "So if the debriefing shows okay after all *those* shenanigans, it means that the stream of past events—"

"—is what we always insisted it was," Esterhazy cut in. " 'Twig-in-the-river' theory," he reminded me brusquely. "The stream of past events is a mighty stream indeed, far from easy to deflect casually, as ought to be obvious. It can happen by accident, as we've learned. Although the consequences were negligible. In any historical context, that is. But we have no doubt, nor did Dr. Danziger, that it *could* be affected by design."

It was hard to even keep my mind on what he was saying, and when he paused I nodded and rather vaguely said, "Well, fine. Colonel, and Rube, I think I've completed my mission. How practical it is to study past events, considering the risk I've demonstrated of getting involved with them, is something you people will have to judge. But right now my own affairs are piling up on me; I've got things to work out. And what I'd like now, if you're through with me"—I smiled—"is an honorable discharge."

Neither of them answered for a moment or so. They looked at me, then at each other. Finally Esterhazy said, "Well, before we take that up, Si, there's something I'd like you to know about. You're free to resign; you've done beautifully, done all that could be expected and more. But I'm certain you'll be interested in what I want you to hear. And then maybe you won't want to resign quite yet."

A girl opened the door; I hadn't seen her around the project before. "The others are here, Colonel."

"Good. Send them in." Esterhazy stood up behind his desk and looked toward the door with a pleasant smile.

Two men walked in, and I recognized them. The first was the young history professor with the big nose and big shock of thinning black hair that made him look to me anyway, like a television comic; his name was Messinger. The man behind him was Fessenden, the President's representative, around fifty, bald, with gray-brown hair combed over the shiny top of his head. They both greeted me, and Professor Messinger walked over to my chair as I stood up, to shake my hand. "Welcome home!" he said, and held up a sheet of mimeographed typescript stapled in one corner; I saw it was my dictated account of this last trip. "Terrific," he said, rattling the papers, "absolutely terrific," even *sounding* like a TV "personality." Fessenden gave me a formal nod, and then in imitation of Messinger decided to add a smile and waggle his copy of my account, which was a mistake; smiling cordiality wasn't really a part of his nature.

Rube was bringing over a couple of folding chairs, opening one as he walked; with his foot he shoved his own chair to Fessenden and gave the opened folding chair to Messinger. When we were all seated in a little curve at the front of his desk, Esterhazy sat down, saying, "This is the board now, Si, except for the senator, who's shepherding a bill through Congress today and can't join us. And Professor Butts, whom you may remember: professor of biology at Chicago. He's an advisory member now, without vote, present only when his specialty requires it. The old board was unwieldy. This is far more practical. Jack, maybe you'd like to brief Si."

Messinger turned to me, smiling easily, pleasantly; I saw Fessenden watching him, and it occurred to me that he envied Messinger. "Well, Mr. Morley—is 'Si' all right?"

"Of course."

"Good. And please call me Jack. We've been busy, too, Si. While you were gone. Doing the same job you were: investigating Mr. Andrew Carmody, though not at quite such close quarters. I've been in Washington, on leave and with a secretary provided. A very capable one, though"—he grinned at Esterhazy—"you might have found one just a shade better-looking. We've been cozily alone together in the National Archives, literally down in the basement, rummaging through papers of both Cleveland administrations, the rest of my team in other sections of the Archives. And Carmody really *was* a Cleveland adviser, one of many, in the years following your visit, Si. He began to involve himself in politics beginning in the spring of 1882 when Cleveland was governor of New York. And from occasional notes of Cleveland's, from the minutes of several meetings, and from references in two letters of Cleveland's, I've learned that he became something of a friend of his during Cleveland's first term. How that came about I don't know; there was nothing on that, not surprisingly. His influence then was zero, so far as I've been able to learn. But Carmody—or as we now know he really was, Pickering —fostered the friendship, and it reached its height, such as it was, during Cleveland's second term. The references we found in the Archives show clearly that Cleveland sometimes listened to Carmody—as of course the records call him, and as I might as well continue to call him. His influence was never large, and never important, except in one instance, and the evidence I found on that is conclusive. Cleveland entered office the second time with a war over Cuba building up with Spain, and being whooped up by several newspaper interests. Cleveland hoped to avoid the war, and a pretty good solution was offered him by a number of people; namely, that he offer to buy Cuba from Spain. This much is well known, a matter of clear record; you can find references to it in any complete account of Cleveland's second term. There was precedent for the plan—in our purchases of the Louisiana Territory from France and of Alaska from Russia. And there was evidence that Spain would welcome a chance to avoid a war they knew they couldn't hope to win. But here, I discover, is Pickering-Carmody's place in history: It was his advice that turned Cleveland against the notion. I don't know what he said; the little I found on it is partly technical and pretty sketchy. But it's certain; no mistake about that. And that's it. His sole role in history of any importance is a negative one, a small one, a footnote he might not care to brag about if he were around to do so. After Cleveland's second term we don't hear of him again so far as I was able to learn."

He stopped, and I sat nodding for a few moments, thinking about what he'd said; I was interested. I said, "Well, I'm glad I was able to contribute the new knowledge, unimportant though it is now, that Carmody was actually Pickering. Personally I'm a little pleased at the thought of old Jake Pickering actually in the White House advising Cleveland."

Esterhazy said, "We're pleased with your contribution, too; damn pleased. We hoped for something like it, and you delivered. It's a contribution far more important than you know. Rube?"

Rube turned to me, swinging a leg over an arm of his chair so he could sit facing me more comfortably, smiling that good smile that made you glad he was your friend and made you want to be on *his* side. He said, "Si, you're bright. You can understand that this project has to yield practical results. It's great that it can contribute to scholarly knowledge, but that isn't enough. You can't spend millions, can't take valuable people off other work, to add a little footnote to history about someone nobody ever heard of anyway. Your success—and how remarkable a thing that is I don't think there are words for—has made the next phase of this project possible. That next phase is an advance on the experiment. As careful and cautious as those that preceded it. And it is potentially of enormous benefit—"

"—incalculable benefit," Esterhazy interjected.

Rube nodded. "—of incalculable benefit to the United States. It has been considered and unanimously passed by this board, and then cleared in Washington with the highest authorities; we were on a scramble phone with Washington for nearly an hour this morning."

Esterhazy had his forearms lying on the desk top, hands clasped together in what looked like a relaxed position. But now he leaned far forward over the desk top toward me, and when he spoke I turned to him and saw that his hands were so tightly clenched the fingertips were white. He couldn't keep himself from interrupting Rube. "We want you to go back one more time. Then if that's what you want, your resignation will be instantly accepted, and with great thanks by a grateful government, I can promise you. When the time comes—not in our lifetime, I think, but eventually—when the time comes that this is no longer secret, you will have a place of distinction and honor in your country's history. Your findings, Si, have made this next step possible, and now we want you to use those findings. You're to go back, and do just one thing: You are to reveal 'Carmody's' secret. You're to expose him as what he really is; namely, a clerk named Pickering—responsible for Carmody's death, responsible for the World Building fire. You won't

386

have proof, of course; he won't be imprisoned, tried, or even charged. But he'll be discredited. As he deserves. Can you do that, Si?"

I was slow, baffled. "But . . . *why?* What for?"

Esterhazy grinned with the pleasure of explaining. "Don't you see? This is the logical next step, Si, a very small and very carefully controlled experiment . . . in slightly altering the course of past events. We've avoided doing that till now, scrupulously avoided it, as well as we possibly could, and rightly so. Until we learned from experience that the accidental risk of altering the course of past events is negligible. And that even when it does happen, the actual effect seems trivial. Now it's time for the next slow advance, a slight and very careful change of events in the past . . . for the benefit of our own time and country. Think about it! We can prevent Carmody—or Pickering, as we know him to be now—from becoming an adviser, minor though he was, to Cleveland. And there is obvious reason to think that this may actually result in a change in the course of our history. If Cuba became a permanent American possession in the 1890's . . ." He grinned. "Well, I don't have to spell out the benefit of *that*. The name Castro will remain what it was, unheard of. The man himself remaining whatever he was, a worker in the sugar fields, I suppose, forever unknown. That's the next step, Si, if it works, a clear immediate benefit—and, even *more* important, a guide to even greater ones. My God . . ." His voice dropped in awe. "To correct mistakes of the past which have adversely affected the present for us—what an incredible opportunity."

We sat in absolute silence then. I was stunned. I was, and I knew it, an ordinary person who long after he was grown retained the childhood assumption that the people who largely control our lives are somehow better informed than, and have judgment superior to, the rest of us; that they are more intelligent. Not until Vietnam did I finally realize that some of the most important decisions of all time can be made by men knowing really no more than, and who are not more intelligent than, most of the rest of us. That it was even possible that my own opinions and judgment could be as good as and maybe better than a politician's who made a decision of profound consequence. Some of that childhood awe and acceptance of authority remained, and while I was sitting before Esterhazy's desk—the room silent, everyone watching me, waiting—it seemed presumptuous that ordinary Simon Morley should question the judgment of this board. And of the men in Washington who agreed with it. Yet I knew I had to. And was going to.

I stumbled, though. I spoke badly and in confusion. I even began with what I suppose was the least important aspect of the entire decision. I said, "Go back and deliberately discredit Jake? Destroy his life? I, ah . . . does anyone have the right to do that?"

"The man's long dead, Si," Esterhazy said gently, as though to a simpleton he didn't want to offend. "We're what counts now."

"He won't be dead where I'll be seeing him."

"Well, yes. But, Si, a lot of men make far greater sacrifices than he will. For the good of the country."

"But he wouldn't even be consulted about it!"

"Neither are they; they're drafted into the army."

"Well, maybe they should be asked, too."

He genuinely didn't understand. "What do you mean?"

"Maybe it's wrong to force a man to join an army and kill other people against his own wishes."

They just looked at me. What I was saying was really incomprehensible to them, and I realized I'd been arguing the wrong point. I said, "Colonel, Rube, Mr. Fessenden and Professor Messinger—listen. Would it be—*right* to alter past events? I mean who *knows* it's a good thing to do? Who can be *sure* of it, I mean."

"Why, dammit, *we* can be sure!" Esterhazy said. "Do you deny that it would be one hell of a lot better if Cuba were long since a U.S. possession instead of a Communist country ninety miles from our mainland?"

I shrugged uneasily. "No, it isn't that I deny it. The point is it doesn't matter what I think; because I might be wrong. Who can be sure Cuba will ever do us any harm? It's awfully tiny, and hasn't hurt us yet."

"They tried, didn't they?" Esterhazy very nearly shouted.

Gently, trying to calm things down, Fessenden said, "The missile crisis," as though politely reminding me of something that might have slipped my mind.

I said, "Well, yeah. Though according to Robert Kennedy it was the military who tried to make JFK think the danger was greater than perhaps it might have been. But I don't want to bog down into a debate about Cuba. Whatever the truth there, I just don't think *anyone* has the godlike wisdom to actually rearrange the present by altering the past. It's going too far! My God, look what has already happened. The scientists make fantastic new discoveries which are immediately taken over by a group, almost a *breed* of men, who always know what's best for the rest of us. Science learns how to split the atom, and they immediately *know* that the best thing to do with that new knowledge is blow up Hiroshima!"

"Don't *you* think it was?" Esterhazy said coldly. "Or should we have allowed hundreds of thousands of American troops to die on the shores of Japan?"

"*I don't know!* Who *does* know? I think the most enormous kinds of decisions are being made by people who *don't know either*. Only in their own opinions do they know. They *know* it's right and necessary to poison the atmosphere with radioactivity. They *know* we should use our scientists' genetic discoveries to breed new and terrible kinds of disease. And that they don't even have to ask the consent of the ninety-nine and nine-tenths percent of the rest of us. And now that still another scientist, Dr. Danziger, has made *this* enormous discovery, he sits at home, squeezed out, unfit to decide what should be done with it. But you aren't. Once again you *know* that the best thing to do with his discovery is eliminate Castro Cuba. Well, *how* do you know? Who's given this new little breed of men who've polluted the entire environment and who may actually wipe out the human race—who *gave* them the power of God to control the lives and futures of the rest of us? Most of them we never heard of, and we sure as hell didn't elect them!" I sat looking from one to the other, then lowered my voice. "Even if you're right about Cuba, as you may be, look what it leads to. It leads directly to bigger and bigger changes, with a handful of military minds rewriting the past, present, and future according to *their* ideas of what's best for the rest of the entire human race. No, sir, gentlemen; I refuse."

Esterhazy's nostrils were so rigidly flared in rage that the edges were white. His teeth clenched, he drew a long sighing breath, a prolonged inhalation through his nostrils, filling his lungs to explode at me. Rube saw it and before Esterhazy could speak he said, "Let me!" and I heard the ring of command, and understood in astonishment that it was an order—from Major Prien to Colonel Esterhazy—and I knew I hadn't begun to understand the real relationships here in the project. Esterhazy forced his lips tight together, obeying. Rube turned to me and spoke in a flat calm voice; not catering to me one bit, not out to mollify me at all, but simply explaining the facts, take it or leave it.

He said, "We'll be sorry if you refuse; you're the best operative we have. Our recruiting has continued without letup, and it hasn't become one bit easier to find qualified people. But still . . . they *can* be found, and they have been. Furthermore, other portions of the project have continued; yours hasn't been the only one. The man who spent a few seconds in medieval Paris has done it again. Four days ago we reached Denver, 1901, for twenty minutes. We failed in North Dakota, failed at Vimy Ridge, failed in Montana. And we've had important trouble with the Winfield, Vermont, project. The man there succeeded. He made the transition twice, and never returned the second time. We don't know why; there is an obvious guess, but we don't know. Now, what am I driving at? I tell you frankly and honestly that we have serious difficulties and problems. I tell you that you may be the best operative by far that we will ever find. I tell you that we hope very much that you will reconsider. But I also tell you that *if you do not—*" He stopped, and sat looking at me, no smile at all in his eyes; then he finished the sentence, quietly and flatly: "—we'll simply get somebody else. And if the experiment cannot be made in New York City, 1882, with Jacob Pickering, then another will be made at some other place, some other time, and with somebody else. I'm not interested in arguing with you. Just understand this: It is *going* to be done."

Rube sat for several seconds, not moving, staring directly into my eyes. Then he allowed just a ghost of the old smile to appear. He said, "I agree with—not all, and not the most important part—but with a very great deal of what you said, and what you think. What you feel does you credit. But, Si, I can only repeat: With every possible precaution we are nevertheless going to do it. Now, take your time; sit and think; then tell us what you want to do. Whatever it is, it will be accepted instantly with no further argument or discussion."

I sat there for several very long slow minutes; and I thought more intensely, I suppose, than I'd ever done before. Once Messinger started to speak, but Colonel Esterhazy's hand shot up, and he said, "Hold it!" I'd looked up, and Esterhazy sat back in his chair, deliberately relaxing, taking his time, to let me know I had all the time I wanted. Silence again, for a long time, then presently I looked up at them.

I said, "All right; my conscience is clear. I did my best. I did my very utmost to persuade you of what I still feel is right. And if any record is to be made of these proceedings, I'd like the record to show that I did. But now—all right, Rube; there's no answer to what you say. If this is going to be done no matter what I think, feel, or do, then I want to be in on it. I started this, and rather than someone else finishing it, I want to. Because there's one thing I can do better than anyone else, and I ask now that I be allowed to. I'll do what you want because I know it, or something else like it, is going to be done anyway, but I ask you to let me be as easy as I possibly can on Jake Pickering. I came into his life unasked, and I've done him harm, though I think it was justified. But I don't care to destroy him. Let me do just enough so that he is discredited only in the immediate circle that matters to you. It will accomplish what you want just as much as wrecking the man completely. His future is grim enough; let's let him keep something, for crysake. If you'll agree to that, I'll do it. But then I resign."

Everyone was pleased, Rube and Esterhazy agreeing immediately. We were all standing then, everyone shaking my hand, assuring me I wouldn't be sorry, that they weren't foolhardy, that they'd had to convince some very sober, responsible, and extremely important people in Washington that every safeguard would be taken. They'd be phoning Washington again now; when could I leave? I said I had to have a little time to take care of my own affairs; how about a week? And Rube said a week was fine. I asked about Oscar Rossoff then, and Martin Lastvogel; I liked them, and would have liked to see them. But Esterhazy told me Oscar had left the project; he had his own practice to take care of, and the time he'd agreed to stay was up, unfortunately. It was possible, of course, even probable, but I didn't believe it; the thought rose up in my mind, though I knew I might be wrong, that Oscar had quit in protest against the course the project was taking. Martin was gone, too: back to teaching.

Standing in the office, all of us chattering away, I'd managed a smile by now, and I made what amounted to a miniature three-sentence speech, I suppose. I said, "Well. We're all set now. I did my best to change your minds; I think I had to do that. But I have to admit . . .

since you're going on with or without me, I'd one hell of a lot rather have it be with me." And they all grinned, and actually applauded with a quiet token clap or two.

I'm not going to say too much about my visit with Kate. It was awkward, for one thing; she was waiting for a delivery and couldn't leave the shop, so we had to talk there for quite a while, occasionally interrupted when a customer would come in. Then I'd have to wander around the shop, waiting for the customer to get the hell out and trying not to show it.

I told Kate about the "trip," of course—the project word for it that I'd gotten into the habit of using, too. And of course she was fascinated. The delivery arrived during the last of it, and Kate had to check through four cartons of carefully wrapped antique glassware, verifying the contents and condition before she signed for it. And then, finally—it wasn't closing time but late enough—Kate locked up, and we went upstairs.

First thing she did upstairs after starting some coffee was to go to her bedroom and bring out her red-cardboard accordion folder. And while I finished my story we looked once more at the long blue envelope and the note inside it. When finally I finished talking, Kate read the last sentence aloud: " 'So, with this wretched souvenir of that Event before me, I now end the life which should have ended then.' " She looked up at me and nodded; the questions she'd wondered about most of her life were answered now. She said, "I've pictured it so often: The shot sounded, and the woman who lived as his wife came running."

"To the body with *Julia* tattooed across the chest."

She nodded. "Yes. So she washed, dressed and laid him out alone: No one else was to see that tattoo."

I had the blue envelope in my hand, and I gave it a last look, then handed it back to Kate, and took the little snapshot she held. Again I stared down at the clear sharp image of the tombstone under which Mrs. Andrew Carmody had finally laid Jake. No name on it; she'd live with him as her husband but she wouldn't bury him that way. There on the face of the stone outside Gillis, Montana, were the dots, the time-eroded pits forming a nine-pointed star in a circle. Only now it no longer looked like a tombstone. Rounded at the top, the sides straight, the short little stone looked to me as it had looked to the woman who

392

ordered it made: It was Jake Pickering's boot heel in stone, the final touch to the melodrama of his nineteenth-century life.

Kate put her folder away, she poured our coffee, we sat sipping it, talking, waiting till what had to be said was spoken. And presently I said it, clumsily. "It hasn't worked out for us, has it, Kate?"

She said, "No. I don't know why. Do you?"

I shook my head. "I thought it was going to; I was sure of that. But it reached the point when it ought to have . . ."

She didn't want to go on about it. "And it didn't. Well. It happens, Si. What else can be said? It's not a matter of fault; it can't be forced. Don't blame yourself."

We talked much more, of course; quite a lot, surprisingly, even laughing at things that had happened in the past. And when I left, finally, I think we felt pretty good about each other, and I knew that when some time had passed, our new relationship an old fact, I'd be pleased if I saw Katie again someday.

On the walk home, the doubts struck, and everything turned bleak. Was it possible for me to go back and live out my life with Julia? Could I do that, knowing the future? Could I live in nineteenth-century New York and look at infants in their carriages, knowing what lay ahead for them? It was a vanished world, actually, nearly every soul in it long since dead: Could I ever really join it?

During the next week I let the question lie in the back of my mind, not trying to force an answer. Instead, I finished up several sketches and began this account, working steadily and rapidly in longhand since I had no typewriter, stopping for meals and taking a walk now and then, but not doing much else. In an oblique way it was helping me think what to do, my mind on what mattered yet not directly. Occasionally I thought about Rube Prien, and was amused; if he knew what I was doing he'd want every page stamped CLASSIFIED—or, better yet, burned. Which is what I'd have to do with it unless I joined Julia and took it with me. I have a friend, a writer, and I'm very certain he is the only man ever to look through a great decaying stack of ancient religious pamphlets in the rare-book section of the New York Public Library. If I were to join Julia, I could finish this, I thought, and then whenever it was—1911?—that the library was built, I could place this where I knew he'd come onto it someday. Sitting at my kitchen table working, I smiled, liking the idea; it gave the feeling, at least, of a little further purpose to the doing of it. But the real purpose wasn't achieved; the question in my mind didn't answer itself.

Rube phoned each day, and dropped in on me twice during that week. He was careful to phone first to avoid any appearance of checking up on me, which was just what he was doing, of course. Each time we talked I took the trouble to let him know I hadn't changed my mind.

On the last day I phoned Dr. Danziger. He was in the book, and he answered on the fifth ring, just as I was thinking of hanging up, my conscience clear. As we spoke I wished I'd hung up one ring sooner because, in the mysterious way that this sometimes happens, he'd suddenly turned old, I realized, and I was relieved not to see him. His voice had a quaver now, he was old and beaten, and it struck me with the force of certain knowledge that he was living the very last of his life. I told him what Esterhazy and Rube had told me—he insisted; and I thought he deserved that knowledge if he wanted it. He hadn't known, nobody had told him. And he was so disturbed, his voice trembling almost to breaking, that I was horribly afraid he might actually cry but of course he did not. I should have known he wouldn't; he was old suddenly and very likely dying, but this wasn't a man to let himself change that much. He was angry. "Stop them!" he cried, his voice tiny in the receiver at my ear. "You've got to stop them! Promise it, Si! Say you'll stop them!" And of course I said yes, I certainly would, listening to my own voice, hoping it sounded as though I really meant it.

A week after my return I was back in the Dakota, back in the clothes that seemed almost more natural to me now than those I'd left behind in my apartment. I'd spent last night here and most of this next day, not because I any longer needed them to reach the state of mind necessary to step out into what I thought of now as Julia's time. It was because I was even more alone here than I'd been in my apartment, and more free to try to think through the most important decision I'd ever make, here in a limbo between two worlds and times.

It didn't snow but it was a drab February sky all day, visibility low, as though it might snow soon. And finally, well after dark this time, I walked out of the apartment, down the stairs, and turned toward the street and the park just ahead. There were cars on the street, their tires sounding wetly on the pavement, and I stood waiting at the curb. Then the traffic light clicked green, and I crossed, walked far into the park, found a bench to myself and sat down. I waited then, deep in the park, in the silence, and—simply allowed the change to happen, almost to *accumulate*. And when finally I stood up, looking around me at the bare trees visible by the light of the night sky reflected from the snow, the park looked no different. But I knew where I was with absolute certainty, and when once again I walked out onto Fifth Avenue, a light delivery wagon rattled slowly by, the horse tired, his neck slumped, a kerosene lantern swaying under the rear axle. On the walk a woman in a feathered black hat, a fur cape over her shoulders, walked past me, holding her long dark skirt an inch above the wet paving stones.

I turned south, down narrow, quiet residential Fifth Avenue, glancing into yellow-lighted windows as I walked, catching glimpses: of a bald bearded man reading the evening paper, the light from a fireplace I couldn't see reflected redly on the windowpane; of a white-aproned, white-capped maid passing through a room; of a month-old Christmas tree, a woman touching a lighted taper to its candles for the pleasure of the five-year-old boy beside her.

I walked a long way, not thinking but just waiting to see what I felt. Then I stood across the street beside the iron railings of the park fence staring over at the tall lighted windows of 19 Gramercy Park. I stood for some minutes, and once someone passed quickly by a lower front window, I couldn't tell who. I stood till I was cold, my feet numbing. But I didn't go in; after a while I walked quickly away.

And then, north on Broadway from Madison Square, I walked along the Rialto, the theatrical section of New York when Broadway was Broadway. The street was jammed with newly washed and polished carriages. The sidewalks were alive with people, at least half of them in evening dress, the night filled with the sound of them, and the feel of excitement and imminent pleasure hung in the air.

But I wasn't a part of it. I hurried past the lighted theaters, restaurants, and great hotels, until I reached the Gilsey House between Twenty-ninth and Thirtieth. There, at the lobby cigar counter, I bought a cigar, a long thin cheroot, and tucked it carefully into the breast pocket of my inner coat. Outside I crossed Thirtieth Street, and stopped before a theater that looked and was brand-new: Wallack's. THE MONEY

SPINNERS, said the big block letters of the printed signs beside the entrances. Just ahead of me a man carrying a silver-headed cane collapsed his opera hat, then held open a lobby door for the girl with him. They walked in, and I followed, stepping into a lobby so magnificent it was overpowering. It was all dark blue and maroon velvet, gilt and silver ornamentation, dark polished wood, and ornate chandeliers. Twin staircases, one at each end of the lobby, curved up to the balconies. I walked over to the ticket window, before which stood a short line, and read the framed price schedule beside it: PARQUET ORCHESTRA OR ALL DOWN STAIRS, $1.50. DRESS CIRCLE FIRST ROW, $2.00, SECOND AND THIRD ROWS, $1.50; NEXT FIVE ROWS $1.00; NEXT ROWS, 75¢ AND 50¢.

I glanced out through the glass door panels then; the woman I was waiting for still wasn't there, and I stood to one side by a wall, listening to the excited hum of the lobby, but apart from it. Minutes passed, maybe four or five; then I saw her, back bent, feet shuffling. She was white-haired, wearing a buttonless man's overcoat tied at the waist with a rope, her shoes split at the sides, a rag of a scarf tied under her chin. On one arm she carried a small basket two-thirds filled with polished red apples, and she stopped in the middle of the walk and began an endless cackling spiel: "Apples, apples, apples. *Get* your apples, get 'em now. Apples, apples, Apple Mary's best! Hurry, now, hurry. Apple Mary says *hurry*." I stood watching; only one man of the three or four that I saw hand her a coin actually took an apple, and he didn't come into the theater but walked on, eating it. The others came in or stood on the walk.

Carriages had been steadily dropping off their parties at the curb. Now another stopped, and a family got out, all in evening dress: a bearded father, a ruby stud in his stiff white shirtfront; the mother, a pleasantly smiling woman in pink dress and gray cloak; and two girls, one in her twenties, the other younger. Each girl carried her cloak folded over an arm, shoulders bare; one wore a gray dress trimmed with red bows, and the younger wore a marvelous velvet gown of untrimmed, unrelieved spring-green velvet. When she smiled, as she did now, passing through the door her father held open for the party, she was lovely.

In the lobby they met friends, and now they stood talking, laughing, and I wanted to eavesdrop but couldn't: I stood staring out at Apple

Mary chanting on the walk. And in less than a minute here he came, in evening dress, clean-shaven except for a mustache, moving deftly through the groups on the walk, a slim, very tall, handsome man in his twenties. The lobby doors beside me opened and closed steadily, and as he stopped out on the walk beside Apple Mary I heard him speak the words I could almost repeat with him. "Here you are, Mary. Good luck for you and good luck for me!" and I saw the wink of gold as the coin dropped into her hand. She stared at her palm, then looked up at him. "Bless you, sir; oh, *bless* you!" she said aloud, and then my lips moved silently, almost in unison with hers. "This evening *will* be blessed for you; mark my words!"

I glanced quickly to my left. The family party were saying goodbye to their friends, turning slowly toward the staircase as their friends turned toward the main-floor doors. And the man I'd watched on the sidewalk was striding toward my door, his hand reaching out for the handle. My own hand was lifting from the breast pocket of my suit coat, the other pushed open the door. I said, "Excuse me, sir," smiling, blocking his way, and I slowly raised the cigar in my hand to my mouth. "But do you have a light?"

"Certainly." He brought out a match, lifted one foot to strike it on the dry part of the sole, then raised the sputtering match, shielding it with one hand, to my cigar. Sick at heart, I ducked my head, unable to meet his eyes, and puffed my cigar into light.

"Thank you," I said then; from a corner of my eye I could see the far stairway to the balcony, and the girl in the pale green dress was climbing it. "You're welcome"—the man just outside the door shook out the match, then stepped past me into the lobby, glancing around it. But there was nothing now to catch his interest. On the staircase there was a last flick of pale green velvet but I don't think he even noticed it. Taking a ticket from his white vest pocket, he crossed the lobby on into the theater.

As I walked along the dark side-street east of Broadway, my hands shoved into my overcoat pockets, it was queer to realize that if I were again to—though I knew I would not—walk into the great brick warehouse labeled Beekey's, it would be into an interior of six concrete floors filled with stored household goods, nothing else. And that if, through the army, I were to track down a major named Ruben Prien, I might eventually find him, a tough little former football player with a wonderful smile. He'd be at a desk somewhere, in his neat khaki uniform, planning in absolute good faith and with an utter certainty God knows what terrible mischief. And he wouldn't know me at all.

To Dr. Danziger, on the phone, I'd repeated as a promise the decision I'd made on the day I confronted Rube Prien and Esterhazy. Now I'd just kept my promise. And the man—the facial resemblance had been very strong—who would have become Dr. Danziger's father, and the girl in green who in time would have become his mother, now never would be.

But these were thoughts that weren't of my time anymore. Now they were of a far-off future I no longer belonged in. I touched the unfinished manuscript in my overcoat pocket, and looked around at the world I was in. At the gaslighted brownstones beside me. At the nighttime winter sky. This, too, was an imperfect world, but—I drew a deep breath, sharply chill in my lungs—the air was still clean. The rivers flowed fresh, as they had since time began. And the first of the terrible corrupting wars still lay decades ahead. I reached Lexington Avenue, turned south and—the yellow lights of Gramercy Park waiting at the end of the street—I walked on toward Number 19.

A FOOTNOTE

I'VE TRIED to be factually accurate in this story. Horse cars really ran where Si rode them; El stations actually were located where he got on and off trains; the things he saw in the lobby of the old Astor House were really there; quotations from newspapers he read are verbatim; and the arm of the Statue of Liberty did indeed stand in Madison Square, a truth that especially pleases me. Occasionally my efforts at accuracy became compulsive, as in my account of the World Building fire and events just preceding it, in which I became obsessed with getting times of day and exact details of changing weather during the fire, and names of tenants and even the room numbers of that unmemorable old wreck of a building correct or close to it. I even tell myself that my fictional solution to the mystery of that forgotten fire's origins blends so well with the known facts that it might have been accepted as truth at the time. This kind of research becomes time-wasting foolishness, but fun.

I haven't let accuracy interfere with the story, though. If I needed a fine old Dakota apartment building in 1882, and found it wasn't finished till 1885, I just moved it back a little; sue me. So there are some deliberate inaccuracies, and maybe even an outright error or two; it's only a story, offered only as entertainment. But—with the enormous help of Warren Brown and Lenore Redstone, who did a great deal of knowledgeable, imaginative research—I doubt that I made too many.

Si's photographs and sketches were not, of course, products of his own hand. Many of the best illustrations were searched out with endless patience, kindness, and intelligent judgment by Miss Charlotte La Rue of the Museum of the City of New York. Others were kindly lent to me by Brown Brothers (pp. 265, 266); by Culver Pictures, Inc. (pp. 236–37, 247, 270 bottom, 272); by the Home Insurance Company (pp. 117, 347); by the Museum of the City of New York (pp. 155, 241, 242, 244, 257 top, 257 bottom, 258, 259, 268, 269, 270 top, 271); and by The New-York Historical Society, New York City (p. 243). The photographs and sketches represent the time pretty well, I think, even though they couldn't all be strictly of the eighteen-eighties. Before 1900 things didn't change so fast as now—one more reason why Si so wisely decided to stay back there.

J.F.